D0722291

NEELY JONES:

The Medusa Pool

NEELY JONES:

The Medusa Pool

•••

M. K. WREN

Thomas Dunne Books
St. Martin's Minotaur
New York ≈

MYS
W945ne

THOMAS DUNNE BOOKS.
An imprint of St. Martin's Press.

NEELY JONES: THE MEDUSA POOL. Copyright © 1999 by Martha Kay Renfroe. All rights reserved. Printed in the United States of America. No part of this book may be used or reproduced in any matter whatsoever without written permission except in the case of brief quotations embodied in critical articles or reviews. For information address St. Martin's Press, 175 Fifth Avenue, New York, N.Y. 10010.

Design by Jane Adele Regina

Library of Congress Cataloging-in-Publication Data

Wren, M. K.
    Neely Jones: the Medusa pool / M. K. Wren. — 1st St. Martin's Minotaur ed.
        p. cm.
    "Thomas Dunne books."
    ISBN 0-312-24223-9
    1. Afro-Americans—Oregon Fiction. I. Title. II. Title: Medusa pool.
 PS3573.R43N44   1999
 813'.54—dc21   99-22252
                                                                   CIP

First Edition: October 1999

10   9   8   7   6   5   4   3   2   1

Acknowledgments

I'M CONSTANTLY AMAZED AT PEOPLE'S generosity with their knowledge and time. What more precious possessions do we have? For sharing those treasures with me, I offer my thanks to Sheriff John Raichl and Chief Criminal Deputy Daniel P. Laughman of the Clatsop County Sheriff's Office, as well as Lieutenant Dale Kahn of the Clark County Sheriff's Office; to Rita Johnson for reading the manuscript and offering a perspective only she could provide; to T.C. and Charles Vollum for opening a door into a new world, one in which they live so gracefully; and, finally, to Diane Hankins, writer and, until recently, deputy sheriff and dispatcher for the Clatsop County Sheriff's Office and (with her husband, John) member of the CCSO Search and Rescue Team, for patience and contributions far above and beyond the call of friendship.

Chapter 1

BLOODRED AND NIGHT BLACK, CHROME flashing like a biker's chains, the big customized pickup rumbles north, headlights sweeping vacant asphalt. At this hour—nearly midnight—the pickup encounters no traffic in Westport, except a semi heading south.

The first Tuesday in November.

And keenly cold, yet the sky is as clear as summer. The moon shimmers on the lamé surface of the Pacific Ocean, gleams on the asphalt seam of Highway 101, the Coast Highway, traces the pale outlines of an angular construction, built from the trunks of two alder saplings, lying in the bed of the pickup. A five-gallon gasoline can rattles against the tailgate.

Westport, Oregon, population 4,207, seat of Taft County, is divided vertically, but not evenly, by Highway 101; on the west side, only a few blocks separate the highway from the beach. On the east lies the mass of the town, sequin lights, pink-gold and blue-white, clustering around Chinook Bay, a dark, irregular square that might be a landlocked lake except for the narrow passage to the sea in the northwest corner. High above the churning waters in that rockbound passage, a bridge soars on neo-Gothic arches of steel.

The red-and-black pickup rumbles over the bridge, gaining speed, then flashes past rows of restaurants, shops, and tourist traps, all closed except for the Salty Dog Tavern. As the pickup passes the tavern, the twang of country music escaping its open door strikes a brief dissonance with the boom of hard rock from the truck's radio.

At the corner where 101 meets Highway 13, the pickup barrels through a red light. Northeast of the corner, the Taft County Courthouse stands square and brick-solid. Lights glow in the elections office on the second floor, where the last ballots are being counted. Beyond the courthouse, the pickup swings left, boom-booming along a residential street for three blocks, turns right, and accelerates up North Front Drive with a brassy roar, hitting sixty within six blocks.

Then abruptly it shrieks to a stop.

A side street strikes east from North Front: Kittiwake Drive. The pickup's radio and headlights switch off as it turns and prowls around the curve where Kittiwake hooks north toward a dead end.

The four houses along the street are tucked into jack pines on a ridge just high enough to give them an ocean view: three short-term rentals, empty at this time of year; an A-frame with two wings—kitchen on the north, garage and makeshift dojo on the south.

There's a light in the A-frame's loft bedroom.

The bloodred-and-night-black pickup growls at idle, and three men emerge, unload the truck bed, then move like dark leaves blown along a gutter toward the A-frame. Moonlight glances on shaven heads and on silver swastikas adorning the backs of black leather jackets.

The leader carries the gasoline can. The other two pant under the shared weight of a crudely cobbled cross.

Chapter 2

IN THE A-FRAME'S LOFT BEDROOM, Neely Jones sleeps, too exhausted by a week of double shifts to be disturbed by the reading light and, for the moment, unaware of the midnight moonlight men outside.

Neely lies curled on her side, the pillow wadded under her head, her bronze skin glossed by the gold reflected from the fir paneling. Her dark hair, cut short and left natural, defines a long, narrow skull and absorbs the light, and under the deep, convex curves of her eyelids, a dream plays out in shadows of motion.

Next to her, close enough to touch her, Jan Koto sits propped with pillows against the headboard, his wire-rim glasses slipping down a nose that offers no purchase, while he focuses intently on a slim treatise titled *Cnidocyst Neurotoxins in Medusae of the Eastern Pacific Rim.*

He doesn't hear the distant rumble obscured by the constant rush of the surf.

But the next sounds are closer, louder.

Shouts, echoes of rowdy, abandoned laughter.

The sounds seep into a dream Neely will never remember, and she comes abruptly awake, listening, black eyes wide, fiercely unblinking.

The shouts and laughter fade, but she can still hear the distant rumble, and she knows exactly what it is. With an adrenaline rush that explodes her out of bed, she mutters, "Riker!" Jan stares at her while she shrugs on her *hapi* coat then reaches for the leather gun belt on the chair near the bed and unholsters the Glock 9-mm semiautomatic.

Deputy Neely Jones's duty weapon.

An aging Alinco DJ580 transceiver is clipped to the belt. She grabs it and heads for the stairs, spirals down to the living room.

But at the foot of the staircase, she stops, staring through the huge, black triangle of glass at a blinding cross as tall as a man, a cross of flame. Her heart pounds erratically, but she can't be sure whether fear or rage impels it.

Neely, honey, if you can't tell the difference between mad and scared, better use the mad to think with and the scared to get you moving.

So said Gramma Faith Jones, and it seems all her equivocal scraps of wisdom hide, ready to emerge at any time, in the recesses of Neely's memory.

No, Gramma, it's the mad that gets *me* moving.

And it's the yellow obscenity outside that sends her bolting across the living room to the glass door. She unlocks it, slams it back against its metal frame, and steps out onto the deck, the Glock raised and ready.

The cold of the wood under her bare feet registers at the same moment she recoils from the heat and the stink of smoke tainted with gasoline. Hungry flames gulp the night air and spit it out, rippling-hot and roaring. The blaze illuminates the length of Kittiwake Drive, but it's empty. No red-and-black pickup. And she knows it was Riker's pickup she heard. That sound she can't and won't forget.

Eugene Buxman, aka Dirk Riker, the fish-white, skinny-shanked, bald-shaven representative of the Aryan master race who, with his two similarly masterful sidekicks, are the tip of the iceberg of racism in lily-white Westport, Oregon.

Three times this year Eugene and his merry men have decorated the house with spray-painted swastikas and graffiti: JAP MONGRIL! NIGGAR BITCH! DIE NIGGAR FUCKER! The representative of the master race can't even spell.

But there's no graffiti this time: only this ultimate Christian symbol turned to viciously unchristian purpose.

Neely pulls out the tranceiver's antenna. Charlie Eckholm should be on dispatch now. Not that that's anything to shout about. "Charlie? This is Neely Jones. We have a cross burning in progress at our house. I need a deputy as witness, and make sure he has a video camera."

Charlie replies through a rattle of static, "Neely, we ain't got the men to check out every kid's prank in the county, and you know it."

"I'm reporting a *crime*, Charlie! Who's available?"

According to Charlie, no one is available at the Taft County Sheriff's Office. All six of the men on duty are out on calls or on patrol.

Neely stands with the Glock heavy in her right hand, listening to the voracious panting of the fire, bitterly aware that even if there were twenty men sitting on their butts at the TCSO, Charlie wouldn't admit it. He won't even bother to scribble a note about a cross burning.

A kid's prank.

"Charlie, at least put out an APB on Eugene Buxman. Riker! Whatever he calls himself."

She signs off, letting her rage drown out the despair underlying it.

"Neely?"

She turns. Jan Koto is standing in the doorway, like Neely barefoot and clad in a hastily donned robe. His right hand is clenched on the frame of the glass door. A strong hand, and she knows all too well how strong.

He taught her karate, the art of the "empty hand."

And that's how he has always approached life: Strong hands empty, as he seeks the way of peace and harmony.

The firelight reflects on the lenses of his wire-rim

glasses, sheens his silk black hair, flashes in his black eyes, but there's more bewilderment there than anger. He looks at the cross and says succinctly, "Shit!"

Neely nods, facing the flames as she places the transceiver and the Glock on the railing. Her hands are shaking. "That honky *bastard!* I'll never get used to it, Jan. *Never!*"

She feels his arms slip warm and easy around her.

"Why should you, Neely, any more than you get used to murder and beatings and kids stoned on crack?"

"This is different. This is personal." She turns in the circle of his arms and bends her head into the curve of his shoulder. "For both of us."

Sometimes Neely wonders if one of the reasons they find such comfort in each other is that they both understand certain things. Her great-uncle was lynched by the Klan in New Orleans. Jan's father was a child when his family was shipped to an internment camp during World War II. That was the past, yes, but it isn't over. Neely closes her eyes, holding on to Jan. To hope.

My prince of the empty hands, seeking peace where discord prevails, making harmony where it never existed. In my heart, at least.

Yet Jan Koto hasn't a clue about this flaming obscenity. Not really.

In the Westport Oceanographic Center, the science-focused institution where he's worked for two years, there's a mix of races and ethnic origins among the twenty scientists on the research staff, and Westport treats all of them with respect.

But then the center provides a respectable payroll and, with its museum aquarium, a respectable tourist attraction.

This white-bread town likes its bread.

It's a different town for her. She works in an understaffed, underfunded, all-white-male department where she's Sheriff Gifford Wills's token woman and token African-American in one. Her world is in the darkness behind closed doors and in midnight alleys, where people reveal all that is worst in human nature, and where she tries to light small candles of hope for the survivors.

Jan's world is the sea, a magnificent and infinite mystery, and every day he tugs at the veils of the mystery and sometimes catches a glimpse of an answer and treats it as a gift from a capricious goddess.

In time, Neely has come to share his joy in the sea's revelations. That's his gift to her.

Maybe someday she'll believe it's her world, too.

The cross shivers. Neely looks around in time to see its arms crack and break off, fall in a hissing rain of orange sparks. Finally, Jan says, "I'll get the fire extinguisher," and disappears into the house.

Neely waits at the railing until Jan returns with the red cylinder of a fire extinguisher and goes down into the yard to blast the flames with spewing white clouds that take on a coral light until they succeed in suffocating the blaze. Something within Neely rebels at the desecration of a crime scene, but she's documented Buxman/Riker's "pranks" before, and Sheriff Giff Wills wasn't interested.

When nothing is left of the cross but a blackened post, the November chill sweeps in around her as if into a vacuum. Jan returns to the deck and draws her close to him, kisses the soft, yielding hair at her temple.

"Come on, Niri-san, let's go back to bed."

She smiles at that ironic pet name. He pronounces it with an exaggerated Japanese accent: *Nee-ree-sahn*. He's fourth-generation American, and she knows his Japanese vocabulary extends only a few words past *sayonara* and *sushi*.

They retreat into the living room, and Jan has just locked the glass door when the phone rings. He says, "I'll get it," as he crosses to the table at the end of the couch and reaches for the phone.

Neely climbs up to the loft, puts the transceiver and gun in their proper places on the leather belt, then gets into bed and pulls the covers up against a chill that won't let go. She hears Jan's voice but not his words. At least it isn't a call from the TCSO ordering her to report for duty. Jan's laughing.

She's still exhausted, but she knows she won't sleep soon. She finds herself gazing at the wall above the chest of drawers where a samurai sword in a brocaded sheath is mounted. That lethally beautiful weapon, Jan told her, was presented to him when he came of age, by his father, Ando Koto.

But Jan also joked to her that he ordered the sword from the Franklin Mint.

The chill has subsided by the time Jan climbs the stairs to the loft. He sits down on the bed next to her, regarding her with a secretive smile that makes no sense, and says softly, "Congratulations."

"For what?"

"Congratulations on your election as *sheriff* of Taft County."

Neely sits up, staring at him. "What are you talking about?"

"That call was from Lydia Quigley, and—"

"Lydia! What did *she* want?"

"To talk to you, but I managed to put her off. Which she took with some grace, actually. At least she didn't seem surprised."

Neely begins irritably, "Lydia's *never* surpr—" Then with a sensation in her stomach that reminds her of her first ride on a roller coaster, she asks, "What did you say about the election?"

"You *won*, Neely!" He takes both her hands, smiling proudly. "The first time a write-in candidate has won a major position in this county, and definitely the first time an African-American woman has been elected sheriff. You'll be sworn in on New Year's Day!"

"Oh, Jan, that's crazy. Lydia must be drunk."

But Neely is grasping at straws. Lydia Quigley, éminence grise of Taft County politics, stinging gadfly among the good ol' boys, a teetotaler with the willpower of a Puritan, albeit a liberal Puritan—Lydia drunk?

Jan is still grinning as he adds, "Lydia said there's plenty of margin. No chance the absentee ballots will tip it. She wanted you to come to her house for the victory celebration tonight."

"*Victory?* Damn it, I *told* her I didn't *want* the job!"

"Right. If nominated, you won't run. If elected, you won't serve."

She hits his shoulder with a hard fist. "Jan, it's not funny! The men will never tolerate *me* as sheriff! And Giff—nearly two *months* to live with Giff Wills before I'd be sworn in? Ever since the Barany case—I mean, if I *did* beat him . . ." Her voice fails her as the full import of those words finally sinks in.

Then like a woman drowning, she flings her arms around Jan. "Baja! *Poseidon*'s leaving Thursday for Baja, isn't she? Take me along. I'll cook for the crew. Anything!"

"Neely, you can't cook, and you know I'm not going on this voyage. I saw all I needed to see of gray whales in September. I don't know why Ben scheduled another expedition to Baja so soon after the last one—unless it's the R and R in Cabo San Lucas. Anyway, if I go on any research jaunts, they'll be closer to— Oh, damn."

"What?"

"Nothing important. I just remembered I can't have lunch with you tomorrow. We're going scuba diving off the Lands End Point. Mersky offered to take us out in his boat, and with him, we have to strike while the iron is hot—or while his boat's working."

Neely hasn't been focusing on what he's saying, but she does now.

"You and Andrea the Amazon?"

"Hey, don't give me your Benin sorceress look." There's a defensive cast in his tone now. "If Andrea's analyses show any decent results, we'll all be rich and famous one day."

Neely knows Jan thinks she's jealous of Andrea Olenick, chief biochemist at the center. But she's not. She just knows that Andrea's in love with Jan, and since he discovered the new jellyfish—now officially named *Chrysaora kotii*—and the rare chemistry of its stings, and since Andrea pointed out its potential value as an analgesic, he's had to spend a lot of time with her. But as far as he's concerned, Andrea is in it for the money. Not for him. Not even for science.

Jan doesn't pursue the subject of Andrea Olenick. With solemn pride, he cups Neely's face in his hands. "You'll be the best damn sheriff this county ever had. You've got more training than the rest of them put together, and you *can* survive two months under a lame-duck Giff Wills. You're tough, and I've never seen you wave a white flag."

She's had no choice about *tough*, but Jan can't imagine what she'll be facing if she accepts this "victory" Lydia Quigley has dumped on her. But Neely has nothing to prove here, no reason to accept a no-win situation.

"Of course, I can resign tomorrow."

"And let *Giff* win?"

"The better part of valor. And Chief Kleber will give me a job. He said he'd love to have me, and it's only a thirty-mile commute."

Jan doesn't argue with her. In the five years they've lived together—three in San Francisco, two here in Westport—he has always respected the decisions that are hers alone to make.

Only once did he express any doubt about a decision of hers.

That was when she resigned from the San Francisco Police Department to encourage him to accept the post at the Westport Oceanographic Center.

It meant exchanging her sergeant's stripes for the bottom-rung rank of deputy, but Jan could only carry out the research he finds so compulsively engaging in a place like Westport. Here he has access to the technical facilities he needs, and in the waters offshore the medusoid populations he's made his specialty to proliferate.

Where Jan Koto goes, she goes. It's that simple.

She gently removes his glasses and leans close until their lips whisper together. "Jan, I love you. . . ."

He sighs, giving in, and perhaps neither of them understand what he's giving in to, as he pushes the covers aside and stretches close against Neely, and they both laugh. And if they don't understand that laughter, either, after what this night has brought them, it doesn't matter.

Tonight laughter and love and making love are a triumph.

Chapter 3

As DISTRICT ATTORNEY OF TAFT County, Owen Culpepper is no stranger to telephone calls in the middle of the night, but at the moment, the ring of the phone so close to his ear is particularly unwelcome. He spent much of this night celebrating another successful political campaign and the assurance of another term as the county's top lawyer.

And now his head is pounding in the dark, and he's at the edge of the bed on the verge of falling out. How can Glenda always manage to nearly push him out of a king-size bed when she's so skinny? No hips, no breasts, all angles and hard spots.

The phone rings yet again while he feels for it on the bedside table, and Glenda mutters, "*Oh*-wen, for Christ's sake, answer the *phone*!"

"I'm *trying* to!" Finally he has it. "H'lo? H'lo!" He reaches for the light switch. The glare feels like knives sinking into his eyes.

Owen Culpepper doesn't always look so bloated, but he does normally look pale, as if his skin is too thin and getting thinner with age. So is his hair, fine and colorless, too wispy to cover the bald spots. "Who the hell *is* this? Damn it, it's . . ." The clock is a blur without his glasses, but the hands seem to be pointing straight up and down.

"Owen, don' tell *me* what goddamn time it is!"

"Giff?" Jesus, not Sheriff Giff Wills this early in the morning.

"Yer goddamn right! Or'd you figger you'd never hear from me again? I'd jus' fade away like . . . like . . ."

Culpepper can nearly smell the bourbon through the telephone, and the memory snaps into place. It's not *Sheriff* Giff Wills anymore. At least, it won't be on January first. Giff lost the election.

Culpepper can hear Glenda tittering behind him. He sits up on the edge of the bed. "Giff, I'm really sorry about—"

"*Tell* me 'bout sorry! Here I was with a houseful of people, havin' a little party, when ol' Tom down at the *Gazette* calls and tells me the results're in—and I lost! I *lost* to that nigger cunt!"

"Jesus, you didn't say that to Tom, did you?" The DA runs his hand through his scant hair. Tom Jordan would *love* a quote like that. Of course, in a family newspaper, he can't use it verbatim. Glenda is sitting up now. Still tittering.

Giff slurs, "Don' know what I said, but you gotta *do* somethin'!"

"What do you expect *me* to do about it?"

"I wanna invessigation! Fraud! 'Lection fraud! No way that black bitch coulda beat *me* without fraud!"

The DA grimaces at the sour taste in his mouth. Damn strawberry daiquiris. And the media will be all over the courthouse tomorrow—this morning. A black woman winning with a write-in campaign . . .

It'll probably get picked up by the networks.

"There was no fraud, Giff."

Glenda is laughing out loud now; Culpepper turns to give her a glare, but she just laughs harder.

"Hadda be! Dammit, I 'spect you to—"

"Look, just go to bed and sleep it off. When you sober up, we'll—"

"I *am* sober! Mos'ly. Owen, I ain't standin' for this. If

the cizzens of Taff Counny want that smart-ass nigger for sher'ff, then, by God, they can have her! *I'll quit!*"

Glenda apparently hears that, since it comes out in a bellow, and she whoops with laughter, pummeling a pillow. Culpepper snaps, "Jesus, Glenda, what's so damn funny? No, Giff, that's—never mind! Damn it, you *can't* quit *now*. We need some sort of transition period—"

"Fuck you, Owen!" The phone goes dead.

Culpepper gazes at the receiver numbly, and Glenda says, "Oh, *poor* little Giffy. All upset because he lost the election?" She breaks into another seemingly uncontrollable spasm of laughter. "I told you, Owen, I told you years ago, that man is an idiot. It's about time he got put out to pasture." She begins shifting back to her own side of the bed.

The DA says plaintively, "She said she didn't *want* to be sheriff."

"Neely?" Glenda settles her angular body and pulls the duvet up. "She didn't. But Lydia Quigley wanted it for her. It's a new era in Taft County politics, Owen—an African-American *woman* sheriff!"

He eyes his wife suspiciously. "I bet you voted for her."

"What goes on in the sanctity of the voting booth is none of your business." Then she adds archly, "As a matter of fact, I *did* vote for her. If you're getting up now, try to be quiet. I've got an awful headache."

Culpepper sighs. So do I, he thinks. So do I.

Chapter 4

"I'M GOING TO RESIGN, JAN. It's the only way."

On the morning after the election, those are Neely Jones's last words when she drops Jan off at the Westport Oceanographic Center on the north shore of Chinook Bay.

Then, stomach roiling with what she refuses to call dread, she drives their blue Toyota pickup the four blocks to the courthouse. It's 7:40 A.M., the sun just topped the Coast Range, and the air sparkles like fire opal, but she can't muster her usual enthusiasm for the new day.

She approaches the Taft County Courthouse from its south flank on Highway 13. The building faces west onto 101 from a lot the size of two city blocks: The courthouse and its well-kept lawns occupy the front third; the back two-thirds is paved for parking. The courthouse was built in 1948 of red brick, with big windows that actually open. The single-story wing at the back was added twenty years later. Still, the brick is almost the same color, the windows similarly generous and functional, though they're all one-way glass. A pair of glass doors are centered on the east wall. The morning sun flashes on the bronze letters above them:

Neely wonders if she'll miss it.

No way. Miss the inadequate facilities, the lax protocols, miss being treated as Giff's factotum and sometimes PR flunky?

Of course, the latter probably backfired on him.

He hates those obligatory appearances at civic organizations and schools, so he usually sends Neely as his stand-in—in part, she knows, to show off his token black female deputy. *See? We're really not redneck racists/sexists at the TCSO.* As a result, she's spent a lot of time in the small towns, most of them along 101, where Taft County's citizens live and battle the problems inherent to any human community, as well as those peculiar to a seasonal tourist economy. In the two years she's been with the TCSO, she's had more personal contact with the citizens of the county and their problems than Giff has in two terms.

Neely idles through the parking lot. It's already nearly full; the county offices and courts will open in a few minutes. The fifteen slots to the left of the TCSO entrance are reserved for its staff, and they're all occupied. The six mismatched patrol cars were purchased at police auctions, given a degree of uniformity with tan paint and star logos. The personal vehicles are unanimously made in the USA, all pickups or four-wheel-drives, except for Sgt. Curtis McMinn's metallic gold 1960 Thunderbird convertible. That expensive toy—along with the gun collection he's always bragging about—probably explains why he moonlights as night watchman at the Westport Oceanographic Center.

Sheriff Giff Wills's brown Ford pickup is absent from the lineup.

Neely finds an empty slot in the public parking area, turns off the motor, and closes her eyes, trying to get the queasiness under control.

Jan was right: Giff *will* consider her resignation a victory.

The day Giff hired her, he made it clear that he was doing so only because the state requires ethnic and gender diversity, nor did he mince words: "We don't need *your* kind here." She never told Jan that.

Neely occasionally fantasizes about introducing Giff to her mother, Dr. Helene Cleary-Jones, professor of astronomy at Berkeley, a quietly forceful woman who happens to be snow-white, blue-eyed, and blond, although now her hair has grayed to a warm pewter.

But no doubt Giff is of the "one drop of colored blood" school.

And by most people's definition—and by her own—Neely is black, whatever her mother's color. Except to some blacks, who consider her tainted, despite her father's color. Yet she wonders where in this country any reasonable person would expect to find anyone who isn't "tainted" with white blood or black. Or yellow or brown or whatever.

Only nutcases like Dirk Riker believe in racial purity.

Neely looks at her watch. 7:50. The day shift begins at 8:00. Her last shift.

Maybe.

No: Definitely.

She gets out of the pickup and checks her reflection in the side window. She won't let Giff or the other deputies catch her looking sloppy. Thus the brown jacket and tan twill uniform are immaculate, the tie in a perfect knot, the Stetson at an exact horizontal, collar brass aligned symmetrically, the seven-pointed star of her badge gleaming. She slides her hands down to the gun belt that hugs her waist reassuringly: Glock 9-mm semiautomatic, two loaded clips, handcuffs, flashlight, Mace, radio. Everything in order.

Neely turns and marches briskly to the TCSO entrance.

And opens the door, to find the small lobby packed.

They come at her like an avalanche, shouting questions, waving mikes and cameras, their strobe lights blinding her.

This, she didn't expect.

"How does it feel to be the first African-American sheriff in Taft County?"

"Will you be hiring more black women deputies?"

"Is it true you're going to fire all the white men on the staff?"

"Will we see a new design in uniforms—dashikis, maybe?"

"What does Sheriff Wills think about losing the election to a black woman?"

That last question almost makes her smile, but she ignores it, too. As she elbows through the surging crowd, she glances to her left; the door into the reception office is closed. On her right, the jail entrance is closed, too, but it always is. She reaches the door to the central hallway, keys ready in her hand. The clamor stops when she shuts the door behind her.

It locks automatically. She takes a bracing breath, looking down the long, empty hall. It divides the wing lengthwise: Criminal Division on the left; Corrections Division on the right. But there are no doors into the jail wing along this hall. At the far end, a door opens into the courthouse; it also locks automatically.

She squares her shoulders and starts down the hall, glancing into the first door on the left, the Dispatch Center, where Senior Deputy Lonsdale Weaver attends his electronic consoles, looking like a middle-aged Wizard of Oz in his secret control room.

The next door on the left is the briefing room.

The sudden silence that marks her entrance is profound and as unnerving as the flood of noise that greeted her in the lobby.

But this she *did* expect.

It's a big room, shaped like an upside-down, reversed L. A dozen drab gray metal desks; drab gray metal file cabinets lined up between the three windows on the far wall and between the doors to the two small offices and the evidence room on her right. And in this room where she would usually find a handful of people—there are only six deputies on the day shift—she finds another crowd.

A silent, hostile crowd.

Twenty-two uniformed men, perched on desks, slumped in chairs: every member of the TCSO staff from both divisions, Criminal and Corrections, and all three shifts, including three reserves. And Heather Blessing, Giff's strawberry blond secretary/receptionist, five and a half feet tall in spike heels, pink sweater snug over her breasts, a scrap of burgundy wool skirt showing off legs sleek in smoky panty hose.

Heather is at the table to the right of the door, pouring coffee for Owen Culpepper, and his presence is another surprise. The DA seldom leaves the courthouse's second floor, where his office is grandly ensconced between the circuit and district courtrooms. He nods vaguely at Neely, then focuses on Heather as she hands him a mug.

Heather turns to Neely, her eyes shining—they're green today—and says softly, "Congratulations, Neely."

At this moment, that seems bitterly inappropriate, demonstrating either the airheadedness Neely has always attributed to Heather or—and the possibility makes Neely do a double take—a lot of courage.

But there'll be no congratulations from anyone else in this room.

Yet didn't she expect this collective hostility?

Yes, although in the past, most of the men ignored her or treated her as an unavoidable inconvenience. A few had even been politely friendly.

Among those was Chief Criminal Deputy Foster "Buck" Dolin, Giff's second in command. He leans against the doorjamb of the first office, arms folded. He's a big man, bulky with muscle, but he moves well. A weight lifter and probably a football player at Westport High in his youth.

Before Vietnam. Gossip has it that Buck is part Indian, and he looks it now, with his eyes reduced to dark slits fixed on Neely.

She turns to Heather and asks, "Where's Giff?"

With a glance at Culpepper, Heather whispers, "We don't *know*."

Neely nods, then walks into the silent room, the rubber soles of her flawlessly polished shoes squeaking on the green linoleum. She turns left at the corner of the L, walks past the inner door of the Dispatch Center to her desk, which faces the inside wall next to the partition separating Giff's office from the briefing room. Where he can keep an eye on her. The partition is glass from the wainscoting up, with a glass-paneled door in the middle. It's closed now, in Giff's absence.

Where *is* he? Sulking? Sleeping it off at home?

Neely hangs her jacket over the back of her chair, places the Stetson on top of the file cabinet to the left of the desk, and checks for messages, but there's nothing on her desk that wasn't here yesterday. Buck Dolin, as shift supervisor, should be giving out orders for the day.

Damn it, what is everyone waiting for?

She rolls a sheet of paper into the old electric typewriter and begins typing, the click of keys echoing in the silence. She dates the letter and addresses it to Sheriff Gifford Wills.

Maybe this is what everyone is waiting for: her resignation.

Sir: This letter will serve as notification that

She pauses when Sgt. Curtis McMinn drapes himself over the file cabinet. His sandy hair is growing out from a buzz cut, and his upper lip is decorated with a woolly Chuck Norris mustache. He says loudly, "Y'know, Neely, Giff ain't gonna put up with this shit."

No doubt he thinks he's speaking for everyone present. She ignores him and continues to type:

as of this date I am tendering

"*Nobody's* gonna put up with this shit. Just 'cause you got yourself elected sheriff don't mean you're ever gonna *be* sheriff!"

She keeps typing:

my resignation from the Taft County Sher

"*Where the hell is she!*"

Neely winces at that hoarse bellow: Sheriff Giff Wills has arrived.

Chapter 5

NEELY PULLS HER SHOULDERS BACK as she rises and strides past McMinn. But two paces beyond the corner of the L, she stops, staring at the man standing just inside the hall door, his chin lowered bullishly.

It's no secret that Giff Wills is a dedicated drinker, and he's often come to work hungover. But today, he's more than hungover; he's still drunk and looking like a gone-to-pot wino who found a discarded sheriff's uniform at Goodwill. He has his gun belt on, but his hat and tie are AWOL, his shirt grease-spotted, his fly unzipped two inches, and his stubbly moon face scrunched into an expression of indignation that incongruously reminds Neely of a Cabbage Patch doll.

Until he bawls, "You fuckin' nigger bitch!"

Heather gasps, while the DA's eyes roll heavenward. Neely stands silent, feeling her body go stone-hard to contain the rage, the familiar rage she learned so early in life. And fear. She recognizes the part fear plays in that rage. Fear that she can be hated, hurt, damaged, devastated for no reason except the color of her skin and the contours of her features, her heritage from a father she was justifiably proud of, whom she loved and mourned as only a child can.

Gramma Faith Jones used to say, *The devil isn't black or white, Neely, honey. He's the color of fire and torment.*

But right now, to Neely, the devil seems to be pinkish beige.

Giff announces to the room at large, "I got jus' *one* thing t'say! I spent a lotta years here, makin' this the best damn sher'ff's office Taff Counny ever seen. And this's what I get. Throwed out on my ass . . ." He seems to realize he's lost track of the one thing he had to say. Neely glances at Chief Buck Dolin, who's watching from his office door, a curl of distaste on his thin lips. She wonders what it's for: Giff's unforgivable behavior or the fact that he's out of a job.

"I got jus' one thing t'say!" Giff reiterates. "If the cizzens of Taff Counny wanna nigger bitch for sher'ff, by God, they got 'er! *I quit!*"

Neely blinks. *She's* the one who's going to quit. *Giff* can't quit.

"Giff, you *can't* quit!" Culpepper wails. "Not till January *first!*"

"Who *says* I can't?" Giff looms over the DA, who retreats a step; no doubt having Giff breathe into his face is not a pleasant experience.

"You wannit in *writing,* Owen?"

Giff sways to the chalkboard on the east wall and scrawls in foot-high letters "I FUCKIN QUIT!!!" He signs it "G. Wills Ex-sherrif."

Then he draws his gun, an enormous Colt .45, and lurches toward the DA, who backs into the coffee table. "Giff, what're you *doing?*"

"Turnin' in my weapon!"

Buck Dolin clears his throat. "Giff, that's *your* gun. You don't have an assigned duty weapon."

"Oh." He holsters the Colt, glaring at Culpepper as if he were trying to steal it, then rips his badge from his shirt and hands it to the DA. "Okay, Owen, you got my badge; you got my ressination in writin'!" He turns his glare on Neely. "I hired you 'cause I figgered it was the right thing t'do. Helpin' out the unnerpriv'leged. Din't know I was hirin' a goddamn snake in the grass. Well, it's all yours now—the whole shitteree! And I hope you fuckin' *choke* on it!"

With that, he turns and careens out the door.

In the ensuing silence, the deputies focus as one on Neely. She can feel their resentment like a wind off a glacier.

When she hears the hubbub from the lobby, she realizes Giff must be trying to run the media gauntlet. A PR disaster in the making, but she finds it difficult to give a damn at the moment. The silence in this room stretches taut, crackling with hostility. No one attempts to break it.

Finally, the noise in the lobby fades and Neely turns to the DA, who looks like a man who's been shot but doesn't know it yet. She hears herself say, "Mr. Culpepper, we need a legal opinion. The county can't afford to have the chain of command in the TCSO in limbo for two months."

A still, small voice within her—it sounds a lot like Jan's—says, *I thought you were going to resign.*

So, I changed my mind.

Did I?

Why not? Maybe she *will* fuckin' choke on it, but she won't be put down by a redneck jerk and a room full of white men.

Culpepper frowns at Giff's badge, still resting in his hand. "An opinion? Well, I, uh, don't recall any precedents. . . ."

It's Sgt. Jimbo Ventry, supervisor of the late swing shift, who responds to that, his scowling black eyebrows nearly meeting, the lower half of his face gray with stubble. "Jesus, Owen, I don't care how that fuckin' election came out, you can't make *her* sheriff!"

Neely watches Culpepper and realizes she probably should be grateful for Ventry's obtuseness. First, District Attorney Owen Culpepper doesn't take well to being addressed by his given name by someone he considers an inferior. Second, the reference to the election reminds him that more citizens of Taft County voted for Neely than any other candidate, and those citizens might be the ones whose votes *he'll* need in the next election.

At least that's Neely's interpretation of his thought processes. They seem so transparent.

Now he's thinking that maybe the best way to get rid of Neely permanently would be to throw her into the job now, without any transition period for her or the staff, and let her sink or swim.

He's betting she'll sink.

"Since Deputy Jones *is* sheriff-elect..." Culpepper grins like a cat contemplating a cornered mouse. "Well, I don't know any reason why, in light of Sheriff Wills's resignation, she shouldn't assume her duties as his successor *now*. That is, before the usual January first swearing-in. I don't know of any *legal* reason at all why not."

Every deputy has something to say, but Culpepper waves them to silence. "Just remember, boys, we're all public servants. You guys may not be hired *directly* by the people, but the sheriff *is*. It's up to the people—or the county commissioners—to determine who's going to be sheriff. And for *how long*."

That, Neely thinks bitterly, makes it clear enough. Put up with the snake-in-the-grass nigger bitch until the commissioners or voters get a bellyful and fire or recall her. Or until you can drive her to resignation. The DA didn't mention that possibility, but he doesn't have to.

The deputies get the message. No one protests when Culpepper smiles indulgently at Neely and says, "I'll make arrangements for a judge to swear you in as soon as possible. Meanwhile . . . well, like Giff said, it's all yours—*Sheriff* Jones."

Then, still grinning smugly, he beats a hasty retreat. Neely can hear his footsteps as he hurries down the hall to the courthouse door.

Again, she is the focus of every eye.

She remembers her father, Sgt. Michael Abraham Jones, SFPD, comforting his ten-year-old daughter after she witnessed a white officer bad-mouthing him: "Don't worry about small things or small people, Neely. All you have to worry about is doing the right thing and doing it the very best you can."

Sure, Dad, but how can I do my very best when I'm surrounded by so *many* small people?

When it comes to people, honey, the only thing you can be sure of is you can't be sure of anything.

Gramma Faith Jones again.

Neely finds Buck watching her. He's the key. If she can bring him around, the others will follow his lead.

A big *if.*

And one of the few things she's sure of now is that the worst thing she can do is to force a confrontation. This is the time for diplomacy.

Sure.

Neely says calmly, "The DA is right about one thing: We're all public servants. The people of this county depend on us to keep them safe. If any of you forget that, if you get so busy playing games with me that you don't do your jobs, then people are going to get hurt and maybe killed. Keep that in mind." No response, but that doesn't surprise her.

She chooses two men from the swing and late swing shifts. "Deputy Anderson and Deputy Hoffstead, clear those reporters out of the lobby. They're blocking a public entrance."

The deputies look to Buck, but his gaze is still locked with Neely's. Finally he concedes, "Sounds like a good idea, Neely."

Neely. Definitely not *Sheriff.*

But at least Anderson and Hoffstead are on their way to the door. She tells them, "When you've taken care of that, you're off duty." Neither of them even break step. She hears the hall door open and close on a chorus of protests as the deputies wade in.

"Okay, swing shift and late swing, you're off duty. Reserves . . ." She glances around and finds the three volunteer deputies. "You'd better stay on." She pauses, but no one makes a move. She says clearly, "Everyone but day shift and reserves, you're free to go."

She's beginning to feel rooted to the spot, like a tree strangling in vines. *You're free to go.* Yes, there's diplomacy. What she really means is, *Get the hell out of here!*

But diplomacy—or probably some subtle signal from Buck—works. For a while, the briefing room is filled with the scraping of chairs, muttering voices, and finally only the day shift deputies and the reserves are left. And Heather Blessing, still looking worried, yet, as always, pert and pretty. That's the way Giff liked his secretaries.

Neely goes to the coffee table and fills a mug, then turns to face Buck. "Chief, you've checked the radio log for last night?"

Diplomacy again, making such a polite question of that. Damn, she's getting better at this.

Buck purses his lips thoughtfully and finally admits, "They're on my desk." He starts into his office but pauses when Senior Deputy Lonsdale Weaver emerges from the Dispatch Center.

Neely asks, "What is it, Lonnie?"

His reply is directed to Buck: "Got a log truck jack-knifed on the bridge. State Patrol's on the way, but they'll need some help."

Buck doesn't move except to turn his head to give Neely a patently challenging look. She nods. "You take that, Chief. You'll need a couple of men till the OSP shows up. Lonnie, did you radio the EMTs?"

Weaver shrugs as he returns to the Dispatch Center. "On their way. And the fire department."

Buck grabs his jacket from the coat rack just inside his office. "Okay, Darrell, you and . . ." He points at one of the reserve deputies. "Jimmy, you can ride with me." The three of them hurry out the door, pulling on jackets and settling their Stetsons. Within seconds, Neely hears two patrol cars peel away, sirens shrieking.

When the sound fades, the two remaining reserves go

to the coffee table; Curtis McMinn sits down at his desk, zips a form into his typewriter, and starts pecking out a report; Lt. Whit Chaffee unfolds his lanky body from behind a desk and mutters, "I'm due in court," and heads for the door; Lt. Adam Booker, the jail commander, stubs out a cigarette, nods at Deputy Mike Swenson, and together they saunter out the door without a word to anyone. It occurs to Neely that the jail has been left unguarded except for Molly Teller, secretary and erstwhile matron. She's the only staff member who wasn't present for the festivities here. But the redoubtable Molly is quite capable of handling the jail on her own.

Only Heather Blessing seems to recognize Neely's existence. She asks, "Neely—uh, Sheriff, shall I go round up some empty cartons?"

"What for?" Neely heads for her desk, with Heather at her heels.

"Well, you'll need to move your stuff into the—your office. We can put Giff's things in cartons till he comes to get them. I mean, I don't guess you can run the sheriff's department from that desk."

Neely looks at "that desk," cramped into the corner. She pulls her unfinished letter of resignation out of the typewriter and tosses it into the wastebasket, then turns to look into Giff's office—former office.

"Okay, Heather, go see what you can find in the way of cartons."

Heather hurries away, spike heels clacking, and Neely goes to the glass-paneled door. Opens it.

Her office? It doesn't seem real.

But, damn it, the people of Taft County want her in this office. At least, enough of them to give her the right to be here.

Jan's going to laugh uproariously when he finds out.

No. He'll just smile and say, Congratulations, Niri-san.

Chapter 6

NEELY STANDS JUST INSIDE THE sheriff's office door, thumbs hooked in her gun belt. It's familiar enough, this office. Too familiar.

Yet today she has the feeling she's seeing it for the first time: the dark veneered walls; the tan carpet, a little threadbare; on the south wall to her right, two windows with enough space between them for three file cabinets; a single window on the east wall with a view of an acre or so of parked cars; in the corner to the left of that window, a couch and armchair, upholstered in ugly brown Naugahyde; copies of *Field and Stream* and *Law and Order* displayed on a chunky coffee table—along with a well-read *Sports Illustrated* swimsuit issue. The head of a six-point buck stares glassily from its mount above the couch.

In the middle of the room, a mahogany desk faces the north wall. The chair behind it is also upholstered in ugly brown. Shit brown, Giff's favorite color, apparently. The chair in front of the desk is armless and wheeled. It once lurked behind someone else's desk, and the staff has learned not to try to sit in it. Centered on the north wall are two doors: the one on the right is open into Heather's office; behind the other door is a bathroom.

Jesus, a private bathroom, when everyone else has to use the facilities in the two cramped locker rooms down the hall.

Neely crosses to the desk, grimacing at the stink of cigar stubs in the ashtray. She sinks into the chair, finding it too soft for her taste. The phone is ringing in Heather's office. Neely wonders if there's a phone under the scrap-paper heap on this desk—a chaos of file folders and loose papers, along with the remains of a few take-out meals.

She has almost decided that maybe she *can* run the Sheriff's Office from "that desk"—assuming she can run it at all, with a staff near mutiny and a DA anticipating her failure—when the door connecting Heather's office and the lobby opens and a mobile stack of cartons moves in. The cartons push on into the sheriff's office, and when they're released to fall to the floor, Heather is behind them.

"There's plenty more cartons down in the basement, if we—"

"Miz Blessing?"

Heather hurries back into her office. "Hi, Jimmy. Is that for us?"

Neely recognizes the youngest son of the Lamberts, owners of Hearts and Flowers, the local flower shop. Heather takes delivery of a potted plant, and when Jimmy departs, she brings the plant to Neely.

"Oh, Sheriff, isn't it pretty? It's for you."

Neely eyes the pot dubiously. At least it doesn't have a bow or any of that god-awful florists' foil on it. A nice pot, actually, with a deep blue-green glaze. From a cluster of big pointed leaves, a wirelike stem rises, bends to horizontal, and along the stem, six white blossoms, two inches in diameter, grin at her like smug little monkeys.

Heather smiles fondly back at them. "Jimmy says it's a moth orchid. Oh—here's the card."

Neely rises and takes the tiny envelope, pulls out the card: *Congratulations, Sheriff Jones. I'm sure you'd like to kill me at the moment, but the people of this county need you.*

Heather asks, "Who's it from?"

"Lydia Quigley," Neely replies, trying to keep any bitterness out of her tone, but at the moment, Lydia may well be right: Neely *would* like to kill her.

"Oh, that's sweet of her."

"It's yours, Heather."

"What? Oh, no, Sheriff, I couldn't take it. It's a gift. Besides, I kill plants. I really love them, but they tend to die on me. Here, let's put it on the coffee table. Might dress the place up a bit." She carefully centers the pot on the coffee table and observes, "Strange, orchids don't seem to have any perfume. But I guess they don't need it."

Neely frowns toward the open door into the briefing room. On the far side of the room, one of the reserves is sitting on the corner of Curtis McMinn's desk. They're talking quietly, with occasional glances at her.

"Sheriff, I'm getting an awful lot of calls from media people. Shall I tell them you'll have a press conference later?"

Neely shifts her attention to Heather. "I don't want to have a press conference *any*time."

"Oh, you'll have to, but I can put them off till you're sworn in."

"Please do. Or indefinitely."

"Okay. Well, we'd better get you moved. Why don't you let me go through the stuff on top of the desk. Most of it needs filing anyway."

Neely nods and grabs an empty carton as she heads for her desk outside the glass-paneled door.

It takes only a few minutes to empty her desk, and its contents neatly fill the single carton. She is well aware that McMinn and the reserve deputy, joined now by the other reserve and by dispatcher Lonnie Weaver, are watching her every move, but she decides against acknowledging that scrutiny now.

Another thing she used to fantasize about was how she'd shape up this department if she were sheriff. That was when becoming sheriff wasn't even a remote possibility. Now it's less remote, if not quite a done deal, and her inclination is to dress McMinn and his buddies up one side and down the other for sitting on their asses, wasting time.

Not yet. She hasn't been sworn in yet.

And even if she had been, this is still the time for diplomacy.

Right.

Jan could handle this sort of thing. He has the patience of a saint. But she can't even ask his advice now. He's probably already out to sea aboard Mersky's fishing boat with Andrea the Amazon.

Neely sighs. Andrea Olenick *is* in love with Jan. The signs are blatant. Yet the gentlest, kindest man she's ever known can't see them.

Poor Andrea.

Neely smiles faintly to herself as she picks up the loaded carton and carries it into the sheriff's office.

Heather has performed a small miracle on Giff's desk. It's almost bare, its surface shining, with a few file folders stacked in one corner, a memo pad next to the telephone on the left, pens in the holder on the right. The ashtray has vanished.

Neely puts the carton on the floor by the desk while Heather explains that the folders on the desk are ongoing case files.

"Mostly ongoing," she hedges. "Giff never filed anything, even when a case was resolved. That cabinet there—" She points to one of the three file cabinets behind the desk. "There's probably case files in there dating back to Lewis and Clark. It's locked, by the way. Giff never would let me into it, and I'd love to take the old files downstairs to store. We need the room for new files. I think he just lost the key and won't admit it."

"Well, one of these days I'll pick the lock for you. Damn, look at this phone."

"Yes. Giff sure loved his high-tech toys. State of the art, he says."

The gleaming beige instrument is certainly more state of the art than the telephones in the briefing room. The deputies consider themselves lucky to have Touch-Tone phones rather than rotary dialers.

Heather points out the phone's features. "That light means it's on Giff's—I mean, your private line. This button is the intercom for me. Here's the redial button. Automatic dial for the numbers on this list. Conference phone, answering machine, recording function—"

"And caller ID. I could've used that a few times."

Heather starts to pull out the middle drawer of the desk. "I'll empty the drawers into cartons. I don't think Giff'll get so upset if I do it—*ow!*" She has the drawer out perhaps a foot when it suddenly balks, breaking one long burgundy nail. She frowns at it, says, "Oh, *darn!*"

Neely moves around to get a grip on the drawer, but she can't budge it. Something is jamming it. She gets a better grip and pulls hard.

Abruptly, the drawer surrenders, and Neely finds herself sitting in the ugly brown Naugahyde chair with the drawer in her lap.

She hears laughter, and her face goes hot. In the briefing room, McMinn, the two reserves, and Lonnie Weaver are finding her battle with the drawer highly entertaining.

Don't say it. Your time will come, but don't waste it on trivialities, she thinks.

Good advice, but it takes a few seconds before she can convince herself. And it's distraction more than good judgment that allows her to ignore the deputies.

Something fell to the floor when she pulled out the drawer.

A small manila envelope.

Chapter 7

NEELY SHIFTS THE DRAWER TO the top of the desk, then leans down to pick up the envelope. Torn strips of Scotch tape stick to the carpet.

Heather asks, "Is that what made the drawer stick? What *is* it?"

"I have no idea." It's just a plain brown clasp envelope, about seven by ten inches. The outside is creased from the jamming, but there are no other marks. The flap is sealed, and there's something inside. Pliable, less than half an inch thick. Neely puts the envelope on the desk, careful not to touch the tape. It's a perfect medium for fingerprints.

Why should she be worried about preserving fingerprints?

She can't answer that, but something about this envelope gives her the atavistic sensation of rising hackles.

She tips the drawer up and looks under it, sees the torn ends of tape strips stuck to the plywood. Seven tape ends, although there are only two strips on the envelope. Other areas of the plywood are slightly sticky to her touch.

Was Giff trying to hide something by taping it under the drawer, out of sight—not just this once but many times before?

It doesn't strike Neely as a likely explanation.

She looks toward the briefing room. The deputies aren't laughing now, but they're still watching her. She stares at them, willing her face into the expressionless mask Jan calls her "Benin sorceress look." One by one, they turn away. But they don't leave the area of McMinn's desk.

Neely says, "Heather, would you mind shutting that door and closing the blinds?"

"Sure, Sheriff." She crosses the room to cut off the view, then returns to wait attentively by the desk.

Neely picks up the envelope, finds a letter opener, and slits the bottom of the envelope, then slides the contents onto the desk, while Heather gasps, "Oh my Lord!"

Two stacks of bills, each bound with a rubber band.

Well-circulated twenty-dollar bills. Serial numbers random. Neely counts them. Fifty altogether, twenty-five in each stack.

One thousand dollars. Nice round number.

Heather whispers, "Why would Giff keep all that money under that drawer?"

"A good question." Neely doesn't add that it's highly unlikely Giff *kept* the money there. That's probably just where he expected to *find* it.

A payoff of some sort. For what? A little influence peddling? Encouragement to look the other way? Blackmail?

But why is this money here *now*? Why would Giff leave it here, when he intended to resign?

Of course, Giff couldn't have decided to resign before he learned he'd lost the election, which had to be around midnight last night. He probably started drinking well before that—Giff's election-night parties were legendary—and judging by his state this morning, he hadn't stopped since. Maybe this morning, in his rage- and bourbon-fogged state, the payoff just slipped his mind.

But he must've known about it. In any kind of payoff scam, the recipient has to know where and when to expect the delivery.

The bits of tape and the stickiness on the bottom of the drawer, where another tape was pulled away, suggests that this isn't the first such delivery. It's probably a regular occurrence. The first Wednesday of every month? Or Wednesday of every week? Or every day? No. Daily or even weekly deliveries would be too risky. Monthly, maybe.

So, exactly when was this particular delivery made?

Giff didn't pick up the envelope when he was here—and sober—yesterday, therefore, it wasn't here for him to pick up. It was left during the evening or night or early morning.

Who's the courier? Who has access to this office?

Heather, of course.

But if she's the courier, she could simply hand Giff the envelope at any moment during the day when she happened to be alone with him. As his secretary, there'd be plenty of opportunities. Which means she may be the only person in Westport Neely can eliminate as a suspect.

Someone on the custodial crew? Possibly, although the TCSO offices are cleaned on Monday, Wednesday, and Friday nights. None of the custodians would have had a legitimate reason to have been here last night.

One of the deputies?

That seems more likely, simply because a deputy wouldn't be noticed wandering around the TCSO at any time. Or in this office. Giff made a point of his "open-door" policy. He never locked the door into the briefing room and seldom even closed it.

The day shift is out. Giff was here yesterday for the day shift.

Which leaves swing and late swing shifts.

Chancy, though, for the courier, especially after seven, when the late swing goes on. From seven until midnight, the shifts overlap, since that's the high crime period, and more deputies are likely to be needed. That means more people around to notice the courier taping something under Giff's desk drawer.

The ideal time would be between 3:00 and 8:00 A.M.

The downtime. Deputies are always on call in those hours, but none are actually present in the TCSO, except the dispatcher. The dispatchers run consecutive shifts—no overlapping. So, Deputy Charlie Eckholm would be on duty in the Dispatch Center, but he couldn't see anything going on in Giff's office unless he left his post.

"Sheriff?"

Of course, Charlie might be the courier.

Hell, any of them might be the courier, and if Neely thought she had problems before trying to establish a working relationship with the staff, those problems are compounded now. Who can she trust? None of them. The Corrections Division staff? Same potentials.

"Sheriff?"

And she hasn't yet asked the jackpot question: Who is the *source* of the payoff?

"*Neely?*"

Neely takes a deep breath. "Yes, Heather?"

"Sheriff, you don't suppose—I mean, this couldn't possibly be . . . well, a bribe or something?"

"Yes, it could." Neely returns the money to the envelope, then looks around in frustration. "I need a large paper evidence envelope and some evidence tape."

"I'll get them for you."

While Heather goes to one of the file cabinets behind the desk, Neely delves into the carton she left on the floor and finds her address book. When Heather brings the envelope and tape, Neely puts the manila envelope inside, tapes the flap, writes the pertinent information on the tape, and signs it "Deputy Neely Jones." She hasn't been sworn in yet. Of course, *Sheriff* Neely Jones might get faster service at the Oregon State Police Fingerprint Lab.

But she has a friend in Salem.

She dials the number she finds in her address book and asks for Lieutenant Bivins. At length, the lieutenant comes on the line with an unrepentant Texas drawl and a harried "Bivins, what can I do for ya?"

"Neely Jones, Mary Jo. I need a—"

"Neely! Well, why didn't you say so, girl? Hey, I heard about you gettin' elected sheriff. Way to go!"

"Maybe. I'm not sure Taft County is ready for me yet."

"Well, honey, enough of 'em must be ready, or they wouldn't've voted for you. So, what can ol' Mary Jo do for you today?"

Neely laughs at that. *Old* Mary Jo is not yet thirty. "I have a manila envelope and some cash. I need fingerprints and whatever else you can tell me about them."

"Funny money?"

"I doubt it."

"Shoot! The real stuff's always tricky. Too many smudges. Better chance gettin' something off the envelope."

"I'll be grateful for anything. Oh—you'll find my prints on it."

"Your prints'll be in the files, honey. You gonna bring it over?"

"I can't, Mary Jo."

"Then send one of your guys with it."

Sure, Neely thinks. One of *my* guys, any of whom might be the courier.

"Can't do that, either. Could you get someone from the Oregon State Patrol to pick it up? I'd call them, but you have more clout."

"And you almost a sheriff? Okay, I'll take care of it. ASAP."

"Thanks, Mary Jo."

Neely hangs up, frowning at the evidence bag. Heather is waiting patiently on the other side of the desk.

"Heather, is there a safe here?" She damn sure can't put this in the evidence room, where every deputy would have access to it.

"Yes. Over there behind that picture." Heather points

to a faded Remington reproduction on the wall to the left of the bathroom door.

Neely rises. "Who knows the combination?"

"Well, just Giff. And me. And Buck, I think."

And whoever else Giff decided to trust with the combination.

Neely's attention shifts abruptly to the briefing room door when, without a knock or a word of warning, Chief Criminal Deputy Buck Dolin opens the door and saunters into the office. Speak of the devil, Neely thinks irritably, and it seems the open-door policy still pertains as far as Buck is concerned.

He says, "You wanted Riker; we got him."

Buck is wearing his mirrored shades, and Neely can't be sure, but she has a distinct impression that he's well aware of the evidence envelope in her hands.

She asks, "Where'd you find him?"

"The Salty Dog. Spotted his rig on the way back from the bridge. He was having a beer with his buddies. Beck's."

"Did you bring his buddies in?"

"The APB was for Riker."

Neely nods. So, that's the way it's going to be. He will follow her direct orders—to the letter—and volunteer nothing. She says, "I don't suppose you brought in his pickup."

"No"

"Right. Nothing in the APB about his truck. Where is he?"

"Interrogation A."

"Thanks, Chief." Is there an edge of sarcasm in that? Well, she's new to this diplomacy business.

He nods and starts toward the door, then stops. "I did take a look in the back of his rig, Neely."

"Anything there?"

"Couple of empty gas cans and a lot of bark. Alder, probably." Then he strolls out of the office, leaving the door open.

And Neely wonders whether that was a concession or even a peace offering. Or was he just rubbing her nose in the fact that the evidence in Riker's pickup is meaningless.

Hauling extra gas cans or alder wood is not a crime.

Heather asks, "You want me to close the door, Sheriff?"

"No. And you can open the blinds. But first—" She frowns at the evidence envelope, then looks intently into Heather's startled green eyes. "Heather, I want you to promise me something."

"What, Sheriff?" It comes out in a husky whisper.

"Promise me you'll never tell anyone about this envelope. Not your mother or father or brother or sister or best friend or priest or minister or lover. No one."

She nods so enthusiastically, the wispy curls around her face bob. "Oh, Neely, I promise. On my *soul!*"

That solemn oath is convincing, especially since Neely is sure Heather takes her soul seriously. "Thanks. Okay, when the OSP officer gets here, I'll be in Interrogation A."

Chapter 8

THEY'RE THE OLD-FASHIONED wooden telephone booths, with glass-paneled doors that fold shut. A pair of them are tucked under each of the two staircases framing the courthouse lobby.

The caller turns his back to the lobby and the noise of busy people hurrying across the terrazzo floor. He likes this booth under the north stairs. The overhead light doesn't work, so he's not as likely to be noticed. Of course, the dim light makes it hard to see the numbers on the old rotary dial. The phones are old-fashioned, too.

He listens impatiently to the ringing on the other end. Two rings. Three. Five. "Shit!" He's about to hang up.

"Hello?"

The caller asks, "Can you talk?"

"Uh . . . yes. But this had better be an emergency. You know better than to call me here—"

"It goddamn well *is* an emergency! Listen, Giff *quit.* Came into the briefing room stinking drunk and just quit, right then. Culpepper was there, and he said since that nigger bitch was sheriff-*elect* . . . well, *she's* the new sheriff. As of *today.*"

"My God! I can't *believe*—" A brief silence, then:

"Never mind. I can handle Neely. Don't worry about her."

The caller checks his watch. Nine-thirty. He can't stay away from his desk too long. "Yeah, but you haven't heard the worst yet. I put the envelope under Giff's desk, just like always, but—"

"You *what*? Didn't you know he lost the election?"

"How was I s'posed to know that at six in the morning? Stupid radio station doesn't come on till seven in the winter, and you can't pick up any of the Valley stations."

"The Valley *newspapers* are available at six in the morning!"

"Yeah, well, I guess I didn't think about—"

"Precisely. There's too much you don't think about."

"Goddamn it, even if I *did* know Giff lost the fuckin' election, how would I know he'd quit *today*? He was s'posed to stay on till Janu—"

"I assume there's *more* to this story?"

The caller tries to swallow his resentment at that smart-ass attitude, but it sticks in his throat like a wad of sand. "Yeah, there's more. Giff didn't pick up the envelope. Didn't even go into his office. Just quit and walked out. And as soon as Owen said the bitch could be sheriff, she decided she was gonna move in."

"Move into Giff's office?"

"Yeah. And she *found* it. She found the fuckin' envelope!"

The silence that follows that announcement stretches so long, the caller begins to wonder if the line has gone dead.

No. He hears a long sigh, like a breath held too long then let go.

"What did she do with it?"

"I . . . uh, I'm not sure, except when she went over to Corrections a few minutes ago, I slipped into the office. Giff's phone has a redial button, and when I punched it, I got . . ." He hesitates, then rushes through it: "I got the Oregon State Police Crime Lab. Fingerprint Division."

Another silence. He expects more sarcasm, but the voice is calm now. And that's even scarier.

"Did you leave any prints to be identified?"

"Hell, no! I always use gloves. What about you?"

"Don't be absurd. Well, Giff will have to be dealt with. Unpredictable people are dangerous."

"Yeah, but what about . . . you know, the evidence."

"I'll deal with that, too. And I'll deal with *you,* if you can't keep your brain in gear. I'm warning you now. *Don't screw up again!*"

The caller winces. "Now, wait just a goddamn—" But the line has definitely gone dead this time.

"Shit!" He slams the receiver into its cradle.

But it's an old-fashioned phone, heavy and tough. It doesn't break.

Chapter 9

THE THREE INTERROGATION ROOMS IN the Corrections Division are all alike: eight by ten feet, no windows, the walls painted a rancid pink that's supposed to soothe the most pathologically savage breast.

The evidence envelope is tucked under Neely's arm as she enters Interrogation A and closes the door behind her. Eugene Buxman, aka Dirk Riker, badly in need of a shave—both his face and head—slumps in a chair at the table in the center of the room. He looks up at her with greenish eyes narrowed in arrogant assessment, and for a moment, it seems she can smell the bitter stink of burning, gasoline-soaked wood.

But Riker will never see her rage, never know he's anything but another dumb punk in her eyes.

She can even find him laughable, if she gets in the right frame of mind. He sports a black leather jacket over a black turtleneck, with black Levi's and steel-toed boots. But he's too anemic to carry off this costume. Besides, on some men, shaved heads look good, but Riker's stubbled skull looks like his mother carried him around in a cradle board.

Of course, it's unlikely his mother carried him around

in anything. Neely knows his history, and she wouldn't wish it on any child.

Knowledge in this case does not translate into sympathy.

Corrections Division Deputy Mike Swenson, looking like the tall blond hunk next door, lounges in the chair across the table from Riker. Swenson grins at Neely coolly as he rises. "Well, have fun, Neely. I gotta get back to the cells."

Neely feels like she's been gut-punched.

Damn him. He knows state protocols require two deputies to be present for any interrogation. And he knows Neely can't argue with him in front of Riker. He'd think she's afraid to be alone with him.

Deputy Mike Swenson is into the game, too—the game whose object is to take down the nigger bitch who would be sheriff.

As Swenson opens the door, he says, "We got a screamer in the cells. Lieutenant Booker's waiting for me to go in with him and settle the guy down. Big nigger buck, drunk out of his head. And mad. Oh, man, is he *mad*. Maybe we should put ol' Dirk in the cell with him."

Riker glares at him. "Fuck off, pig!"

Neely knows the "nigger buck" is an invention, but she wonders if the fiction was aimed at Riker or at her.

She watches Swenson leave, waits for the click of the lock, then sits down and lays the evidence envelope on the table, facedown. Swenson has made her position untenable. It wasn't promising when she came in, since all she could hope for was an incriminating slip of the tongue. Still, she turns on the tape recorder mounted at the end of the table and gives it the necessary cover information.

Riker crouches forward and shouts at the machine, "You got no right to hold me, you pickaninny pig! I know my rights, and I wanna lawyer!"

"You *should* know your rights by now, Yew-gene,"

Neely says calmly. "You've had them read to you often enough."

"Damn right! And nothin' stuck, did it?"

"Not in the four years since your juvenile record was closed."

"I wanna *lawyer*!"

"Fine, Yew-gene, but you'll have to pay him yourself."

"What're you talkin' about? Shit, I'm *indigent*."

"Yes, of course you are, Yew-gene. But you're not under arrest."

His eyes are down to slits, hands in fists on the table. Pale hands that look oddly childlike; the Iron Cross ring seems ready to fall off his pinkie finger. He demands, "So, what the hell are you holdin' me for?"

"Questioning."

"Shit, I'm outta here!" His chair scrapes back as he rises and heads for the door.

"Yew-gene, you know better," Neely says indifferently. "I have rights, too, and one is the right to question a suspect in a felony."

"I don't know what you're talkin' about, bitch!"

"Sure you do, Yew-gene. Tell me about last night. Where were you and your buddies at midnight?"

He slinks back to his chair, making a show of nonchalance as he slumps into it. "Midnight? Not sure I can remember that far back. Figure *you* can, though. I bet you're *burnin'* to tell me about it."

"Tell me about burning, Yew-gene."

"You mean how you're just *burnin'* to let a real man get his dick into you, instead of that pukin' little Jap?" He lets her know with a growling laugh how much he anticipates that possibility.

She stares at him without blinking for a count of ten, then says, "Midnight, Yew-gene. Where were you?"

"Shit, I don't know. Nowhere near *your* house, for damn sure."

"Why would you assume I thought you were near *my* house?"

He looks down, fumbling with his ring. "Fuck off, bitch."

"And why did Buck find a couple of empty gas cans and bark from alder saplings in the back of your pickup?"

"That's an unlawful search. I never saw a search warrant."

Neely shakes her head. "Yew-gene, where did you pick up your law? Watching TV at MacLaren?" The reference to the state juvenile detention facility elicits a glare from Riker; then she goes on: "It wasn't a search, Yew-gene. Not with something as visually accessible as the back of your pickup. So, what were you doing last night at midnight?"

"None of your fuckin' business!"

"But it *is* my business, Yew-gene. That's what I get paid for—cleaning up the garbage off our streets."

Every time she uses that sarcastic treatment of his given name, he responds, if only with a muscular tic. Now—finally and predictably—he surges to his feet, leans close to her, his hands planted on the table.

"My name is Dirk Riker, bitch! Not Eugene!"

She rises, too, bracing herself with her left hand, keeping her right hand free. "*My* name is *Deputy* Neely Jones. Not bitch!" Then she smiles with cold amiability. "But it'll be *Sheriff* Neely Jones soon. Keep that in mind."

"You're shittin' me."

"Well, Yew-gene, I know you don't believe in democratic elections, and I'm sure you don't follow the results, but in this case, you should, because yesterday . . . I was elected sheriff of Taft County."

He starts to laugh, but apparently something he reads in her face sobers him. He sags into his chair. "You mean . . . *you* beat ol' Giff?"

"I mean I did. Now, ol' Giff was willing to turn a blind

eye on your fun and games. You and Giff have a lot in common, actually. But *I* take hate crimes very seriously, and I damn sure won't turn a blind eye on you. One of my teachers at the L.A. Police Academy used to say, 'Perps always fuck up, sooner or later. You just have to watch and wait.' And that's what I'm going to do, Yew-gene, watch and wait."

She expects an outburst, and his silence makes her uneasy. So does the charged hatred in his eyes. It occurs to her that however satisfying it was to threaten him, knowing someday there might be some substance to the threat, she has made a tactical error.

Eugene Buxman, aka Dirk Riker, doesn't play by the rules, but he has his own twisted sense of justice. He will have retribution, but he'll strike in the dark, strike when her guard is down.

And he is quite capable of striking her through whatever and whomever she loves.

Jan Koto. The "little Jap" who could take Riker down in a few seconds if the confrontation were hand to hand, but who is too gentle and too preoccupied with the magical world of the sea to keep his guard up against an enemy who lies in ambush in the shadows of night.

A forceful knock on the door startles her. She picks up the evidence envelope before she goes to the door, knocks once. And when the door opens finds Corrections Division secretary/matron Molly Teller there, a big-boned woman with steel gray hair and a no-nonsense steel gray suit. Neely knows that away from the TCSO, Molly has a wry sense of humor and a wonderful laugh, but when she's on duty, she cultivates an intimidating presence.

She says tersely, "Somebody here to see you, Neely."

Behind her stands an Oregon State Patrol officer. He nods and says, "I had a call from Lieutenant Bivins to pick up something, ma'am."

She hands him the envelope, feeling a tangible relief when he takes it. "Fast service, Sergeant. Thanks."

"My route's between Westport and Skinner Junction. Didn't have far to go. Well, I'll be on my way. The lieutenant wants this ASAP."

Molly says, "I'll let you out, Sergeant. Neely, what about him?" She cocks a thumb toward Riker.

"Yew-gene?" Neely looks around at him.

There's lots of cockleburs on the road of life, Neely, honey. If you've got good stout shoes on you just step on 'em. If you're barefoot, you gotta tiptoe round 'em.

Well, I've got good stout shoes, Gramma Faith.

"Let him go, Molly. I'm through with him."

Neely turns away and hears Riker's shout behind her: "I ain't through with *you,* bitch!"

Chapter 10

THE MORNING DOESN'T SEEM DESTINED to improve.

Rumors of Giff's resignation and Neely's promotion to sheriff have already swept through the courthouse—and Westport—and that means more official phone calls and, in the case of Elspeth Prentiss, mayor of Westport, a personal visit. El is worried about the city's contract with the TCSO for law enforcement within the city limits. Neely assures her, "We'll still do our best with our very limited resources." A sugar-coated barb to warn El that Neely will fight to force the city to pay a larger share of the TCSO budget.

Rumors have reached the press, too. Heather has been referring callers from the media to the DA's office, a ploy that tests Culpepper's patience, and he orders Neely to come to his office for a press conference. She tells the reporters nothing they don't already know, which pleases the DA, who does most of the talking anyway.

Then Danny Beecher, the Animal Control deputy, gets an anonymous tip about a cockfight in a barn in north county, and Buck Dolin and Whit Chaffee go with him to check it out. The result is an empty barn, three deputies unavailable for two hours, and a patrol car disabled on a muddy, mountain road.

This on top of the more usual calls: anti-Semitic graffiti at Sterne's Antiques—which Neely chalks up to Riker and his buddies—a car theft, a juvenile shoplifting, and an altercation involving switchblades at the high school.

Neely and Heather work sporadically at boxing up Giff Wills's possessions. Rather, Heather works at that. Neely manages to get her cartonful installed in the desk amid other demands, including spelling Lonnie Weaver at the dispatch board while he takes his lunch break. No one else is available. And it turns out to be a long lunch.

It's deliberate, of course. The men never refuse a direct order, but they continually manage to misunderstand her and try her patience in small, annoying ways.

More cockleburs on the road of life, right, Gramma?

Lonnie finally returns at 1:15, at which time Neely goes into the office—she still can't think of it as *her* office—and asks Heather to bring her a couple of sandwiches and a milk from the courthouse cafeteria.

When Heather departs, Neely sinks into the chair behind the desk. At the moment, the only regular deputy on hand is Darrell Logan, whose desk is nose to nose with Curtis McMinn's. Logan is the office Romeo, or so he likes to think: curly dark hair, blue eyes with long lashes, a heavy jaw with a cleft chin.

Oh, be still my heart, Neely thinks bitterly as he pulls out a comb and rearranges his hair. Perhaps he feels her gaze. He sends her a dazzling "eat your heart out" grin.

The phone on the desk rings, and she frowns, trying to figure out which line is represented by the blinking pink light. Giff's private line. She picks up the receiver and snaps a crisp "Deputy Neely Jones."

At first, there's no response. Only the sound of slow breathing.

My God, not a heavy breather.

She makes a note of the number in the caller ID window. A Westport prefix. She motions to Logan, but he's suddenly intently busy typing a report.

"Neely Jones . . ."

The words are a harsh whisper. The speaker's lips must be right on the mouthpiece. She can't tell whether it's male or female. She listens for background sounds while she finds the record button.

"Word of warning, Neely Jones," the whispering voice continues, and she again tries to get Logan's attention, again in vain.

She says into the phone, "A word of warning about what?"

"About rocking the boat. A risky thing to do. Very risky."

There's something melodramatic about that pronouncement, and she has a clear image of two or three deputies gathered around a telephone, smirking, while one whispers into the receiver.

Just another shot in the war of attrition.

Neely says sarcastically, "I'm all a-tremble." Then, putting some punch into her voice, she adds, "Now, get your asses back here!"

She starts to hang up, but the whisperer says, "This is *not* a joke!"

A male voice? The stressed word sounds too deep for a woman. No. It's well within female range. Is that a car horn in the background?

"Convince me," she says.

"Giff Wills found it profitable to be accommodating."

Neely feels a sudden emptiness under her ribs. No, this isn't a joke.

She waits, and finally the whisperer continues: "You can find accommodation profitable, too, Neely Jones."

"How profitable?"

A soft laugh. Something familiar in it, but she can't pin it down.

"Silence is golden. In your case . . . silence is worth a hundred times the amount Giff received for his accommodation. A onetime payment, of course. Payable upon your resignation."

A metallic crashing sound in the background.

"A hundred K for my resignation? Maybe I should be flattered."

"And your silence."

"About Giff's accommodation?"

"Precisely. Besides, you didn't *want* the job of sheriff. So you said."

"Maybe I changed my mind."

"Oh, I wouldn't advise you to do that. It could be very dangerous."

"Dangerous how?"

A passing truck in the background. An outdoor location, near a highway. Pay phone, probably.

"Police officers die every day in the line of duty."

That's enough to send a chill down her spine, but the chill intensifies when the voice adds, "Sometimes those nearest and dearest get caught in the crossfire. Think about it, Neely."

A click. The line goes dead.

Neely does think about it, especially the part about "those nearest and dearest," while she gets a phone book out of the top drawer, calls the phone company's local office, and asks for the manager.

"This is Jeffrey Walker. How may I help you?"

"Deputy Neely Jones, TCSO. I want to know the location of a phone." She gives him the number. "It's probably a pay phone."

He puts her on hold and subjects her to a Lawrence Welk polka.

"Did you want something, Neely?"

Deputy Darrell Logan lounges in the briefing room door. Neely busies herself putting the phone book away, rearranging the bouquet of pens and pencils—anything rather than recognize Logan's presence.

Finally, the manager rescues her from the polka. "You're right—it is a pay phone. It's at one one four two Highway Thirteen. That'll be the Eastgate Mall."

She nods. The metallic crashing she heard was a bagger stacking grocery carts at the Thriftway. "Thanks, Mr. Walker."

When she hangs up, she looks at Logan, considering whether to send him to the mall to ask around about someone making a call from the pay phone. A wild-goose chase, yes, but Logan deserves it.

No. Right now, Logan and two reserves are the only deputies available. She was the one who warned the staff about playing games.

"I don't need you, Deputy Logan."

He looks irritably disappointed as he returns to his desk.

She rewinds the tape and listens to it again. She can't rid herself of a sense of familiarity, but neither can she identify the voice.

Finally, when Heather comes in with a carton of milk and two sandwiches—ham and cheese and egg salad, both on wheat—Neely turns off the recorder and places the note listing the pay phone number and location in the top drawer.

Heather sighs gustily. "Sorry to take so long, Sheriff. Long line. And everybody's talking about you."

"What are they saying?" Then she laughs. "Never mind. You'd better take your lunch break now."

"I already did. I had some yogurt while I was waiting in line." She looks longingly at the sandwich Neely is unwrapping. "Oh, it must be lovely not having to count every calorie that crosses your lips."

Neely studies Heather's perfect, size-six-petite figure. It never occurred to her what a price she pays to maintain it.

The phone in Heather's office rings, and Neely finds herself tensing, glancing at the phone on her desk to see if the pink private-line light is on. It isn't, but she realizes now that if the whisperer's purpose is to make her nervous, he has succeeded.

Damn him! Or her or it or whatever.

Chapter 11

BEFORE SHE ENTERS THE LOBBY at the Taft County Sheriff's Office, Willow Thornbeck checks her old Timex. Nearly three. Should be a good time. She wonders if Neely will remember her. They've often met on the beach when Neely and her young man were jogging and Willow was giving the dogs their early run.

No, Neely probably won't remember her. Just another elderly, overweight woman on the beach. Westport is full of them. And most of them cut their white hair short, as Willow does, although she can't be bothered with those curly perms. And most of them wear tennie runners and pants with elastic waists and bright-colored windbreakers. And most of them have at least one dog.

Something to keep them company. They're so often widows.

Willow Thornbeck has been a widow for thirty years, although she tends to think of herself as a spinster. She didn't find marriage particularly agreeable, and it was almost a relief when John Quincy Thornbeck, the proselytizing health nut, had a heart attack at the age of thirty-seven while climbing Mount Hood.

Willow pauses in the lobby, then turns left into the receptionist's office, where Heather Blessing is at her desk. Pretty little thing. She doesn't know she's been a model for three different heroines.

Heather looks up and says brightly, "Oh, hi, Mrs. Thornbeck."

"Hello, Heather. I want to see the sheriff. The *new* sheriff."

Heather looks toward the open door into the sheriff's office, where Neely Jones is at the desk. Before Heather can say a word, Neely calls out, "Mrs. Thornbeck? Come on in."

Well, that's a good sign.

The sheriff's office is in a state of flux, with loaded cartons strewn about. To Willow's relief, the decapitated deer has been removed. Neely waves her to the chair in front of the desk with a warning: "Watch out for that chair, Mrs. Thornbeck."

"Please, call me Willow." She eases into the chair, remembering its wayward habits.

"Okay, Willow. And you might as well call me Neely. I haven't been officially sworn in yet. Is there something I can do for you?"

Oh, my, what a difference. And Neely might make a good heroine, too. Willow wonders if her editor would insist on making any character based on Neely white. That wouldn't work at all.

"Yes, Neely, there *is* something you can do for me." As she speaks, she feels the knot of anger and grief tightening in her stomach. "I . . . I want to report a dognapping."

"Is your dog lost?"

"Not *lost*. Stolen. Benny. He's such a little thing. Terrier mix, mostly Cairn. And I *know* he didn't just wander off. I have a six-foot chain-link fence around my property. Well, not the rental half. It's a duplex, you see, and I rent out the north half. But Benny couldn't get out of my yard unless he dug his way out, and I didn't find any sign of digging. And he isn't a wanderer; he was neutered."

Neely leans back in her chair. "When did you last see Benny?"

"Last Monday at nine in the morning. I have—*had*—three dogs. That day, I let them out in the yard about eight-thirty and went back inside to work. But at nine, when I went out to call them in, Benny was *gone*. Oh, damn . . ." She digs in her jacket pocket for a Kleenex. She didn't intend to get weepy. After a moment, she asks, "Did you ever have dogs, Neely?"

She seems surprised, as if the question brings up buried memories. "No. None that were really mine. Some of my cousins and friends had dogs. Did you ask about Benny at the Humane Society?"

"That's the first thing I did, since that's where I got him. All my pups have come from the pound. Except Sal. But that was a long time ago. I had her when I first moved here. Miniature poodle. Actually, poodles are marvelous dogs, if you don't give them those atrocious trims." Oh, dear, she's getting garrulous. The sheriff will think she's just another dotty old lady. Willow adds firmly, "I also put a notice on the radio and in the paper and talked to my neighbors. And I called your Animal Control officer, Deputy Beecher."

"Oh? What did he say?"

That seems so guarded. Almost suspicious. Willow replies, "He said he only deals with animal nuisances or mistreatment. I don't know why I even bothered him this time."

"*This* time?"

"Benny's the *third* dog I've had stolen in a little over a year. That's why I don't think they were just lost. I think someone's stealing them to sell to a laboratory. But when I told Sheriff Wills—and I did, both times before—he just said not to worry, that they'd come back when they got hungry. Then he told me how busy he was and shooed me out, and after I waited over an hour to see him the first time and two the second!"

Neely's eyes are narrowed and glittering. There's a definite animosity there, and Willow finds that as reassuring as her words.

"I apologize for my predecessor, Willow. No citizen with a complaint should be treated so badly."

"Thank you. I suppose . . . well, I know a lot of people think I'm just an eccentric old woman." Willow laughs at that, dabbing at her eyes. "It's just that I get so attached to my pups, and I'd only had Benny two months. Same with the other stolen ones. I'd just had them a short time. They had such hard lives before I got them, then . . ."

"Okay, Willow, let's start with the first disappearance." Neely reaches into her shirt pocket for a notebook and pen. "When was that?"

"September fifth last year. Katya."

Neely begins writing. "What kind of dog was she?"

"Oh, a sweet dog. So playful and full of joy."

"No, I mean—well, can you describe her?"

"Oh. Yes, of course. She was a sheltie-shepherd mix, three years old, two feet tall at the shoulder, tawny brown, with very big ears."

"What were the circumstances of Katya's disappearance?"

"Just like Benny's, really. Although it was earlier in the morning."

"And the second dog?"

"Button. Same story. That's what's so *strange* about it."

"Did the other dogs bark or give any sort of alarm?"

"No. But then, Kili's a basenji. He *can't* bark. He makes a sort of whining noise, but it's not very loud. And Abby, well, she's quite elderly and doesn't see or hear well. She hardly ever barks."

Neely nods. "Tell me about Button."

"He was a black Pomeranian-poodle mix, about ten inches tall. And my best guard dog. I mean, best for sounding the alarm. He wasn't big enough to do any real damage, but he thought he was a wolf. They all do." Willow opens her purse and rummages inside, thinking ruefully what an old-lady's bag it is, floppy and huge, stuffed with rattling odds and ends. Finally, she finds the small album.

"I have photographs of them," she says, flipping through the plastic envelopes. "Here. The last three."

Neely dutifully looks through the album. She says, perhaps a little too casually, "You've had a lot of dogs."

"That album covers a period of thirty years, and I was just fostering some of them. Like a couple of years ago when the Chinook flooded and so many homes were damaged. The Humane Society found foster homes for the pets until the families could get on their feet enough to take care of them. I fostered three dogs then."

Neely reaches across the desk to return the album to Willow. "I wish I could offer you some hope for your dogs, but—"

"I know you can't get them back. It's just—well, I can't go *on* like this, grieving for my pups. Oh, I hate even thinking about what happened to them. They're innocents, you know. It's just not right for someone to make them suffer."

"No. Nor to make *you* suffer." Neely picks up her pen. "Okay, I'll need your address and phone number."

Willow provides them, adding, "I'm just a few blocks from your house—that duplex on the beach south of the Sea View Motel. Cedar shingles. The garage in the middle between the units."

"I remember it. You must have a gorgeous view."

"Oh, yes. I bought it back before beachfront property became the perquisite of the rich. Fortunately, the rent covers the property taxes. But I never take short-term rentals. That's the ruin of a town, making motels of neighborhoods. And I've been lucky with my renters."

"You have a renter now?"

"Yes. He moved in . . . well, let's see, about a year and a half ago. Yes, late July of last year."

Neely's dark eyes are suddenly hooded. "What's his name?"

"Gordon Wyland. He's such a considerate renter. No

late parties or loud music. He even mows both our lawns. Of course, I don't see him much, since he works a late shift. He's a bartender at the Beachside Lounge. Works from six in the evening until two in the morning, and he says it takes another couple of hours to wind down enough to sleep. Bartending is so nerve-racking. But he says he likes the late shift. He's a night person. You know, that's so hard for me to understand. I'm always up and about by six. I do my best work before noon." Then, realizing she's getting garrulous again, Willow rises. "Well, I won't keep you any longer. Thanks for listening to my troubles."

Neely comes to her feet. "That's my job, Willow. I just hope I can do something about these particular troubles."

As Willow departs, she feels almost light-headed with relief and hope. At least she knows Sheriff Neely Jones will *try*. Writing Neely's name in on that ballot was the smartest thing she's done in a long time.

Chapter 12

ALL IT TAKES IS ONE, Neely. Get one good person on your side, and the Lord behind you, and you're an army.

Neely isn't so sure about having the Lord behind her, and she doesn't feel much like an army. Still, Willow Thornbeck was a tonic.

"Sheriff?" Heather comes into the office with a sheaf of papers. "Somebody left these on my desk while I was in the ladies' room. Here's the paperwork from Vehicle Maintenance and some requisition—oh, for heaven's sake!"

"What?"

Heather hands Neely a requisition form—for a size 44D, brass-lined bra; color, black.

Another shot in the war of attrition. Yet Neely finds herself laughing. She says, "Darrell."

Heather nods. "Who else?"

Neely takes the form and goes into the briefing room, where Darrell Logan and Danny Beecher are at their desks, looking busy. She drops the requisition form on Logan's desk as she passes. "Sorry, Darrell. The uniform allowance doesn't include your underwear."

Beecher snickers, but Logan apparently has nothing to say. Neely continues to Buck Dolin's office. He looks up at her from behind his typewriter, waiting for her to initiate any conversation.

"Chief, do you know anything about a man named Gordon Wyland? He's night bartender at the Beachside Lounge."

Buck leans back in his chair, big hands laced behind his head.

"Met him once. Called us on a D and D at the Beachside. Had sort of a chip on his shoulder, but he was polite enough." Buck's eyes go into a thoughtful squint. "Quiet. A very quiet man."

"Thanks, Chief." Neely goes into the Dispatch Center, and while Lonnie Weaver watches her obliquely, she checks priors for Gordon Wyland on the Law Enforcement Data System computer. LEDS has nothing on him.

"Lonnie, I'll be out of the office for about half an hour."

He makes a noncommittal sound, and as she reaches for one of the sets of car keys on the board by the hall door, she wonders if he'd radio her for anything less than an attack on the courthouse by terrorists.

When she leaves the building, she's vaguely surprised to find it's a perfect autumn day, the sun shining, a light, warm wind blowing. She drives east on Highway 13, past Eastgate Mall, a cheapjack collection of small shops, dominated by a supermarket. She notes the pay phone near the supermarket. It reminds her of the Whisperer. She's beginning to think of him, her, or it with a capital letter.

Two blocks beyond the mall, she turns left into the gravel parking area in front of the flat-roofed building that houses the Humane Society's pound. She goes into the lobby, where a volunteer assures her the director is in and waves her to a door on the right wall. When Neely opens the door, she's greeted by a fusillade of barking.

The dog is standing on Janie Dial's desk. It looks like a miniature collie, with long fur, gold shaded with sable, a white ruff and legs, and a thin white line down its long nose.

Janie is standing behind the dog, wielding a wire brush. "Hi, Neely. And congratulations, *Sheriff* Jones! Hush, Vixen. It's okay, sweetheart. She's a friend."

The dog doesn't seem convinced, but when Janie whispers in its ear, it stops barking. She has that knack with animals. A tall, rail-thin white woman with chestnut hair cut shoulder length and wide brown eyes, Janie looks as if she just finished her adolescent growth spurt, but, in fact, she's Neely's age and has a master's degree in human services. Neely often wonders how Janie went from human to animal services.

"This is Vixen," Janie says.

"She's . . . pretty." Something about the dog makes Neely uncomfortable. Maybe the direct gaze. It never seems to blink.

Janie continues brushing. "Pretty? She's gorgeous. Pedigreed Shetland sheepdog. Her people dumped her here an hour ago. Said the neighbors complained about her barking. We get a lot of dogs with that excuse. Shelties, Poms, and terriers, especially. They all tend to be vocal." Janie runs a hand along Vixen's head, and the dog opens her mouth in what almost seems a smile. "If no one adopts Vixen within a week, we'll have to kill her."

Janie never bothers with euphemisms.

Neely asks, "How do you stand this work, Janie?"

"I just remember all the animals we *do* find good homes for. Well, I doubt you came for the ten-cent lecture. What can I do for you?"

"I had a visit from Willow Thornbeck a little while ago."

"Good. Giff Wills would hardly give her the time of day. Willow's one of our volunteers, and I've known her for years. Oops! Sorry, Vixen. You've got a bad tangle back here. And, Neely, no way has Willow lost touch with reality. You can believe anything she says."

"I do. Have you heard of any other cases like this in the area?"

"You mean spayed or neutered dogs disappearing from loving homes surrounded by six-foot chain-link fences? No. Not a one."

"What about Willow's theory that they were stolen to sell to labs?"

"Selling animals for experimentation does happen. Some city pounds even sell animals they'd have to euthanize otherwise. But with Willow's dogs . . . I don't know. Why would a dognapper concentrate on *her* dogs? And at intervals of months?"

Neely finds herself avoiding Vixen's unflinching gaze. "Do you have any ideas about what happened to Willow's dogs?"

"Well, in this business, we always say, *Cherchez le voisin.*"

"Find the . . . what?"

"Neighbor. The *complaining* neighbor. Although Willow said she's had no complaints from any of her neighbors."

Neely nods. "Maybe we're looking for a quiet man. A *very* quiet man." Then without thinking about it, she reaches out to touch the sheltie's head. The short fur around her face is like satin.

"Janie, no way can I have a dog in my life."

Vixen looks up at Neely and smiles. A sad smile, it seems, as if she understands her probable fate. Neely turns and heads for the door.

"Thanks for the information, Janie."

By the time Neely gets back to the TCSO, it's nearly four o'clock, and the swing shift is coming on. Only four deputies, including Wayne Gerlach, the dispatcher, but they'll be augmented with two more when the late swing shift comes on at seven.

Neely informs the swing shift supervisor, Lt. Brad Skinner, that she'll be staying on this evening. Skinner, a man whose answer to tension is food, and whose middle-aged body shows the cumulative effect, grunts noncommittally.

She leaves Skinner and Buck discussing the day-shift radio log and goes into the sheriff's office.

Heather is there, searching through one of the file cabinets. "I'm looking for the department protocols file you asked for, but I can't find it. Giff never worried much about protocols."

"He probably filed it under *F* for Forget It." Neely sinks into the chair behind the desk. She's beginning to get used to it, and it feels almost comfortable. "It's quitting time, Heather."

"Is it? Well . . . I could stay for the swing shift."

"What? No heavy date tonight?"

Heather blushes winsomely. "Thomas has a basketball game."

That would be Thomas Stockton, assistant coach at Westport High. "Well, you should probably be there to cheer for the home team."

"Yes, I suppose so. Trouble is . . ." Heather gazes upward as if in search of divine absolution. "I don't really *like* basketball, and after a game, that's all Thomas can talk about—every little play and all the tiny details." She pauses for a sigh. "But I guess I *do* love him. I learned all the rules of basketball by heart."

Neely laughs. "It must be love, then. Go on home, Heather. And thanks for your help today."

When Heather departs, Neely realizes she's suddenly tired. Stress-tired. What she needs is a run on the beach or a session in the dojo with Jan. No. All she needs is Jan. He must be back from his expedition with Andrea by now. She leans forward to pick up the phone, startled when it rings before she can touch it. The private line.

She snatches up the receiver but doesn't speak. What she hears is audible breathing. The Whisperer.

She presses the record button.

The voice begins, "Neely Jones . . ."

"No, it's Oprah. What do you want?"

A soft laugh. "Oh, Neely, such a sense of humor. I've told you what I want. No—what I *expect.*"

Neely jots down the number in the caller ID window. It's different from this morning's call. She considers trying to get one of the deputies' attention in the hope of locating the phone and sending a patrol there before the caller departs.

No. The Whisperer is too canny to give her that much time. And which of the deputies can she trust with that assignment?

"What you expect," she repeats. "You mean my resignation?"

"Precisely."

"Oh, yes, precisely. For a hundred thou, right?"

"Your memory seems to be quite clear."

"Well, that sort of thing tends to make an impression."

"Then we can reach an agreement?"

Neely hesitates. She wants the Whisperer to keep calling; otherwise, she'll never get a line on him. Or her. Or it.

She says, "I need some time to think about this."

"Oh, no." The voice is still a whisper, but there's a latent menace in it now. "You've run out of time. You have a choice: the carrot or the whip. There's no other alternative." Then a click and a dead line.

"Shit!"

"Something wrong, Neely?"

Buck Dolin looms in the doorway, frowning slightly.

"Nothing's wrong, Chief. Go home." That comes out with more of an edge than she intended.

He shrugs and returns to the briefing room without another word.

Neely irritably punches the number for the telephone company. A few minutes later, she is informed that the call came from another phone booth, this one at the marina on Chinook Bay.

Why would Buck turn so solicitous at just that moment? *Something wrong, Neely?*

Oh, gee, Buck, not a thing.

Obviously, he isn't the Whisperer, but it's possible he's the courier—the one who left the thousand-dollar payoff for Giff this morning.

What the hell was it for, and who did it come from?

Only the Whisperer knows. . . .

And she's got better things to worry about. Like a small dog named Benny.

She goes into the briefing room, where the swing shift is settling in to wait for the inevitable first call. Their banter was audible from the office, but the moment she steps into the room, a cool silence falls.

Fine. There's enough idle chatter in here anyway.

She studies the available deputies: Lieutenant Skinner, Senior Deputy Sonny Hoffstead, and Deputy Kevin Locksey.

Yes, Kev will do. Kevin Locksey, with his clean-cut good looks, seems to be the essential all-American nice white guy, from an all-American nice white suburb. Kirkland, in fact, a suburb of Seattle. He's the youngest deputy and the most recently hired. He's been with the TCSO less than a year.

Which is why Neely chooses him. She asks, "Kev, have you ever been to the Beachside Lounge?"

Locksey glances at the other deputies before he replies, "No. Melanie and I don't go out a lot."

"Perfect. I need you for a special assignment." She looks at Skinner, challenging him to object.

The lieutenant shrugs and says, "Take him, Neely; he's yours," and can't seem to resist adding a laugh bordering on the gamy.

Neely motions to Locksey as she strides back to the office. "Come on, Kev. I'll fill you in."

Chapter 13

THE SCIENTIFIC NAME FOR THIS species is *Aurelia aurita*. The popular name is "moon jellies." *Jellies*. Even the scientists at the Westport Oceanographic Center use that slang for jellyfish. So does Jan, although sometimes he calls them medusae.

He calls this the medusa pool.

It's the center's newest display, and Neely considers it the most beautiful. But then, she's biased. Jan Koto designed it.

A cylinder eight feet in diameter, made of three-inch-thick Lucite, rising from floor to ceiling. The working parts of this and all the other displays—pipes and pumps to carry seawater from Chinook Bay and back, filters to remove contaminants, temperature probes and salinity monitors, incubators to produce shrimp larvae and other organisms for food—are all out of sight in the maintenance room above the ceiling.

Neely has the museum wing to herself at 5:15, a quarter hour past winter closing time, although she can hear voices from the front of the center. The museum occupies the east wing of the spacious U-shaped building; the west wing is devoted to research. The open end of the U faces south and overlooks the staff parking lot and Chinook Bay. Through the windows at the back of the wing, Neely can see the bay, reflecting gray clouds, and the dock where *Poseidon* is moored, pristinely white and as graceful as the sea creatures she pursues.

The walls and ceiling in the museum wing are a deep blue-green to focus attention on the lighted aquariums lining the walls and jutting out in angular peninsulas. The medusa pool is the only freestanding tank, and within the transparent cylinder, a corps of two dozen moon jellies dances in slow motion, glowing in the light from the spotlights inset in the floor of the tank.

Mindless and blind, all they can do is flex their foot-wide umbrellas, pulsing randomly through the water. Yet jellyfish have pulsed through Earth's seas for half a billion years, evolving into myriad forms. They are virtually all water—living capsules of the sea.

All that, Neely learned from Jan. Before she met him, jellyfish were just the revolting blobs of dead protoplasm she stepped on as a child on rare visits to the beach. Now she watches the living creatures. Radiant white, tinged with pink, they seem creations of delicately embroidered silk organdy, their scalloped edges perfectly hemstitched, fringed with long, fine threads; gathered beneath the organdy umbrella, ruffled lobes and gossamer streamers trail, undulating with the slow pulsations.

"Here for some R and R?"

Jan. She didn't hear him approach. He kneads her tight shoulder muscles, and she closes her eyes. "I'm past R and R. Oh, Jan, that's beautiful. I always dreamed of having a live-in masseur."

"By the way, congratulations, *Sheriff* Niri-san."

She smiles and turns to face him. "I knew you'd say that." And she kisses him, relishing the sweet freedom within the confines of his arms. Finally, she says, "Now, *that's* therapy. Any luck today? Did you catch any of your pet jellies?"

"Yes. Actually, they're more prevalent than we thought. I've got ten of them in the lab and about ten rolls of film to develop."

"How's Andrea?" Neely gives him a glancing smile with that.

"Ravishing in a wet suit," he replies with a quick laugh.

Neither the response nor the laugh surprise her, but she *is* surprised when the laugh fades, to be replaced by an uneasy frown.

"Jan, what's wrong?"

He shrugs and says, "I'm afraid it might be a little awkward in the future, working with her. Maybe impossible." The he focuses on Neely with the smile that always sets the world right for her. "Never mind that, Sheriff Niri-san. Let's go *celebrate.*"

"What? My being crowned sheriff for a day?"

He puts his arm around her shoulders and they walk toward the north end of the wing. "Oh, I think you'll be wearing this crown for many days to come, even years. Damn, I'll be glad when they finish this painting job." Jan detours around the sheets of plastic laid on the floor under the painters' ladders at the front of the wing.

They turn left and walk through the turnstiles and past the ticket counter and gift shop and into the bright lobby centered in the base of the U. Three pairs of glass doors open to the public parking lot north of the building. Neely is surprised to see the center's director, Dr. S. Benjamin Nicholass, holding one of the glass doors as three volunteers depart. He wishes them good night, calling them by their first names.

Ben Nicholass is an adept politician. He has the resonant voice and paternalistic chumminess. Neely wonders if he knows that the staff calls him "Saint Nick" behind his back. Or "Saint Nickel-ass."

He'd like the Saint Nick. Every Christmas, he plays Santa Claus for the Kiwanis children's party. It doesn't take much artifice, since his hair is white—prematurely, he insists—and he sports a beard. The role requires some padding, although his athlete's body seems to be going soft with middle age. His eyes are such a bright blue, Neely suspects the color is augmented by tinted contacts, but the children are probably less suspicious. They probably also think his pink cheeks are a result of life in a cold climate, when the ruddy hue is more likely due to his taste for good scotch.

But he needs the red suit to carry off the role. Now he looks typically Southern California, with his pale yellow turtleneck and baby blue blazer. His white Nikes seem to be his only concession to life in Oregon, the home of Nike.

"Neely!" He strides toward her with a dazzling smile. "I understand congratulations are in order!" He takes her hand in both of his with a familiarity she finds vaguely offensive. She always wonders if he's trying to establish that he doesn't mind touching a black person.

She musters a smile. "I'm not sure I'm ready for congratulations."

Jan laughs. "Whether you're ready or not, congratulation *are* due. I told you—you'll be the best damn sheriff this county has ever seen."

"Precisely!" Nicholass says, finally releasing her hand. "Well, are you two going out for a celebration tonight?"

"It'll be a short celebration," Neely says. "I want to be back at the TCSO before the late swing shift goes on at seven."

Nicholass nods knowingly. "The price of command. Are you parked out front? I'll lock the door behind you. You're the last ones."

Neely wonders why Sgt. Curtis McMinn, in his role as night watchman, isn't locking up, but she doesn't ask. Nicholass ushers them out onto the covered deck with hearty but hurried good-byes.

The public parking lot, interspersed with islands of jack pines and globe lights, is empty except for their blue Toyota pickup. The wind has turned cold, and Neely looks up into the gray sky.

"Storm coming," Jan says. "Mersky was making baleful predictions all day." He pulls his keys out of his pocket as they reach the pickup. "I was planning to take you to the Château la Mer for dinner. My treat."

"*Your* treat? Well, tonight I'll settle for a hamburger at Henny's."

As Neely climbs into the passenger seat, she's distracted by the roar of a car spurting along Chinook, the street west of the oceanographic center. It's Ben Nicholass's white Mercedes SLK. She watches the showy little car brake at North First, then turn left toward the highway, and she mutters, "What is it with men and piston engines?"

Jan only laughs as he turns the key in the ignition and noisily revs the Toyota's engine.

JAN DOESN'T SEEM TOO DISAPPOINTED at trading hamburgers at Henny's, a venerable café a block from the courthouse, for multiple-course delicacies at the ambience-laden Château la Mer.

They sit in a booth upholstered in vinyl nearly the same grating pink as the walls in the TCSO interrogation rooms, enjoying generous hamburgers and mounds of crisp french fries while Neely tells Jan about her first day as sheriff of Taft County. She realizes she's venting her frustrations, but Jan is a willing and sympathetic listener.

By the time they leave Henny's, Neely is sated and calm. Jan tells her he'll walk the four blocks to the center. He has notes to enter into his computer and film to develop. "I'll phone you when I'm finished, Neely. And if you're out on a call, I'll walk home."

The arrangement isn't unusual. Neely knows that when Jan gets involved in his research, he loses all track of time. She's learned not to worry about him when he doesn't get home until the wee hours.

And he had learned not to worry about her when a late call keeps her out until the wee hours.

At least they tell each other they don't worry.

Chapter 14

DOWN EBBTIDE STREET, IN AND out of the pools of light at the corners, Jennifer Kaynard pedals south, her sturdy, muscular legs moving with machinelike efficiency.

And she's thinking that the Walkers not only have really sweet kids but they're totally neat people. They came home early, at nine—poor Mrs. Walker was sick to her stomach—yet Mr. Walker paid Jennifer for the full three hours they expected to be gone. He offered to drive her home, but she wouldn't let him. Not with Mrs. Walker so sick.

Besides, it's only twelve blocks. Just a few minutes on her bike.

Jennifer Kaynard is fifteen, and grown-ups always seem to like her. Mrs. Walker calls her "a darling girl." But when Jennifer looks in a mirror, she calls herself ugly: too short, too chunky, hair the color of mud, face always producing a zit at the worst times.

Her mom says it's just as well she isn't pretty. Pray for acceptance; pray for understanding of true beauty in the eyes of the Lord.

Jennifer prays, but not for acceptance.

Up ahead, Ebbtide ends in a T with North First Street

just in front of the Westport Oceanographic Center's parking lot. Normally, she'd turn left and stay on North First to Kelp Street, where she lives, but tonight she stops before making the turn.

Jennifer loves the center building, with its cedar walls and shake roof. It looks so natural, as if it belongs here, surrounded by jack pines and wild rhododendrons. And she takes a personal interest in the center, not only because she works part-time in the gift shop but because she's decided that one day she'll be an oceanographer.

She's never told anyone that. Only Mr. Lutz, her science teacher.

But what stops her tonight is the light in one of the windows to the right of the main entrance. She can't see through the window; the miniblinds are closed.

That's Dr. Nicholass's office. Maybe he's working late.

It's odd, though. She's never heard of Dr. Nicholass ever working late. Maybe she should just check the staff parking lot behind the building to see if his white Mercedes is there.

A glare of headlights distracts her: a car driving north on Chinook, the short street that runs along the west side of the center property and gives access to the staff parking lot. There's a streetlight at the corner of Chinook and North First, and she gets a good look at the vehicle before it turns left and drives away from her.

A dark blue minivan, the kind with the sloped windshield.

An unfamiliar vehicle coming out of the center's staff lot brings on a frown; then she remembers that Chinook also connects with Bay Road, which runs west to Highway 101.

Jennifer pushes off and crosses North First. She coasts through the public parking lot with a whir of spokes, angling toward the museum wing. But she's barely halfway across when she stops again. The light in Dr. Nicholass's office has gone out. And it's only now that it occurs to her that it was probably Sergeant McMinn who turned the light on. Just making his rounds, checking the offices.

She should've figured that out.

Again, she's distracted by a vehicle heading north on Chinook, which seems like a lot of traffic for a short street at night. She shivers, suddenly cold, when she recognizes the big red-and-black pickup.

Dirk Riker, the wanna-be Nazi. He looks so stupid with his head shaved. But Riker and his buddies aren't the kind of guys anybody wants to meet up with on a dark night.

Jennifer pedals hard away from the pickup to the east entrance of the parking lot. Once out of the lot, she doesn't turn left to return to North First. She just wants to get out of sight fast, so she crosses Frigate Street and continues east on South First.

She glances back. The pickup is gone. Her breath comes out in a sigh of relief.

A pothole shimmies the front wheel. She's never been on this street at night. *South* First. It always seemed weird that two streets only a block apart have the same name, except one is North and the other South. But Westport is full of odd stuff like that.

The street is narrow and bumpy, and after two blocks, she runs out of pavement and out of houses and streetlights. Still, it's only a couple more blocks to Fairgrounds Road. She'll turn north there. The tires chatter on gravel, but she can see a streetlight ahead and the high, board fence surrounding the fairgrounds. And up ahead, a stop sign.

She dutifully stops, even though Fairgrounds Road seems deserted. That's when she hears voices and loud laughing. She looks to her left. The streetlight shines on a car parked on the near shoulder, maybe fifty feet away.

Jeff Amato's red Taurus convertible. And the idiot has the top down, like he thinks it's summer or something.

Jeff is a senior, and all the girls think he's *such* a hunk. So does he.

She wonders who's with him. That's Dylan Unger. The

one with the bowl cut, blond hair. She gets a whiff of something sweet.

Marijuana.

That figures. Jeff Amato thinks he can do anything he pleases, just because his father is a big lawyer and filthy rich.

She's *got* to turn north here, and that means she has to pass them. Jennifer begins the turn, heading for the far shoulder to put as much distance between her and the guys as possible. She hears a chorus of shrill whistles: the kind a person would use to call a dog. Bastards!

Mom would be mortified that Jennifer even knows that word.

Headlights flash on, blinding her. But she keeps pumping, bending over the handlebars like a racer.

"Hey, Jennifer!"

Shadow shapes loom out of the light. "Hey, slow *down,* baby!"

"Lookin' fer somethin', Jennifer?" Footsteps slap the asphalt.

T. J. O'Neill. Another one of Jeff's buddies, laughing like a maniac. Right in front of her. Stupid clod! He's grabbing the *handlebars.*

She screams as the bike spins out from under her, and it seems like a huge invisible hand grabs her, pitches her off the bike, and the asphalt heaves up, smashes into her. She hears something snap, and part of her mind knows it's her left arm breaking, but the rest of her mind is an endless shriek of pain that blots out everything else.

At least until she stops sliding along the asphalt.

Somebody's trying to move her.

"No, don't touch me! Don't! Oh, *please* . . ."

They're dragging her, laughing, shouting foul-sounding words she doesn't understand, and she's drowning in pain, screaming with it. Down into the ditch. Cold, wet, dead grass submerges her, and she keeps screaming.

"*Shuddup,* bitch!" Dylan hits her with his fist.

Hits her again. And again. Somebody's jerking at her legs. Pulling her jeans down, ripping her panties, and Dylan's straddling her. Other hands like iron bands on her wrists and ankles, crucifying her in the grass. Can't breathe. Can't see. She can smell the root odor of dirt; she can smell beer, marijuana, and hot, musky sweat.

Dylan panting and laughing, and Jeff and T.J. are laughing, too. Not even human, that sound. Nowhere near human. Her mouth is full of blood, her muscles spasming, while Dylan's grunting weight grinds her into the dirt, while his thick, hard *thing* jams into her.

I'm a virgin! I'm a virgin, and Mom told me to save myself for—

And why can't she faint? Why can't she *die*?

Chapter 15

WESTPORT GENERAL HOSPITAL IS AN attractive single-story building on a hill southwest of Chinook Bay, which gives it a spectacular view, and perhaps the patients who use its fifty beds appreciate that. No doubt they appreciate more having a hospital less than an hour's drive away—a convenience they've enjoyed only for the last ten years.

But there is no view from the emergency room.

The call came into Dispatch at 9:32 P.M. from Senior Deputy Sonny Hoffstead in his patrol on Fairgrounds Road. He was driving north, approaching a parked red Ford Taurus convertible, when three male Caucasians leapt into the car, made a U-turn, and drove away at reckless speed. Sonny got the license number, but he didn't pursue the car, because that was when he saw the wrecked bicycle.

He found Jennifer Kaynard lying in the drainage ditch.

It's now ten minutes before midnight, and Neely waits in the curtained cubicle for Dr. George Standish to finish Jennifer's pelvic exam. She lies in stoic silence, eyes closed. Her left arm is encased in an air cast from wrist to elbow; her hands and forehead are raw with asphalt burns, her mouth and the left side of her face swollen and bruised.

Standish said she's lucky her jaw wasn't broken.

Lucky.

There's nothing lucky in any of this for Jennifer Kaynard.

On the girl's left, Kelly Bower, her silver hair worn defiantly long and free, whispers assurances. Kelly is a counselor at the women's shelter and the recently appointed Taft County Victim's Advocate.

On Jennifer's right, her mother stands gaunt in an old gray cloth coat. There's no *Mr.* Kaynard. He long ago departed and left no forwarding address. Grace Kaynard holds her daughter's hand and mutters about praying for forgiveness.

"A judgment," she says. "This is a judgment."

And Neely wants to ask her what kind of god would inflict a judgment so severe on a shy, pleasant teenager. But she doesn't ask. Nor did she ask Standish why it took him so long to get to the ER, when he was the physician on call. An orthopedic surgeon was paged when Jennifer arrived, and he was here within fifteen minutes to take care of her broken arm. But Standish kept Jennifer waiting an hour and a half.

Neely suspects that was because the nurse who called him told him it was a rape case. To him, that meant there was no hurry. A nurse could have done the exam, but hospital protocol demanded an M.D.

Finally, Standish finishes. He puts the last swab in a plastic bag, marks it with his name, the date and time, and the victim's name. Then he strips off his gloves, tosses them on the floor, and hands the bag to Neely as he sweeps out of the cubicle.

She slips the plastic bag into the rape kit, along with the nail scrapings, hair samples, Poloroid photographs, and clothing, then pushes aside the curtain. Sonny Hoffstead is waiting outside.

Sonny is not a nickname. It's the name on his birth certificate, and it has long ago ceased to be appropriate, since he's a balding man a few years short of retirement. He's worked under three sheriffs and seems indifferent to Neely's sudden rise to the rank.

She finds indifference something to be grateful for.

"Sonny, would you take this and sign it into the evidence room?"

He nods. "How's Jennifer?"

"I . . . well, she's in a lot of pain."

"Damn shame. She's a nice girl. Baby-sits for my son's kids."

"Anything on that license number?"

"Yep. Car's registered to Jeffrey Amato. Francis Amato's boy. You know, the lawyer."

Neely knows, and she grimaces at the prospect of dealing with a lawyer who considers himself the Oregon coast's Melvin Belli.

"Okay, Sonny. I'll try to get a statement from Jennifer."

Grace Kaynard apparently heard that. When Neely steps back into the cubicle, Mrs. Kaynard is shaking her head. "No statements. Jennifer must make her peace with the Lord, not with the law. No statements!"

"*She's* done nothing wrong, Mrs. Kaynard," Neely says. "And if the boys who did this to her aren't brought to justice—"

"Justice! There'll be no justice, except the Lord grant it!"

Kelly Bower comes around the bed to embrace Mrs. Kaynard. "Grace, the Lord *will* grant it, and Neely is—"

"No! Oh, I can't let her go *through* this."

"She's already been through the worst part," Kelly assures her.

"Mom . . ."

"No, she *hasn't*! The worst is still to come."

"Mom . . . please!" Jennifer's words slur through cut, swollen lips. "What about Tim and Ted? Who's looking after them?"

"Mrs. Hamlin. The woman's a saint. Had to wake her up to—"

"She's eighty years old, Mom. Can't leave her with two ten-year-old boys too long. They'll give her a heart attack." Jennifer tries to smile with that. "Please, Mom . . . go on home. They'll take good care of me here."

After more argument, finally Mrs. Kaynard leaves. Neely moves to Jennifer's left side, and the girl says calmly, "Sheriff, I *want* to make a statement."

Kelly puts in, "Jennifer, you know you don't *have* to talk about it now, don't you?"

"It's okay." She looks up at Neely. "You gotta understand about Mom, though. It's . . . hard for her. It happened to her, too."

"She was raped?"

"Yeah. Says it ruined her life. I guess it did. But I . . ." Her eyes close for a moment; then she goes on: "I won't let those guys get away with this. I'll do whatever I have to. Even . . . testify in court."

Neely says softly, "Jennifer, you have a lot of courage."

"If I really had courage . . . I would've stopped them somehow."

"There were *three* of them. Courage can't overcome those odds. Look, in the next few days, you're going to spend a lot of time with Kelly. She'll help you deal with questions like that. Meanwhile, *my* job is to get these scumbags convicted." Neely takes a palm-size tape recorder from her jacket pocket and turns it on, prefaces her first question with the date, time, and names, then says, "Okay, Jennifer. Do you know who raped you?"

She nods, staring at the tape recorder. "I know. Dylan Unger raped me. The other guys . . . helped. Jeff Amato and T. J. O'Neill."

"I need to know exactly what happened. Your mother said you were baby-sitting with Mr. and Mrs. Jeffrey Walker's kids tonight."

"Yeah. Mr. Walker offered to drive me home. Guess I should've . . ."

For the first time, her bruised eyes shine with tears.

Kelly says, "That's what you have to learn *not* to think about, Jennifer—what might have been."

Wincing, the girl nods, and Neely says, "Let's start when you left the Walkers' house. You were riding your bicycle?"

"Yes. I rode down Ebbtide to North First. I usually turn left there, but that night . . ." She sighs. "It's still to-night, isn't it? Anyway, I saw a light in the oceanographic center, and I thought I should check on it."

Neely frowns at that. "Where was the light?"

"Dr. Nicholass's office. It went off, though. Probably just Sergeant McMinn checking the office. But that's why I was on South First when I got to Fairgrounds Road. And then I saw Jeff Amato in his car. It was parked on the side of the road. Dylan and T.J. were with him. I smelled pot. And later, beer. They started yelling at me, and I *tried* to get past them, but T.J. grabbed the handlebars, and that's when I fell and broke my arm. I . . . heard it."

She pulls in a shaky breath before she continues: "They dragged me into the ditch. Pulled my jeans off and held me down. Don't know exactly who was doing what, but I know they were all three there, and I know it was Dylan who . . . who was on top of me, who raped me. And they were all laughing . . . *laughing*!"

Kelly Bower murmurs, "Well, they won't be laughing now. Not when they're arrested."

"Oh, I hope not. I hope not . . ."

BEFORE NEELY LEAVES THE HOSPITAL, she phones the Westport Oceanographic Center to see if Jan's still there and gets a recorded message informing her of the center's hours. She tries their home number, but there's no answer there, either. Then she calls dispatcher Charlie Eckholm and gives the order to bring in Jeffrey Amato, Dylan Unger, and T. J. O'Neill for questioning, adding that they must be kept separated.

Neely is waiting at the TCSO when the three boys are brought in and placed in separate interrogation rooms with their irate parents. Jennifer's testimony provides probable cause to give the boys Breathalyzer tests and urinalyses. The results of the Breathalyzers show BACs ranging from .08 to .12. The urinalysis tests will have to go to the state police crime lab.

The interrogations are predictably inconclusive. Francis Amato won't allow his son to answer a single question. Dylan Unger and T. J. O'Neill claim they were at Jeff's house studying all evening.

Obviously, they've had time to work on their stories.

Neely releases them and goes to her office. She takes a perverse pleasure in calling District Attorney Owen Culpepper at this hour—1:30 A.M.—to bring him up-to-date on Jennifer Kaynard's rape. Culpepper is appalled when she informs him that Jennifer has identified her attackers. They are, after all, scions of some of Westport's leading families. He insists that no arrests can be made until a case strong enough to withstand Francis Amato's challenges is built.

It *will* be built, Neely promises him, carefully and by the book.

She spends another half hour filling out reports, then finally, at two o'clock, wearily makes her way to the Toyota and drives home.

A cold rain is falling. She's shivering by the time she reaches the A-frame, too exhausted to feel more than a fleeting annoyance when she sees the remains of the cross in front of the house. She unlocks the sliding glass door and goes inside, expecting to be met with warmth and a sleepy greeting from Jan.

But the house is cold and Jan isn't home.

Damn. But she won't worry about him. He has no sense of time when he's working on his pet jellies.

Neely turns up the furnace and sags onto the couch,

her body aching, as if she'd just finished a marathon. She reaches for the telephone and punches the oceanographic center's number.

Nothing but the recording again.

She lets her head fall back against the cushions and closes her eyes. Maybe she'll just rest a few minutes, then drive down to the center.

Within seconds, she's asleep.

Chapter 16

THE PHONE RINGS. NEELY JERKS out of a bad dream, yet she wakes totally, as she always does. But for a moment, nothing makes sense.

She's slumped at the end of the couch, and in the dusky gray light, it takes a moment to remember where she is. The phone rings again, only a foot from her ear. She fumbles for it, gets out a husky "Hello."

"Neely? Jesus, is that you?"

Jan? No, it isn't Jan. Where is he? Upstairs in the loft? She asks, "Who is this?"

"Curtis McMinn. Oh, shit, Neely, you gotta get *down* here!"

"Down where, Curtis? And why?" Her first thought is that McMinn is setting her up for a practical joke.

"The center. I'm at the center. Neely, we got a *murder* here!"

"You've got a what?" But McMinn has hung up.

Bastard!

He *is* setting her up. Something about that act didn't ring true.

She pulls herself to her feet, groaning as she flexes her stiff back muscles. She'll have to play along. As newly crowned sheriff of Taft County, she can't ignore a call about a murder.

But sooner or later, she'll get McMinn for this.

Neely tucks in her rumpled shirt. Damn, she didn't even take off her gun belt before she fell asleep last night. This morning. What the hell time *is* it?

Her watch reads 6:15 A.M.

That's when she becomes fully aware of the silence around her. The only sound she can hear is the faraway murmur of the surf.

"Jan?"

She listens, feeling the gray of the clouded dawn press against the windows, feeling the panic within her press against her ribs.

"Jan!"

She turns on the overhead light, runs up the spiral staircase to the loft, turns on more lights. The bed is empty. For one inexplicable moment, she stares at the samurai sword on the wall.

Downstairs again. Into the kitchen, utility room, dining room, the dojo, turning on more lights. The house blazes with light.

"*Jan!*"

He's at the center. In the lab. Or probably in his office, asleep over his computer.

The center.

We got a murder here.

No. Oh, no. That's insane.

But she's already on her way out the front door.

It takes less than three minutes to drive the mile and a half to the oceanographic center through a misty rain that makes the windshield wipers shriek. And in less than three minutes, she has time to imagine a multitude of scenarios, but she refuses to recognize any of them consciously.

Except one: Curtis McMinn is having his idea of fun with her.

Her route takes her south on Abalone Street to Highway 13, then east to Ebbtide Street, where she turns south again and remembers Jennifer Kaynard, who bicycled along Ebbtide last night and into the center's public parking lot, exactly as Neely does now.

What was it Jennifer said about a light in the center?

Neely skids to a stop in the yellow-striped section in front of the entrance deck. No patrol cars in the lot. That means McMinn hasn't called for backup.

And that means she's probably right: This is a setup.

McMinn is standing behind one of the glass doors. The lights in the lobby are on, and as she crosses the deck, she sees that he seems to have lost parts of his uniform: His hat and tie are missing. And his gun belt. Curtis McMinn, who loves his Glock 9-mm, and all the other guns in his collection, almost as much as he loves his toy T-bird—McMinn without his gun belt?

He waits until she reaches for the push handle before he opens the door, putting her slightly off balance when she enters the lobby. Oh, the subtleties of the game of Get Neely.

She wonders if he's been drinking. That might explain why he's missing parts of his uniform, and why there's a fresh bruise on his left cheek. Probably ran into a door—literally. Yet he's got on those damned black leather gloves. She always suspected that they're reinforced with metal over the knuckles.

"Okay, Curtis, what the *hell* is going on?"

He says brusquely, "In here," and sets off for the museum wing.

Neely follows him, their footfalls echoing on the cloud gray vinyl as they move past the gift shop, the ticket counter, the turnstiles, the painters' tarps and scaffolding, away from the lights and into darkness.

In the museum wing, no lights are on, not even in the aquariums.

Except in the medusa pool, where the pink-and-white silk-organdy moon jellies dance in slow motion in the spotlights.

McMinn heads for the Lucite cylinder, then stops a couple of paces short of it. Neely doesn't stop until she's an arm's length away.

DIE NIGGER FUCKER! JAP MONGREL!

The graffiti, interspersed with swastikas, is sprayed all around the cylinder in a vicious, random pattern. The letters range from one to three feet in height. They look black with the light behind them, except where the paint has dripped and thinned to reveal its true color: blood red. Over and over, the same bloody messages of mindless hatred.

Riker. Dirk Riker, aka Eugene Buxman. That creature of shadows and ambush. *I ain't through with* you, *bitch!*

The graffiti distracts her for what seems a long time. Or perhaps she simply doesn't want to see beyond the words of hate to the dark shape floating near the bottom of the tank.

Perhaps she knew it would be here.

She sinks to her knees, hands pressed against the cold curve of Lucite, dry smears of paint against her palms.

The water is pinker than it should be. She understands that only now when she sees the source of the discoloration: wispy shadows of blood like smoke eddying around the dark shape.

Around the body.

Facedown, arms and legs extended, relaxed, it seems; fine black hair veiled around his head. The curved wall of the tank and the column of water it contains make an enormous lens, distorting the image into mocking illusion.

But she knows it's real.

She knows what and who it is.

Jan.

She hears a whimpering wail and knows the sound comes from within her.

Take me with you. Oh, Jan, take me with you. . . .

Did I tell you I love you? When I spoke my last words to you, did I tell you that you have enriched my life with hope and joy?

Did I tell you?

A reflection wavers against Jan's black turtleneck. Neely stares at it, wondering if it's her own face. No. Another face, stretched in the lens of Lucite and water. Fuzzy mustache. And a smirking half smile.

Curtis McMinn.

She was right. He *did* call her here to set her up for a joke:

We got a murder here.

No way did McMinn not know the identity of the murder victim.

And no way did he not know of Jan's relationship with Neely. She and Jan had never made a secret of it, and in a small town, such a secret could never be kept anyway.

Yet McMinn hadn't told her *who* had been murdered when he called her, nor had he radioed for backup.

He had lured her down here alone to play the ultimate joke on her, to let *her* find Jan's body, while he watched. And smirked.

Rage flashes over within her, fueled by the pain of a grief whose dimensions she can't yet fathom.

And there's a white-hot clarity in that rage. She understands what she needs to know now, what she needs to do. Understands that this rage will carry her through the next few minutes, hours, days, weeks, months, years. It will burn hot and clear until she finds out who murdered Jan Koto.

Until she sees justice done.

One way or another.

She rises with feral swiftness, pivoting on her toes, legs spread and braced, right hand clenched in a palm-up karate fist, and the raging power surges from her feet through her legs and back and shoulders to her arm and drives the fist into Curtis McMinn's belly like a sledge hammer.

She watches his smirk collapse, feels his breath forced out in a sudden cough while his legs buckle under him, and he crumples to the floor, clutching his gut.

Neely says softly, "*That's* how it feels, you bastard."

Chapter 17

WHILE MCMINN CURLS INTO A fetal position on the floor, his face purple as he gasps for air, he gives Neely a look of stark bewilderment.

Maybe he didn't think the nigger bitch had it in her.

She snaps, "Sergeant, you're the first deputy at the crime scene. Have you called for backup? Secured the crime scene? Checked for suspects in the building? Put out an APB for Riker?"

He wheezes, "Shit, Neely, I just *got* here!"

"You were here fifteen minutes ago to call *me*. When did you find . . . the body?" She gets the word out with only a brief stuttering of her heart. Still, she keeps her back to the medusa pool.

As he struggles to his feet, McMinn groans, "*I* didn't find it. Jesus, I think you busted a rib." His knees are still loose, but they hold. "Ben found the body. Him and Dr. Olenick got here about six o'clock."

Neely winces. Andrea the Amazon is the *last* person she wants to see now. "Where are they, Sergeant?"

"Ben's in his office. Don't know where Olenick is."

"You don't *know*? Christ! Come on, we've contaminated the crime scene enough already." Her concern for the integrity of the crime scene is genuine. She just doesn't add that it's pushing her self-control to the edge to be so near Jan's body.

She leads the way out of the museum and back to the lobby, where the light coming through the glass doors is pale and cold, draining the color from the mosaic of marine life on the wall across from the doors. She takes her radio from her belt and calls Dispatch, orders Charlie Eckholm to notify Buck Dolin, send every available man to the center, and inform Culpepper that there's been a murder here. The last chore is technically hers, but she's not ready to deal with the DA yet.

Her final order is to renew the APB on Dirk Riker, as a person of interest in a murder investigation. "Top priority, Charlie. Out."

Then she faces McMinn. "What do you mean, you just got here?"

"I, uh, wasn't here last night. I was home, sick as a dog all night. Got some bad food, I guess."

Neely returns the radio to her belt. Her hand is shaking, and it's only now that she realizes she shouldn't have used the radio to call Dispatch, and certainly she shouldn't have used the word *murder*. Too many people—including journalists—have scanners.

Concentrate, damn it. You can't fuck up this investigation.

"Go on, Sergeant."

"Well, this morning a little before six, Dr. Nicholass phoned me, told me to get down here fast. So I threw on some clothes and got here about ten after. He showed me . . . well, that's when I called you. I mean, Culpepper says *you're* the sheriff now."

McMinn shows his old cocky belligerence with that, and Neely welcomes it. It helps her hold her focus.

"You entered through the loading dock doors?" Then at his nod, she asks, "Are they locked now?"

"Yeah. They lock automatically."

"What about emergency exits?"

"There's four altogether, but they don't open at all from outside, and if anybody opens 'em from inside, it sets off the security alarm. After thirty seconds, it signals the TCSO."

She nods. "Sergeant, stay here until our backup arrives. Meanwhile, no one else gets in. Understood?"

McMinn glares at her, and when she crosses the lobby and starts down the hall toward the research wing, he yells, "If you busted a rib for me, I got half a mind to file a report with the state board!"

Neely turns, refraining from commenting on his half a mind. "Curtis, do you really want every deputy in the state to know you got knocked on your ass by a woman—a *black* woman?"

She takes some satisfaction in his suddenly red face as she continues down the hall to the second door on the right. It's marked in gold leaf: DR. S. BENJAMIN NICHOLASS, DIRECTOR.

The door opens into his secretary's office. Nicholass's sanctum is through the door on the left-hand wall. Neely walks in without knocking and finds herself in an unexpectedly austere room: white walls and carpet, black enameled furniture, white miniblinds closed over the big window on the wall to her right. She notes the door on the left wall: Saint Nick's private entrance into the hall. A glass-topped desk faces the inner door. To the left of the computer workstation behind the desk, there's a bookcase filled with texts and journals and, on the bottom shelf, a binocular microscope mounted with a 35-mm camera. Its gray vinyl case rests on the floor next to a carton with an Intel logo—the only evidence of clutter. The only color is provided by two framed posters, one from the San Diego Zoo, the other from the St. Louis Zoo.

Reminders, Neely thinks uncharitably, of Dr. S. Benjamin Nicholass's sterling qualifications. He worked for both institutions.

No, there *is* another splash of color in the room: the man himself.

Jaunty in a yellow silk shirt and rosy tan jacket, with designer jeans and his usual white Nikes, Nicholass is near the window, searching through a file cabinet. When he sees Neely, he switches on an expression of sympathy and strides toward her. For a moment, she's afraid he intends to hug her.

"Dr. Nicholass, I need a telephone."

His hands drop to his sides. "You can use mine, Neely. Or if you'd like privacy, you can use the phone in Carla's office."

"Thank you. Where's Dr. Olenick?"

"I, uh, assume in her office. Neely, if there's anything I can do . . ."

"There is. Don't leave this room until I get a statement. And I need a list of your employees with their addresses and phone numbers. I also need to know which ones have keys to the building or know the security system code." An exercise in futility, probably, in light of the graffiti on the medusa pool, but she has to go through the motions.

Nicholass says, "Everyone on the research staff has keys to the loading dock doors and knows the code. Curtis does, too, of course, and he has a master key."

"Does that mean it opens every lock in the building?"

"Yes." Then he hedges. "Well, not my office—I have a separate key for that—but every other lock."

"Does anyone else have a master key?"

"Well . . . *I* do."

"I'd better have it."

Santa Claus's blue eyes turn hard as marbles. "But I . . . I'll have no way to get into the building."

That's the idea, but Neely doesn't say so. "It's a matter of your convenience. We'll need access into all areas of the center. I don't want to bother you to unlock every door."

Nicholass can't seem to find an argument for that. Lips tight, he unfastens a key from his key ring and hands it to

Neely. Then he says, "I was wondering about *Poseidon*. I assume our departure will be, uh, delayed, but I'd like to give the crew some idea how long—"

"Indefinitely, Dr. Nicholass." She turns and goes to the door into Carla's office. "And don't contact the crew about the delay or its cause yet." With that, she closes the door behind her.

The call goes to the Oregon State Police in Salem, to Crime Scene Investigation. The TCSO is definitely not equipped to handle the forensics on a case like this. She speaks to Division Chief Steve Travers, identifying herself as *Sheriff* Jones, outlines the situation, and asks for a state crime-scene team.

Travers asks a few questions, then, says "Okay, Sheriff, I'll send Lieutenant Heathman. It'll be a couple of hours before he can get a team down there."

She has just hung up when Nicholass emerges from his office to ask, "Neely, would you like me to notify Jan's parents?"

This new world she inhabits now is full of land mines that shatter her friable mental focus.

She hasn't thought about Ando Koto, Jan's father, whose dignified bearing hints at extraordinary self-discipline. Ando is retired, but he was an architect of repute in San Francisco. Nor has she thought about Miko, Jan's mother; even at seventy, exquisite as a lotus blossom. They have always been gracious to Neely, although she knows they don't approve of her. Not for their son. Kim Miyu, Jan's older sister, is more accepting. But how will Kim and her parents accept this?

Neely, honey, there are some things that'll never be easy, but it doesn't hurt to pray while you're going through them.

Right, Gramma. But does it *help* to pray?

"*I'll* inform the Kotos, Dr. Nicholass."

Neely leaves him and his unctuously sympathetic expression and walks out into the hall. She turns right, passes Nicholass's private door, and continues, rounding the corner where the hall makes a left turn into the research wing. Fluorescent lights glow the length of the long sea green corridor, all the way to the loading dock doors at the end. On both sides of the hall, wooden doors are inset at irregular intervals. Behind them are laboratories, storage facilities, a library, and staff offices.

Jan's office is the third door from the end, on the right.

Andrea Olenick's is the fourth from the end. Neely stops there and looks through the small window set at eye level. Andrea is at her desk, in profile to Neely, facing her computer, but her eyes are closed. The monitor is occupied with a screen saver. Colored fish.

It occurs to Neely to wonder why Andrea chose Jan to lavish her affection on. She's an attractive woman, with long, thick auburn hair and a body honed to athletic perfection. This morning, the body is displayed in matching red turtleneck and stirrup pants. Her face might be a little short of ideal Caucasian beauty, but there's something seductive about it. It would seem that a woman like Andrea could have any man she wanted. Why did she choose the one who didn't want her?

Neely moves on to the next office, stares for a moment at the name plate: DR. JAN KOTO.

Over the inside of the window, there's a curtain that wasn't there before. She reaches into her hip pocket for a pair of latex gloves, pulls them on, and tries the door. Unlocked. She opens it and steps inside.

It's not a curtain. An ochre sweatshirt is tacked across the window. It's Jan's.

She flips the light switch and looks around the small room. One wall is lined with shelves filled with neatly segregated books, journals, notebooks, and computer discs. On another wall is a NOAA map of the world's ocean beds. Jan had added a paper arrow pointing to the location of the oceanographic center, with the legend "Here there be monsters."

His jacket is hung over the back of the chair behind

the desk. The dustcover has been removed from his computer and tossed with atypical carelessness on the floor, but the computer is off. No discs in its slots or on the desk. The hundreds of color photographs piled in the center of the desk look as if they'd been hastily dropped there. Without touching them, she studies the ones visible to her. They're the photographs Jan took yesterday while scuba diving with Andrea.

Something happened on that expedition. Something that made Jan say it might be difficult working with Andrea in the future.

Neely studies the blue-gray vinyl floor. Between the door and the desk, there's a big dull patch, as if the wax shine had been scrubbed off. She squats down to study an indentation in the vinyl an inch from the metal leg of the desk. The desk has been shifted toward the door. She gets down on her hands and knees. Scratch marks circling the metal.

She checks the other legs. None have similar marks. And when she's behind the desk, examining the fourth leg, she sees something metallic in the shadows under the desk.

Jan's gold wire-rim glasses.

She recoils, hands in fists to stop the overwhelming need to reach for the glasses, to hold them clasped to her heart. She beats her fists against her thighs, fighting for control.

Find your rage. Hold on to it.

Yes! She feels the rage again, relishes the cold clarity it engenders.

But she has to get out of this room.

Neely rises, coming up behind the desk, startled to see someone in the doorway.

Dr. Andrea Olenick seems equally startled. Her gray eyes are wide as she stares at Neely. "What're *you* doing here?"

"No, that's *my* line, Andrea."

"I heard somebody in here when I left my office."

As Neely comes around the desk, she notes the big

black leather purse slung over Andrea's shoulder. Neely takes her arm to urge her into the hall, then closes the door. "Andrea, I hope you weren't planning to leave just yet."

She jerks out of Neely's grasp. "Why not? Am I a *suspect*?"

Neely almost laughs. Somehow Andrea doesn't seem the type to paint hate graffiti.

But does that eliminate her?

It's the graffiti, Neely realizes, that has fixed only one suspect in her mind.

Rage may keep the grief at bay, but she can't let it skew her objectivity. Probably the most obvious suspect *is* the perpetrator. That's how it works in the real world. But that's no excuse for closing her mind to other possibilities.

And there's something about the graffiti on the medusa pool. . . .

But she can't face that even in thought, right now.

"You're a witness, Andrea, and I need a statement, but it will have to wait until my backup arrives. Please, stay in your office for now."

Andrea glares at her, but she goes into her office, slamming the door behind her. Neely looks at her watch: 7:05.

Where the hell *is* her backup? Playing Get Neely again? *Well I'm not in the mood for games.*

Chapter 18

CHIEF CRIMINAL DEPUTY BUCK DOLIN charges into the lobby of the TCSO, through the door into the hall, and as he makes a fast left into the Dispatch Center, he checks his watch. It's five after seven, and he hasn't had breakfast or even a cup of coffee. He is not a happy man.

"Charlie, what the *hell* is going on?"

Deputy Charles Eckholm, who still wears his hair in an army crew cut, although he's long past his army days, swivels his chair around. "Beats me. That's why I called you. Neely radioed in with some sort of bee in her bonnet. Wants every available man at the oceanographic center—like we're ass-deep in available men this time of the day."

"So, who'd you send?"

"Hell, Chief, I figured I better check with you first."

Which means, Buck realizes, that Charlie hasn't called anybody.

Charlie adds, "She wanted me to phone the DA, too, and tell him there was a *murder* at the center." He looks at Buck, ready to laugh, but gets no encouragement. "Curtis must be at the center, Chief, so why didn't *he* call it in, if there was a murder? I tried reaching him, but he's not answering."

Buck grabs the keys to one of the patrols. "You figure Neely'd tell you there'd been a murder if there hadn't?"

"Hell, maybe she's having her period or something. I damn sure wasn't gonna roust out half a dozen guys till I—"

"Charlie, you dumb shit," Buck says softly, leaning over the dispatcher's chair. "It's not up to *you* to question what a deputy in the field says. *Any* deputy. Besides, Neely studied homicide investigation at the LAPD Academy. I figure she'd know a body when she saw it." He straightens and heads for the door. "Get your ass in gear and call everybody on the day shift. It's starting now—at the center. Tell the swing shift they're on standby. And, damn it, phone the damn DA!"

Charlie mutters, "Yessir," but Buck is already out the door.

When Buck reaches the Westport Oceanographic Center, it's 7:13. He parks next to Neely's blue Toyota pickup and heads for the front entrance, where McMinn is holding open one of the glass doors for him.

"So, what's comin' down here, Curtis? Charlie says you haven't been answering his calls."

"Well, I, uh, left my radio at home."

"You *what?*" Buck realizes then that McMinn apparently left his entire gun belt home. "Where's your duty weapon?"

But Buck tunes out McMinn's stuttering explanation, distracted by footsteps in the hall to his right. Neely Jones strides toward him like a soldier on parade. She asks, "Chief, where's the backup I called for?"

"It's coming."

And Buck feels skewered by the look in those hooded black eyes. It's like something's been revealed to him he never imagined was there.

She says coldly, "Charlie fucked up again, right?"

Buck doesn't answer that, and maybe she doesn't expect him to. She says, "Here's the situation, Chief. Curtis was sick, and he wasn't on duty here last night. At six this morning, Dr. Nicholass and Dr. Andrea Olenick came to the center. Nicholass found a body, and instead of calling nine one one, he called McMinn. Who called me." She doesn't even look at McMinn, but something flashes in those black eyes. "The victim is Dr. Jan Koto, one of the staff biologists here."

Buck whispers, "Jesus X. Christ, Neely..." and he feels like somebody's just punched him in the gut. Vaguely, he realizes that McMinn is pressing a hand to his own belly.

But Buck is focused on Neely. He knows who Jan Koto is—was. Knows what Koto was to Neely.

And Buck knows that what he's feeling now is half flashback, remembering the day, ten years ago, when a doctor told him Val didn't make it through the last surgery for the cancer they never suspected until it was too late—the cancer she was too young, too vital to have. He was a basket case then and for a long time afterward. But here's Neely, reeling off the victim's name like she just read it on a crime report.

Buck says huskily, "Neely, I'm so damn sorry. Look, you better go on home. I can take over here."

"No!" she snaps, and she's vibrating like a tuning fork. "This one's mine, Buck. I won't let *anyone* fuck it up!" A deep breath, and she's ice-solid again. "I told Charlie to inform the DA. Did he at least do that?"

"It's taken care of," Buck hedges.

"Good. I've called for a state crime-scene team. They'll be here about nine. But I want to videotape the scene now. I didn't come in a patrol, obviously. I need the camcorder and tape recorder from yours."

Buck hands his car keys to McMinn. "Go out and get 'em, Curtis."

When McMinn leaves, Neely continues: "The center staff will be arriving soon. All the scientific staff have keys to the loading dock doors, so we'll have to seal them and detour everyone to this entrance. All we can do till the crime-scene team arrives is send them home with orders to

• 101 •

stay near their phones. Not the best arrangement, but we can't handle them at the TCSO, and they'll be needed for comparison prints and statements. Did Charlie renew the APB on Riker?"

"I'll check with him." Buck starts to pull out his radio, but Neely shakes her head.

"Not by radio. I already made that mistake." She frowns as McMinn crosses the deck toward them, and once he's inside, she puts the small tape recorder in her jacket pocket, then takes the camcorder. "Sergeant, find a telephone and make sure Charlie renewed the APB on Dirk Riker. And when our backup arrives, let me know immediately. Come on, Chief. The victim is in the museum."

Neely marches down the hall toward the museum wing and doesn't seem to notice the sour look McMinn gives her. Buck notices it, and he says, "Curtis, we got work to do—all of us."

Then Buck sets off after Neely, catching up with her past the turnstiles, where she's stopped to videotape the floor under some scaffolding. The floor is bare in an area about ten by ten feet. "One of the plastic tarps is missing, Chief, and I know it was here yesterday about five. And look at that." She indicates an aerosol can under a ladder. Spray paint: Fourth of July red.

She videotapes the can, then heads for the big jellyfish tank in the center of the display area. Buck follows her, looking around in the dim light for the body. At first, all he can see is the graffiti on the tank. Which explains why Neely wants Dirk Riker so bad.

Then Buck sees the body.

And he realizes it must've been the same for Neely—seeing the graffiti first, then, finally, the body.

Yet here she is, the camcorder up to her face, taping the graffiti. And Buck keeps flashing back to ten years ago, to the moment when he couldn't even stand up, when somebody had to help him to a chair.

But now Neely's turning away from the tank, knees

going slack, her eyes full of the kind of pain Buck under-stands too well.

He grabs the camcorder and puts his arm around her to support her, but she stiffens, pushes him away. "Finish that up for me, Buck. I . . . I need to interview the witnesses."

He watches her go, wondering how long she thinks she can keep this up.

Buck begins methodically videotaping the tank from all sides, watching where he puts his feet. The jellyfish move like slow pink smoke, like escaped souls, through the pink water. Finally, he squats down for a close look at the body.

Jesus, why would anyone want to kill Jan Koto? But when Buck realizes he's looking at Koto's body through the O in the words JAP MONGREL, the answer to that question seems clear enough.

Buck figures Neely's worked it out, too. But she's going to run this investigation by the book.

Chapter 19

WHEN NEELY PASSES MCMINN AT his post in the lobby, he's opening the door for Deputy Danny Beecher. Beecher, who also serves as the TCSO's Animal Control deputy, is redheaded and freckled, almost as wide and tall as the door itself, and none of it fat. She gives Beecher instructions about guarding the door; then she turns to McMinn. "I understand you have a master key, Sergeant."

He eyes her suspiciously. "Yeah?"

"Let me have it," she says, holding out her hand.

McMinn balks, but Neely waits, meeting his angry stare with cold determination. He blinks first, reaches into his pants pocket for a key ring, and surrenders one key to her. She nods. "Okay, I want to get some preliminary statements, and I better get you on record, too."

He follows her to Ben Nicholass's office, where the director is at his desk, signing papers with his left hand while he holds the telephone receiver to his ear with his right hand, but when he sees Neely, he concludes the call with a curt "I'll let you know."

She raises an eyebrow, and he says, "That was Captain Olsen. I just remembered he was planning to oversee loading *Poseidon* this morning. We can't even set foot on that ship until he unlocks the boarding gate. I just told him not to come. And, no, I didn't tell him why. Andrea can verify that."

Andrea Olenick is sitting in a chair in front of the desk. She looks up at Neely, her features perfectly ordered, except for an equivocal light in her icy gray eyes that Neely reads as contempt. Neely doesn't comment on the fact that Andrea didn't stay in her office as she'd been instructed.

"Yes," Andrea says, "I can verify that. Now, for God's sake, how long are we going to be kept incarcerated here?"

There's a second chair in front of the desk, and Neely claims it, leaving McMinn to stand. She places the tape recorder on the desk and takes out her notebook. "I just need preliminary statements now."

"Preliminary?" Andrea cries. "I suppose that means—"

"Andrea, we must be patient," Nicholass interrupts. "After all, this *is* a murder investigation." Then he turns to his computer workstation and retrieves a sheaf of paper from the printer. "These are the names and addresses you wanted, Neely. I've starred those staff members who have keys to the rear door and know the security code, and I printed two extra copies, in case your men need them."

"Thanks. I appreciate that." Neely puts the lists on the desk, turns on the tape recorder, and gives it the necessary information, then, "Dr. Nicholass, what time did you arrive at the center this morning?"

"About five or ten minutes before six."

"Do you usually come to work so early?"

"No, but I have so much to do before *Poseidon* sails. Of course, our departure date is now . . . well, moot. But I hope you understand that we have a limited window on the gray whale birthing in the gulf."

Neely doesn't comment on his limited window. "Tell me in your own words what happened here this morning."

"Well, Andrea drove in at the same time I did—into the staff parking lot, I mean—and we came inside together."

"Through the loading dock doors?"

"Yes."

"Were they locked?"

"Yes, and the security system was on."

"Okay. Go on."

"Andrea went to her office, and I continued to mine, and I was just outside my door—the private entrance—when I noticed a faint light from the museum wing."

"It was unusual to see a light there?"

"Precisely. We try to maintain a natural diurnal rhythm for our little creatures, so the lights are always turned off at night. Well, I thought the cleaning staff had left a light on, but—"

"Who does your cleaning?"

"Pinkley's Janitory Service." He adds indulgently, "That's how Mrs. Pinkley spells it. Janitory. We always like to do business with locals when we can, of course, and Jenny is totally trustworthy."

"Does she have a key to the building or know the security code?"

"No. She and her girls come in just before closing time. When they're done, Curtis lets them out and resets the security system."

McMinn puts in, "What difference does it makes who the hell has keys or knows the code? You seen the shit painted on that fish tank."

She ignores that. "Dr. Nicholass, who's doing the painting in the museum? Is that also locally contracted?"

"Yes. Billy Huff is the contractor. No, he doesn't have a key or know the code. His crew always works during regular museum hours."

"Okay, what happened this morning when you saw the light in the museum wing?"

"I went down there to check it out, of course, and when I saw the jelly tank . . ." He looses a gusty sigh, and Andrea closes her eyes.

Andrea, don't turn on the tears. You don't know the meaning of tears.

But maybe she does. Maybe Neely despises Andrea's threatened tears because they make it so much harder to hold back her own.

Nicholass goes on: "As you can imagine, I was stunned. I went to get Andrea. I probably shouldn't have subjected her to . . . but I don't think I believed my own eyes then."

Andrea nods. "He came running down the hall shouting my name, and he was so distraught . . ."

"I'm sorry, Andrea. I wasn't thinking at all clearly."

Neely asks coolly, "What did the two of you do then?"

"We went to the museum wing," Nicholass replies, "and . . . well, I *had* to believe my eyes then. And poor Andrea was so shocked."

Andrea mumbles, "I felt nauseous, and I had to run for the rest room. The one in the museum wing."

"How long were you in the rest room?"

"I don't know. Maybe five minutes. Then I went to my office. I wanted to be alone. And I didn't leave until I heard you in Jan's office."

"Which was about seven-oh-five A.M.," Neely puts in for the tape. "Dr. Nicholass, what did you do after you discovered the body?"

"I was so befuddled, I couldn't think who to call, except Curtis. He *is* a deputy, after all. So I came here to my office to call him."

Neely swivels her chair to look at McMinn. "You were at home when Dr. Nicholass phoned you, Sergeant? What time was that?"

"About six. Like I told you, I was sick. Stomach flu, I guess. Sick as a dog all night."

"What happened to your face? The bruise on your left cheek." That's for the tape. *Always get everything on tape, whether it seems important or not*—so said Lieutenant Wollanski of the LAPD Academy. He also said that women would never make it in police work because they were short on testosterone.

"I, uh, slipped on the bathroom floor," McMinn replies. "Hit the sink. Hell, I spent most of the night in the bathroom."

Neely swivels back to Andrea. "Do you usually come to work so early?"

"I often come in early. Morning's the best time of day for me. I'm a lark." Then she adds, as if Neely wouldn't know, "Jan was an owl. He liked to work at night."

Neely feels a tremor running through her body. Bitch. She didn't need to say that. "Andrea, where were you last night after seven o'clock?" That was the last time Neely saw Jan alive.

"You think *I* killed Jan? Oh, Neely, why in God's name would I kill Jan? He was . . . a dear friend."

"Maybe because you were working with him on a jellyfish he discovered that has unusual chemistry in its stings. It could lead to a brand new analgesic. That little jelly could be worth millions. Maybe you didn't want to share."

Andrea glares at Neely. "Oh, that's ridiculous! We didn't know whether *that little jelly* would be worth two cents, much less millions."

Neely doesn't reply, only looks at her steadily.

And finally, Andrea glances at Nicholass apologetically. "I'm sorry, Ben, but we'll *have* to tell her." Then before he can respond, she says to Neely, "Last night after seven o'clock, I was with Ben. We had dinner at his house— salmon filets, baked potatoes, artichokes, and a lovely Sokol Blosser Riesling. Afterward, well, I . . . spent the night with him."

Neely catches a fleeting surprise in Nicholass's eyes. Is he surprised because Andrea is lying, or because she's revealing something he didn't expect her to expose? Neely tries to imagine the two of them at Nicholass's three-level beachfront house, sharing a glass of "lovely" Riesling on one of the balconies, with the wind tossing Andrea's auburn hair, while Saint Nick nibbles at her ear.

"Yes, it's true," Nicholass admits cautiously. "I, uh, would prefer to keep it between ourselves. The center's board doesn't approve of . . . well, close relationships among staff members."

Neat, Neely thinks. Two alibis for the price of one. Not that it will probably matter a damn. If Andrea isn't the type to spray-paint hate graffiti, Nicholass seems even less likely. He might get paint on his pastel shirt and white Nikes.

But she can't resist asking Nicholass, "How long have you and Andrea been . . . dating?"

"For a little over two months. Since *Poseidon*'s last voyage to Baja, in September." Then he adds, with a self-conscious laugh, "I guess there's something about those tropical nights."

Andrea smiles, but she's not looking at Nicholass. That cold smile is for Neely, and there's an edge of triumph in it.

Neely asks, "Dr. Nicholass, after Curtis arrived this morning, what did you do?"

"Well, nothing. I stayed here in my office."

"Andrea?"

"I told you—I stayed in *my* office."

Neely considers that a moment, then closes her notebook. "That's enough for now. We may need to question you further later." She turns off the tape recorder, and at that, Andrea lifts her hefty purse off the floor and slips the strap over her right shoulder as she rises.

"*Now* can I go? I feel like hell."

"Yes," Neely says, knowing she can't legally justify holding Andrea here against her will. "Just stay close to your phone."

Andrea stalks out of the office without saying a word to her supposed lover of last night. Neely motions to McMinn. "Escort her to the front door. Yes, I know she's parked in back. She can walk around the building. I don't want anyone touching the loading dock doors."

He mutters something under his breath as he departs. Neely doesn't ask him to repeat it. She hears cars and voices outside and crosses to the window to push up one slat of the closed miniblinds. The cloudy sky seems only a little brighter than when she first arrived.

An hour ago. It's a lifetime. A deathtime.

Hold on.

Her backup has finally arrived. Buck is outside getting them organized. Three patrol cars, three men. With Mc-Minn, Beecher, and Buck, that makes six. The whole damn day shift, plus one: Deputy Kevin Locksey, from the swing shift.

She turns away from the window, to find Nicholass watching her. He says gently, "Neely, I wish there was something I could do to help."

"Just stay here in your office, Dr. Nicholass. I've called in a state crime-scene team. They'll want to talk to you."

She picks up the lists he provided and leaves before he can say anything more. She heads for the front entrance, where Beecher is still on guard, and goes out on the deck. For a while, she simply stands there, pulling in long breaths of cool rain-scented air.

Buck has the men setting up folding barricades at the parking lot entrances. Out on North First Street, a small traffic jam has formed, some drivers stopping to ogle the police activity, others trying to get into the lot. The old VW van belongs to Tom Jordan, owner, publisher, reporter, editor, and compositor of the *Gazette*, the local newspaper.

Buck joins her on the deck, stonily anonymous in his mirrored sunglasses. She hands him one of the lists. "Center staff," she explains. "The starred names have keys to the loading dock doors and know the security code. Is anyone loose to seal and padlock those doors?"

"Kev's taking care of that. I better call the OSP for some help with traffic. I don't figure it's going to clear up by itself."

"Right. Chief, you might as well go back to the courthouse. You've got things organized here, and I'd like you to run a priors check on the staff and on Jenny Pinkley and the employees who worked here last night."

"Jenny?" He laughs. "It'll be a cold day in hell when you find any priors at Pinkley's Janitory."

"Yes, I know. Just going through the motions. Billy Huff and his painting crew, too. What I really want, though, is for *somebody* to tell me they've found *Riker!*" That comes out with more of an emotional charge behind it than she intended.

Buck seems to be looking toward the street. With those damn glasses, she can't be certain.

"Neely, you sure you're up to this?"

Suddenly she wants to scream, *No! I'm* not *up to this!* And just as suddenly, she's angry.

"Whether you like it or not, Buck—or even whether *I* like it or not—I'm sheriff now. Acting sheriff, anyway. You're needed at the TCSO. This won't be the only crime in the county today."

He turns in her direction, finally nods, then heads for his patrol.

Neely closes her eyes. Maybe he's right: Maybe she's not up to this. But she has no choice.

Chapter 20

HEATHER BLESSING ALWAYS COMES TO work half an hour early, and she maintains a strict schedule. First, the coffee. Then, while it drips, she goes to the courthouse cafeteria for a big box of doughnuts. By the time she gets back, the coffee is finished, and she fills a mug for herself and takes it to her office, where she sorts the mail and checks the answering machine for messages.

But this morning, she doesn't get past the doughnuts before everything seems to go wrong.

Dispatcher Charlie Eckholm comes out of the Dispatch Center just as she takes the cover off the doughnut box. Charlie *does* love his doughnuts. He goes off duty at eight, but he always gets his share before he leaves.

Heather doesn't really like Charlie—maybe it's that awful crew cut on a man old enough to be her father—but she puts on a smile for him.

"Good morning, Charlie."

" 'Morning, sunshine. No raspberry jellies today?"

"Sorry, no. Did you have a quiet night?"

Charlie reaches for a sugared doughnut. "Well, the *night* was quiet enough. Wasn't till about six that the shit hit the fan."

She tries to ignore the swearword. The guys think it's funny when she turns red at some of the things they say. "What happened?"

"Had a murder."

Her stomach goes all hollow. Yes, they have murders in Westport, especially when the summer people and tourists are around, but murder isn't something that happens every day, thank goodness.

"A murder, Charlie? Where? Who got murdered?"

"The oceanographic center, that's where." He takes a bite out of the doughnut, sugar snowing down on his brown tie. "It was one of them scientists. The Jap. Koto, his name was."

Heather stares at Charlie, and she can feel the trembling starting inside her. "Koto? Oh, no . . . not Jan Koto?"

"Yeah, I think that's his name."

"Oh, Lord help us. Poor Neely! Does she know?"

"Well, sure. She's down at the center making like the sheriff."

"She's *there*? Oh, this is *terrible*!"

Charlie asks around a mouthful of doughnut, "Whadaya mean?"

"Don't you know who Jan Koto *is*?" When Charlie only shrugs, she says angrily, "He's Neely's boyfriend! They're practically married!"

"Oh, yeah. I remember she was shacking up with—"

"Charlie, you're awful! You—you—oh!"

"Now, Heather, I didn't mean—Heather, don't *cry*. . . ."

She hurries away, through the briefing room and the sheriff's office, to her office, sits down behind her desk, and holds her head in her hands.

Murders never happen to people she knows.

Not that Jan Koto was a close friend or anything, but she talked to him sometimes when he came to pick up Neely. He was a sweet man. She always thought he and Neely looked so good together.

Oh, dear . . . this will break Neely's heart.

At that thought, Heather gives herself up to unrestrained weeping.

It's only when she sees two of the men from the swing shift cross the lobby that she realizes this just won't do. She reaches for the Kleenex box on her desk, presses a tissue to her eyes. It comes away smeared with mascara and eye shadow. She's ruined her makeup, and she hates crying with her contacts in. They make her eyes feel awful.

Heather takes her purse out of the foot well, repairs her makeup as best she can, then resolutely continues her morning schedule. It's eight o'clock when she goes into the sheriff's office, takes the dirty coffee mug from the desk into the bathroom and rinses it out, then uses it to carry water to the moth orchid.

"You'll just have to be brave and get used to me," she murmurs to the flowers. "You're so beautiful, and I don't want you to die on me."

Die.

And that reminds her of the murder again. She doesn't realize she's speaking aloud when she says firmly, "No, I *won't* cry!"

Oh, this is turning out to be a really awful day.

Chapter 21

AT 8:45 A.M., NEELY JONES stands looking out through the glass doors into rain that falls in silk-fine veils. Danny Beecher is still at his post at the middle set of doors, apparently fascinated by the traffic jam on North First. Whit Chaffee and Darrell Logan are in the midst of it, trying to clear a path for a small caravan of anonymous pastel green vehicles. Neely isn't surprised to see Tom Jordan of the *Gazette,* along with a dozen other oglers, standing under a tree just outside the parking lot, protecting himself and his camera from the rain with a yellow poncho. But she is surprised at the KEEN-TV logo on one of the vans caught in the jam. That's from Portland—Oregon's largest city.

At last, the pastel green caravan streams across the parking lot and lines up in front of the center: the medical examiner's station wagon, the state crime lab van, and two sedans. Neely has in the last hour surrendered to an innervating numbness, but her pulse rate kicks up at the presence of these vehicles and the experts they bring.

These people will get some answers.

She recognizes the man in the ME's station wagon. Dr. Gregory Feingold, with his unruly black hair and the black-rimmed glasses perched on a prow of a nose. He was stationed in Westport for a while, although he now works out of the new state ME's office in Portland.

But Feingold isn't the first to leave his vehicle.

From the lead sedan emerges a man in a tan raincoat, unbuttoned over a dark three-piece suit. Must be a native Oregonian, Neely thinks. No umbrella not even a hat to protect the bald spot at the crown of his head. Short, dark, kinky hair. Like hers.

He's African-American, and the rush of emotion this shadow-skinned man striding across the deck generates in her makes her pause. What does she expect? That he'll be a friend because they're both black?

Just because birds are of a feather doesn't mean they're chums.

So said Gramma Faith.

But there's something mighty lonely about being the only bird in the flock with odd feathers.

Right, Gramma, and I've been odd bird out all my life, no matter what flock I flew with.

She opens the door for the man and offers her hand. "I'm Neely Jones."

White teeth flash as he shakes her hand. "*Sheriff* Jones. Been hearing a lot about you lately. I'm Lt. John Heathman."

Neely looks out at the van, where five men and a woman, all white, are unloading gear. She turns to Danny Beecher, who's having a hard time keeping his jaw from dropping. Maybe he didn't expect the ranking member of a state crime-scene team to be black. She says, "Deputy Beecher, see if you can give those people a hand."

"Okay, Neely." Not Yes, Sheriff or even Yes, ma'am, but at least he accepted her order with unusual alacrity.

The lieutenant says, "Sheriff, I want you to understand that we're acting solely as . . . well, expert consultants. It's still your show. Yours and your DA's. Is Mr. Culpepper here?"

"No. I have instructions to phone him when you arrive.

Come on, I'll introduce you to Dr. Nicholass. He's the center's director. Oh, you'll need this." She reaches into her pocket for one of the master keys and hands it to him. "This will open every door for you—at least here in the center."

Heathman smiles at that and walks with her down the hall toward Nicholass's office, but before they reach it, she stops him. "There's one thing you should know, Lieutenant. The victim and I were . . . close."

Heathman studies her, and she realizes his eyes are more gray than brown. He asks, "Is that going to be a problem?"

"No."

"Okay, then. Let's get the amenities over with and get to work."

THE RESEARCH LIBRARY IS COMMANDEERED as an incident room. Heathman gathers his team there for a strategy session, along with Neely and the two deputies she chooses—Lieutenant Chaffee because he'd get his nose out of joint otherwise, and Kevin Locksey because she thinks the experience won't be wasted on him—and Owen Culpepper, who arrived in a briskly officious mood but has the sense to shut up once Heathman begins the session.

Following the briefing, the team withdraws to the museum wing.

So does Culpepper, but after a glance in the medusa pool, he withdraws altogether, claiming he has a case on the docket this morning and instructing Heathman to keep him informed.

Neely stays out of the way as the crime-scene team goes to work, except to accompany Heathman and two of the criminalists upstairs into the maintenance area. From this perspective, the medusa pool seems like nothing more than an outsized hot tub with hoses and probes hung over the rim. The floor around the rim is still damp with splashed water. She doesn't try to get close enough to look down into the pool.

Later, she takes Heathman to the front of the museum wing to show him the spray-paint can and bare area where the painters' tarp is missing. He writes in a notebook, then frowns at the medusa pool.

"Did you and Dr. Koto get a lot of that?"

That, she knows, is the graffiti, and he doesn't have to say more; they both understand exactly what is encompassed in *that*.

Neely replies, "There've been eight incidents in two years. The perps are three local skinheads. I have an APB out on the ringleader—Eugene Buxman, aka Dirk Riker."

"What kind of incidents are you talking about?"

"Decorating our house with this sort of . . . artistic expression. The last incident was a cross burning. That was just—" For a moment, she feels disoriented; she can't even guess what day it is.

Thursday. This is Thursday.

"It was Tuesday night," she says, "about midnight. We pulled Riker in yesterday but didn't have enough evidence to hold him."

I ain't through with you, *bitch!*

She stares at the tank, at the obscene bloodred and night-black lattice of words and symbols. There's something wrong, but she can't grasp it; something that keeps sinking away, like the dark shape—

"Sister, you okay?"

Neely nods, turning away from the tank. "I'd like to show you Jan's office. I think that's where he died. At least where he was attacked."

"Okay, let's have a look."

He follows her, and as they pass the front door, Danny opens it for two of the research staff, here to leave their fingerprints and statements: Dave Townsend, Jan's closest friend on the staff, and Lili Spenser, director of the museum. When they see Neely, both begin halting expressions of sympathy, but Neely puts them off with promises to talk to them later.

But she won't. Not soon, at least. She can't deal with their sympathy, however well intentioned. Not yet.

In Jan's office, Heathman stands in the doorway while she points out the evidence that led her to the conclusion that Jan was attacked here: the dull area on the floor, the shifted desk, Jan's glasses under the desk. The lieutenant listens intently, nodding occasionally.

"That's weird," Heathman says finally, "about the sweatshirt. Like he was trying to keep somebody from seeing what he was doing in here. So, what *would* he be doing?"

"Normally? Studying the photographs he'd just developed, or, since the cover is off his computer, entering his notes. He spent most of the day yesterday scuba diving with Dr. Olenick."

Heathman frowns at Jan's computer. "There's no diskette in the slots. Or didn't he make backups?"

"He backed up everything. He was compulsive about it. And, yes, he usually left the backup disc in the computer."

"What about those on the shelf there?"

The discs he indicates are in the manufacturer's boxes, marked with dates and subjects in felt-tip pen. Neely explains, "Those are full discs. At least, that's what they're supposed to be, I'll check them."

"Okay—*after* my people go over this room."

Neely nods and moves out into the hall, just in time to see Ben Nicholass coming toward them with a briefcase in one hand and, in the other, the heavy gray vinyl case she noticed in his office.

As he approaches, Nicholass says almost cheerfully, "Neely . . . Lieutenant. I've been fingerprinted, debriefed, and informed that my presence is no longer needed, so I'll get out of your way. I'll be at home for the foreseeable future. My phone number's on that list, Neely."

Heathman smiles pleasantly and takes a casual step into the center of the hall, blocking Nicholass.

"I'm sorry, Dr. Nicholass, but nothing leaves this building."

Neely is relieved that Heathman is taking the initiative on this. It saves her from having to assert authority that Nicholass would probably not recognize without a confrontation.

And he seems ready to confront Heathman. "What do you mean? Look, Lieutenant, I have a great deal of work to finish before *Poseidon* departs. I have grant proposals from five of our scientists in here—" He hefts the briefcase. "—and I don't mind telling you, they're difficult reading. I also have ten résumés to read and—"

"I understand that you're a busy man, Dr. Nicholass," Heathman says levelly. "But I must operate under certain rules. One is, nothing leaves a crime scene."

Nicholass's blue eyes flash with anger; then he seems to get himself under control. "Very well, then. I'll take these back to my office."

"I appreciate that, Dr. Nicholass. By the way, what's in the case?"

"Hm? Oh, it's equipment I'll need on the voyage. A Zeiss Ikon binocular microscope with a camera mount. I just wanted to check it."

He pauses, perhaps waiting for Heathman to comment, but the lieutenant only says amiably, "When you leave, Dr. Nicholass, use the front entrance, if you don't mind."

Nicholass gives him an annoyed frown over his shoulder as he turns and stalks away down the hall. When he's out of earshot, Heathman mutters, "I better make sure he leaves that stuff here. I know his type. Doesn't think rules apply to him, and damn sure doesn't like taking orders from an uppity nigger."

Neely laughs. "You got him, Lieutenant."

AT 11:30, THE BODY IS REMOVED from the medusa pool.

Neely doesn't watch that process. She goes out to the front deck and waits. The rain has stopped; the sun sends searchlight beams through breaks in the clouds. She can hear water dripping from trees and chattering down a heavy chain hung from an eaves trough. Out in the street, two Oregon State Patrol officers have arrived to help unjam the traffic. There are now three vans with dish antennas on top caught in the jam, and Tom Jordan has been joined in his vigil by a woman and two men wielding video cams.

Nearly half an hour later, Neely hears a metallic clank. Danny and Kevin are bringing a stretcher out. The body is encased in black plastic.

Neely looks into the lobby and sees Dr. Feingold. She keeps her eyes fixed on him to avoid watching that stretcher being loaded into the ME's vehicle. Feingold pushes through a glass door and crosses the deck to her, frowning uncomfortably. He was stationed in Westport when Neely first came here. With Jan.

"Damn, Neely, I don't know what to say."

"Right now, I wouldn't want to hear it. So, what can you tell me about the victim at this point?"

"The . . . victim?" Feingold takes off his glasses and polishes the lenses with a yellow handkerchief. His eyes look small, like an inquisitive mole's, without the thick lenses to magnify them. "Well, time of death's going to be a bitch, since the body was submerged in cold water. You, uh, have any idea when the last meal was ingested?"

Neely catches her breath. "About six yesterday evening."

Feingold takes a notebook out of his breast pocket and scribbles in it. "Okay, cause of death is probably drowning, but there's a bullet wound left upper thorax. Close range. I don't think the wound would've been fatal, but it caused a lot of bleeding and possibly unconsciousness. No exit wound, so I can retrieve the bullet. There's . . . some marks on the hands and face. Probably jellyfish stings."

That means Jan was still alive when he was thrown into the tank. Neely nods, swallowing at the rush of saliva in her mouth.

Feingold continues, focusing on his notebook: "Some bruises around the left wrist. Not rope or cloth burns, just bruises. And contusions on the left side of the jaw, cuts inside the cheek, and a loosened lower-left bicuspid. And that's all I can tell you till I do the autopsy."

Neely looks up into a searchlight beam of sunshine, closes her eyes. Hold on. She feels the light move away and opens her eyes to face Feingold. He looks miserable.

"When will you do the autopsy, Greg?"

"I have a feeling this thing'll get top priority just because it's so weird, so I'll probably do the autopsy as soon as I get back to Portland."

"I'll have to notify the family. They live in San Francisco. They'll want to know when . . ."

"When I can surrender the body to them? Probably by next Monday. Have them give me a call. Well, I, uh, better get going."

"Thanks, Greg." She watches him hurry to the station wagon, drive across the empty asphalt to North First, where it takes two deputies and two OSP officers to get him out of the parking lot.

"Hey, Neely!"

She turns, annoyed, to see Beecher holding one of the doors open.

"What is it, Danny?"

"Phone call just came in from Buck. He says Culpepper wants to see you at the courthouse. He's got Judge Lay waiting to swear you in."

Neely's inclination is to let Judge Lay keep on waiting, but she knows better than to antagonize a man in a position to sign such vital documents as search warrants.

Besides, she has a phone call to make, one she'd prefer to make in the privacy of her office: a call to the Kotos.

Chapter 22

IT'S A BRIEF CEREMONY. BY the time Neely arrives, Judge Harvey Lay is fuming at giving up part of his lunch hour, and in the book-lined, Karistan-carpeted solemnity of his chambers on the courthouse's second floor, he administers the oath of office in what must be record time. The only witnesses are Owen Culpepper and the judge's secretary, Sally Blessing Greenleaf. She's Heather's sister, and Neely has often heard Heather call Sally her "beautiful sister," as if Heather were the ugly duckling.

When Neely has sworn to uphold the laws of the county of Taft, the state of Oregon, and the United States of America, Judge Lay casts off his judicial robes and heads for the door. It's left to Sally Greenleaf to congratulate Neely, who manages a smile. The good wishes seem sincere.

But when Sally turns sincere about "Dr. Koto's passing," Neely cuts her off with a brief "Thanks, Sally" as she follows the DA out into the hall. "Mr. Culpepper, I need to talk to you about Jennifer Kaynard."

Culpepper is in a hurry to get to lunch, too, but he sighs and leads Neely to his office. In the anteroom, his plain, plump, and middle-aged secretary, Thelma Clapton, is brown-bagging it. Neely notes, with a little surprise, that the book she's reading is *Push* by Sapphire.

In his office, Culpepper sits down at his desk and waves Neely to one of the chairs in front of the glistening antique. He says, "I'm surprised it's the Kaynard case you want to discuss. I'd think you have your hands full with, uh, the affair at the center."

"There's nothing I can do until the crime-scene team finishes."

"Yes, of course. Neely . . . well, are you sure you feel up to handling the center case? I mean, since you are . . . were . . ."

She says coolly, "I feel up to it. Now, have you talked to Jennifer?"

"Uh, well, no." He clears his throat. "I did have a call from Grace Kaynard. She tells me her daughter won't testify against the boys."

"What does Jennifer say?"

"Well, I, uh, haven't had a chance to . . . Besides, you know, the whole thing was probably a simple misunderstanding. The boys just got carried away. No real harm done, after all, and I—"

"No harm done!" Neely shouts, surging to her feet, reckless with anger, because at this point in her life, so little matters to her. "No *harm*? Go look at Jennifer, look at the photographs I took of her last night. Go *talk* to her before you tell me about no harm done!"

The DA stares at Neely in amazement. "Really, I just meant—"

"You meant you don't want to get into it with Jeff Amato's lawyer father. Well, I will *not* let you slip-slide out of this one!"

She's shaking, and she knows that if she doesn't leave, she'll do something she'll regret. Like burst into tears. Right now, tears are waiting to overwhelm her at any moment, and she knows the real cause, but she won't give the DA an opportunity to misinterpret them.

So she turns on her heel and slams out of the office. She doesn't even register Thelma's quiet "Tell him, sister!"

When Neely reaches the TCSO, she hasn't cooled down, but she has herself under control. She finds Buck Dolin in the Dispatch Center with Lonnie Weaver. Buck gives her a brief report of activities at the TCSO this morning. No major incidents or complaints, and no problems in the Corrections Division, except one prisoner who had an appendicitis attack. Lieutenant Booker called an ambulance, and the prisoner is presently in surgery.

Buck also reports that he personally checked Dirk Riker's trailer at the Camden Loop Mobile Home Park, as well as his usual hangouts, but didn't find him. "Nobody I talked to has seen him today."

Neely asks sharply, "Where the *hell* would he go?"

It's a rhetorical question, but Buck answers it. "Maybe he left town. The APB went out statewide, though. Fancy rig like he drives, somebody'll spot it sooner or later. Anyway, we ran LEDS and NCIC checks on the center staff. The only person with a gun registration is Andrea Olenick. S & W nine-millimeter semiautomatic."

"Andrea?" Somehow it hadn't occurred to Neely that Andrea would think it necessary to own a gun. "What else?"

"Ran Jenny Pinkley and her staff and Billy Huff and his painters. Nothing. I sent Sonny out to get comparison fingerprints from Billy and his guys, and I notified Jenny and the girls who worked with her last night to go to the center for prints and statements."

"You've been busy, Chief."

He shrugs. "I'm about to order sandwiches from Henny's for me and Lonnie—"

"Ham and cheese," Lonnie puts in, looking up from his console. "American cheese. None of that Swiss shit."

Buck laughs. "Okay. Neely, you want something?"

Even the thought of food makes her stomach lurch. She shakes her head and turns to leave, but Buck stops her with a casual "By the way, there's somebody waiting for you in Giff's office."

Giff's office? Neely says irritably, "I can't talk to anyone now."

"Better talk to *this* guy. He's DEA."

She catches herself before asking Buck what a federal drug enforcement agent is doing in Westport. She'll ask the man himself.

Neely goes into the sheriff's office—*her* office—just as Heather places a steaming mug next to a file folder on the coffee table. The folder apparently belongs to the man sitting on the couch. He looks like an insurance salesman on vacation: middle-class white, bland and anonymous, light brown hair, glasses with plain plastic frames, Levi's and running shoes, a tan windbreaker. He rises when he sees Neely.

But he doesn't have a chance to say anything. Heather turns, and abruptly her lavender eyes are swimming with tears. "Oh, Neely . . . I'm so *sorry* about Dr. Koto. . . ."

Don't, Neely thinks, teeth clenched. "Heather, would you mind bringing another cup of coffee?"

"Oh. Yes. Yes, of course." And she hurries into the briefing room.

The man offers a hand. "I'm Special Agent Scott Sayson, DEA."

A firm grip. He doesn't shy from contact with black skin. Some white people do, as if blackness were contagious.

She goes to the armchair at the end of the coffee table. The monkey faces of the moth orchid seem to grin at her maliciously. "What can I do for you, Agent Sayson?"

He sits down and picks up his mug. "Call me Scott, for one thing. I've worked undercover so long, I don't know how to answer to a rank." He smiles with that, then sobers as he adds, "I just want to let you know I'm in town. I've got two agents working with me, running a surveillance. It started about sixteen months ago, and I alerted your, uh, predecessor then for the same reason I'm telling you now."

"So I won't do anything to jeopardize your surveillance, like arresting you or your fellow agents as Peeping Toms?"

"More or less."

Heather returns with coffee for Neely, then, sniffling discreetly, retreats to her office and closes the door behind her.

Neely says, "I can't guarantee anything, Agent—uh, Scott, but I'll do my best to make sure no one at the TCSO blows your cover. Where are you headquartered?"

"We're renting a house at five twenty-two North Abalone."

Neely glances at her watch. At the moment, she can muster little interest in Sayson's surveillance; she has a phone call to make, and however much she dreads it, she wants to get it over with.

But Sayson seems determined to explain himself. "Our subject calls himself William Johnson. Claims to be a retired stockbroker. Owns a beachfront house at five twenty-six North Front Drive."

"William Johnson is an alias?"

"His real name is George Tarbet. Drug smuggler and distributor. Used to work out of San Diego. Small-time independent, with a limited but very profitable upper-class clientele. Tarbet was a little shark who always managed to stay out of the big sharks' way. Until five years ago, when his boat blew up in the San Diego harbor. Supposedly, he was aboard. We know now he faked his death, but it wasn't because we were anywhere near an arrest." There's a cast of bitterness in Sayson's tone with that. "Word on the street was he got into a territorial dispute with a bigger shark."

Neely sips at her coffee. "He staged his death and moved *here*? To Westport, Oregon?"

"Why not? You've got a nice little harbor. Tarbet likes to be on the water. That's how he did most of his smuggling—by boat. But we didn't know he was here until July of last year. One of our guys spotted him on Grand Cayman and tailed him back here. He has a beachfront place on the island, too, only on paper, it belongs to *Robert* Johnson."

"Any relation to William Johnson?"

"So to speak. Tarbet's palming him off as his nephew. Sandro Spinski, known as 'Sandy.' He was Tarbet's bodyguard, enforcer, and occasional hit man in San Diego. And live-in nurse."

"Nurse? Why does he need a nurse?" Neely finds herself intrigued with Sayson's story in spite of her impatience. For one thing, she's wondering why Sayson is bothering to tell it to her in such detail.

He opens the file folder on the coffee table and hands her a five-by-seven black-and-white photograph. The image is grainy. An enlargement, probably. It shows a tall, thin man standing on a dock, his spine bent in an agonized curve, supporting himself with two canes. His face is shadowed by the brim of a Panama hat.

"Rheumatoid arthritis," Sayson explains. "He's fifty-eight years old and looks eighty. Hell, you'd think he'd be willing to retire. That's what my boss thinks—that he's retired. But I know George Tarbet. He'll *never* retire. Likes playing the game too much."

Perhaps today Neely recognizes the edge of anger in Sayson's voice more than she would on another day. She says, "You have a personal stake in this, don't you, Scott?"

He fixes her with a hard stare, his anonymity suddenly gone. "Yeah, I got a stake. I almost had him five years ago. Found a witness willing to testify against him. God, that woman had guts. And . . . well, I cared about her."

Oh, yes, Neely thinks, we're on the same wavelength, and I can't take too much of it. Yet she has to ask: "What happened to her?"

"She was shot. The bullet was a forty-four Magnum. Spinski carries an Israeli Desert Eagle forty-four Magnum automatic. But we couldn't touch him or Tarbet. A month later, Tarbet's boat blew up, and Spinski just disappeared."

"Case closed."

"Yeah."

Neely studies the photograph, thinking of the paradox that if she saw this man on the street, she'd feel sorry for him. But she hasn't seen him on Westport's streets. "Scott, I don't remember ever seeing this man, and with that spinal curvature, I'd notice him."

"You haven't seen him because he hardly ever leaves his house. Spinski run the errands. Just loves tooling around in his white Porsche. He sometimes goes up to the Indian casino, too, or down to the Jade. Must like the girls there; he's a regular."

Neely nods, a memory coming into focus. "I've seen *him*. Blond guy, six two or three, about thirty."

"That's Sandy."

"So, if Tarbet never leaves home, how is he running a drug business? Does Spinski do all the legwork?"

Sayson's eyes go to suspicious slits. "You figure I'm just beating a dead horse?"

"Is that what your boss thinks?"

"Yeah. But I didn't say Tarbet *never* leaves his house. He and Spinski made two trips to Grand Cayman. Spinski drove them in the Lexus to Portland International, and they flew from there. First trip was in December last year. This year it was in September. He only stayed a few days, and he stopped at his bank both times."

"Maybe that's the purpose of the trips."

"Probably. He damn sure doesn't pick up his drugs there. The money has to be for his middlemen. Another thing—when he's home, he doesn't go out, but people come to him. Spinski brings them to him, actually. Picks them up at PDX. Business types, usually male. They stay at Tarbet's place maybe an hour, then Spinski drives them back to PDX."

"Have you put a name on any of these visitors?"

"Just one. My little project isn't exactly top priority, so there's never anybody available to tail these guys. Except me. Most of them I lost at PDX, usually in the damn parking garage. But I got lucky with this one guy. Maurice Danko, Vancouver, BC. Runs a fancy shop up there called Treasures of the First People. Vancouver PD checked him out for me. No priors, no known connection with drugs. Of course, you could say the same about Tarbet. He just never gets *caught*!"

Neely notes the tension that wrenches the last word out so forcefully. "Scott, did you tell Sheriff Wills this much about your surveillance?"

"No."

"Then why tell me?"

He studies her for a moment, then, "I've done a little checking on you. Let's just say you seem more . . . trustworthy. The other reason—well, I'm desperate. My boss gave me the word: I've got till December first to come up with something. If I don't, Tarbet and Spinski will just keep on doing what they do best, and I *still* can't touch them."

"I hope you're not depending on the TCSO to pull something out of a hat for you. We're shorthanded and up to our behinds just trying to keep tabs on our little county."

"I know, and you've got a murder on your hands now. But, like I said, I'm desperate. Hell, I'd be happy with just a parking ticket."

Neely laughs. "That's desperate. You're sure it's drugs Tarbet's into now? We may have a nice little harbor, but we also have a fleet of fishermen who tend to be conservative and watchful, plus a Coast Guard station at the mouth of the harbor. If I were smuggling drugs by boat, I think I'd want a more private place to land them."

"I don't really know what he's into. I just know he isn't retired. Besides, he's always been in the drug business, so why would he change now? Perps are creatures of habit."

"Any pattern to the visits from the business types?"

"Well, there's been a total of twelve visits in sixteen months, and all of them took place within a month or two of his trips to Grand Cayman. Damn it, there *is* something to find! I just can't get the resources to—"

The phone on the desk rings, and Sayson looks at it, startled. Neely rises and crosses to the desk.

And sees the light on the personal line.

She hasn't forgotten about the Whisperer. Just put him/her/it on the back burners of her mind. Of course, this call may not be from the Whisperer. It may be perfectly innocent. But who knows this number?

Answer the damn phone!

She punches the record button and picks up the receiver. Waits. And she hears that husky whispering voice: "Neely Jones . . ."

She makes a note of the phone number, still waiting.

The voice says, "Playing coy? Well, it doesn't matter. Just a question for you, Neely: Have you learned your lesson yet?"

She sinks into the chair, knees giving way. Still, she says nothing.

"A hard lesson, I know, Neely. Bad things happen to good people. And they'll keep on happening until you resign and leave Westport. After all, there's nothing to keep you here now, is there?"

"You *bastard*!"

Damn it, she didn't mean to let the rage take the shape of words, of any kind of reaction the Whisperer could hear; didn't mean to let the pain slip through the armor she's been building around herself in the long hours since this day began.

There's nothing to keep you here now . . .

But the Whisperer is wrong. There's everything to keep her here now. All that's left to her is the rage that will keep here here until . . .

She says coldly, "I'm *not* resigning. I'm *not* leaving."

A long silence, then the voice hisses, "There's a point when stubbornness becomes stupidity, Neely Jones!" The line goes dead.

She frowns at the phone without seeing it. *Bad things*

happen to good people. Is the Whisperer claiming credit for murdering Jan?

But the graffiti . . .

One thing she's sure of—probably the only thing she's sure of at this moment—is that the Whisperer is not Dirk Riker.

"Neely? What's wrong? You got a heckler?"

She looks up at Scott Sayson; he's standing in front of the desk.

"Yes," she says. "A heckler."

"Anonymous, right? These guys never have the guts to spew their garbage to your face. Well, you're busy, so I'll get out of your hair." He places the file folder on the desk. "This is a duplicate. Maybe if you get a few minutes, you can go through it."

Neely musters a smile. "I'll try, Scott. Good luck."

"Thanks. I figure we'll both need some luck."

Chapter 23

THE WHISPERER'S LATEST CALL CAME from a pay phone on Bay Road. Neely makes a note and adds it to the others in the top drawer, remembering how relieved her mother had been when Neely told her she was moving to Westport. Helene Cleary-Jones admitted she would miss seeing her daughter so often, but she was relieved because she thought Neely would be safe in a small town.

Sorry, Mom. Even small towns have gangsters and hate crimes.

And vicious murders.

We have this grief in common, Mom, for the men we loved.

For a moment, she's overwhelmed by a need to call her mother.

She'd be here within hours if she knew about Jan; here to comfort, to hold Neely while she weeps. And that, Neely knows, is the last thing she needs. She has no time now to be her mother's hurt, aching child.

But she does have a phone call to make. To the Kotos to tell them *their* child is dead.

Neely finds her address book and turns to to the *K*'s. Ando and Miko Koto. Beneath that listing is one for Jan's sister, Kim Miyu Naito.

Maybe she should call Kim first. And maybe it's the coward's way out, but Kim has always been easier to talk to.

Easier? Nothing will make this easier.

Gramma Faith used to say, *The Lord wouldn't give us strength and courage if everything was going to be easy.*

Neely picks up the receiver and punches the numbers.

Kim answers cheerfully: "Naito Data Services. May I help you?" A printer is buzzing in the background. Kim is a CPA, working out of her home. She's also the mother of two boys, eight and ten years old. At least there will still be male heirs in the family, although they won't bear the Koto name. Will that be any comfort to Ando Koto?

"It's Neely, Kim. I . . . I have some bad news."

Then she rushes through the pitifully inadequate words that tell Kim the brother she loved is dead. Murdered. The words that will be a benchmark in Kim's life, as they are in Neely's. Afterward, Neely can't remember exactly what she said, but it doesn't matter.

Kim is lost in a dazed silence. It's a long time before she says softly, "I can't believe it, Neely. I mean . . . yes, I believe *you*, but . . ."

"I know." Yes, she knows, and the tears she hears in Kim's voice burn like acid in her own eyes.

No! You can't let the tears start. They'll eat you alive.

"Neely, who *did* this? Why would anyone want to kill Jan? *Why?*"

"It's too early to even guess, Kim. But I *will* find out who killed him." *If it kills me, I'll find out.*

"Does it have anything to do with . . . well, Jan told me you'd been having trouble with some skinheads."

"It may. I can't be sure now." Yet she *was* sure only hours ago. Before the third call from the Whisperer.

And before she became aware that there was something she should have noticed, something she missed. . . .

"Kim, I haven't called your parents yet. I thought—"

"No, *don't* call them. It'll be better if I . . . if I tell them.

But I'll have to do it face-to-face. Besides, you have enough to deal with now. Oh, Neely, he loved you so much."

"Kim, I can't—" She stops, breathing slowly, deeply. "I'll give you the phone number of the pathologist who's doing the autopsy."

"Autopsy? Oh. Yes, of course, they'll have to do an autopsy."

Neely finds Greg Feingold's number in her address book and reads it to Kim, adding, "I know Dr. Feingold. He'll do everything he can to help you and your parents."

"Thanks. I'll let you know about . . ."

Neely knows what Kim started to say, the words she can't get out: *the funeral.* "I'll be there, Kim."

"Oh—" She clears her throat. "There's something . . . it'll mean a lot to Dad. Jan's sword, the samurai sword. It's been passed down from eldest son to eldest son in our family for three hundred years."

Three hundred years.

Three hundred years ago, Neely's ancestors might have been living in Africa. Or they might have been among the first to be captured and sold as slaves in the new American colonies. That's on her father's side. On her mother's side, the Clearys might have been farmers in Brittany or merchants in England. She doesn't know. Immigrants to a new world don't always want to remember the old. And slave owners didn't encourage their chattels to maintain family traditions.

"Kim, I'll bring the sword with me when I come to . . ." the word *is* hard to get out; it's so final—". . . to the funeral."

"Thanks for calling me first, Neely. I'll talk to you. . . ."

She might have had more to say, but Neely hears the first hopeless sobs before Kim hangs up.

Neely cradles the receiver and closes her eyes, but in that darkness, she's overcome with dizziness, as if she were poised at the edge of a cliff above a cauldron of roaring surf.

It's real now. You can't even imagine it's a dream now, a nightmare. All that's left is the reality.

"Neely?"

She opens her eyes, heart pounding for no good reason. Deputy Kevin Locksey is standing in the briefing room door. She asks numbly, "What are you doing here, Kev?"

"Well, I'm on my meal break. Lieutenant Chaffee's letting us go for half-hour breaks two at a time."

"Any problems at the center?"

"No. The crime-scene team's still at it. I was wondering if . . . well, I'd like to give you a report on my, uh, undercover assignment."

Neely doesn't know what he's talking about until he adds, "About Mrs. Thornbeck and her dogs. I can come back some other time, if—"

"No, I want to hear about it." Which isn't entirely true, but Kevin seems so anxious to tell her about it, she won't discourage him by putting him off. "Come in and sit down."

He crosses to her desk, sits carefully on the wayward chair, and takes a notebook and tape recorder from his inside jacket pocket. "I've got the whole thing on tape—my conversation with Gordon Wyland."

"I'll listen to it later. Just give me an oral report for now."

"Okay. Well, I got to the Beachside Lounge at seven P.M. and sat at the bar. Wyland was on duty. I had a beer and just rapped with him for a while. Mostly about the Blazers game on the TV." Kevin grins and shakes his head. "Had a scare about ten minutes after I got there. I could see the front door in the mirror behind the bar. Well, Curtis McMinn walked in, and I was sure he'd spot me and say something. But he didn't see me. Went back to a booth and sat down with some guys. Looked like loggers. They all knew each other."

Neely holds her face expressionless, reigning in her annoyance. Apparently, McMinn's illness didn't strike until well after he was supposed to go on duty at the center at five. She says, "They were probably relatives. There are a lot of McMinns around here. Did you notice when Curtis left?"

"About nine. Just a few minutes before I left at nine-fifteen."

"So, what did Wyland have to say?"

"A lot. There weren't many customers, so he had plenty of time to talk. I told him I'd just moved to Westport, and I was on my own because my wife was visiting her mother in Portland for a week. Well, I hadn't talked to him long before I figured out he's the kind of guy who has to one-better whatever anybody says. So I started complaining about my neighbor's dog barking and keeping me awake. And he had to one-better me. Told me about his landlady's dogs. First thing in the morning, they start yapping, he says, and since he's on the night shift, he's not ready to wake up at dawn. I said I didn't see how he had a problem. He's just renting, so he could always move out, but I told him I had a mortgage. I couldn't just pull up stakes and move. He came back with how he had a really sweet deal: beachfront duplex for two seventy-five a month. His landlady says that's what the place rented for when she bought it thirty years ago, and it's just too sweet a deal to give up. So I said, 'I guess the only answer for both of us is earplugs.' "

Neely smiles at that, appreciating the way the deputy worked Wyland. She asks, "What did he say to that?"

"He started giving me some advice about how to solve the problem. Said the main thing was to be real friendly with the dog and the owner. Then when the owner isn't looking, you grab the dog, take it to your house, and give it some hamburger laced with sleeping pills. Wyland told me he has a prescription for Seconal, since he's always had trouble sleeping. As soon as the dog nods off, you throw it in the trunk of your car, then drive up the river and drown it. Says it doesn't hurt the dog, and you get a good night's sleep for a change."

Neely remembers Willow Thornbeck's eyes filling with

tears of grief, and she mutters, "That scumbag . . ."

"He's a piece of work, all right. Anyway, I have all that on tape. Lot of background noise from the TV, but old Gordon comes through loud and clear."

"Good job, Kev. Now, as soon as you can, take that tape to Judge Lay and get a search warrant for Wyland's house and car. You'll be looking for Seconal and dog hairs."

"I'll see if I can catch the judge before the afternoon court session starts." Kevin heads for the door, then pauses. "I know it isn't a big deal—Mrs. Thornbeck and her dogs—but it still feels good."

Neely watches Kevin disappear around the L in the briefing room.

Yes, it *does* feel good. In the emotional havoc of this day, one small triumph is a treasured gift.

Chapter 24

IT'S 1:45 WHEN NEELY REACHES the Westport Oceanographic Center and threads through the traffic jam. A grand entrance, thoroughly photographed and videotaped. She parks behind the crime-scene team's vehicles and hurries to the entrance, where Curtis McMinn is on duty.

She considers asking him what he was doing at the Beachside Lounge last night, but he'll just say Kevin was mistaken, and no doubt Trina, his loving and, it seems, ever-pregnant wife, will swear on a stack of Bibles that Curtis was home all night. Sick as a dog.

Besides, sometimes it's a good idea to save certain information for the right moment.

Thus she passes McMinn with only a nod and goes to the museum wing in search of Lt. John Heathman. He's there, conferring with two of the criminalists. When he sees her, he walks over to her.

"I hear you're now officially sworn in, Sheriff."

She gives that a brief laugh. "I guess so. How's it going?"

"Okay. We've finished printing and taking statements from the staff." For a moment, his gray-brown eyes search her face. "I'd like you to look at the victim's personal effects. They're in his office."

Neely nods, grateful that he doesn't ask if she's up to it. They walk in silence to Jan's office, where they must duck under the yellow crime-scene tape to get in. Nothing has been moved, but now there's a large evidence envelope on the desk. Heathman opens it and offers it to her. Inside is a handful of smaller manila envelopes.

Neely takes them out and opens them, willing her hands not to shake. Two pens, one black, the other red. A plastic key ring/flashlight in the shape of an unlikely fish. A class ring from Berkeley. A wallet—still damp. Nothing unusual in it; nothing missing. In the next envelope, she finds the gold and onyx yin-yang medallion she gave Jan last Christmas. She drops that envelope, ambushed by memories, and hurriedly takes out another envelope.

Jan's bent wire-rim glasses.

She frowns at the desk. The case for the glasses is next to the computer, but the computer's off and there are no journals, books, or notebooks on the desk. She looks through the photographs, finds some exquisite views of marine life, but nothing else.

She says, "Jan developed these last night, but he hadn't even begun to sort them. He just dropped them here. And he wasn't reading. There's nothing for him to read. No steno pads, either, so he wasn't transcribing his notes. Yet he must've been using the computer. The cover is off, and he was wearing his glasses. They were only for reading or the computer." She turns toward the door, wondering again why Jan tacked his sweatshirt over the window. What was he doing that he didn't want anyone in the building to know about? *Who* in the building? Curtis McMinn? He left the Beachside Lounge about nine, but she doesn't know where he went from there.

Heathman reaches into the evidence envelope and hands her another small envelope. "You have any ideas about this?"

Neely slides the contents out into her palm. A flat black metallic rectangle, about three by six inches square, with an Intel logo printed on it.

"What is this?" she asks. "Some sort of microchip?"

"According to Ben Ottley—our team hacker—it's a Pentium Three Xeon processor. He says they run maybe a thousand bucks apiece."

"Damn, it should be mounted in gold."

"I wondered if Dr. Koto might've been trying to fix his computer."

"Jan?" She almost laughs, until she realizes that if she laughs at any of Jan's remembered quirks, she'll end up crying. "He didn't know zip about how his computer worked. Where did you find this?"

"In the back pocket of his Levi's."

She stares at Heathman. "Where would Jan get a thousand-dollar Pentium processor?" Then she sighs. "I'll check his computer. I want to see what he was working on, anyway."

Heathman nods and begins putting the small envelopes back into the big one. "The personal effects will have to go to the lab, but we'll return them to you as soon as possible."

She has more than once spoken the same words to families and loved ones of victims. "Yes, I know."

"Yeah. Sorry. Well, I'll be in the other wing if you need me."

Heathman closes the door as he leaves, and Neely sits down at Jan's desk, facing his computer, placing her fingers on the keyboard where he had placed his.

Concentrate!

Methodically, she boots up the computer. The screen shows her the neatly arrayed document icons. She shifts the VIEW menu to dates, searching for the document he worked on last. But as far as this machine is concerned, Jan didn't touch it yesterday. Of course, it's possible he didn't actually use the computer, that he was about to but was interrupted.

Again, she orders herself to concentrate. What would Jan have been working on? After his field trip with Andrea, a document on the new medusa. *Chrysaora kotii.*

She tries the FIND function. No *C. kotii.* She opens every folder, examines the documents by name, size, kind, label.

And finally, she realizes that everything on the new medusa is gone.

Neely goes to the bookshelf where the full backup discs are stored in their marked boxes. She checks the subject listings and isn't surprised that there's nothing on *C. kotii.* She could go through the discs to make sure the ones she's seeking didn't get misplaced, but that would be a waste of time. Jan was meticulous about such things.

She moves to another bookshelf to check the steno pads he used as field notebooks. Each is marked on the cover with dates and subject.

And again, there is nothing on *C. kotii.*

The office door was unlocked this morning. Anyone could have gotten in.

No, not anyone. Andrea Olenick.

Who else would have any use for Jan's files on *C. kotii?* None of the other staff scientists are working on jellies.

And it was Andrea who came to the center at six this morning. Andrea who said that after recovering from the shock of seeing Jan's body, she went to her office and stayed for at least half an hour—time enough to go into Jan's office, grab the field notebooks and backup discs, and delete everything on the medusa from the hard drive.

What happened on the scuba-diving expedition? Did Andrea come on to Jan, make it obvious even to him, who was so naïve where she was concerned, that she wanted more from him than scientific collaboration? Or was it something else?

Neely leaves the office and goes to the next door along the hall. It's locked. But she has the master key.

Which gets her into Andrea's office, but not into her computer: That requires a code word.

Neely storms down the hall and across to the museum wing. When she finds Heathman, she asks, "Is your computer expert available?"

"Sergeant Ottley? Well, he's a fiber specialist in real life. He's upstairs now. I'll send him down."

Ben Ottley is a young white man who looks more like a college linebacker than the stereotypical hacker—or criminalist, for that matter. He tries. For half an hour, he tries, but he finds no way around Andrea's code word.

He also tries when Neely asks him to help search Andrea's office for Jan's notes and backup discs. Andrea isn't as orderly as Jan was, and the search takes another half hour. And turns up nothing.

"Her purse," Neely says finally. "That saddlebag of a purse. Damn, I should've searched it before I let her go home."

Ottley frowns. "A personal search? Shaky legal ground there."

"Yes. Well, thanks, Sergeant. Sorry it was such a waste of time."

"Most of what I do is a waste of time." Then he shrugs. "Never can tell, though."

Chapter 25

AT 3:30, DISTRICT ATTORNEY OWEN Culpepper arrives at
the oceanographic center and calls for a conference: Heathman, Neely, and himself. He wants to know what progress
had been made.

Heathman leads the way to the research library, where
the bagged evidence nearly covers a conference table. He
explains everything—in detail. By four o'clock, Culpepper
is checking his watch every few seconds, and finally he
opines, "Well, it all seems clear enough."

Neely's jaw drops. Throughout Heathman's inventory,
it seemed obvious to her that nothing about this case is as
clear as she first thought.

Culpepper nods judiciously. "Yes, the man we want is
that skinhead. What does he call himself?"

Neely supplies the name: "Dirk Riker."

"Yes. Neely, you'll have to put out an APB—"

"There's been an APB out on Riker since six-thirty this
morning, and Chief Dolin made a personal check of Riker's
trailer and known hangouts. The APB is statewide, in case
he decided to leave town."

"Well, there you are, then."

"*Where* am I, Mr. Culpepper?"

"Riker's your man. Found out about the APB and did a bunk."

"Sir, I don't think we can jump to any conclusions—"

"Considering the garbage sprayed on that fish tank, I think it's a *very* small jump. After all, you and Dr. Koto had trouble with this Riker before, didn't you? That's what Chief Dolin told me today."

"Some graffiti on our house and a cross burning."

"Exactly. I wish you'd reported the incidents, Neely. We might've had some idea what we were dealing with."

"I *did* report the incidents," Neely retorts, "to Sheriff Wills."

"Oh." Culpepper checks his watch again and announces, "I've scheduled a press conference outside the center at four, and it's five after now. I'd like you and Lieutenant Heathman to be present. But just, uh, let me do the talking. I've had more experience with the press."

Neely shares a foreboding glance with Heathman.

LATER, NEELY WATCHES THE LAST of the photographers and reporters trail out of the parking lot. The press conference was short and relatively painless. Culpepper, as promised, did most of the talking.

And Dr. S. Benjamin Nicholass.

It was the DA who invited Nicholass to the press conference. Saint Nick was earnestly concerned about "this senseless violence," full of praise for Jan Koto, "a promising young scientist, cut down in his prime," and brimming with confidence that the new sheriff and the state crime-scene team would "bring the guilty man to justice."

The guilty man, according to Culpepper, is Dirk Riker. Then he hedged to say that at least Riker was a "person of interest."

Now Neely stands on the deck next to Heathman, watching Culpepper and Nicholass in whispered consultation. As the afternoon wanes, the clouds have thickened again. In the empty parking lot, gulls peck at the scattered contents of a potato-chip bag one of the reporters left behind.

Culpepper turns to Neely. "Dr. Nicholass was wondering when his maintenance staff can get into the museum to begin cleaning up."

"I don't know. Certainly not today."

Nicholass protests, "But, Neely, the aquariums have to be checked and maintained, or the specimens will die."

"Dr. Spenser can take care of whatever basic maintenance is necessary—under my supervision or Lieutenant Heathman's."

"Well, perhaps I can help her."

"Lili knows every detail of the museum displays. She won't need any help, Dr. Nicholass."

Nicholass looks to Culpepper, and the DA seems on the verge of countermanding Neely, but she doesn't give him a chance. She says firmly, "This building is now a crime scene. Until the evidence has been analyzed, and we're sure nothing has been overlooked, the center is off-limits to anyone except police personnel."

Culpepper looks at her sharply, but Nicholass turns sympathetic. "Yes, of course you're right, Neely. I'll call Dr. Spenser. I suppose . . . well, I was wondering about *Poseidon*. I mean our scheduled voyage."

"I'll let you know, Dr. Nicholass."

The DA puts in, "Don't you think you're being a little hard-nosed about this, Neely?"

"That's my job," she counters. "We've just begun the investigation, we don't have Riker, and we can't be sure he's guilty. Until we *can* be sure, I do *not* intend to let potential suspects leave the country."

Nicholass seems honestly shocked. "Oh, Neely, you don't think any of the research staff—"

"I don't *know*. That's the bottom line. When we have a viable suspect under indictment, I do not want him—or her—to walk because I was anything *less* than hard-nosed."

"Quite right," Nicholass concedes. "You're under a

great strain, Neely, and I certainly don't want to add to your burdens." He gives Culpepper a brief smile. "Good-bye, Owen. I'll talk to you later."

"Okay, Ben. We won't inconvenience you any more than is absolutely necessary." Culpepper sends Neely a meaningful look with that, which she chooses to ignore by turning on her heel and marching into the center. Heathman is only a few steps behind her.

Once they're in the lobby, Heathman says casually, "Nicholass seems to be a fair-haired boy around here."

"Oh, yes. A pillar of the community. And Culpepper's another. They seem to spend a lot of time propping each other up."

"I can see that. Well, we're almost finished here for today. I'll send the rest of the crew back to Portland, but I'll stick around until Dr. Spenser takes care of her fish. And I might as well stay over tonight. Any good motels around here?"

Neely laughs at that. "A few. If the state's paying, try the Glencove Resort at the south end of town. I think I'll go talk to Andrea Olenick. She's the only staff member with a gun registered to her."

Heathman raises an eyebrow. "You're really not convinced Riker's our man, are you?"

"I'd like to believe it's that simple, Lieutenant."

"Maybe it is."

Neely nods. "Maybe."

Chapter 26

NEELY JONES DRIVES SOUTH ON Highway 101 through a hard rain, slowing as she crosses the bay bridge to look out at a choppy gray sea vanishing to a dark horizon; a fishing boat is coming into the bay through the open arms of the jetties that make calm waters for a vessel too insignificant to survive the muscular swells of the open sea tonight.

She is tired, weary beyond her comprehension, yet she feels an elusive electric buzz along her nerves. It reminds her of her sophomore year at Berkeley. Finals week, and she succumbed to a friend's offer of Dexedrine to get through the last exams. The same feeling: electricity under the skin, and a conviction that she could do anything.

Now she has no choice but to believe that.

At the end of the bridge, she turns left on South Bay Road, following it as it curves past a row of shops, then skirts Chinook Bay Park. The two-story Bayview Manor looms on the right side of the road, aligned east and west, so all the apartments face the park and bay; breezeways with staircases divide the building into five units. Neely drives into the parking lot behind the apartments. Andrea's red Saab convertible is parked behind the unit farthest to the west.

Neely should be armed with a search warrant, but she's not.

She stopped by the courthouse at five o'clock and caught Judge Lay as he was leaving his chambers. He wasn't impressed with her theory that Andrea Olenick stole Jan's discs and notebooks and deleted every document pertaining to the new jelly from his computer.

"Neely, you don't have reasonable cause to assume she stole anything. If her fingerprints show up on Dr. Koto's keyboard . . . well, that would be different. Besides, it's a hate crime. Simple as that. I talked to Owen, and he told me about the graffiti. So, if you'll excuse me, I have an appointment—with a rare steak at Henny's."

Now Neely considers the ethics of a judge discussing with the district attorney a case he might one day be trying.

She parks the patrol directly behind the red Saab, then runs through relentless rain to the breezeway. She hears the thump of music before she hits the first step, and by the time she reaches the last step, she identifies it as someone's electronic version of "Louie, Louie." Andrea's apartment is upstairs at the end of the building, and it's the source of the music. Neely has to ring the bell three times before the door opens.

Andrea's gray eyes turn icy when she sees Neely. Her profligate auburn hair is tied back with a beaded cord, her muscular body sheened with musky sweat and a skin-tight blue-and-orange spandex leotard.

"What do you want, Neely?" She has to shout over the music.

Neely shouts back, "I need to ask you some questions."

Andrea seems on the verge of slamming the door in her face, but instead, she opens it wide enough for Neely to enter and apparently satisfies herself by slamming the door behind Neely.

Neely looks around the living room, a room so blandly ordinary—the furnishings unexceptional, the walls and carpet a generic beige—that the Bowflex exerciser in the center of the room seems exotic and bizarre, like a huge robot insect. Neely notes the absence of a computer, then surveys the bookshelves lining the west wall, but she sees nothing in the way of notebooks or computer discs.

"Nice apartment," she says softly, knowing Andrea can't hear her.

"What?" Andrea crosses to the stereo on the south wall and cuts off the music in mid "Louie."

"I said this is a nice apartment. How many bedrooms?"

"Three. No, I won't show you around. If you're interested in renting an apartment, talk to the manager. If you want to search the place, get a search warrant." Andrea goes to the Bowflex for the towel hung on one of its appendages and wipes her face and arms. She doesn't ask Neely to sit down. "You said you wanted to ask me some questions—as if I haven't answered enough already."

"Oh, I think you have some answers left. Like, where's the handgun registered to you—a Smith and Wesson nine-millimeter semiautomatic?"

For a moment, Andrea seems to freeze, then she drapes the towel around her shoulders. "Everett, Washington, probably."

"Everett?"

"A guy I used to go with gave it to me. We broke up two years ago, and I gave the damn thing back to him. It never occurred to me to do anything about the registration."

Neely takes out her notebook. "What's your ex-boyfriend's name?"

"Donald Grabenhorst."

"Address?"

"I have no idea."

"But he lives in Everett?"

"Could be. When he left Westport, he said he was offered a job managing a restaurant in Everett."

"What's the name of the restaurant?"

"Who knows? We didn't part friends. Shit, if we'd been married, we'd still be in litigation."

"You didn't stay in touch with him?"

Andrea gives that a bitter laugh as she sits down on the Bowflex, hands propped on her knees, legs apart. There is about her something intimidating. The honed body is too golden, too perfect, as if she weren't made solely of flesh and blood. Her athletic shoes are molded into a design so rakishly abstract, they make her feet look like weapons.

She says, "I haven't heard from Don since I packed his belongings in cartons and left them outside our apartment door. That gun was in one of those cartons. No, wait—" Her lips curve in a slow smile. "I *did* hear from him. Once."

"Heard from him how? A letter? Phone call?"

"A wedding announcement. It was about six months after I threw him out. Yes, Donny the Prick got married. I guess he thought I'd be prostrate with grief. I just feel sorry for the poor woman."

"You didn't happen to keep that announcement." It's not a question.

"Strange as it may seem, no. But it wouldn't make any difference if I *had* kept it. He marked out the nuptial couple's address, and there was no return address on the envelope."

Andrea seems to enjoy telling her that, as if she knows how much trouble it could be to locate Donald Grabenhorst without an address.

Neely changes the subject. "I'm amazed you and Dr. Nicholass managed to keep your relationship secret so long."

"So we're discreet. What business is that of yours?"

"Since Nicholass is providing your alibi, it's my business."

"Alibi? You think I . . . did that to Jan? Christ, Neely! That's sick." Then abruptly, her shoulders sag; her face is stamped with pain. "Oh God, he was a dear, kind man, and I . . . depended on him so much."

You bitch! Don't tell me *what a dear kind man he was.*

Neely doesn't speak the words boiling up in her throat.

She asks, "Are you going on the next voyage to Baja?"

"Yes. If and when it ever happens."

"I didn't realize you were so interested in gray whales."

"I'm not. I've been doing water-chemistry analyses for Dave and Carla Townsend and Eric Winslow. They're our cetacean experts."

"Have you gone on all the Baja trips?"

"Yes. And all the Juan de Fuca trips and the Gulf of Alaska trips."

"What's the code word for your computer?"

Andrea snaps, "That is *definitely* none of your business. Why do you want to get into my computer?"

Neely hoped to catch her off guard, but it was a faint hope at best. "Because of what's missing from Jan's computer."

A hesitation no longer than the blink of an eye, then Andrea asks, quite convincingly, "What the hell are you talking about?"

Neely ignores that. "It's too bad, since Jan was such a dear friend, that your last day with him was ruined by that . . . disagreement."

Again, a brief pause, then: "You're not making any sense, Neely."

"Oh, I think I am." Neely puts her notebook and pen away. "Thanks, Andrea, for your cooperation."

Andrea gives her a potent glare that seems to focus the energy in her powerful body. Neely wonders if it's powerful enough to drag another body from an office in one wing of the Oceanographic Center to the other wing and up the stairs to the maintenance area above the medusa pool.

Neely turns and leaves the apartment. Within seconds, "Louie, Louie" again assaults the airwaves. She doesn't go to her patrol yet. Instead, she knocks on the door of the apartment below Andrea's.

She's invited in by the retired couple who live there—Maggie and Geoffrey Hunsaker. Andrea's music is audible, and that's what Neely asks about.

"Last night?" Geoffrey repeats, rolling his eyes toward the ceiling. "It's on *every* night. Till ten or eleven."

Maggie nods. "Every night of the world."

"We've complained to the manager," Geoffrey adds. "He always says he'll talk to her, but I don't think he ever has."

"You're sure you heard the music last night?"

"We're sure," Maggie says. "Heck, it was still going when we went to bed about ten."

"Yes," her husband agrees, "but it stopped about an hour later."

"Did you notice if Dr. Olenick's car was parked outside last night?"

Maggie says, "Had all the shades pulled last night, but this morning when I opened the kitchen shade, that red car was gone."

Neely tries not to reveal any tension in her face or voice as she asks, "What time was that, Mrs. Hunsaker?"

"Oh, about seven, wasn't it, Geoffrey?"

"About then, yes."

Neely makes a note of the time, but only for the Hunsakers' benefit. She already knows where the red Saab was at 7:00 A.M.: in the staff parking lot at the center. She puts her notebook away. "Well, I won't bother you any more. You've been a great help. Thanks."

"You sure are welcome," Maggie says. "You know, Geoffrey and I voted for you."

"I, uh, hope you won't be sorry."

As Neely drives away from Bayview Manor, she considers Andrea's alibi. Of course, just because the stereo was on doesn't mean she was home. If she did spend the night with Nicholass, she might have left the music on in her apartment inadvertently, or purposely—to make potential burglars think she was there. One of those multiple CD players would go on for hours.

But if she *was* home last night, did she lie to give herself an alibi or to give Ben Nicholass one?

Chapter 27

RAIN HAS ITS ADVANTAGES. PERPS are as averse to getting wet as most people, which offers some hope for a quiet night at the TCSO. At seven, when Neely returns, the late swing shift is coming on. She checks with the dispatcher and shift commander, then goes to her office and sits down behind a desk littered with files and reports. She reaches for the phone, thinking about Andrea Olenick and how difficult it is to be objective about her. *He was a dear, kind man . . .*

Shit.

Neely dials directory assistance for Everett, Washington's area code and tells the operator, "I'm trying to reach Donald Grabenhorst."

"Just a moment, ma'am."

Neely waits, expecting either no number at all or a long list to call in search of Andrea's ex-boyfriend. Thus she's surprised when the operator turns on a recorded voice that reels off one phone number.

My lucky day, Neely thinks, but her luck runs out. The number only gets her another recorded voice, asking her to leave a message. She considers calling the Everett PD to find Grabenhorst, then refrains. This isn't an emergency.

For now, she satisfies herself with an official and urgent message.

She hangs up just as Heather comes in from her office with a thermos in one hand, a spoon and mug in the other.

"Heather, you should be home by now."

"I *have* been home, Sheriff." She opens the thermos and fills the mug. "It's chicken soup."

Neely almost laughs at that. "I didn't know you were Jewish."

"Oh, I'm not. I'm Methodist. I'll bet you haven't eaten a thing all day, and I . . . I understand, but you've got to keep up your strength. Try a little of this." She offers the mug, adding hopefully, "It's homemade."

Neely spoons up a mouthful, taking it like medicine. It's probably delectable, but it seems her taste buds have been disconnected. Still, she works at it, because Heather is right: She must keep up her strength.

"It's . . . wonderful, Heather."

"You know, I can stay at your house tonight. You shouldn't—"

"I'll be fine," Neely insists. "And thanks for the soup."

Heather sighs. "Okay. But if there's *anything* I can do, *call* me."

As Heather departs, Deputy Kevin Locksey appears at the briefing room door with two plastic evidence bags. "Got a minute, Neely?"

"Sure. I'm taking my meal break, I guess."

Kevin perches on the chair in front of the desk. "I just got back from serving the search warrant on Gordon Wyland."

"Any problems?"

"No. Wyland was there, and he was really pissed, but it was all talk. And, you know, I don't think he even recognized me."

Neely nods. "The uniform. People don't look past it."

"Yeah. Anyway, I found this bottle of Seconal. Called

the pharmacy, and Wyland's been taking it since he moved to Westport. And this." He hands her the other bag. "Dog hair. Well, I think it's dog hair. Came out of the trunk of his car."

Neely studies the strands of hair. "Beautiful, Kev. Take this to Janie Dial at the Humane Society tomorrow and ask her if they're consistent with a terrier mix, a sheltie-shepherd mix, and a Pom-poodle mix. Janie can offer an expert opinion that'll get you an arrest warrant; then we'll send the samples to the Forensic Wildlife Lab in Ashland for an opinion that'll stand up in court. You'll need to talk to the DA."

Kevin grins. "I'll see him first thing in the morning."

When Kevin leaves, Neely finishes the mug of soup, then begins a second, willing her stomach to acceptance. She's almost finished the second mug when she looks up and sees Buck at the briefing room door.

Startled, she asks, too sharply, "What're you doing here?"

"Well, I checked Riker's RV and the Salty Dog. Nada. So, I'm going down to watch the RV for a while."

"That won't be necessary, Chief. Go on home and get some sleep."

"What about you? You planning on working three shifts again?"

Why does that question annoy her? "I have to write a case report."

"I can help you with that."

"I don't *need* any help."

"Neely, I figure you need all the help you can get."

"Go *home*, Buck."

He shrugs. "Maybe you should think about doing the same."

When he's gone, Neely closes her eyes, shivering. The truth is, the reason she won't go home is that she can't face a house empty of Jan.

It's an equivocal thing, her acceptance of his death.

One part of her mind recognizes the gaping hole in her life created by his death, but she imprisons that realization in a mental genie bottle.

If she uncorks it, the pain inside will paralyze her.

Then there's a part of her mind that refuses to believe Jan is dead. He's just somewhere else. At home, waiting for her. If she doesn't go home, she won't have to believe he isn't there and never will be.

She listens to the rain against the windows, hears voices and a typewriter from the briefing room. Finally, her gaze fixes on a file on the cluttered desk. KAYNARD.

Damn, she's hardly thought of Jennifer Kaynard all day. She can only hope someone else did, someone who could help her deal with the horror she suffered last night.

Neely frowns, remembering one small detail of Jennifer's story—a detail Neely had forgotten.

She rises and grabs her Stetson off the top of a file cabinet.

Chapter 28

THERE'S NOBODY IN THE OTHER bed in the hospital room, and Jennifer is of two minds about that. It was nice not to have anybody listening this afternoon when she talked to Kelly Bower, the Taft County Victim's Advocate, or when her mom was here a little while ago.

Mom was crying; couldn't seem to help herself. And it was scary. It meant Jennifer had to be the strong one, and she didn't *feel* strong.

But having the room to herself isn't so cool now. Eight o'clock, and it feels like midnight, the hospital so quiet, the rain rattling on the window to her right. She looks up at the dark screen of the television on the opposite wall. Her mom can't afford to pay for TV, and the insurance won't cover it. There's a lot of things it won't cover.

Jennifer closes her eyes, conscious of the chorus of drug-muted pain emanating from different parts of her body: the left side of her face thumping with every heartbeat; her left arm buzzing like a really bad toothache; and between her legs . . .

Maybe that pain is more in her head, in her heart. . . .

"Jennifer?"

The ceiling lights are off, and the reading light barely

reaches the door, but it flashes on the gold seven-pointed star on her visitor's uniform.

"Hello, Sheriff."

Neely Jones comes over to the bed, and Jennifer remembers what Mom told her about Neely's boyfriend. That he was murdered.

"Oh, Sheriff, I'm so sorry about your friend."

She touches Jennifer's hand—just a quick feather touch. "Please—call me Neely. The nurse said you'll be released tomorrow."

Jennifer starts to nod, but it hurts. It hurts to talk, too, and the words come out slurred. "Dr. Standish said I should stay home from school for a week."

"Did Kelly talk to you about school?"

"Yeah, but it's still . . ." Jennifer had a look at herself in a mirror this morning, and it was horrible. "It'll be hard, going back to school. I mean, everybody will *know*. They'll know I was *raped*!"

"And what will they think?"

"They'll think—" She stops, realizing she doesn't know the answer to that. Will they think she asked for it? That she's such a cow, a boy wouldn't look at her otherwise? Will they think she *wanted* it?

Jennifer says, "Well, it doesn't matter what anybody thinks. Besides, I never expected to be invited to the senior prom, anyway."

"Proms aren't that big a deal," Neely assures her, then laughs. "I can say that because *I* wasn't invited to the senior prom, either."

That silences Jennifer until she blurts out, "But—but you're beautiful. Lots of guys must've wanted to take you to the prom."

"Well, I happened to be at a high school that was ninety-seven percent white. You know, Jennifer, it'll be hard for you *not* to let it matter what other people think."

Jennifer nods. "Maybe, but I *can't* let it matter, because I'm not giving up school, and I'm going on to college. Mr.

Lutz—he's my science teacher—he thinks he can get me a scholarship. Anyway, I won't let those guys ruin *my* life like Mom's was ruined." She takes a shaky breath. "And I haven't changed my mind about testifying in court."

"What does your mom say about that?"

"Oh, she doesn't like it. She says *I'll* be the one on trial, and maybe I will, but what those guys did—" For a moment, she feels suffocated by anger and pain. "If they *are* convicted, what'll happen to them?"

"Unless they're tried as adults—which they could be— they'll be sent to MacLaren. When they turn eighteen, they'll be released and their records wiped clean."

Jennifer can hear the bitterness in that, even though Neely's trying to be cool about it.

Jennifer asks, "*Will* they be convicted?"

"We have DNA evidence, we have Deputy Hoffstead, who can identify the car and license number. And, above all, we have you. They'll be convicted."

"Then it'll be worth it." She closes her eyes. Pain wears a person down. She never really understood that before.

"Jennifer, you've got a lot of courage. I hope you don't pay too high a price for it."

"Don't worry about me. You've got lots of bigger things to worry about now. I mean, with . . . with the murder."

Neely nods. "Yes, and one of the reasons I'm here is that I need to ask you more about what you saw at the center last night."

"What I saw?" Jennifer frowns, but that hurts, too. "All I saw was the light in Dr. Nicholass's office."

"I know. Could you tell if anyone was inside the office?"

"No. The blinds were closed."

"You're sure it was Dr. Nicholass's office?"

"Well, it was the third window from the lobby. The first window's the accounting office, the second is Dr. Nicholass's secretary's office, and the third is his. Is there something . . . suspicious about that light? I just figured it was Sergeant McMinn checking the office."

"Except that Sergeant McMinn's master key won't unlock the door on that particular office."

"Oh. Well, was it Dr. Nicholass?"

"I don't know." She looks out the window, dark eyes hooded. Then she asks, "Did you see anyone around the center? Or any cars?"

Again, Jennifer tries to nod, and then regrets it. "I *did* see a couple of cars. Actually, one was a van and the other was—well, it was Dirk Riker's pickup. You know, that lifted custom rig? Red and black?"

"I know it." Neely takes out a notebook and writes in it. "Tell me everything you remember about it."

"There's not much to remember. Right after the light went off in Dr. Nicholass's office, I headed for the east entrance of the parking lot, and that's when the pickup came roaring north on Chinook Street."

Neely's eyes seem to glitter. "From the staff parking lot?"

"I couldn't see the entrance to the staff lot, so I don't know where it came from. Might've gotten to Chinook from Bay Road, and that connects with the highway."

The glitter goes out of her eyes. "Right. You said there was a van?"

"Well, a minivan, really. One of those with the swept-back windshield? Dark blue. Anyway, it came up Chinook a minute or so *before* Dirk Riker's pickup."

"Driving north?"

"Yes. Then it turned left at North First."

"But you couldn't see whether the minivan came out of the staff parking lot, either."

"No."

"Could you see the driver at all?"

Jennifer sighs. "No. Sorry."

"What's to be sorry about? You're a very good witness." Neely puts her pen and notebook away. "Have you talked to a lawyer yet?"

"No . . . I well, I don't see how Mom can afford a lawyer."

"Sometimes they work on contingency or even pro bono. I know one who might be interested in your case. Her name's Susan Benedict. Do you want me to ask her if she'll talk to you?"

Jennifer still feels doubtful. Probably that's because her mom hates lawyers so much. "Well, maybe . . . I mean, just to talk, you know."

"I'll call Susan tonight. One thing I'm sure she'll advise you about: You should think past the criminal trial to a civil trial. Parents are liable for what their children do. That means the boys' parents should be financially responsible for your hospital bills, at least a year of counseling, and maybe punitive damages—enough to see you through college."

Jennifer stares at her. "I . . . I never even thought about . . . you know, money."

"Francis Amato will think about it. He understands money, if not justice. Meanwhile, thanks for the information, Jennifer. And try to get some sleep." Neely smiles as she turns and walks to the door.

"Good night, Neely. . . ."

When the door closes behind Neely, Jennifer looks out at the rain-streaked lights and sighs.

Yes, maybe now she *can* sleep.

Chapter 29

IT'S NINE O'CLOCK AND THE rain is letting up when Neely returns to the TCSO from the hospital. The briefing room is empty. Lt. Brad Skinner, the swing shift supervisor, is in the small office Whit Chaffee occupies for the day shift. Skinner is munching Doritos while he types a report. He tells her that Kevin Locksey is on guard duty at the oceanographic center, Sonny Hoffstead is checking out a D and D at the Marina Tavern, Sgt. Jimbo Ventry is checking out a vehicular theft on Camden Loop, and Deputy Andy Anderson is driving patrol on 101. A relatively quiet night, for which Skinner professes gratitude as he reaches for another handful of chips.

Neely goes to the Dispatch Center, where Deputy Wayne Gerlach is on duty. She tells him, "I'm available, Deputy."

He greets that news with the enthusiasm of a weary basset hound.

In her office, Neely checks the phone for messages, half-expecting another communication from the Whisperer, but there's nothing. Then she calls Susan Benedict, who is ready and willing to take Jennifer's case on contingency. Whatever happens, Susan promises, the parents of the three young men will pay dearly. Financially, at least.

When Neely concludes the call, she pulls in a deep breath and surveys her desk. She has work to do.

She spends the next hour organizing her desk and filling out a case report on the Koto murder.

Yes, the Koto murder.

She *can* be objective. Coldly, hard-as-nails objective. It doesn't matter that she's shaking by the time she finishes the report. Finally, she adds a Post-it note to Heather, instructing her to make copies for the shift supervisors, and takes it to Heather's desk.

When Neely returns to her own desk, she's well aware that she should go home and get some sleep. But she also recognizes the sensation of panic she feels when she thinks about going home.

Not yet.

She rubs her burning eyes. A long day. A long two days. It seems impossible that she laid claim to this office, this desk, this chair, only yesterday morning.

The payoff envelope. She's almost forgotten it. Tomorrow she must call Mary Jo Bivins to see if she turned up any prints.

Damn Giff Wills!

What kind of game was he playing? And with whom?

And what kind of game was Saint Nickle-ass playing— or whoever it was who turned on the light in his office last night?

And where did Jan get an Intel Pentium III processor worth a thousand dollars?

Intel. That rings a faint bell. But she doesn't know why.

And what does that dark blue minivan Jennifer saw have to do with anything?

And was Riker driving out of the center's staff parking lot last night, or just taking a shortcut from Bay Road to Chinook to who knows where?

And where the *hell* is Riker now?

She realizes she's going around in circles and getting nowhere.

Rest your mind's eye now and then, Neely. Look at something else, so you can see what you missed.

Okay, Gramma Faith. It's worth a try.

Neely finds the file Special Agent Scott Sayson gave her on Tarbet/Johnson, a subject in which she can muster little interest, and that's why she chooses it.

After a few minutes leafing through the file, she comes to the conclusion that Scott Sayson is a man just a hair away from obsession when it comes to George Tarbet and his sidekick, Sandro "Sandy" Spinski. The surveillance reports chronicle day after night after day of such exciting action as "2:33 P.M.: Spinski left house, drove the Porsche to Thriftway in Eastgate Mall, arriving at 2:45. 3:10 P.M.: Exited market with two sacks of groceries. 3:21 P.M.: Returned to house."

But then the monotony was occasionally broken by the arrival of the "business types" Sayson talked about. Did they come to Tarbet's house to deliver or to pick up something? Drugs? That's Sayson's assumption. But he recorded only twelve visits in sixteen months. Drug dealers can't maintain their customers with such sporadic deliveries. And why would the one man Sayson managed to identify come all the way from Vancouver, BC, to pick up drugs? Vancouver is a major port. It doesn't make sense that the man couldn't make connections in his hometown, if he was dealing drugs.

Maurice Danko. Owner of Treasures of the First People. An upscale antique shop, according to the next page of the report.

Neely flips through more pages, stopping when she comes to a sheaf of telephone company printouts. Tarbet and Spinski made virtually no outgoing calls. Of the incoming calls, she notes that two of them came from telephone booths in the Westport area. Sayson scribbled a note that the phone-booth calls—one on December 28 of last year, the other September 25 this year—are both dated a day before Tarbet flew to the Cayman Islands to visit his bank.

Those dates ring a bell for some reason. Damn, she hates these tinkling bells in her memory that she can't—

"Neely!"

Startled, she looks up to see Lieutenant Skinner in the briefing room door. He's almost panting, his double chins quivering. There's an odd reluctance in his tone as he tells her, "Charlie just got a fire call. He radioed Art Hager to call out his volunteers."

Neely closes the file and rises. "What's the location, Lieutenant? Does Art need backup?"

"Well, I . . . I don't think he needs backup. The, uh, address . . . Neely, it's *your* house!"

For a long time, she can only stare at him, trying to translate those words into meaning.

"*My* house?" That's part of her confusion: She never thought of it as *my* house. It was *our* house.

"Yeah. Norma Addisill called it in. Her and Harry own the Sea View Motel down on the beachfront."

"Was she sure? I mean, was she sure it was . . . my house?"

"Harry drove up to Kittiwake Drive to see which house it was."

My house is on fire. The house that is no longer *ours*.

Fly away home, ladybug. Your house is on fire, and your children will burn. Only she doesn't have any children.

She doesn't have anyone in that house now.

Chapter 30

THE RAIN HAS STOPPED, AND a nearly full moon shines through breaks in the clouds, lining them with iridescence. She looks out at the moon's reflection on the infinite, ancient skin of the sea.

But she can't hear its reassuring murmur.

Neely stands on the shoulder of Kittiwake Drive, across the road from the two fire trucks and Chief Art Hager's band of volunteers. She can't hear the sea because its murmur is overwhelmed by the roar of the fire. She turns to face it again, staring at it in detached fascination.

It is incredibly beautiful.

The flames whip up a whirlwind of sparkling ashes like stars escaping to the sky. The fire seems sentient, a beast of no substance, only searing power. Counterpointing its predatory roar, she hears the explosions of windows shattering, the hiss of high-pressure hoses arcing hundreds of gallons a minute into the radiant heart of the beast. It has consumed the A-frame's roof and the two wings. The black skeleton of angled beams and ridgepole resists still. And the stone chimney. It will be the only thing left standing when it's all over.

Everything she owned, everything she and Jan owned

together, is in that house, eaten alive by the ravening yellow beast. Yet at the moment, she can remember only one object lost to the beast.

Jan's samurai sword.

Three hundred years, from father to son, and it ends here. How will she tell Ando Koto it's been destroyed? Like his son.

Fire Chief Art Hager tramps toward her out of the bitter smoke, a big lean slab of a man, weighted with his equipment and boots and smoke-streaked macintosh. He shouts against the roar, "Not much we could do to stop this one. Arson. Had to be arson. Too damned hot, and when we first got here, I could still smell gasoline."

Arson.

Neely looks at him, jarred out of her numbness by the word.

"Art, are you sure?"

"As sure as I can be right now. I'll make sure after it cools down." He shakes his head and tramps back to the fire.

Arson. She should've suspected arson. Riker is still at large.

There's nothing to keep you here now . . .

The Whisperer is also at large.

She reaches for her radio to call for backup, but when she glances south toward the curve of Kittiwake Drive, she realizes her backup is already here. A patrol blocks the road, bar lights flashing hectically.

When did Buck arrive?

And it *is* Buck Dolin. He's leaning against the fender of the patrol, surrounded by perhaps a dozen onlookers. She hurries toward him, wondering why he's here. Maybe Charlie called him. Buck is talking to a middle-aged couple. Addisill. Yes. Harry Addisill, president of the Lions Club. Neely has been a guest speaker at a number of Lions Club affairs. He and his wife own the Sea View Motel a few blocks away.

"Chief . . ."

Buck turns, frowning at first; then his expression shifts into something she doesn't understand until he asks, "You okay, Neely?"

"I wasn't home when it started. Art says he thinks it's arson."

Warning shouts, a rumbling crash, and Neely looks around in time to see the skeleton of the house collapse in an incandescent geyser that sucks up the flames, the shimmering sparks, the smoke, even the air around it, until she can't find air enough to breathe.

". . . figure you'd want to hear what they have to say."

She turns away from the fire. "What?"

Buck says, "The Addisills got a look at the perps."

Harry Addisill nods, his pugnacious jaw thrust forward. He's a wiry white man, with a full head of hair untouched by gray, although she knows he's old enough to be a Vietnam War vet.

Putting his arm around his wife's shoulders, he asks, "Sheriff, you remember my wife, Norma?"

Norma offers a hand. She's as wiry as her husband, but barely five feet tall. "Yes, we've met. Oh, I can't tell you how sorry I am about your house and—well, everything. Terrible! It's just terrible!"

"Mrs. Addisill, if you saw something—"

"Just call me Norma. Harry, you better tell her."

"Right. Well, we'd been playing pinochle with some friends down on North Front Drive. They're only a block from us, so we walked. It was about eleven-thirty when we started for home, and not a bit of traffic, until this van came ripping along behind us. Lord, I thought the maniac was going to run us down. Well, when it passed us, I saw the license plate and memorized it."

Buck says to Neely, "I already called it in."

"Good. What kind of vehicle was it, Harry?"

"An old VW Vanagon. Oh, maybe '85 or '86. Light green."

Neely frowns at that. "Not . . . not a pickup?"

"No. It was a VW. Anyway, Norma and I kept on walking, and we'd just reached the motel parking lot when we saw that same Vanagon come out of Kittiwake Drive onto North Front, hell-bent for leather. But the damn fool didn't have his headlights on. Well, we've got a streetlight at the entrance to the parking lot, and when he came under the light, damned if it wasn't that skinhead at the wheel. Calls himself Riker. Now, I know he usually drives that black-and-red pickup, but I also know it was *him* in that VW."

Which might explain why no one had turned Riker up. The APB described the pickup. Neely asks, "Was he alone?"

"There was another guy in the passenger seat. Head was shaved, too. But I don't think I could identify him for sure. I was concentrating on Riker, and I only had a second or two."

"That's okay. Riker's enough. What happened then?"

"We watched him hot-rod down Front till he hit the turn at Fourth. Hell, he almost didn't make it. Well, we knew you'd had trouble with those punks before, so I thought we better call you, but by the time we got to the office, Norma saw a fire up here on Kittiwake."

Norma puts in, "I could see this awful orange glow. And smoke. The moon's so bright, I could actually see the smoke."

Harry nods. "Well, I didn't know which house it was, or if anybody might be inside, so Norma went in the office to call nine one one, and I hopped in our car and hightailed it up here. Good thing you weren't home. The whole house was aflame by the time I got here. I said to myself right then, That sure isn't any kind of *natural* fire."

Neely sees the light of the flames on their faces, on the faces of the onlookers gathered behind them. She turns, stares at the fire, and her mouth burns with the taste of bitter smoke.

Buck says, "We'll need statements from you, if you wouldn't mind coming down to the TCSO in the morning."

"Sure. We'll be down as soon as we get our units cleaned up. Only have three rentals tonight. By the way, Neely . . ."

She focuses on Norma Addisill. "Yes?"

"You'll need a place to stay for a while, so you might as well camp out in one of our units. The Commodore, don't you think, Harry?"

"Sure. Don't have much call for it this time of year. Got a Jacuzzi and a kitchenette."

Neely feels a perverse compulsion to refuse that offer, but she has to sleep somewhere. If she ever sleeps again.

She manages a smile. "Thanks. But it might be a while before I get there. I want to find Riker before he disappears again."

Buck says irritably, "Damn it, Neely, you won't turn him up tonight. He's had nearly an hour's head start, and if he dumped his pickup and stole that van, he knows we're looking for him. He won't go to any of his old haunts, and he damn sure won't go back to his trailer. So just go on with these folks and get some rest."

A wave of trembling anger encompasses her. Where does Buck get off being so damn patronizing? It isn't *his* call.

She doesn't put her anger into words, but only because she's distracted by the plump white-haired woman who comes up to her and gently touches her arm. Willow Thornbeck.

And distracted by the dog leashed at Willow's side. Vixen.

Ridiculous that on seeing the sheltie in Willow's care, Neely wants to hold the dog close and feel her soft fur against her face, to weep with relief that Vixen has found a home.

That she won't die.

Willow nods at the fire and says, "This is the sort of

thing that made me give up trying to believe in a god. It's just not *right*. Anyway, my house is down the street from the Addisills. If there's anything I can do, give me a call."

Neely nods, suddenly so tired, she feels faint, and Willow walks away into the shadows. Vixen looks back at Neely. It seems she's trying to ask a question.

Little dog, I don't have any answers.

Except . . . just live. Stay alive.

Chapter 31

NEELY DOESN'T GO DIRECTLY TO the Sea View Motel; she has to drive the patrol back to the TCSO and get the Toyota. She goes inside only to leave the patrol's keys in the Dispatch Center, but there Charlie Eckholm distracts her with "Y'know that Vanagon Buck called in? That's the rig Jimbo got the call on about nine. Swiped from a house on Camden Loop. Near the trailer park."

Neely smiles tightly. "Now we know where Yew-gene got his new wheels. Put a description of the VW in that APB for Riker. It should include Riker's sidekicks, too. One of them was with him tonight."

Charlie is writing on a notepad. "Names?"

"Burton Lisker, aka 'Lash.' Male Caucasian, about six one, one hundred and sixty pounds, hazel eyes, shaved head, black leather jacket with a silver swastika on the back. Jeremy Buhl, aka 'Bomber.' Also male Caucasian, about five six, one hundred and ninety pounds, brown eyes and shaved head, same jacket."

"*Buhl*?" Charlie asks. "That's funny. He's the D and D Sonny brought in. Booked him about eleven."

Neely stares at Charlie, anger knotting under her ribs. "Why the hell wasn't I notified? Is there anyone on this staff

• 173 •

who *doesn't* know that Buhl is one of Riker's buddies? Is there anyone who *doesn't* know there's been an APB out on Riker since Thursday morning?"

Charlie regards her blankly. "The APB was just for Riker."

"Shit!"

They're still playing games with her. She storms out of the Dispatch Center, down the hall to the lobby, left to the Corrections door, hits the entry bell, and waits impatiently until Deputy Jason Fleming lets her in and locks the door behind her.

"I want to talk to Jeremy Buhl," she snaps as she marches down the hall to the booking desk. "Bring him to Interrogation A."

From behind the desk, the other guard on duty, Senior Deputy Ev Malachowski, opines, "Wouldn't do no good if we *did* bring him to A."

She leans over the counter. "Why *not*, Deputy?"

"Passed out. You couldn't wake him up for Judgment Day."

Neely takes a slow breath. Finally, she says, "Okay. But do not—I repeat, do *not*—let Buhl loose until I've talked to him." She turns on her heel and heads for the door. "Jason, let me the hell out of here."

It's 1:30 A.M. WHEN NEELY reaches the Sea View Motel, but Harry Addisill is waiting for her in the office. He leads her down the covered walkway fronting the motel to number 12, the Commodore. It's a spacious unit paneled in knotty pine, with two double beds at the south end, a kitchenette on the east, a bathroom, complete with advertised Jacuzzi, on the north, and on the west, a deck overlooking the ocean.

She says, "I really appreciate this, Mr. Addisill."

"No problem for us, this time of year. It's yours till you find a place to—" He's stopped by a knock on the door. He opens it, then offers a welcoming "Well, Heather, nice to see you."

"Hi, Mr. Addisill. I just brought this stuff for the sheriff."

He holds the door open for her, then says to Neely, "If you need anything, just ring the office."

As he leaves, Heather, in jeans and a sweatshirt, as informally comfortable as Neely has ever seen her, crosses to the nearest bed and deposits a lavender leather suitcase on it.

"Oh, Neely, it's not *fair*. I mean, your house burning down when . . . well, when you've already lost so much. Reverend Dill says the Lord never burdens you with more than you can handle, but sometimes I wonder." She snaps open the suitcase. "I'll call the uniform place first thing in the morning, and they can UPS some uniforms for you overnight. Oh, you better tell me your size. Looks like about a ten tall?"

Neely sinks into an armchair near the bed. "Uniforms? But I have—" She almost said she has three clean uniforms at home.

Until she remembers that she has nothing but the clothes on her back. Well, there's the spare uniform she keeps in her locker at the TCSO. Finally, she nods. "Yes, Heather. Ten tall."

Heather begins taking things out of the suitcase. "Brought you some clothes and stuff. I figured you were about Sally's size. My sister. Let's see, Levi's, sweatshirts, T-shirts. Some pajamas and a robe and slippers. The slippers may be too big. You know, that's the only thing about Sally that isn't perfect. She's got big feet. And here's a brush and comb, blow-dryer, toothbrush. I didn't put in any makeup. You don't wear makeup, do you? Anyway, my colors won't work for you."

Neely almost laughs at that. No way, baby. Not unless I want to make myself up in whiteface.

It doesn't seem to occur to Heather that for an African-American, the word *color* in any human context is emotionally charged. Heather doesn't have a clue. She thinks the difference between herself and Neely is a matter of complexion, and *color* only describes the shades of foundation and blush that will complement their skin tones; the lipstick, eye shadow, and mascara that will flatter their eyes and hair.

But maybe that's the way it should be, and Neely wonders if she's given up hope that it ever will be that way, that Heather will be just a blue-eyed—usually—fair-skinned strawberry blonde; and Neely a brown-eyed, dark-skinned . . .

Nigger?

There's a charged word, acid charged by history, and why did it come to her now? Heather has never used it, and Neely doubts she's even thought it.

Abruptly, Neely stiffens. "Oh my God . . ."

"Neely? What's wrong?"

Nigger.

That's what kept pricking at her memory when she thought about the graffiti on the medusa pool, that hideous red lattice of hate.

But it isn't that simple. Hate? Possibly, but mainly . . .

Calculation.

One thing she's sure of, Eugene Buxman, aka Dirk Riker, didn't learn to spell overnight.

Heather is hovering near her. "Neely, please—what's *wrong*?"

"What? Sorry. I just realized there's no way Riker murdered Jan."

"But . . . but what about—"

"The graffiti? That's why everyone assumed Riker was the perp—that damned graffiti. But Riker can't spell worth a damn. He always spells *nigger* with an *a* and *mongrel* with an *i*. Everything on the medusa pool was *correctly* spelled. But I think—" She stops, closing her eyes. "Yes. The swastikas were backward, and Yew-gene *does* know how to make a proper Third Reich swastika."

Heather whispers, "But if Riker didn't . . . well, who *did*?"

"I don't know. I *do* know Riker torched our house, but this eliminates him as a suspect for . . ." She almost said *the Koto murder*. But she's suddenly lost her cold objectivity.

She can't speak the words.

And what she needs now more than anything is to be alone. She rises, managing a smile. "Heather, I'm so grateful to you and Sally for this CARE package, but I'm . . . a little tired now."

Heather looks at her, eyes shining with tears. "You must be totally worn-out. You know, I can stay with you if—"

"I'll be fine."

Heather sighs, then nods as she heads for the door. "See you in the morning, Sheriff."

When the door closes behind Heather, Neely stands motionless in the empty room, and the only sound she can hear is the rush of the surf. She goes to the windows to close the curtains.

One thing she does not need tonight is to lie in bed and look out at the moon shining on the ocean.

On Jan's magical world, his goddess of mysteries.

Chapter 32

AT 8:30 THE NEXT MORNING, Neely Jones is in Interrogation A, facing Jeremy "Bomber" Buhl, while Deputy Mike Swenson sits at the end of the table, looking less like the blond hunk next door than the spoiled punk next door. His nose is out of joint. Before Buhl's arrival, Neely made it clear that Swenson would never again pull a stunt like leaving her alone to interrogate a prisoner—not if he valued his job.

If she thought about it, Neely wouldn't say she's feeling good, but she's feeling better than she expected to, as long as she disciplines her mind not to focus on certain subjects. This morning, after she woke at six in a cold, trembling sweat with a dream she didn't try to remember, she put on a pair of Sally Greenleaf's jeans, her purple sweatshirt, and her size-ten tennis shoes—made functional with wads of tissue in the toes—and took a run on the beach. Not a jog. An all-out run, until she could think of nothing but her body.

The run awakened her appetite enough so that she decided to stop at Henny's on the way to the courthouse. She might have gone elsewhere if she had known that her waitress would be an old hand named Sheree, who never censored her contempt for blacks or "Japs." She was always on the edge of surly, her blue-lidded, mascaraed eyes rock-hard. Yet today, when she dropped Neely's plate of bacon and eggs in front of her, she muttered, "Sorry to hear about your house."

Nothing about Jan's death. Only sympathy for the loss of a house. Neely knew she'd never understand the tangled rationalizations of racism.

When Neely reached the TCSO, she called her insurance agent, Joan Newberry, and wasn't surprised that Joan had heard about the fire and already talked to Fire Chief Art Hager and set the slow but fine-grinding wheels of the insurance bureaucracy in motion.

Now Neely faces Bomber Buhl, who reminds her of a lumpy pumpkin in his jail-issue orange sweatpants and T-shirt with the black TCSO across the chest. He's so hungover, he can barely move.

Buhl isn't a handsome specimen under the best of circumstances. Short and overweight, with that effeminate, subcutaneous layer of fat typical of whites whose ancestors lived in cold climates, his brown eyes are bloodshot, the skin around one puffed and purple, his soft pink lower lip cut—the results of the tavern brawl that landed him in jail last night.

Neely gives the tape recorder the necessary information, then smiles at Buhl. "Jeremy, have you ever thought of joining AA?"

He focuses on her with apparent difficulty. "Go fuck yerself."

"You've been advised of your rights. Do you remember that?"

"I remember. So why the hell don't you let me outta here? The other guy pressin' charges?"

"No, Jeremy, the other guy was smart enough to split from the tavern before you did. We're not holding you on the D and D."

He thinks about that. "So what the fuck *are* you holdin' me on?"

"Suspicion of conspiracy to commit arson."

Buhl jerks upright, then groans, pressing both hands to his stubbly head. "Oh shit. Listen, I told Dirk—" Then abruptly, he shuts up.

Neely waits. But he remains silent, holding on to his head. Finally, she says, "Decorating our house with obscene graffiti, even the cross burning—you figured that was just fun and games. But arson . . . well, that's serious shit. Five to ten years."

"Oh, Jesus Mary . . . Look, I don't know nothin' about whatever Dirk's doin'. I ain't even *seen* him since . . . hell, what day is it?"

"Friday."

"Zat all?" Buhl's soft hands fall limp on the table. "Well, I ain't seen Dirk since yesterday about noon. Him and me don't run in the same circles no more."

Mike Swenson apparently decides to give up his pout and take a speaking role. "Buhl, you and ol' Dirk've been joined at the hip for years. You want us to believe you had a parting of the ways?"

"I don't give a fuck *what* you believe. I didn't have nothin' to do with him or anything he did. Nothin'!"

"Sure," Swenson says doubtfully. "So, what was it he did?"

"I dunno."

"Then why'd you say he did something?"

"I never said that!"

"You want me to play the tape back?"

Again, Buhl lapses into stubborn silence.

Neely says, "Come on, Jeremy. We know Dirk did the arson. He was seen leaving the scene with another perp. Was it you?"

Buhl's good eye widens. "Me? Goddamn it, I was at the Marina Tavern all afternoon and last night till you bastards picked me up. I ain't done nothin'! Talk to Lash Lisker.

He's the one that stuck with—" Again, he stops himself.

Neely asks, "Lash stuck with Dirk? For the arson?"

"I got nothin' to say."

"Jeremy, do you think your buddies wouldn't flip on *you* if they were up against a felony conspiracy charge?"

"I told you—I got nothin' to say!"

As it turns out, he doesn't, although Neely and Swenson keep at him for a while. Finally, she tells Swenson to take Buhl back to his cell.

When Neely returns to her office, her phone is ringing. The private line. She feels a fluttering chill as she reaches for the receiver.

But it's not the Whisperer.

Lieutenant John Heathman.

He tells her, "I'm at the center with a couple of guys from my team. We're just picking up on a few things we didn't get to yesterday. By the way, didn't you say you're keeping the crime scene closed for a while?"

"Yes. Someone giving you an argument on that?"

"So to speak. Dr. Nicholass."

"What did he say?"

"That you told him it was okay for him to go to his office to work."

"I didn't tell him any such damn thing."

Heathman laughs. "Yeah, I thought so. Well, he didn't get in, and I told the deputy on duty here the scene is still closed. *No* exceptions. Anyway, Nicholass went away mad." A pause, then, "I heard what happened to your house. You think it's your local skinheads?"

"I know it is. Art Hager's checking out the site today. He's our fire chief, and he's had arson-detection training. And speaking of skinheads—whatever crimes he *is* guilty of, I'm sure Riker didn't murder Jan." She explains why she came to that conclusion, and Heathman believes her—a profound relief, since she knows she won't be believed in other quarters. Riker is too convenient a scapegoat.

She says bitterly, "Weird, isn't it, Lieutenant, that I find myself defending a vicious little honky like Yew-gene Bux-man?"

"Well, maybe your reward will be seeing him do time for arson."

"My reward will be figuring out who *did* kill Jan."

When Neely hangs up, Heather comes into the office with an armload of file folders. "Mr. Culpepper is trying to get hold of you, Sheriff. Says to call him as soon as possible."

Neely winces. "What about?"

"He didn't say." She carries the folders to the file cabinets and stacks them on top. "Oh, I wonder when Giff is *ever* going to come pick up his stuff. Maybe he has the key to this file cabinet."

Neely rises, reaching for the small tool kit she keeps on her gun belt. "Here . . . I'll open that thing for you."

The one lock controls all four drawers, and it's a primitive affair. She could probably open it with a bobby pin—if she possessed one. It takes about five minutes with her tools.

"Okay, Heather. Now you can sort to your heart's—"

The ring of the phone stops her. The private line again. And again that ring, that damned pink light, triggers a shiver of fear. She doesn't speak when she picks up the receiver.

"Neely Jones . . ."

The Whisperer.

She hits the record button as she sinks into the chair, reaching for a pen to write down the phone number.

"I know you're there, Neely. Perhaps you're beginning to learn."

She asks guardedly, "Learn what?"

"That an uncooperative attitude can be very expensive."

"Especially with people like you around to up the ante?"

"Precisely."

"Maybe you're the one who has a few lessons to learn."

"Oh, no. *I'm* the teacher. I teach cooperation. You seem to be a slow learner, but you can still remedy that. The original carrot is still yours to claim."

Neely swallows. Her mouth feels dry as dust. "And if I don't want to claim it?"

"That could be a dangerous decision. You can't keep looking over your shoulder all the time. Now, here's a tip: You'll find Giff Wills at his house. He forgot how to cooperate. You'd better learn."

"Giff? What're you—" But the line has gone dead.

She replaces the receiver, her breathing shallow and fast. Heather is standing beside the desk, staring at her. Neely says, "Heather, go get Buck. Don't make a fuss about it. Just ask him to come in here."

Heather hurries away, and Neely rewinds the tape a few inches.

Why did she immediately think of Buck? Yes, she needs backup, but can she trust him any more than the other deputies—at least one of whom was the Whisperer's courier for a payoff to Giff?

"What's going on, Neely?"

She waves Buck in. "Close the door."

Squinting dubiously, he shuts the door, then strolls to the desk. She plays the recording for him, but only the few sentences beginning with "Now, here's a tip . . ."

When she turns it off, Buck mutters, "Jesus X. Christ, who the hell was *that*?"

"I don't know. What's Giff's phone number?" She punches the numbers as Buck reels them off.

There's no answer.

She lets the phone ring ten times; then she heads for the door.

"Come on, Chief. Let's roll."

Chapter 33

GIFF WILLS'S HOUSE IS A mile east of Westport up River Road, on an isolated lot that stretches south a hundred yards from the road to the Chinook River. It's a manufactured home with the panache of a mint green boxcar; double garage at the west end, and nothing breaking the straight facade except a stoop at the front door. Giff's brown pickup is parked in front of the garage.

Neely parks on the shoulder of the graveled road, thirty feet short of Giff's concrete driveway, and she and Buck get out to survey the house. Giff apparently has an aversion to trees: He must've bulldozed every tree on the lot, which gives Neely a clear view of the boat dock behind the house, where a sparkling fiberglass speedboat is moored.

An expensive plaything, but then with an extra thousand magically appearing under his desk drawer now and then, Giff can afford it.

She leads the way to the driveway, then pauses. At some time, a vehicle turned into the driveway but missed the concrete just enough to leave a curving impression in the mud. "Someone coming from town," she says, "or heading back that way." She looks at Giff's pickup. "Not Giff. He's got mud tires." Then she kneels for a closer look.

"This track was made after it stopped raining last night. Look how sharp it is."

Buck nods. "Wonder what time it was when the rain stopped."

"I know it cleared by midnight." Just in time for a house burning.

They walk up the driveway to Giff's pickup, then along the narrow sidewalk to the front door. Neely punches the doorbell, but even after three rings, there's no answer or any sound inside the house.

Buck tries the door, frowning when the knob doesn't turn. "Giff never locks his doors. What the hell's going on here?" He bangs at the door with his formidable fist, yelling Giff's name. Finally, he mutters, "Shit," and strides back to the pickup, with Neely only a pace behind. He reaches through the open driver's side window, flips down the visor, and presses the bar on the Genie. The garage door rattles up.

It's obvious now why Giff's pickup isn't in the garage. There's no room. It's been converted into a carpentry shop, with a workbench on the far wall and, above it, on a Peg-Board panel, what seems like every carpenter's tool, manual and motorized, ever made, all shining clean. Or new. One-by-six boards are stacked near the table saw in the center of the garage. Pinkish sawdust with the pungent smell of cedar films the floor.

"Giff's building himself a deck out back," Buck explains.

There's something oddly plaintive about that observation. Neely only nods as she goes to the southeast corner of the garage, where there are two doors. The one on the south leads to the backyard; the one on the east opens into the house. It's unlocked.

The door opens into a kitchen separated from the living room by a counter and hanging cabinets. The kitchen is a shambles, littered with dirty glasses, empty beer cans, liquor bottles, bags and bowls of peanuts and chips and crackers and molding dip, ashtrays overflowing with cigarette and cigar butts. The smell is stultifying.

Buck says, "This mess is left over from Giff's election-night party."

Neely doesn't comment on the mess because she is just realizing that it's more than the detritus of a party. Drawers are open, utensils, silverware, and linens scattered about. Cabinet doors are open, jars and containers littering the floor. At first, she thinks vandalism, but the destruction seems inadvertent. Things have been moved, even dropped and broken, but not thrown or capriciously destroyed.

"Chief, someone's been looking for something here."

Buck grunts agreement as Neely goes into the living room, where again the mess is a mix of leftover party and a reckless search: papers and bric-a-brac tossed randomly, furniture overturned, the cushions on the couch and arm-chairs unzipped, their foam-rubber stuffing torn out. In the center of the room, a brown leather BarcaLounger faces the television set to the right of the front door. There's a nearly empty fifth of Jim Beam on the side table.

Buck stalks through the debris to stand in front of the chair, and his usually stony face is suddenly laid naked to shock and anger. He murmurs, "Jesus X. Christ . . ."

Neely crosses the room to stand next to him. Unlike Buck, she isn't shocked by what she sees in the chair: She expected it.

Sheriff Gifford Wills is still in his wrinkled, stained uniform, jaws peppered with stubble, mouth hanging open. He might've fallen asleep—or passed out—with the television remote in one hand.

But the television is off, and there's a red star-shaped hole, haloed with gray, in the center of his forehead.

He forgot how to cooperate.

And he won't be given a second chance.

Jan's murder seemed a death of opportunity or necessity, but this is a clean execution. In fact, there's nothing to link the two murders.

Except the Whisperer.

Neely reaches into her back pocket for a pair of latex gloves and pulls them on as she crosses to the telephone on the counter between the living room and kitchen. The instrument is a twin of the one on her desk at the TCSO, and she wonders if the taxpayers of Taft County didn't provide both of them. She picks up the receiver.

Buck asks sharply, "You calling for backup?"

"I will," she replies, "but first I'll try to catch Heathman at the center before he—"

"Heathman!" Buck strides toward her. "Damn it, Giff Wills had his faults, but he was one of ours. We take care of our own!"

"That's what a defense lawyer likes to hear, Buck. If you want any evidence collected here to stand up in court, you won't collect it. You'll be accused of bias. That's why I'm calling a *state* criminalist."

"Jesus! You are the coldest bitch I've ever run into!"

Neely flinches involuntarily, and she knows he isn't just talking about her response to Giff's death. She saw a hint of this look in Buck's eyes yesterday; the look that asks why isn't she hurting, why isn't she on her knees.

The anger coiled within her trembles to be unleashed, but she doesn't let it go. She says, "I have a job to do. So do you."

She sees Buck's mask of imperturbability restored. Strange, but she never knew before that it was a mask. Finally, he nods. "Yeah. But there's no reason I can't look around in case the perp is hiding in a closet somewhere. I mean, that's standard procedure."

"Okay, but we look for any hidden perps together. Chief, this phone has a redial button, and this is one piece of evidence we *can* collect. I can't call out without destroying it, and I have to phone Dispatch." She doesn't add that she won't make the error of advertising *this* murder by radio.

She holds the receiver so Buck can listen while she

punches redial. A distant burr, repeated four times, then a recorded message kicks in: "You have reached the residence of Dr. S. Benjamin Nicholass. I can't come to the phone now, but if you'll wait for the tone—"

Neely doesn't wait. She hangs up and wonders aloud, "Why would Giff be calling Nicholass? And when did he make the call?"

"Well, the phone company can tell us when. Who's on the memory index?"

The names are written under a plastic sheath: TCSO Dispatch; SueAnne Fritch, Gill's housekeeper and rumored lover; Curtis McMinn's and Owen Culpepper's home phones; and the county commissioners' office.

Neely checks the message and recording tapes, but they're blank. Finally, she punches the center's number and waits impatiently while the phone rings. It's answered with a crisp "Lieutenant Heathman."

"This is Neely Jones. I've . . . got another murder for you."

A silence stretches tight until he asks, "Who's the victim?"

"Sheriff Gifford Wills."

"Wills!" Another silence, then: "I'll make some calls to Portland and get the rest of the team together. Where's the body?"

She gives him directions, hangs up, and tells Buck, "He'll be here as soon as possible. Why don't you call Dispatch? Tell Lonnie to phone the OSP. We'll need a roadblock."

Buck nods once as he pulls on a pair of latex gloves. While he makes the call, Neely returns to the body.

Several points seem obvious. One, Giff was unconscious—he'd probably OD'd on Jim Beam—when he was shot. The TV remote in his right hand tells her he didn't move while someone approached him from the front and shot him, point-blank, probably with a large-caliber weapon, exactly in the center of the forehead. The killer had plenty of time to place that shot. And the cold nerve for it.

The MO has the earmarks of a professional hit.

And she knows of only one professional killer in the area: Sandro "Sandy" Spinski. That's according to an obsessed DEA agent.

But what connection would Giff have with an ex–San Diego hit man? Maybe the connection was with Spinski's boss, George Tarbet. Sayson told Giff about his surveillance when he first set it up. Giff might have investigated on his own and come up with information to blackmail Tarbet with, which might explain the payoff.

But the Tarbet-Spinksi connection is tenuous, and Neely wastes little time considering it. What she finds intriguing is the contrast between the body's resting place and the remainder of the room, where the evidence of a frenzied search is so obvious. Since every piece of upholstered furniture in the room has been searched down to the stuffing, why is the BarcaLounger untouched?

One answer is that the searcher found what he was looking for elsewhere, making it unnecessary to search the BarcaLounger.

Another is that the searcher was reluctant to move the body, and that suggests another question: Would the person who could coolly put a bullet in the exact center of an unconscious man's forehead be so squeamish that he couldn't bear to touch the body?

Or were the killer and the searcher two different people?

She finds herself referring to both as *he* only because of the limitations of the language. Either one might just as well be *she*.

Buck hangs up the phone. "Whit's bringing three deputies, and he can get three reserves if we need them. Don't know about the OSP. There's been a four-car pileup on Highway One-oh-one at Seal Point. You know, somebody's going to have to tell Culpepper about this."

And, obviously, it isn't going to be Buck.

Neely goes to the phone and punches the DA's office number. She gets Thelma Clapton, Culpepper's secretary, the middle-aged white woman who reads *Push* on her lunch break. She says the DA is in court. Neely hesitates, then decides Thelma is probably a woman to be trusted.

"Thelma, this is an emergency. Giff Wills was murdered. I need to let the DA know—but no one else."

"Oh, of course not. I—oh, dear, I guess I better take a message to Mr. Culpepper in the courtroom."

"Thanks. I'm at Giff's house." She hangs up and turns to Buck. "Okay, Chief, while we're looking for this concealed perp, I want to see how far the search went. It might help us figure out whether he found what he was looking for."

"Neely, what do you know about whoever it was who tipped you about Giff?"

Briefly, she considers telling him about the Whisperer, but some nagging doubt deters her. "Nothing." And she sets off down the hall.

There are three bedrooms and two baths, and every room shows signs of a search, and in every room, the curtains are drawn. Obviously, the searcher didn't want to call passing motorists' attention to the house with lights in the windows, which probably means the search took place late at night.

There's no indication that the search stopped anywhere. Neely and Buck go out to the garage, careful to walk in the tracks they left when they arrived. The garage has also been searched, although the searcher was more careful here, or else there simply aren't as many spaces that can't be examined without moving things. The sawdust on the stacks of wood is untouched, but the searcher ineptly swept the floor to eradicate footprints. And he missed one near the kitchen door. No, two. One is a partial.

"Chief, did you ever see Giff wearing athletic shoes?"

He squints at the footprints. "No, but we better check his closets."

"Heathman's team can check them." She frowns at the sound of a siren in the distance. "What smart-ass turned his siren on? Might as well send Tom Jordan and his cohorts an engraved invitation."

Buck heads out of the garage, and although his pace seems casual, he stays within his own tracks. "Probably Darrell. I'll talk to him."

By the time Buck and Neely reach the road, three TCSO patrols are approaching, throwing up a cloud of dust. Neely leaves it to Buck to wave them to the shoulder behind the patrol she and Buck arrived in, and to give Darrell Logan the word about his siren. She walks down to the end of the line, where a green sedan is coming to a stop.

Lt. John Heathman gets out of the car, nose wrinkling at the dust. Then his gray-brown eyes go hard as he studies the house. "Sometimes I think you can tell a house where there's been a murder. Something . . . empty about it." He shrugs. "Let's get on with it."

Chapter 34

DISTRICT ATTORNEY CULPEPPER MAKES HIS obligatory appearance at Giff's house at 10:30 A.M. By then, Heathman has made a preliminary examination, and he's waiting for the rest of his team and Feingold to arrive. No one is pleased at the prospect of yet another person tramping through the crime scene. Neely serves as the DA's guide, taking him through the garage and reminding him to watch his feet.

"Neely, I was viewing crime scenes before you were born."

But this one has some surprises for him. In the kitchen, he looks around dazedly. "What *happened* here? Some kids have a wild party?"

"No, sir, I'm sure no kids were involved." Neely leads him into the living room. "Giff's there. In the lounger."

Culpepper crosses to the chair and for a long time stares at Giff Wills's mortal remains. Finally, he shakes his head. "My God, what's happening in our town, Neely? Random violence. Violence for the thrill of it. That's what the world's coming to."

"There's nothing random about this violence, Mr. Culpepper. It's more like a professional hit. Look how carefully the bullet was placed."

He doesn't seem inclined to look too closely. "But this house—it's been trashed! Viciously trashed! Is anything missing?"

"Nothing obvious. TV, VCR, microwave, radio, liquor, prescription drugs—none of that has been touched."

The DA nods as if that proves his point. "This is the work of drugged kids gone berserk. Some sort of gang or even a cult."

"Or this is simply the result of a thorough search."

"Search!" He laughs contemptuously. "What would Giff be hiding that anybody'd kill him for? Giff Wills served Taft County well and courageously for many years—"

"Save it for the eulogy, Mr. Culpepper," Neely cuts in impatiently. "First, I know Giff was receiving money in thousand-dollar increments. For what, I don't know yet. Second, I was told I'd find Giff here by an anonymous caller, and I quote: 'Giff Wills forgot how to cooperate.' "

Culpepper's face goes from a sickly white to bright pink. "Do you realize what you're *saying*? You're accusing Giff Wills of taking bribes! By God, you'd better have something to back that up, girl!"

"Do you think I'd make that kind of accusation if I couldn't back it up? And don't *ever* call me 'girl.' It's *Sheriff* Jones."

So much for diplomacy, Neely thinks as the DA snaps, "We'll *see* about that!" He takes one last look at the body, and the pink fades to a sickly white again. "Oh hell, let me *out* of here!"

Culpepper stumbles out of the house—through the front door, despite Neely's objection that the door hasn't been fingerprinted yet—and doesn't stop until he reaches the road. Neely follows him, arriving in time to hear Culpepper throw a few words at Heathman and Buck as he gets into his car, then makes a tight U-turn, spinning gravel as he accelerates toward Westport.

Buck tips his Stetson back. "He better slow down before he gets to the barricade." Then Buck sighs. "Owen and Giff go way back, and ol' Owen always had a hard time with bodies."

"Hope he never runs into a popper," Heathman says blandly. He turns to ask Neely something, but he's distracted by a spewing roar.

An empty log truck is barreling up the road toward them. The men at the barricade were instructed to let no one through who didn't live on River Road, so Neely assumes the driver is a neighbor of Giff's.

The huge huffing rig stops, and the driver climbs down from the cab, leaving the motor growling at idle. Buck waves him over. "How're you doing, Nate?" Then in an aside to Neely: "Nathan Jablonski. Lives up River Road about a mile."

Jablonski is a hirsute young man with a beard and long hair that any male hippie of the sixties would have envied, although Neely is willing to bet he's a Rush Limbaugh fan. He has an easy smile for Buck, but she and Heathman get long, cool looks, and when he speaks, it's to Buck. "Didn't know you had *two* niggers at the Sheriff's Office now."

He says it as casually as he might comment on the weather.

Neely puts on her sweetest smile and says, "And I didn't know we had more than one honky living up River Road." She never lets up with her smile, and Jablonski looks thoroughly confused, as if he's not sure he heard her right.

Buck gives Neely an annoyed glance, then asks the trucker, "How's the wife and kids, Nate?"

"Hmm? Oh, they're fine. Say, the guys down at the barricade said there'd been some trouble at Giff's house. He get robbed or somethin'?"

"Yeah, there was some trouble. You didn't happen to be driving through here anytime last night, did you? Say, after ten?"

Jablonski scratches at his cheek through his beard. "Nope. This morning, though, I drove out about five-thirty. Got a contract to haul logs over to Willamina from a cut south of here. Only got in two runs today before they shut down the cut. Ever' time the humidity drops a point, them nervous Nellies at the Forest Service close us down."

Buck shakes his head sympathetically. "They'll put every logger out of work before they're through."

Sure, Neely thinks, when the loggers finish cutting down all the trees, except the weedy toothpicks they plant. But she doesn't voice that thought. She's content now to let Buck handle Nathan Jablonski.

Buck asks, "Did you see anybody around Giff's house this morning? A car or truck, maybe, that didn't belong here?"

"Not right at Giff's place. But, y'know, I *did* see a strange car. Thought it was peculiar, that early in the mornin'."

"What kind of car?"

"One of them little sports cars. White, it looked like. Headed into town. I first saw it" —he waves in the general direction of Westport— "oh, maybe a quarter mile down the road. I come up behind it and just had it in my headlights a second or so when that thing took off like it had a firecracker up its tailpipe."

Buck looks no more than politely interested, but his eyes are down to black slits. "Didn't happen to get a look at the license plate?"

"No. That car was *movin'*. Couldn't even tell what make it was."

"That's okay, Nate. Thanks."

"Sure. Tell Giff I'm sure sorry he got robbed. Why'd anybody pick on a sheriff to rob? Sounds kinda dumb to me." Jablonski laughs and climbs back into his rig, sparing Neely and Heathman not so much as a glance. The truck moves out with a ground-shaking roar.

When the noise and diesel fumes fade, Buck says to Heathman, "Nate just doesn't always know what's coming out of his mouth, Lieutenant." Heathman only raises an eyebrow, and Buck adds, "At least he gave us something to chew on. This is a dead-end road, and there aren't many folks living along it. Maybe ten or twelve houses in eight miles. Makes you wonder what a strange car was doing here at five-thirty in the morning."

Neely puts in, "There aren't many white sports cars in Westport, but we can't be sure the perp is local."

"I can think of one white sports car in Westport," Buck says. "A Porsche. Belongs to a guy named Bob Johnson."

Neely looks at Buck, trying to read his stony squint. Does he know that Robert Johnson is an alias for Sandy Spinski? It's possible. Giff might have told his second in command about Sayson's surveillance.

Neely doesn't comment on that possibility, nor does she mention that she knows of another white sports car in Westport: Dr. S. Benjamin Nicholass's Mercedes SLK.

Chapter 35

WHEN DR. FEINGOLD AND THE rest of Heathman's crime-scene team arrive at Giff's house at noon, Neely leaves Buck in charge. There's nothing she can do at Giff's, and she has another murder to think about.

She returns to the TCSO, goes to her office, and has just settled in the chair that's beginning to seem comfortable, when Heather appears.

She says, "Oh, Sheriff, I'm sorry about the mess." Neely only looks at her blankly, and Heather adds, "Behind you. I'm trying to clear out the old case files in that filing cabinet—the one you picked the lock on—but I keep getting interrupted."

Neely swivels her chair around, and only now does she notice the stacks of file folders on the floor and more filling a carton. "No problem, Heather."

"The *phone* keeps ringing. Reporters mostly. How ever do they find *out* about these things? Sheriff, is it true?" Tears gather in her turquoise eyes, threatening to spill over. "I mean . . . about Giff?"

"Yes, it's true. He was murdered last night."

"Oh." Heather sinks into the chair in front of the desk, managing to stop it when it tries to roll out from under her.

"Oh, dear, I just don't understand. I mean, it's not like we're in a big city. Two murders in two days? It's just . . . weird."

Neely nods wearily. "Yes, it is."

Heather dabs at her eyes with a tissue, careful not to smear her mascara. "Oh, I almost forgot. Mr. Culpepper called. Three times. He wants to see you in his office the minute you come in."

"Does he?" Yes, Owen prefers to conduct business—or dress down subordinates—in the comfort of his office.

Heather goes on: "Some reports on the, uh, Koto case came in by fax from the state crime lab. They're in that top file on your desk."

Neely reaches for the file. "I was hoping these had arrived."

"Is it all right if I work on the old files—oh, darn, there's the *phone* again." And she marches into her office to answer it.

Neely opens the file on a sheath of photographs. These, she puts aside. The first report is the autopsy, and that's hard enough to face, but at least the rational scientific language puts some distance between her and the reality in the pictures.

Time of death, between 9:00 P.M. and midnight Wednesday. Cause of death, drowning, and the water in the victim's lungs was chemically identical to the water in the jellyfish tank. A 9-mm bullet was recovered from a nonfatal gunshot wound in the upper-left thoracic area. The bullet entered five centimeters below the left clavicle and eight centimeters from the sternum and lodged against the left scapula.

The rest of the autopsy reiterates what Greg Feingold told her yesterday: the bruises from a hard ligature around the left wrist, the contusions on the left side of the victim's jaw, and the loosened tooth, "indicating that the victim was struck by a blunt instrument, possibly a right-handed person's fist." That sounds like Greg. Morgue humor.

But one piece of information is new: "Flecks of dried paint, blue-green in color, were found in the victim's hair and clothing."

Neely shuffles through more pages until she comes to a report on Jan's office. The floor had been scrubbed, but Luminol revealed traces of blood. There were also microscopic flecks of paint—and here's what she's looking for: ". . . which match in composition and color the paint presently being applied to the walls in the museum area."

The missing painters' tarp.

She flips through more pages. "A plastic painters' tarp, ten by ten feet, was missing from the front of the museum area. According to Billy Huff, the painting contractor, it was in place when he and his employees left the Westport Oceanographic Center at 5:00 P.M. Wednesday. A search was subsequently made for the tarp, but it was not found."

Neely leans back, eyes unfocused. When Jan was moved from his office to the medusa pool, he was probably unconscious from the blow to the face and/or the bullet wound. Someone had to carry him. Maybe to avoid getting bloodstains on his or her clothing, that person used a handy sheet of plastic to wrap Jan in, a sheet of plastic decorated with drops of dried paint that sloughed off in minuscule fragments.

In that case, there should be flecks of paint upstairs around the top of the medusa pool, too. She scans page after page, but there's nothing on the maintenance area. Apparently, that report hasn't been completed.

Disappointed, she turns to a fingerprint report, looking for one name, and finally finds it. "Fingerprints on the case and keyboard of the victim's computer belong to the victim and to Dr. Andrea Olenick."

Gotcha, Andrea baby!

Now Neely can get a search warrant for Andrea's apartment.

Otherwise, all the fingerprints in the center ID'd so far belong to staff members. Except one: a print on the Pentium III Xeon processor found in the victim's pants pocket.

INTEL INSIDE . . .

Intel is the tallest tree in Oregon's "Silicon Forest" near Portland. Neely can see the loose circle of the company logo in her mind's eye. But she's seen it somewhere else, and not long ago. Where?

In a TV ad, probably.

But where in hell did Jan get that damned Pentium processor?

And who does that odd fingerprint belong to?

And on the subject of fingerprints . . .

She dials the number for the Oregon State Police Fingerprint Lab and finally reaches Lt. Mary Jo Bivins, who answers with a concerned "Neely, I heard what's been going on down there. Land sakes, girl, you okay?"

"I'm hanging in, Mary Jo. Thanks. I was wondering about that envelope I sent you. . . ." When? Only Wednesday? Two days ago?

"Well, I sure do hate to tell you this, but we couldn't pick up any prints on it—except yours."

Neely sighs. "That's not a surprise."

"You want me to send the envelope back to you?"

"Uh, no. Just keep it for a while."

"Okay. By the way, y'know, if you ever find a good suspect, it just might be possible to get a DNA match."

"DNA?"

"Saliva, honey. Somebody probably licked that envelope to seal it. I'm not sure there'd be enough traces left, but it might be worth a try."

"Yes, it might. *If* I could find a good suspect. Thanks, Mary Jo."

Neely hangs up, frowning at the telephone and thinking of its twin in Giff's house. Why was the last person Giff called Ben Nicholass? Did the two of them have frequent conversations? And what did they talk about? There's one way to learn about the frequency, if not the subjects, of their conversations.

She calls the manager of the phone company and asks him to fax her a message unit detail sheet on Giff's calls for the last month. While she's waiting, she continues reading the forensic reports, but nothing gives her the sensation of rising hackles she's hoping for.

Within ten minutes, Heather brings her the MUD sheet.

Neely has to get out her reverse directory to check most of the numbers on the list. The names she recognizes. SueAnne Fritch, Buck Dolin, County Commissioner Vernon Clack, Fire Chief Art Hager, and other names she knows belong to Giff's drinking and fishing buddies. On last Wednesday, at 6:00 A.M., Giff called Owen Culpepper. The DA must've loved being wakened at that hour after he'd been out celebrating his election victory.

Also on Wednesday morning, at 8:45 A.M., which was about half an hour after Giff so theatrically resigned, he made the first call to Nicholass. A short call. Then on the same day at 12:10 P.M., Giff received a call from a pay phone. Then another call from Giff to Nicholass Thursday afternoon at 1:03 P.M. The last call Giff made.

Calls from pay phones . . . There's something she meant to check, something that *did* raise her hackles, but she can't remember what—

Neely looks up from the report. Voices in Heather's office: Heather's raised in alarm, a male voice raised in anger.

The door bursts open, and the DA strides in. It's only then that Neely remembers she was supposed to report to his office. He looms over the desk and shouts, "Damn it, I am *not* accustomed to having to trail after people like some messenger boy!"

Neely rises and goes to the briefing room door to shut it, then, as she returns to her chair, says levelly, "I'm sorry, Mr. Culpepper, but I've been very busy today."

The apology seems to mollify him slightly. He sits down, and when the chair starts to roll, he has to do a fast shuffle to keep his seat. "Jesus, where'd you get this mantrap?"

"Original equipment. What did you want to talk to me about?"

She expects his answer to concern her accusations

against Giff Wills. Instead, he replies, "The Westport Ocean-ographic Center. I see no reason why it can't be opened to the staff at least, since there's considerable cleanup to be done. Not only that there are plant and animal specimens—some of them quite rare—that require constant tending or they'll die. I also see no reason why *Poseidon* can't embark as soon as possible. The window of opportunity for observing the gray whale birthing is very narrow."

"I know. I heard the same speech from Ben yesterday."

"Well, Dr. Nicholass came to see me this morning. Neely, he's one of our leading citizens, and the center is vital to the city's tourism economy. It simply doesn't make sense to put that in jeopardy or antagonize someone of Dr. Nicholass's stature in the scientific world."

Neely doesn't comment on Nicholass's stature. She says, "Mr. Culpepper, the rare specimens are being cared for by Dr. Spenser, the director of the museum, who's also a marine biologist. As for unsealing the crime scene, I can't do that without consulting Lieutenant Heathman, and he has his hands full right now. As for the center's economic value to Westport, this is November—not exactly the height of the tourist season. As for *Poseidon,* the window of oppor-tunity will be there next year. I do not feel comfortable let-ting anyone leave the country. Not until we know who murdered Dr. Koto."

Culpepper surges to his feet, and the chair goes scut-tling. "But we *do* know who murdered him! That skin-head!"

"No, we do *not* know—"

"*I* know! And I'm the one who's going to prosecute this case! All *you* have to do is *find* him! That is your first and *only* priority."

"Well, there *is* the matter of Giff Wills's murder . . . sir."

Culpepper glares at her, his anger magnified by the thick lenses of his glasses. "I had hoped," he says coldly, "that since you and I are the top law-enforcement officials in this county, we could develop a relationship of cooperation and mutual—"

"That's the *last* thing you hoped!" Neely rises, palms braced on the desk. "What you *hoped* was that I'd fold, one way or another. You didn't give a damn about cooperation and mutual anything. Now, I'm busy, Mr. Culpepper. I have two murder cases to investigate, and I intend to handle both of them by the book—carefully and thoroughly. If that's a problem, I'm sorry, but that's the way it's going to be."

He holds his glare on her for another few seconds, then, without a word, stalks out, slamming the door behind him.

Damn, Neely thinks, I'll never get this diplomacy thing down.

She sags into her chair, willing her pulse to a reasonable rate and trying to recapture her train of thought before the DA's arrival.

Phone calls. Something about phone calls. She looks at the files on her desk for a mnemonic nudge, and finds it in an unexpected place: the Tarbet file. Last night, she was trying to figure out why two dates in that file rang a bell. She opens the file and leafs through it.

And finds the page she was reading last night when Brad Skinner told her that her house was afire.

In the sixteen months of the surveillance, George Tarbet had two telephone calls from local phone booths. The first was on December 28 of last year. The second on September 25 of this year.

She begins digging through desk drawers, looking for her Sierra Club engagement calendar. Finally, she finds it and turns to the front, where there's a page for the last week of the previous year.

Yes. December 28. The notation is in her own writing: "Jan returned from Baja."

Which means that was the day *Poseidon* docked at the end of that voyage.

She flips through the pages to September 25. And

there's the same notation, same words, but with an exclamation point: "Jan returned from Baja!"

And those are the dates on which George Tarbet received calls from local phone booths and a day later departed for the Caymans.

Coincidence?

It doesn't seem likely, but coincidences never seem likely.

And the September 25 voyage was the one on which Andrea Olenick supposedly succumbed to the charms of tropic nights and Ben Nicholass.

Which is probably beside the point. Neely frowns, focusing her thoughts on George Tarbet. And Giff.

If Giff did learn something to blackmail Tarbet with, that would explain the payoff. But when Giff lost the election and went on an alcoholic bender, maybe he became more of a liability than a threat, and maybe Tarbet killed him—or had Spinski handle that detail. Yet Giff must've had evidence of some sort against Tarbet hidden away as insurance. That would explain the search at Giff's house: Tarbet wanted to recover whatever evidence Giff was holding.

Tarbet might even be the Whisperer.

Neely grimaces sourly. Somehow she can't imagine a man so bent with rheumatoid arthritis that he can't stand up without canes bopping around Westport from one telephone booth to another.

Maybe Spinski drove him.

In the Lexus that Sayson mentioned? A man who never left his house except for his trips to the Caymans? A man under constant surveillance by federal agents?

Or maybe Spinski does the calling. And whispering.

And maybe she's chasing her tail. As Gramma Faith put it, *A dog can chase his tail all day, and even if he catches it, all he's got is a mouthful of dog.*

Still, at the moment, she finds George Tarbet and his trusty live-in nurse and hit man downright fascinating.

Chapter 36

IT'S NEARLY TWO WHEN BUCK Dolin walks into the briefing room. He fills a mug with coffee, knowing he shouldn't drink it on an empty stomach. Not when it's so queasy. He can't get rid of the image of Giff in that lounger with a bullet hole in the middle of his forehead. Whatever his sins—and Giff had plenty—he didn't deserve that.

Giff took care of his own.

The year Val died, when Buck fell apart—drank and picked fights and cried too much, even started having flashbacks to Nam—it was Giff who kept him on the payroll and juggled the paperwork to give him medical leave until he got his act together again.

Buck looks around the empty room. Is *everybody* out on call or at Giff's? No. Curtis McMinn and Lonnie Weaver are coming around the L. They stop dead when they see him. He strolls toward them, eyes slitted. "Who's manning the Dispatch Center, Deputy Weaver?"

"Uh . . . just stepped out for a second, Chief." And he steps back in—fast—and out of Buck's sight.

McMinn's still grinning. "We was listening in on a real catfight." He cocks a thumb toward the sheriff's office.

Buck glances that way. The door is closed. "You got

nothing better to do than listen at keyholes, Curtis?"

"Didn't have to lean over no keyhole to hear that fracas." He strokes his woolly mustache, and Buck notes the bruises on his left cheek and the knuckles of his right hand. Buck wonders who he's been hitting and hopes it isn't a prisoner or, worse, Trina.

"The DA and the coon," McMinn adds. "Goin' at it tooth and—"

"Coon? Curtis, you got a dirty mouth. So just shut it!"

"Ah, come on, Chief."

The smirk is still there. Hell, McMinn was Giff's fair-haired boy, and here he is, joking around, while Giff's on his way to the morgue. Maybe Buck is looking for something to call McMinn down on, and he finds it: the pearl handle sticking out of his holster.

"What the hell is that in your holster, Sergeant?"

That wipes the grin off. "Uh, it's one of my own guns."

"Where's your duty weapon?"

"Well, it's a long story, Chief."

"Shorten it up for me."

"I, uh, well, it—it got . . . stolen."

Buck leans toward him. "It got *what*?"

"Well, see, Wednesday evening, I was sick as a dog, and a neighbor kid was over playin' with Jason. I, uh, hung my gun belt over a chair instead of in the closet. The next morning . . . well, my Glock was gone. I gotta talk to the kid's folks, but I just haven't had time to—"

"Jesus X. Christ! There's a kid out there with a loaded gun, and you haven't had time to do anything about it? Go home. Right now. And if you don't come back with that gun, don't come back at all."

"Okay, Chief, okay!" He backs toward the hall door. "I'll get it, I swear. . . ." When he reaches the door, he crashes into Darrell Logan.

"Shit, Curtis!" But McMinn is gone. Logan looks at Buck. "What's *his* problem?"

"Urgent call. So, where've *you* been?"

"Domestic disturbance. The Peabodys. Ol' Carl started early today. Booked him into our *de*luxe hotel overnight."

Buck is distracted when the door to the sheriff's office opens and Neely leans out to say, "Chief, I need to talk to you," then heads back to the desk, like it never crossed her mind he won't snap to. And he will. With two homicides hitting all at once, this is no time to get sensitive.

Neely's standing behind the desk, frowning a little. The strain is showing. Under her eyes, the dark skin is even darker. He shouldn't have said what he did to her this morning, calling her a cold bitch. People handle grief different ways. He just didn't expect her way.

"Chief, the preliminary reports on the Koto murder came in." Neely hands him a file folder. "Heather made copies for you and all the shift supers. Did Giff ever tell you why the DEA agents are in town?"

The change of subject surprises him. "Yeah. They're running surveillance on a guy named Tarbet. Suspected drug dealer."

"And his sidekick is a suspected hit man. People in that business generally do neat, clean work. Like one bullet to the head."

Buck's queasy stomach clenches up. A professional hit? On Giff? But she's right: It *was* neat work.

"Maybe we should bring Tarbet and his buddy in and talk to them."

She shakes her head. "On what grounds? But I want to meet Tarbet, and the only way to do that is to pay him a visit. I was thinking about the arson. If we didn't have two murder investigations going on, we'd do a door-to-door on the arson. You know, ask if anyone saw a green Vanagon last night around eleven-thirty? Standard procedure."

"You want me to give you backup?"

"No. A woman alone has an advantage sometimes. Men usually don't take them seriously." She picks up a clipboard and grabs her hat. "I just wanted you to know where I'm going."

He says, only half-joking, "If you're not back by three-thirty, I'll round up a posse and come after you."

She looks at him and seems surprised. Then she laughs. "Don't bring it to a vote, if you round up the posse here. I have a feeling the vote would be to leave me with Tarbet."

Chapter 37

FROM NORTH FRONT DRIVE, THE house seems unexceptional, even modest: an old ranch-style, apparently single-story; gray composition roof, gray vinyl siding; double garage on the south, living room on the north, the front door in an alcove in between.

But Neely has seen this unexceptional house from the beach. It sits on a hundred-foot beachfront lot—which makes the land worth maybe a quarter million—and the lot slopes steeply to the beach, providing room for a full story under this one.

She parks across the street. In the last half hour, she made an actual door-to-door canvass of the houses to the north, those visible from George Tarbet's living room. She moved the patrol car twice, and her clipboard is covered with the names of people who didn't see a thing at 11:30 last night. Now she crosses the street to the gray house, well aware of the shadow moving away from the window. She reaches the front door via a sloping wheel-chair ramp and rings the doorbell.

The door opens, and Sandy Spinski looks out at her with ice blue eyes. He's Hollywood-handsome; a weight lifter, probably, with blond hair curling just short of his wide shoulders. But there's a spooky stillness about him, an emptiness. It's almost as if he runs on batteries.

She lifts the top sheet on the clipboard and makes a show of checking a nonexistent list. "Mr. William Johnson?"

"No. Bob Johnson."

"Oh. Well, is William Johnson here?"

"Who's asking?"

"Neely Jones, Taft County Sheriff's Office. I'm doing a neighborhood canvass concerning an arson that occurred last night."

A whining hum, a sound Neely responds to as she might to the dry, shivering chatter of a rattlesnake.

"Bob? Who is it?"

Spinski says, "The sheriff. Something about an arson."

Interesting, Neely thinks, that Spinski identified her as the sheriff. She didn't mention her rank, and she's wearing her old uniform with the deputy's insignia on it.

"Don't leave her standing on the doorstep, Bob. Invite her in."

Spinski doesn't go as far as inviting her anywhere, but he stands aside, and Neely steps into a brown-carpeted hallway that stretches west at least thirty feet, with two closed doors on the left, two openings into brightly lighted rooms on the right.

George Tarbet is seated in a motorized wheelchair in the first opening. Pain seems to emanate from his warped and skeletal body; she can almost feel it. Yet it inspires no sympathy. There is a reptilian sheen in his sunken, nearly colorless eyes. She's seen a few men with that look in their eyes. They were all killers. Spinski has the look, too.

Tarbet smiles pleasantly. "I'm William Johnson, Sheriff Jones. How delightful to meet you. Please, forgive me for not rising." He laughs at his little joke. "Actually, I *can* walk, but it's so much easier to ride. Come in . . . please." The chair whines backward, then swivels around as Tarbet leads the way into the living room.

Neely isn't sure what she expected in the house of an alleged drug dealer, but certainly something more tasteful. Carpet, drapes, and paneled walls are all dull brown, overstuffed furniture upholstered in a gaudy brown-and-orange pattern. Over the fireplace on the far wall hangs a seascape probably copied from a postcard. On the left-hand wall, shelves display assorted bric-a-brac, including an arrangement of vapidly cute pseudo-Oriental figurines: Siamese cats, dancing girls, Fu dogs, Ho Tais, dragons, all fired with gold-colored glazes.

But one of the figurines isn't so cute. . . .

Mr. William Johnson *does* enjoy his little jokes.

It's about five inches tall: a squatting figure with a half-animal face. Toltec? Mayan? She doesn't know pre-Columbian art well enough to guess, but she knows this piece doesn't fit the decor.

She laughs ingenuously as she picks it up. "Oh, look at *this*! Reminds me of my tiki. When I was a kid, my dad gave me a tiki he picked up in Hawaii. Oh, I *loved* that thing. Used to tell it all my girlhood secrets. Till I dropped it and it broke into smithereens. Just plaster, you know." She looks at Tarbet as she puts the piece back on the shelf. He's still smiling. Enjoying his little joke.

But by the weight of the figure, she knows it's not plaster. It's exactly what it seems: solid gold.

She gives Tarbet an embarrassed grin. "Sorry. I didn't mean to get into my childhood memories."

"Ah, but they do sometimes catch one unawares, don't they? Sheriff, can I offer you some coffee? Or some other refreshment?"

"Well, I really *would* like a glass of water. No ice. Just straight out of the tap." She walks toward the fireplace, ostensibly to examine the seascape. The room widens to the left at this end into an area about ten feet square, currently used for television viewing, apparently. There's no west wall; just an arched opening into a dining room whose windows frame an unimpeded vista of beach and surf and sea.

Neely exclaims, "Wow! What a *gorgeous* view!"

Tarbet's chair whines as he follows her into the dining room. "Yes, it *is* spectacular. I never tire of it. Bob, get the sheriff some water."

Spinski grunts and goes into the kitchen to the left of the dining room while Tarbet maneuvers his chair up to the glass-topped table.

"Won't you sit down, Sheriff?"

"Oh, no, thanks." She clicks out the point of a ballpoint and raises her clipboard. "The reason I'm here, Mr. Johnson, is there was an arson on Kittiwake Drive last night. We have a witness who saw a light green VW Vanagon drive away from the fire, heading south on North Front, but the witness didn't get a license number. I'm hoping somebody else along North Front saw that VW—*and* the license plate."

Tarbet looks up at her, head at an angle, his neck canted with the curve of his spine. "What time was this vehicle seen, Sheriff?"

"About eleven-thirty last night."

"Ah. Well, I was in bed by then. Bob? Were you up and about?"

Spinski shrugs as he hands Neely a glass of water. "Nah." Then with a cold-eyed smile, he adds, "Gotta get my beauty sleep."

Neely downs half the water, noting the deck to the north of the dining room and the tripod-mounted telescope. It isn't pointed out to sea, where it might focus on passing ships or whales, but to the east—toward the house where Sayson and his fellow agents are living.

She puts the glass down on the table and makes a note on her clipboard. "Seems a lot of people were getting their beauty sleep about then. Or glued to their TVs. Well, that's all I needed to ask. Sorry to bother you." She finishes the water and takes the glass into the kitchen to leave it in the sink. Like the entire kitchen, it's low: wheelchair-accessible. "I'll let myself out, Mr. Johnson." And instead of going back through the dining room, she takes the alternate route: through the opening into the hallway, then left toward the front door. Spinski is right behind her, and she can hear the wheelchair's whine.

Spinski makes a point of opening the front door for her. She looks back at Tarbet. He seems to float in the chair, one hand on the controls, fingers grotesquely angled from the knuckles. There is a presence about him—something eerie and irrational—and she can understand Scott Sayson's obsession with him.

"The house that was torched last night," she says, "was mine. That's one reason I'd really like to bust the guy who did it."

A flickering light in Tarbet's pale eyes. Did he already know it was her house that burned? He says, "I'm truly sorry to hear that, Sheriff."

She nods, then says, "Thanks for your help, Mr. Johnson." She glances once at Spinski and walks out the door.

It closes behind her with a solid thud.

Chapter 38

ON THE WAY BACK TO the TCSO, Neely stops at the public library in the Westport Center, north of the courthouse, a glass and brick building that also offers a swimming pool, meeting rooms, a senior center, two tennis courts, and a skateboard ramp. It was built six years ago, after a bond issue passed by a scant thirty-two votes, and it's still a bone of contention in town.

The shadows of dusk have already darkened the sky when she reaches her office at 4:30. The swing shift is on, but Buck is still in the briefing room. This, she observes from her desk while Heather explains a stack of phone memos. Heather guesses Neely can ignore the calls from reporters. The DA held a press conference at four about Giff's murder. By 4:20, all the TV vans and half the cars in the parking lot left.

"But this one . . ." She hands the memo to Neely. "He called three times. Said you'd know who he is. All he'd tell *me* is his name is Scott. Oh, and your new uniforms arrived. They've got the proper insignia and everything. I hung them in the bathroom."

Neely nods. "Thanks, Heather. By the way, it's quitting time."

"Yes, I know, but I thought . . . well there's so much to *do*."

"Nothing that can't wait. And you don't need to worry about me tonight."

Heather sighs. "Well . . . okay. But if something comes up, call me. Promise?"

"I promise. Good night, Heather. Have a good weekend."

"Good night, Sheriff." She gives Neely a bright smile as she closes her office door. Neely wonders if that brightness won't eventually wear thin. No. Heather's cheerfulness never palls; it's too authentic.

Neely reaches for the phone and punches the number on the memo. Special Agent Scott Sayson answers, and when Neely identifies herself, he demands, "What the hell are you trying to do? Screw up the whole damn surveillance?"

"We've got a murder that looks professional, Scott, and Spinski is the only professional hit man in town—that I know about. I just wanted to meet him. And Tarbet."

"A murder that—you mean Giff Wills?"

"Yes. One shot, large-caliber weapon, right in the center of the forehead."

Sayson is silent for a moment, then he says, "That's Sandy's MO all right. If it's a forty-four Magnum, there's no doubt about it."

"It's too early for a ballistics report."

"Shit, it doesn't make sense! Why would Sandy do Giff Wills?"

"I don't know that he did, but maybe Giff stumbled onto something Tarbet didn't want the rest of the world to know about."

"Maybe. Like where he's getting his drugs?"

"That's one possibility. Anyway, I did learn a few things on my visit. One is that Tarbet knows about you and your surveillance. He has a telescope trained on your house."

"Yeah, I know, but he can't see anything through *our*

windows. Of course, we can't see much though theirs, either, and I never could get the state AG to give me a phone tap. So, what else did you find out?"

"That there's a room in Tarbet's house, maybe ten by fifteen feet, that has no *visible* access. The County Planning Commission should have the original house plans on record. The builder would have to submit plans to get a building permit. See if there wasn't originally a room between the living room and the kitchen. My bet is Tarbet paneled over the door to an existing room and put in some hidden mechanism to open it."

Sayson says tightly, "So he's got a secret room. Maybe he's doing some cooking along with distributing. Or maybe he's growing. No. I checked his electric bill. Below average, in fact."

"Maybe it's his showroom."

"His *what*?"

"Showroom and warehouse for the merchandise he sells to those night visitors. Small and very valuable items." She can almost feel the weight of the little gold figurine.

Sayson's annoyance shows in his voice. "What *kind* of items?"

"Artifacts. The one I saw—that Tarbet was so sure I wouldn't recognize—was probably pre-Columbian, and it looked to be solid gold. I don't know what that sort of thing is worth, but I doubt it's cheap."

Sayson answers with a long, low whistle, then, "Treasures of the First People—that shop in Vancouver, BC. They must sell Indian stuff. I mean, really *old* Indian stuff. But where the hell would Tarbet get hold of it?"

"Depends on where it comes from, I suppose. Peru, Central America, Mexico—who knows?" Neely stops when the door into Heather's office opens. It's Greg Feingold. She says into the phone, "I'll talk to you later, Scott. The ME's here."

She waves Feingold in as she rises and goes to the armchair. "Have a comfortable seat, Greg. How's it going at Giff's?"

Feingold slumps down on the couch with an explosive sigh. "The place is a mess. Heathman and his team have their hands full just sorting through the debris. He said to tell you he got a great cast of that tire track."

"Good. So, what can you tell me about Giff?"

"Shot point-blank, maybe between ten P.M. Thursday and two A.M. Friday. No other injuries, no signs of a struggle. He was probably passed out at the time. I assume the BAC will be astronomical. The bullet exited the back of his head and buried itself in the cushions of the chair. We got it out. It was in good shape, actually, considering Giff had a fairly thick skull."

"What kind of bullet?"

"Well, just eyeing it in, I'd guess a forty-four Magnum."

That's Sandy's style. . . .

But it proves nothing. It doesn't even explain anything.

"Greg, was the body moved postmortem?"

"No. The exit wound and the hole in the cushions matched. If he *was* moved, somebody took uncommon care putting him back."

She sighs, visualizing that room, almost literally torn apart in a frenzied search, yet the chair wasn't touched.

"Neely?"

She frowns. Buck Dolin has an unnerving habit of appearing without warning in the briefing room door. All the other men sport hard soles that make a lot of noise, but Buck wears thick, soft, silent soles. He leans into the office, his big hands braced on the doorjambs. "Wayne just got a call from Sonny. He found Riker's pickup."

She stands up abruptly. "Where?"

"Behind a shack at the end of River Road. You want it towed in?"

"Yes, of course. And tell Sonny to check the shack."

"He did. Nobody home, and he figures there hasn't been

for a hell of a long time. Roof's caved in." Buck turns away, and Neely hears him passing on instructions to dispatcher Wayne Gerlach.

Feingold asks, "River Road? Isn't that where Giff's house is?"

"Yes, but the road ends about seven miles beyond Giff's." Still, she wonders if there's not a connection.

But then she's grasping at straws of connections at this point.

Feingold rises with a weary groan. "Well, I've got to get back to Portland. Oh—I had a call from Ando Koto."

Ambush. Things keep leaping out of ambush at her.

She doesn't try to speak, and Feingold goes on: "Unless you or Heathman come up with any objections, I'll release the body to Mr. Koto Monday. He, uh, asked about the victim's personal possessions. Particularly some sort of . . . sword?"

Neely only nods, and Feingold heads for the door. "I'll fax the reports on Giff as soon as I finish the autopsy. Damn, sounds like you've got a one-man riot out here."

The riot is in the lobby. Neely follows Feingold through Heather's office and into the lobby, where Kevin Locksey and Lt. Brad Skinner are struggling with a lanky white man in handcuffs, his thin, dark hair stringing down over a face skewed in furious indignation.

"You sonsabitches! You got nothin' better to do than hassle law-abiding citizens!"

Neely smiles sardonically. "Gordon Wyland."

Her guess is proved when the man stops struggling and stares at her. But his diatribe resumes immediately. "You got no right to arrest me. By God, I'm gonna sue the hell out of this two-bit pigsty! Shit, they was just goddamned mutts! Better off dead!"

Neely says, "Nice work, Kev. Lieutenant, book him on everything you can think of, from felony theft to cruelty to animals."

Wyland screams, "Nigger bitch!" and kicks at her, missing only because she dodges back out of his way.

"And attempted assault of an officer of the law," she adds.

She watches the deputies maneuver Wyland through the door into the Corrections Division.

This is for you, Willow. And for Vixen, with her sad brown eyes.

As darkness falls and the streetlights go on outside in the parking lot, Neely tries to ignore the apprehension she feels when she thinks about going to her temporary home and trying to sleep. Alone. But there's plenty to do here. She buys a couple of sandwiches from the vending machine in the courthouse cafeteria, eating them while she types a report on Giff's murder. Even when she finishes the report, she doesn't leave the office, but opens one of the library books. The subject is pre-Columbian art.

Finally, at 11:00 P.M., she surrenders, knowing she must at least try to get some sleep. She remembers to take her new uniforms, but only after she's nearly reached her pickup, so that she has to go back to retrieve them. Once she reaches the Sea View, she takes a long run on the moonlit beach and, afterward, a long soak in the Jaccuzi, then falls into a mercifully dreamless sleep a few minutes after midnight.

The ringing of the phone wakes her at exactly 2:00 A.M.

In the darkness, she can't remember at first where she is, can't find the phone on the small table between the beds, but on the third ring, she manages to pick up the receiver and mumble a hello.

"Neely Jones . . ."

The Whisperer.

Shit! She has no way to record this message.

She fumbles for the light, then searches the shallow drawer for paper and pen to write down as much as she can.

"Neely, you have nothing left to stay here for. Is it worth your life?"

"That's a threat, I assume?"

A laugh. It has a masculine sound. Maybe.

"Precisely. Your only choice now is whether you want to leave Westport alive or dead. Think about your mother, Neely. Such a fine, intelligent woman, Dr. Helene Cleary-Jones. No doubt you're proud of her, as she is of you. And you're all she has left."

Bastard! Or bitch? Whatever, it's done its research. Neely scribbles hurriedly with a pen that's nearly out of ink. She says, "I'll tell you what I think: You're just the average nutcase compensating for a lousy sex life. Does this sort of garbage turn you on?"

Another laugh. "Is that what you think, Neely? Well, don't count on it." The whisper goes even softer: "Tomorrow morning, you will tender your resignation. By tomorrow night, you will be on your way home. San Francisco. Sounds good, doesn't it? Home *sweet* home."

"Go fuck yourself," she says—sweetly. "I'm not resigning."

"Then you're dead."

Click. Neely is left with a silent phone. She hangs up and stares at her scrawled notes, listening to the melancholy sighing of surf beyond the curtained window.

How did the Whisperer know this phone number? Each of the motel units is on a separate line, and they don't go through a switchboard. Norma Addisill carefully explained that to her. This morning, Neely wrote her unit's phone number on a memo sheet and gave it to dispatcher Lonnie Weaver, and Lonnie posted it on the radio console for the other dispatchers to see. And any other deputy who happened to pass through the Dispatch Center.

At least now she can be sure of a direct link between the TCSO staff and the Whisperer.

But she was already sure of that.

Chapter 39

THE BEACH IS VEILED IN an opalescent fog that holds captive the subtle pinks and lavenders of dawn, mutes the crash of the surf, and mists Neely's face as she runs north, leaving a trail of footprints in the damp sand. Sometimes she comes upon the prints she left on the run south, but most have been washed clean by the waves.

The sea is tidy on its borders. . . .

That's what Jan used to say on their runs together.

Neely's pace breaks, and she loses her rhythm. Don't think about Jan. Just run. *Run.* Feel your heart pumping, blood rushing to your muscles. Feel your lungs expanding, air rushing in and out. Feel your feet pound the firm sand, *thud, thud, thud, thud.* Just keep running. . . .

Can't outrun your troubles, Neely. They just run along with you, and they're always faster than you.

Oh, but Gramma, I can *try* to outrun them. I can try.

A popping sound. It hardly registers against her panting, the slap of her shoes on the sand, the rumble of surf. Not until it's repeated, twice, and she sees two minuscule geysers of sand only three feet in front of her. Another pop and another geyser, this one closer.

Gunshots.

From the bank. It has to be, but she doesn't stop to look for the source of the shots. Her adrenaline level was already high, but now it skyrockets, and she runs at an angle toward the surf to put more distance between her and the gun.

Handgun, probably, by the sound of it. *Pop!* Again. She's a moving target—a fast-moving target, moving faster than she ever thought she could—and it's at least a hundred yards to the bank, a distance widening with every stride. Not an easy shot, and she doesn't intend to slow down to make it easier.

Damn! Not a rock or a piece of driftwood in sight big enough to take cover behind. Another shot. How many is that? Six? Seven?

The sand's too soft this close to the water, and now a sneaker wave is sliding in. She splashes through the knee-deep rush of water, scattering foam like snow into the wind.

Two more shots.

Her right foot hits a soft spot, sinks suddenly and deep, and she tumbles into a soup of sand and water, stunned by the chill of a second wave that breaks over her, rolls her twice, and sweeps her up the beach.

Blinded and coughing up salty, organic-tasting grit, too paralyzed with cold to move, she's a perfect target.

But there are no more shots.

As the wave recedes, she lies on her stomach in the sand, head raised to listen. Nothing. A nine-shell magazine? Another, smaller wave moves in around her, skimming the sand. She squints at the bank. South of the motel, the houses are packed side by side on fifty-foot lots. She can see no one moving around the houses, no one on the beach.

Neely doesn't try to race to the bank in hopes of reaching the street behind the houses to see someone drive off in a car she might recognize. No way can she reach the street in time.

Instead, she pulls herself to her feet unsteadily, weighted with water and sand, shivering uncontrollably. She knows that the ocean here, by a quirk of current, is warmer at this time of year than it is in the summer, but it's still too damned cold.

Then you're dead. . . .

Not yet, she thinks bitterly. But close. Too damned close.

Neely looks for her own footprints. The last of them were obliterated by the sneaker waves, but at the point where she first turned seaward, she picks up her own trail. She walks along the tracks slowly.

There. A tiny crater in the sand.

With her bare hands, she scoops up wet sand, winnows the sugary clots through her fingers. And finally, she feels something hard. A bullet. She works it out, wipes off the remaining sand.

Judging by size, she guesses it's a 9-mm.

The caliber of the gun that fired the bullet into Jan's chest. The caliber of the gun Andrea Olenick claims she returned to an ex-boyfriend.

Chapter 40

ON MOST WINTER WEEKENDS, THE TCSO shifts are reduced to a dispatcher, plus two deputies assigned on a revolving schedule for an extra day a month, but this Saturday morning, there's a full shift on hand—plus Heather Blessing—all present on Chief Criminal Deputy Buck Dolin's orders.

Neely is grateful, knowing how unlikely it is that she'd get a full shift on a weekend on *her* orders.

She doesn't mention the exciting finale to her morning run, but as soon as she checks the radio logs and the schedule for guard duty at the center, she retires to her office to make a phone call.

To Donald Grabenhorst of Everett, Washington.

Five rings go unanswered, but on the sixth ring, a voice responds with a sleep-thickened "H'lo. Who's this, for God's sake?"

The speaker is female. Possibly Mrs. Grabenhorst.

Neely identifies herself, then asks, "Is Donald Grabenhorst there?"

"Sheriff *who*?" Then when Neely repeats her identification, the woman asks, "What's this about? Westport? Why are you calling Don?"

"Is he there?"

"I want to know what's going on! He's my *husband,* after all."

There's a muffled exchange and about thirty seconds of silence, then the next voice Neely hears is male, asking "Who *is* this?"

Neely identifies herself yet again, then asks, "Are you the Donald Grabenhorst who lived in Westport, Oregon, until two years ago? I understand you worked in a restaurant."

He hesitates before replying, and in that few seconds, Neely hears a click. Someone is on an extension.

Donald admits, "Well . . . yes. I *managed* the Glencove Resort Restaurant."

"I just need some information, Mr. Grabenhorst. While you lived in Westport, didn't you share an apartment with Andrea Olenick?"

Another pause, then a loud laugh. "Is that what she told you? Look, Dr. Olenick was just a customer at the restaurant. I guess. . . . well, it was part of my job to be attentive to customers. That's what people paid for at the Glencove—attentive service. I'm afraid Dr. Olenick misunderstood my, uh, attentiveness."

Neely considers that, then asks, "Did you date her at any time?"

"No, I did not. Not at *any* time."

"Did you ever give her any gifts?"

"No! I told you—she was just a customer."

"Did you ever give her a handgun?"

"What? No!" Again the loud laugh. "Lady, somebody's crazy, and I know it's not me, and it probably isn't you. I'll say it again: Dr. Olenick was just a *customer.*"

"Okay, Mr. Grabenhorst. Thank you for your time."

He hangs up before she can. She frowns at the phone, wondering whether to believe him. But then, Andrea had been in love with Jan, literally hopelessly, for at least a year.

Maybe she has a problem separating fact from fantasy in her love life.

Which might be tragic for Andrea, but it leaves her with a 9-mm handgun registered to her and unaccounted for.

AT 10:00 A.M., NEELY IS reading Fire Chief Art Hager's report on the arson when Heather tells her there's a call she can't screen out.

"It's Mr. Culpepper," Heather says. "He's in his office, and you know how he *hates* working weekends."

Reluctantly, Neely picks up the phone.

The DA doesn't waste words on niceties. "Neely, I just had a conversation with *Ms.* Susan Benedict and her *client* Jennifer Kaynard and Jennifer's mother. They're not only pressing criminal charges, they intend to press *civil* charges."

Neely smiles at the outrage underlying his words and says pleasantly, "Yes, sir. You have arrest warrants for the rapists?"

"*Alleged* rapists. Yes. I had to call Judge Lay, and he had to come down here on a Satur—"

"Is the judge still in the courthouse?"

"He's here in my office."

"Don't let him leave! I'll be right up."

"What? Now, really, if—"

Neely slams the receiver down, sorts through the chaos on her desk for the right file, then heads for the courthouse at a run.

Half an hour later, she returns to the TCSO savoring a sense of triumph. She has in hand not only arrest warrants for Jennifer's rapists, but a search warrant for Andrea Olenick's apartment. In the briefing room, she finds Buck pouring himself a mug of coffee.

"Chief, these are the warrants for Dylan Unger, Jeff Amato, and T. J. O'Neill. The charges are assault and rape. I think you'd better handle these yourself. And maybe Lieutenant Chaffee."

Buck takes the warrants, whistling faintly. "Jeff's dad isn't going to be real happy about this."

"I doubt Jennifer's mother is real happy, either."

"Yeah, but Francis Amato is more accustomed to raising hell. Okay, I'll take care of it. Oh—we've got to release Bomber Buhl. You said you wanted to know when he was let loose."

"Yes. Damn, I need someone to keep an eye on him. He's our only lead on Riker." She looks around the briefing room, where Curtis McMinn and Darrell Logan are busy at their desks.

Apparently, Buck is thinking the same thing she is. He says, "Neely, you know we don't have anybody with any experience at tailing."

"I know." Is there a bitter cast in that admission? Damn right. "Okay, Chief, tell them to let Buhl go."

"Right. By the way, Heathman's in the sheriff's office."

"That's *Lieutenant* Heathman, Dolin," she says irritably as she heads for her office. At least Buck has stopped calling it *Giff's* office.

John Heathman is in the armchair with a mug of hot coffee. Only his gray-brown eyes betray his weariness. He gives her a smile, a warm flash of white against dark skin. "Any more homicides for me today?"

"No, Lieutenant." She puts the search warrant in the top drawer of her desk, takes out a small plastic envelope, and crosses to the couch. "But someone was *trying* for a homicide. That's one of about nine bullets aimed at me while I was running on the beach this morning."

Heathman's jaw goes slack. "Damn. Any idea who was shooting at you? Or why?"

"No, but that looks like a nine-millimeter bullet. I want a ballistics comparison with the bullet Greg took out of Jan's chest."

"I'll get that taken care of today." He sips at his coffee, his forehead creased with a frown. "I had a call from Culpepper this morning about the center."

• 227 •

"Let me guess. He doesn't understand why it's necessary to inconvenience a pillar of the community like Dr. S. Benjamin Nicholass. He wants the center unsealed."

"Good guess. Thing is, I don't think there's anything else we can do there. But I told Culpepper I'd let him know. It's your call, Sheriff."

She frowns at the moth orchid, its white blossoms smiling at her like knowing monkeys. "Actually, it's the DA's call, legally, but as long as he doesn't pull rank on me—one more day. I'm not really sure why."

"I'll tell him." Heathman sighs as he rises. "I better get back to Giff's house. The lab'll be faxing you some reports this morning."

"Anything you can tell me off the top of your head?"

"Well, the tire track is a Michelin. The footprints in the garage are Nikes. Men's size nine, and they weren't Giff's. He wore an eleven. We didn't find a shell casing. The perp cleaned up after himself. At least from the shooting. We've got fingerprints out the kazoo, and we're still trying to find out exactly who was at Giff's election-night party. The partygoers we've talked to seem a bit vague about that night. And Giff had a BAC of point twenty-four. Yeah. He should've died of alcohol poisoning. And that's about it, so far."

"Thanks, Lieutenant. Good luck."

He laughs as he heads out the door. "I'll need it."

Neely leaves the door open, goes to her desk, and takes out the search warrant. She'd prefer to do the search alone, but she knows better. If she takes anyone with her, it will have to be Buck. There's no one else she can trust. Not that she's so sure about him, but he'll have to do, and that means the search will have to wait.

The phone rings, shrilling along her nerves. The personal line. Neely lets it ring, waiting until she can control the rush of rage the sound catalyzes. Then she presses the record button before she picks up the receiver. She doesn't speak.

"Neely Jones . . ."

The Whisperer. Her jaw is clenched, breath coming too fast. Still she says nothing.

"Ah, playing coy again? Well, it doesn't matter. I must say, you run like a veritable gazelle. A joy to watch, in fact. Just remember this, Neely Jones: Next time I *won't* miss."

Click. She listens to the silence for a moment, then carefully hangs up. Her hand is shaking.

"Well, I figure I better talk to the sheriff, Heather. I think I saw them skinheads ever'body's tryin' to find."

Neely feels like she's been jolted with a cattle prod. She looks into Heather's office and sees a middle-aged man dressed in khakis, with heavy mud-crusted hiking boots.

Neely all but shouts, "Come in! Please. Mr. . . ."

He saunters into the office, nods at her. "Franklin Welby, Sheriff. Met you at one of the Rotary lunches a while back."

"Oh, yes. Did you say you've seen Riker?"

Welby pushes his baseball cap back to scratch his buzz-cut scalp. "Well, ma'am, I figure I did."

"Where? And when?"

"About half an hour ago. I'm a timber cruiser, and I was up on the Minton property, past the end of River Road—"

"Wait. *Past* the end of River Road? I thought it was a dead end."

"Well, it is, as far as the county's concerned. Jake Minton's land is east of the turnaround at the end of River Road. He bulldozed an access road into the property. I was up past the gate, checkin' out a parcel of Doug fir he plans to log. It's not much of a road. Runs along the Chinook for a mile till it peters out. I was about half a mile past the gate when I seen an old beat up VW camper—"

"What color?"

"Sort of a washed-out green. Anyway, there was two queer-lookin' guys with their heads shaved bald, hunkered over a campfire by the river. Both of 'em had on black leather jackets. I could see the back of one of 'em. Had a big swasteeka on it."

Neely almost laughs aloud. "That's Riker and his buddy Lisker. It *has* to be." Then she sobers. "Did they see you or your vehicle?"

"Well, I don't figure they did. I was on foot, walking the road alongside the timber parcel, when I smelled their smoke. Smoke in the woods always makes a man nervous. Could be a wildfire. Then I heard voices. That makes a man nervous, too, these days. Never know if somebody's got a marijuana farm out there, and the guys that grow that stuff, well, they like to set booby traps full of shrapnel."

Neely nods. She's familiar with such cases, although she's never run into any in Taft County. "I understand your caution, Mr. Welby."

"Yeah. Well, I come up on 'em real quiet. River's rough along there, so it makes plenty of noise. They didn't even know I was there. Anyhow, I'll show you the spot, if you want."

"I want, but let me get some backup organized."

Neely strides into the briefing room, swearing under her breath when she remembers that Buck and Whit Chaffee are out arresting Jennifer's rapists. Curtis McMinn and Darrell Logan are the only deputies here. She briefly outlines the situation to them, adding, "Darrell, *no* sirens. This is a stealth operation."

He nods eagerly. "Right. We'll just go in like a SWAT team."

Sure, Neely thinks. All three of us.

Chapter 41

DEPUTY DARRELL LOGAN'S ENTHUSIASM FOR this venture seems to be inspired by his perception of himself as a jungle commando. He'd probably like to daub his face with mud and decorate his Stetson with shrubbery. Sgt. Curtis McMinn—the wanna-be Chuck Norris—also seems caught up in the enthusiasm. Both men carry rifles. Neely's carrying her duty weapon.

With Franklin Welby in the lead, they've walked about a quarter of a mile east up the dirt road, where fern and salal encroach on both sides and brown, rain-crushed grass tangles between the ruts. To the left is a stand of second-growth Douglas fir, a forest unnaturally consistent, all the trees almost exactly the same height and diameter. Yet it has a natural forest's earthy scent. To the right, visible between a rank of pale alder trunks, the Chinook River—more a creek than a river this far upstream—hurries seaward with an incessant, clamoring rush.

Neely stops Welby to ask, "How much farther?"

"Another quarter mile, maybe less," he says, squinting up the road.

"Okay. You'd better go back to the gate and wait for us."

He adjusts his baseball cap. "I'd just as soon go with you, Sheriff."

"Mr. Welby, if I could, I'd deputize you, but it's not as simple as it is in the movies. I can't risk a civilian getting hit with a stray bullet."

"Yeah, I understand. Well, you'll see the VW parked just off the road on the right." He nods to McMinn and Logan. "Good luck."

When Welby tramps off down the road, Logan says, "I'll go on ahead and scout the situation."

"Who's senior man here?" McMinn objects. "Anybody does the scouting, it'll be me."

Neely snaps, "Keep your voices down! *I'm* senior *man* here, and we'll stick together until I say so. Come on."

She ignores their rebellious glares and continues up the road, and a few seconds later, they fall in behind her. The dark soil quiets their footfalls, and the the river provides a cover of white sound. None of them speak in the ten minutes it takes to hike the remaining distance. Finally, as they round a curve, Neely sees the VW at the side of the road about fifty feet ahead.

Riker and his sidekick are twenty feet from the van, watching the river from a log on the bank. Lash Lisker, scarecrow-thin and taller by a head than Riker, rises, but only to toss a beer can into the water. Then he sits down again, reaches in front of the log, where they apparently have a stash of beer, opens another can, and tips it up.

Neely whispers to McMinn, "Sergeant, go up the road to that broken alder just past the van. Wait till I make my move. Go!" To her surprise, he does go, dramatically darting from one tree to another.

She turns to Logan. "Deputy, you stay here. And for God's sake, watch where you point that thing!"

"What? Oh." His face goes red when he realizes he had lowered his rifle and is pointing it at her midriff.

Neely unholsters her Glock and, with her eyes focused on Riker and Lisker, moves along the road toward the VW.

They never once look her way. She stops at the back of the van, studying them and the span of loose river-worn gravel separating her from them. Then she takes three strides out into the gravel, raises the gun in a two-handed grip, and yells, *"Police! Freeze!"*

Lisker's beer can flies in a spewing arc as he throws his hands up. Riker jerks to his feet, his "Shit!" clearly audible.

Neely shouts, "I said *freeze,* Yew-gene!" at the same moment a rifle cracks, three times.

McMinn. *Damn* him!

But all three shots miss—which must be a record of some sort—and Riker suddenly sits, hands in the air. Neely motions to her SWAT team. "Curtis, you take Riker. Darrell, you take Lisker. And *don't* forget to read them their rights. For now, the charge is arson."

The two skinheads are docile as lambs while McMinn and Logan go through the ritual of arrest. Yes, they understand their rights. Neely wonders if Lisker really does. His blood-alcohol count might put that in doubt. But she doesn't intend to question either of them here.

With the prisoners lying belly-down on the gravel, hands cuffed behind them, Logan reaches for his radio and says, "I'll call in to Dispatch, Neely."

"No, you won't. Not by radio. Just keep an eye on these two. Curtis, let's see what we can find in the van." She reaches into her back pocket for a pair of latex gloves as they crunch across the gravel to the VW. She glances at McMinn, noting that he's wearing his black leather gloves, as usual.

The van isn't locked. In fact, the keys are in the ignition. Neely and McMinn begin at the back of the vehicle, and half the challenge is discovering the many storage compartments designed by clever German engineers. Most of what they find undoubtedly belongs to the rightful owner of the van: first-aid kit, camp cooking set, folded tent, and other camping gear. Even a sack of dry dog food.

On the ground, underneath the rear bumper, they find

four empty five-gallon gas cans. McMinn starts to pull one out, but Neely stops him. "Leave them alone. I want to get some pictures and video."

Next, they tackle the VW's center section. The side door is open on an incredible mess. The bed platform is down, and on top of it are two rumpled sleeping bags. Like the floor, the bags are littered with cigarette butts, empty beer cans, take-out containers, chip bags, candy wrappers, and porno mags. Neely unzips one sleeping bag while McMinn starts on the other.

She finds only more garbage, plus one exceptionally odorous black sock. McMinn seems to be having similar luck, although he's spared the sock. Then as he starts to roll the bag up, something slips off the bed to the floor. Something flat and tan. About five by seven inches. He doesn't seem to notice it and even steps on it when he shifts his weight to feel around the sides of the mattress.

Neely asks, "What's that?"

"What's *what*?"

"Under your right foot."

He straightens, banging his head on the roof of the van and knocking his hat off. "Oh shit!" He rubs the back of his head, then, groaning, reaches down to pick up his hat. "I think I got a concussion."

"I doubt that. Where is it, Sergeant?"

"Where's what?" He grimaces as he places the hat on his head.

"The manila envelope that fell out from under the sleeping bag."

"What're you talking about? I didn't see any—"

"*This* envelope," she says as she reaches for it. Only a corner is sticking out from under the bed frame.

An interesting shtick. Did McMinn really not see the envelope, or was he trying to hide it?

And an interesting envelope.

It's the twin of the envelope she found under Giff Wills's

desk drawer. The only difference is that this one has been torn open. She empties the contents on the bed.

Twenty-dollar bills.

Neely counts them. Forty-four bills. Well circulated, random serial numbers. She has no doubt that there were originally fifty.

McMinn asks, "What's a punk like Riker doing with all this cash?"

"For services rendered, probably." Neely looks out at the two prisoners and their vigilant guard, then restores the bills to the envelope and places it in clear sight on the bed. "Let's check the front."

McMinn steps out of the van, and Neely follows him, but she stops when she realizes they've missed something. The clever German engineers fitted a compartment about ten inches wide, extending from the floor almost to the roof, between the side of the vehicle and the bed. She opens the compartment door. A closet. Cramped, no more than a yard deep, but a closet. Two cold-weather jackets are hanging inside. She reaches in and feels around, encountering two pairs of boots on the floor and, at the back of the compartment, something that makes her heart stutter, stops her breath.

She pulls it out into the light: Jan Koto's samurai sword.

Her hands cramp on the brocaded sheath, and she hears a ringing whine like a distant, endless scream, and suddenly, irrationally, she's kneeling in the gravel, the sword across her thighs. She stares at it, unblinking, then, driven by some impulse beyond comprehension, she slowly pulls the sword out of its sheath.

A magic thing, this weapon, because when she draws the bright, shimmering blade, the world turns dark.

She hears a motor rumbling. McMinn speaking to her. It might as well be a foreign language. Logan shouting. Then they're gone.

It doesn't matter.

It doesn't even matter that this is the irrefutable proof she needs that Eugene Buxman, aka Dirk Riker, torched her house.

Their house.

Hers and Jan's.

Now Ando Koto can give this three-centuries-old sword to his eldest grandson. His daughter's son. Not his son's son.

And what will Cornelia Faith Jones have left to prove she once loved a man named Jan Koto with all her heart and soul and would've loved him until she died?

Nothing.

For the first time, she understands what she lost in the fire. All the furniture and household goods they chose together; the books, music, paintings, sculptures, ceramics; the gifts they gave each other; the letters Jan wrote on the few occasions when they were separated.

This terrifyingly beautiful weapon, ringing with history, is all that's left of the love and the life they made together.

But it isn't hers to keep.

First, it will be used as evidence in Riker's trial. Then she will give it to Jan's father.

And have nothing left. . . .

"Neely?"

She opens her eyes, looks down at the flashing reflections of light on the blade, blurred through the tears.

"Neely, are you okay?"

She promised herself she wouldn't let the tears start, because she couldn't stop them.

But she must. She will.

Buck Dolin.

He's down on one knee in front of her, and she's not sure what she sees in his dark eyes. Fear? What could he be afraid of in her tears? She looks past Buck and sees that McMinn and Logan and the prisoners are gone.

Buck says, "Whit Chaffee rode up with me. He and the

other guys are walking the prisoners back to the gate to get an ID from Welby."

She nods as she sheaths the sword in a silken swish of steel. Then she rises, ignoring the supporting hand Buck offers. She says, "We didn't finish searching the van."

"I'll take care of it."

"I want some videotape. The gas cans in the back, the envelope—" She turns to look at the bed. The envelope is still there.

"Neely, I'll videotape everything and bag the envelope. And this. I'm sorry, but it's evidence."

He means the sword. She surrenders it to him. Her hands feel empty without it.

He says, "You better head on down to the TCSO. You should be there to make sure they get those punks booked properly."

She knows what he's doing. He's making it easy for her to get away from this place; he's even making sure she gets full credit for the bust, if she wants it. She nods and starts for the road.

She should thank him, but she can't. She can't even look back at him. She's not sure why.

Maybe because he saw her cry.

Chapter 42

HOW DO THEY KNOW? SOME sort of journalistic radar?

The TCSO entrance is blocked with a clot of reporters when Neely drives the patrol into the parking space nearest the door. Riker is handcuffed and caged behind steel mesh in the backseat; McMinn and Logan have Lisker in their patrol.

Fortunately, Danny Beecher is available to help get the prisoners past the noisy bristle of mikes and cameras. Riker spews an unprintable and unairable diatribe, but Lisker is silent and much sobered. The reporters are left disappointed at the jail door, and the prisoners are escorted to the booking desk, Riker still spewing. Neely stops when one of the interrogation room doors opens, and Owen Culpepper emerges, wearing the look of outrage that seems to be getting habitual.

"What is going *on* out here?"

Neely looks past the DA and sees Jeff Amato and his lawyer father at the table. Culpepper slams the door.

"Well?"

"*Well,* Mr. Culpepper, we've just arrested Burton Lisker and Eugene Buxman." He stares at her blankly, then she adds, "Also known as Lash Lisker and Dirk Riker."

"Riker!" The DA rolls his eyes heavenward. "Thank God! Great news, this is *great* news! I'll have to call a press conference."

He starts for the lobby door, but Neely stops him. "What about Jeff Amato? Have the other boys been arrested?"

"Hm? Yes, of course, but I thought it best to keep them separated."

"What did Jeff have to say?"

"That he wants to make a deal. Actually, Francis said that. Deputy Swenson! I need you to open the door for me."

Neely continues to the booking desk. Lisker's shaven scalp is beaded with sweat, and she makes a mental note to question him first, rather than Riker. But she'll let both of them stew a while. Riker's still exercising his lungs, and finally Neely asks Swenson to let her out.

She expects the lobby to be empty, since Culpepper likes to hold his press conferences in his office: The ambience is classier. But there are still a few journalists left, gathered around a brindle-bearded man in a threadbare topcoat and a three-piece suit two sizes too big for him, with his hair sticking out in tufts from under a navy watch cap. Donny Murchison is an institution of sorts in Westport.

"I saw him! Giff Wills's ghost." He gestures with hands as graceful as a pianist's. The reporters are rapt. Human-interest angle, no doubt. "I *saw* him stepping out of his golden chariot, with his Smokey hat on and his wings in his arms, and the headlights shining through them like silk gauze. Oh, it was *beautiful.* . . ."

Neely frowns. Wings in his arms? Silk gauze? His Smokey hat? Golden chariot with headlights? Odd details for an alcoholic fantasy. She pushes through the reporters and hooks Donny's elbow. "How are you, Donny? Remember me?"

The reporters begin complaining, especially when Neely

steers Donny toward the closed door of the reception office.

Donny grins at Neely. "You're that nice niggra lady. I know you."

Niggra? Yes, there is a hint of southern in Donny's speech, but it's masked by more than a hint of Thunderbird. In a few days, it will be gin, when his mysterious monthly stipend arrives on the tenth of the month.

Neely knocks on the door and calls out to Heather, who opens the door enough to peer out. Then her smile lights up. "Sheriff, congratulations! You caught that awful man—" She blinks and sniffs, but her smile remains steadfast. "Hi, Donny."

The Third Estate clamors, while Neely hurries Donny Murchison in, and Heather closes the door behind them. Neely keeps Donny going into her office, and there she has to physically stop him. He seems a victim of inertia. She guides him to the armchair.

"Sit down here, Donny. Make yourself comfortable. Heather?"

"Yes, Sheriff?"

Neely pulls her wallet out of her back pocket and hands Heather some bills. "Do me a favor. Run over to the cafeteria and get some sandwiches out of the machine. Any kind and as many as that'll buy." Then when Heather takes off at nearly a literal run, Neely asks Donny, "How about a cup of coffee?"

"Can't drink coffee. Upsets my stomach. Yes, it does." He adds hopefully, "Maybe a little white wine?"

"Sorry. We're fresh out."

He nods vaguely, and Neely takes a seat on the couch. "Tell me more about Giff's ghost, Donny. When did you see it?"

"Last night. Maybe the night before. Maybe not. When was it I spent the night in jail?"

"The last time? Let's see, you were booked in . . ." It's so hard to remember, to count the years that seem to have passed in the last few days. "Tuesday. You were booked in Tuesday morning. Election day."

"Then it was the *next* day. Night. You shouldn't let a man like me out after just a day. Really, you shouldn't. And it was raining. Guess the god's were pissed off!" He starts to laugh; then his face turns bright pink over his brindle beard. "Sorry. Where's my manners? Talking like that in front of a lady."

There seems to be no irony in that, any more than there was any intentional insult in the word *niggra*. She wonders why and when Donny Murchison left the South.

"It's okay, Donny. So, you were out in the rain Wednesday night? Why didn't you go to the Methodist shelter?"

"Oh, I *never* go there. No, never. It's full of bums and drunks."

"Ah. Well, where *did* you go?"

He has to think for a while. "The Salty Dog. But Willy threw me out. Into the rain. He did. Wasn't even closing time."

"Where'd you go from there?"

"Recycling center. I always go there when the weather's bad. Always do. Got shelter under the drive-through and plenty of stuff to cover up with. And Dumpsters. No garbage in 'em. Have to watch out for the ones they put the glass in, though. Ol' George doesn't mind, as long as I clear out before opening time in the morning."

"Tell me about the ghost."

Donny smiles beatifically. "Maybe it was an angel. Yes, it could've been. An angel. Well, I'd just settled in the paper Dumpster, and then I heard this rumbling sound. *Rrrrrrrmmmm.* Kept getting louder and louder, and then there was *light.* Oh, beautiful, blinding light! Stuck my head up over the top of the Dumpster, and I was looking into the light, and, oh Lord, I couldn't move, it was so beautiful! The chariot all shining gold, and Giff got out of the chariot with his wings in his arms, and the light shining through them, shining *everywhere.*"

Donny is so transported, Neely only needs to maintain an attentive silence by way of encouragement, and she's not pleased when Heather returns at that point with a box full of triangular plastic packages.

"Here's your sandwiches, Sheriff."

"Damn, you're quick." Too quick, Neely adds to herself. Donny might lose his train of thought. "Just put them here on the coffee table."

"Sure." She puts the box down, then retreats into her office.

Neely reaches into the box and takes out a plastic triangle. Ham and cheese. "I haven't had lunch yet, Donny. Would you join me?"

"Don't mind if I do. No, don't mind at all." He pulls nearly all of the dozen or so sandwiches out, squints at the labels, then decides on one—peanut butter and jelly—expertly opens it, and takes a heroic bite.

Neely waits while he chews, then, before he can take another bite, asks, "How could you tell it was Giff?"

Donny takes another bite.

"Donny?"

And another.

She's convinced she's lost him and the rest of his story as he methodically finishes the entire sandwich. But then he takes a surprisingly clean handkerchief out of his breast pocket, wipes his mouth and hands, and replies, "Well, it *had* to be Giff. He was wearing his Smokey hat. And he died. He did. That's what I heard at the Dog."

Neely doesn't point out that he didn't hear that at the Salty Dog Wednesday night, since Giff was still alive then. Donny's sense of time has always been chancy. He probably heard it *last* night.

She asks, "Did the ghost see you?"

"Oh, no. He couldn't. Different world. For a while, I thought *I* might be dead, but I wasn't. No. Not yet."

"What did he do?"

"I don't know."

"What do you mean?"

"You're not eating your sandwich."

"I will. Later. Did you . . ." He stares silently at the box of sandwiches, and Neely sighs. "Have another one. Please."

Donny grins. "Don't mind if I do." Again, he checks the labels and opts for peanut butter and jelly. And again, Neely waits impatiently while he finishes the entire sandwich and wipes his mouth and hands.

Then he looks straight at her. "I slipped out of that world."

"Uh . . . what world is that?"

"Heaven, maybe. Whatever world Giff was in. You can sometimes slip over into different worlds. I've done it lots of times. Lots and lots of times. So, that's all I can tell you. When I looked over the top of the Dumpster again, the golden chariot and the headlights and the ghost were gone. And it was morning. Yes, it was."

Neely considers Donny Murchison as a potential witness and knows he'd be a disaster. Yet there's truth to be read between the lines of his story. An important truth. Is it enough?

No. But it's better than ignorance.

Ignorance never was bliss, Neely. Just means you'll never know what hit you.

Right, Gramma Faith, and I'm tired of not knowing. Tired of getting hit, for that matter.

"Donny, thanks for sharing that story with me." Neely rises, removes another sandwich from the box for herself, and offers the rest to Donny. "Would you mind taking these? Heather misunderstood me. I really didn't want so many, and they'll just go to waste."

He smiles sweetly. "Don't mind if I do. No, don't mind at all." The sandwiches disappear magically into various pockets; then he hurries to the door, opens it, and looks back at Neely. "I won't vote for you, though. I never vote. No, I don't. Tried once, but they wouldn't let me. Bye, nice lady." And he whisks through Heather's office and is gone in seconds.

Heather watches him from behind her desk and shakes her head. "You know, he's really such a dear man."

Neely nods absently. "Heather, what's the name of the guy who runs the recycling center? George something."

"Oh, that's George Relska."

"Thanks." Neely returns to her desk, opens a local phone book, and finds three Relskas, probably all related, but only one George. She punches the number, and to her relief, the call is answered by George himself. She identifies herself, then, "Mr. Relska, I'm looking for a plastic painters' tarp, about ten by ten feet. It was left in the recycling center last Wednesday night. Any chance you would've noticed it?"

"Good thing you're not looking for milk jugs, Sheriff. Took a ton of 'em to Portland yesterday. Yeah, I did see a tarp, come to think of it. Big sheet of clear plastic?"

"Yes. Has paint smears on it." And probably some blood smears.

"Yeah. Somebody put it in with the plastics, and I can't recycle *sheet* plastic. Just bottles. There's a sign over the bin sayin' so, but nobody pays any attention."

"What did you do with that sheet of plastic?"

"Well, most of the stuff I can't recycle, I truck out to the dump." Neely winces, until Relska adds, "You know, I think I kept that. Yeah. Folded it up and put it in my garage. Figured it might come in handy someday. My wife's always hollerin' about how I'm such a pack rat, but I just hate to throw out perfectly good stuff."

"That's a fine philosophy," Neely says. "But I'll have to take that tarp off your hands. It may be evidence."

"You mean like in a *crime*? Well, you're welcome to it, Sheriff."

"I'll have someone pick it up as soon as possible." She hangs up, allowing herself a whispered "Yes!" Then she calls Giff's house and finally gets through to Heathman.

He's quietly elated at the prospect of getting hold of the tarp and asks her how she found it. She puts him off with, "It's a long story, Lieutenant. A ghost story."

When she concludes the call, she begins jotting some notes on the tarp and its history, but she stops when she realizes Heather is standing in her office door, waiting. Neely asks, "What is it, Heather?"

Perhaps that sounded a little impatient. Heather clasps her hands, her eyes widening. Turquoise today, to match her silk blouse and tiny skirt. "Uh, well, I . . . I just need to talk to you a minute, Sheriff."

Neely calls up a smile. "Sure, Heather. What's wrong?"

"Oh, I don't know if anything's *wrong*. It's just something I found in that file cabinet—the one you picked the lock on." She crosses to the cabinet and pulls out the third drawer. "This is exactly where I found it, right here at the back of the drawer."

A clear plastic evidence bag, no markings on it. Neely takes it out of the drawer and puts it on her desk. Through the plastic, she can see some Polaroid photographs and a small green figurine.

Even without opening the bag, she can tell this much about the figurine: It's carved of jade, and, although she can't be more specific, the style is definitely pre-Columbian.

Again, she reaches for a pair of latex gloves.

Chapter 43

NEELY GLANCES INTO THE BRIEFING room and sees Curtis McMinn, ostensibly working on a report, looking her way. She says quietly, "Heather, would you mind closing the door?"

Heather goes to the door and closes it, even closes the miniblinds, then returns to stand in front of the desk while Neely opens the evidence bag and carefully removes its contents.

The figurine is about three inches tall, and it is exquisite, but she doubts Giff kept it for its beauty. Sensuous curved lips and a headdress like an oversized pillbox hat. Olmec? The scant reading she did in the library books leaves her a long way from being an expert.

She turns to the photographs. Three of them. Close-ups of a box of some sort. No scale to judge its size, except for the handle on the top. Like a suitcase handle. And if it's standard size, the box must be about two feet tall and fifteen inches wide and deep. The front section is a door, and it's open. The box is stuffed with packages wrapped in newspaper, but a few have been unwrapped and displayed in front of the box: nine pieces—jade, ceramic, gold. All small, the largest a pot about five inches across. All undeniably pre-Columbian.

She opens the middle desk drawer and finds her magnifying glass. The newspapers are printed in Spanish, and she can read part of a headline on one crumpled sheet: RISTAS EN CABO SAN LU

Something in Cabo San Lucas. Baja.

R and R in Cabo San Lucas. *Poseidon* always docks there for three or four days on the Baja expeditions. The ship is ideal for smuggling. Customs probably pays little attention to a research vessel from a highly reputable institution. And the morning Jan's body was found, Neely saw this box—or one very similar to it—on the floor in Ben Nicholass's office. It was the case for his Zeiss Ikon microscope.

Ben Nicholass?

Why not?

And/or Andrea Olenick, who also uses a microscope in her work, who always went on the Baja trips, who tried to give herself an alibi for the night of Jan's murder by claiming she spent the night with Ben.

Was that why Jan said it might be difficult to work with Andrea in the future—not because she came on to him, but because he found out she was smuggling Mexican artifacts?

"Sheriff? Are you okay?"

Neely looks up at Heather. "Mm? I'm okay. Just . . . puzzled." She studies the photographs again. The box is on a pale carpet. White or beige—the flash distorts the color—and it's close to a wall that's also white or beige. But there's nothing to give her a hint of the location.

She leans back, frowning.

At least now she knows *why* Giff Wills was murdered. The jade artifact and photographs must be the evidence he used to blackmail someone into providing the cash that appeared magically under his desk drawer. Giff caught the smuggler, singular or plural, red-handed, but instead of arresting him, her, or them, he made a deal, using the photographs—and maybe fingerprints on them and the artifact?—as a guarantee of cooperation. But Giff's scheme fell apart after he lost the election and resigned in an alcoholic fog, and after Neely's discovery of the payoff. Someone decided he was too much of a liability to live.

George Tarbet?

He's the only suspect with a live-in hit man, and the only suspect who displays a gold pre-Columbian artifact amid his ticky-tack bric-a-brac.

Well, she can't be sure Nicholass doesn't have any pre-Columbian artifacts in his house. She's only been inside it once, for a staff Christmas party. The decor was as austere as his office at the center—sort of Bauhaus revival—and she doesn't remember any pre-Columbian accents. But she only saw the living room and a deck.

Nor can she be sure of Andrea's apartment, except for the living room. But at least she has a search warrant for Andrea's apartment. The odds against getting one for Nicholass's house are astronomical.

She studies the jade piece and the photographs again. Someone expected this evidence to be hidden in Giff's house. But Giff had the last laugh. He hid it in his office, where there'd be little opportunity for anyone to search for it without risking discovery.

The photographs are all marked with the date and time: December 28 of last year. The date *Poseidon* returned from Baja. The time: 10:37 P.M. At night, when Sgt. Curtis McMinn would have been on duty as night watchman at the oceanographic center.

There's no doubt now, after Donny Murchison's "testimony," that McMinn was involved in Jan's murder. He disposed of the plastic tarp that was used to wrap Jan in when he was moved from his office to the medusa pool. The transparent plastic, loosely folded and backlighted, translated into wings in the arms of Giff's ghost, and the golden chariot with headlights was McMinn's cherished Thunderbird. But how big a part did McMinn play in the smuggling or Giff's murder or his blackmail scam? Was McMinn the courier for the payoffs?

And is he the only TCSO staff member involved?

Neely takes a deep breath. The problem now is where to put this evidence for safekeeping. In the evidence room, where any of the staff can get at it? Is anywhere in the TCSO safe?

"Heather, I want you to watch what I do carefully and remember it in case you're ever called upon to testify to it."

Heather's iridescent pink lips part. "Okay, Sheriff."

"First, I want you to take a close look at these things."

Heather leans forward, frowning as she examines the figurine and photographs, then straightens. "Whatever *are* they?"

"That's a long story. I need another evidence envelope."

"Top drawer on the left."

"Oh. Yes, here they are." Neely returns the figurine and photographs to the envelope Giff kept them in, puts his envelope inside a larger plastic envelope, then seals and marks it. If Giff was depending on fingerprints on the artifact or photographs to implicate the smuggler, he should've known better than to put them in a plastic envelope, but Giff was never much concerned with the technical aspects of investigation. Maybe they haven't been encased in plastic long enough to make the prints mushy. Neely has her own reasons for using a plastic bag: protection against moisture.

Heather asks, "Do you want me to put that in the safe?"

"Not when I don't know who has the combination." She crosses to the coffee table. "Bring me some paper towels from the bathroom."

With the towels spread on the table to catch the loose dirt, Neely tips the moth orchid out of its pot, supporting the plant at its base with one hand, puts the envelope in the bottom of the pot, then restores the plant, apparently none the worse for wear. The monkey faces still grin at her. She flushes the soil caught on the paper towels down the toilet; then she takes off the gloves and opens the door to the briefing room. McMinn and Logan are still at their desks. They hurriedly look away.

Neely returns to her desk. "Okay, Heather. Thanks."

"Sure, Sheriff. Oh, hi, Buck."

Neely looks around, startled to see Buck Dolin standing in the briefing room door. Damn, he keeps sneaking up on her.

He saunters into the office, giving Heather a smile. "Hi, Heather. How're you doing?"

"Oh, I'm fine, Buck. Need me for anything else, Sheriff?"

Neely shakes her head. "No. Besides, it's Saturday. You're not even supposed to be here. Don't you have something better to do on a nice day like this?"

"Well, Thomas and I did talk about maybe having dinner out before the game. It's a home game, thank goodness. Amity High."

"Then you better go home and put on your prettiest dress."

"Well . . . okay, if you're sure . . ."

"It's nearly quitting time, anyway. Go on."

"Thanks, Sheriff!" And she hurries into her office.

Buck says, "We took the VW over to impound. Any problems booking Riker and his buddy?"

"No. Just a lot of noise from Riker. I'm glad you're back. I need you to help me with something." Neely goes to her desk and finds the search warrant for Andrea's apartment.

Buck raises an eyebrow. "What's this something you need me for?"

Is that reluctance shadowing the question? Or irony at the word *need*? She explains: "I need you to help me serve a search warrant on Andrea Olenick. Let's take care of it now."

He nods and follows Neely through the outer office,

where Heather is hoisting her purse over her shoulder while she presses buttons on the phone console. "Bye, Sheriff."

"Have a good time."

They cross the lobby, and when they reach the entrance, Buck opens one of the glass doors and holds it for her, doing it so automatically, it's obvious that it's something his mother drilled into him at an early age. Neely goes through, pausing outside to find the keys to her patrol in her pants pocket.

She looks up at the rumbling sputter of a motor suddenly gunned through two gearshifts, sees a blue pickup coming at them from the right side of the nearly empty parking lot.

It's the Toyota.

For a shivering, dreamlike moment, she sees the faceless figure at the wheel, and something in her mind puts Jan's face on it. It's their pickup. It must be Jan driving. And the last three days have only been a nightmare, and nothing's changed, nothing's lost. . . .

No!

It's not Jan. Nor is the driver faceless The face is hidden behind a ski mask, and the left arm is stretched out the window, a semiautomatic in a gloved hand.

"*Get down!*" Neely hurls herself at Buck, knocks him off balance, and they hit the asphalt hard, Buck coughing out a shout of surprise, and five shots thud against her eardrums in quick succession.

Cracking glass. A scream somewhere. And the pickup accelerates out of the parking lot and turns east on North Fourth Street.

"Jesus X. Christ!" Buck scrambles to his feet, his duty weapon already in his hand.

Neely's gun is out, too. That's reflex. But she's looking into the lobby. Holes, haloed with cracks, in the thick glass door. And five feet beyond the doors, Heather lies sprawled on the floor.

Neely shouts, "Heather's hit!" Then to Buck, who's already on his way to his patrol, who hesitates at that news, "Buck, go! *Go!*"

She doesn't wait to see what he does, knowing he'll do what he must, which is to pursue the Toyota. Instead, she pushes through the doors and kneels beside Heather.

Five shots, and every one of them was for Neely Jones. And every one of them missed her.

But at least one didn't miss Heather Blessing.

Chapter 44

HEATHER IS ALIVE, TRYING TO sit up, and when Neely kneels beside her, Heather clings to her like a terrified child. "Oh *Lord,* Neely, what happened? What *happened?*"

The lobby is suddenly filled with deputies shouting the same question. Lieutenant Booker bursts through the jail wing's door; Whit Chaffee, Darrell Logan, Kevin Locksey, and Lonnie Weaver come barreling out of the hall door.

"Drive-by shooting," Neely says. "Someone give me a handkerchief!"

Two are thrust at her. Neely presses them hard against Heather's right thigh, where the black panty hose is laddered, and blood pours out, pooling on the floor.

"Whit, you and Darrell," Neely snaps. "Buck took off after the perp—give him some backup!"

Chaffee and Logan head for the doors at a run, but Logan stops to ask, "Where *is* Buck?"

"How the hell would I know? Use your *radio!*" Then while Logan scrambles out the door, "Lonnie, call for an ambulance, and tell them to have the ER ready for a gunshot wound. Then try to find Sally Greenleaf. Kevin, you and Mike start looking for bullets. There should be five, unless Heather's got one in her leg."

Lieutenant Booker asks, "What'd you want me to do?"

"Who's minding the jail?"

"Nobody." And, taking the hint, he heads back into the jail wing.

Heather looks down at her wounded leg and wails, "Oh, darn, that was a brand-new pair of panty hose."

Neely laughs at that. "You should be getting hazard pay."

"Guess so. Oh, Neely, it hurts. It really hurts."

"I know." She eases the pressure on the wound, but only slightly. The handkerchiefs are sodden, her hand wet with blood.

It's at that point that Neely realizes someone is missing.

Curtis McMinn. He was in the briefing room when she and Buck left her office.

"Kev? Where's Curtis?"

Kevin Locksey draws a circle with a felt pen on the back wall of the lobby. "Here's one of the slugs. Curtis? Maybe in the john. I'll go see."

He starts for the hall door, passing Lonnie Weaver, who comes out into the lobby just long enough to tell Neely, "Ambulance is on the way, and they've got a new doc in the ER. Trauma specialist from Portland. And I got hold of Heather's sister. She'll be at the hospital."

Heather murmurs weakly, "Sally? Oh, that's nice. . . ."

Again, Lonnie and Kevin Locksey pass in the doorway. McMinn trails after Kevin.

Neely doesn't ask where he's been. She only says curtly, "Get outside, Sergeant, and keep that door clear."

The vultures are already gathering.

WITHIN HALF AN HOUR, THE crisis is over. Heather has been whisked away to the hospital; four of the bullets have been found, and the other is undoubtedly in Heather's leg, since there's no exit wound; and the reporters and the curious have been been dispersed or lost interest.

But Buck, Chaffee, and Logan are still out looking for the Toyota.

Neely goes into her office, stopping first in the bathroom to wash Heather's blood off her hands. Why is it the innocent seem to be paying such a high price just for being near the new sheriff?

Was that why Jan was murdered?

The Whisperer would have her believe so.

Neely looks into the mirror, shocked at what she sees there. Something hard and bitter in the set of that mouth, the obsidian glint in the eyes. She doesn't remember seeing this face before.

Irritably, she turns away and goes into her office.

And realizes that someone has been in here during her absence. When she left the office, the only drawer open was the third drawer in the file cabinet, where Heather found Giff's package of evidence. That drawer is now closed, and the fourth is open. Two of the drawers in her desk are ajar an inch or so. She opens all the drawers, notes the disarray. This was not a careful search. Curtis McMinn is not a careful man. Then she looks toward the coffee table.

Not a trace of dirt on the table, and the moth orchid hasn't been moved. She smiles at the monkey-faced guardians. Good job, guys.

But if McMinn had time to search this room, did he also have time to phone someone about her discovery of Giff's evidence? McMinn was looking into the office when Heather showed it to Neely. Could he tell what it was at that distance?

Maybe he could guess.

Neely pulls a folded document out of her shirt pocket: the search warrant for Andrea Olenick's apartment. Had McMinn heard her tell Buck about this warrant? Unlikely; but if McMinn *did* hear her . . .

The only deputy Neely trusts is Buck, and he's still out chasing the phantom of the Toyota. The risk in confronting a suspect without backup was indelibly impressed on her at the police academy, but nothing was said about what to do if you don't trust your backup.

Yet Andrea might be expecting the search, preparing for it. This warrant could be worthless if Neely doesn't serve it now.

She can't wait for Buck.

Still, she leaves a message on his desk. The time, Andrea's name and address, and the words *search warrant*.

Chapter 45

AT 4:45 P.M. WHEN NEELY drives into the parking lot behind Bayview Manor, saffron-gray clouds hang oppressively low, and the wind has turned to the southwest again. Andrea Olenick is taking a bag of groceries out of the passenger seat of her red Saab convertible. She heads for the stairs without looking in Neely's direction.

At least Neely feels confident now that Andrea hasn't been forewarned about the search warrant. Otherwise, she wouldn't have been out shopping for groceries. Neely drives up behind the Saab and parks, then hurries to the stairs, takes them two at a time, and arrives on the second-floor breezeway just as Andrea unlocks her front door.

Andrea turns, startled. The wind blows her auburn hair, veiling her face. Her white sweats are the kind that come from exclusive sportswear shops and cost a couple of hundred dollars. The athletic shoes probably set her back just as much.

But they're Converses. Not Nikes.

She demands, "What the hell do *you* want?"

"This is a search warrant, Andrea."

"What?" She puts the groceries down, snatches the warrant out of Neely's hand. "Damn it, this is *bizarre*. I'm calling my lawyer. And I will *not* let you search my apartment until I talk to him."

"Well, I'm afraid you will. That warrant gives me the right to search your apartment whether you approve or not. It also gives me the right to arrest you if you don't cooperate."

"This is *harassment*! And you're enjoying it, aren't you?" Andrea picks up the grocery bag and goes into her apartment, pushing the door back so hard, it cracks against the wall. Neely follows her, catches the door as it bounces back, then closes it behind her. Andrea turns left into the kitchen, dumps the groceries on a counter, then stalks past Neely across the beige living room, around the Bowflex, to the couch by the north windows. "I'm *still* calling my lawyer," she insists.

"That's your privilege." And while Andrea angrily punches numbers on the phone on the end table, Neely looks around the room, concentrating particularly on the bookshelves.

Andrea apparently doesn't collect souvenirs or objects of any sort. She collects books. Nonfiction, mostly, but not confined to her area of expertise. Neely finds shelves of history, archaeology, anthropology, earth sciences, astronomy. She smiles at the thought that Andrea will no doubt find Neely's mother's name in some of the astronomy books.

But there's nothing on these shelves remotely resembling computer discs or the steno pads Jan kept his field notes in.

Andrea's exchange with her lawyer ends with a vehement "Shit!" and the slam of the receiver into its cradle. Neely turns to face her.

"Okay," Andrea says, stalking toward her like an angry lioness. "But the search is limited to the items specified in the warrant." She opens the warrant, scans the fine print, and her face goes slack. "A handgun? I *told* you about that damned gun. I gave it back to Don!"

"I called Donald Grabenhorst at his home in Everett to verify your story."

Andrea would've made a good actress, Neely thinks as she watches her strong, expressive features register disgust and contempt. She says, "I suppose Donny the Prick told you I still have the gun."

"No. He said he never gave you a gun. *Or* anything else. He said you were only a customer at the restaurant he managed, that he never dated you, and certainly never shared an apartment with you."

Andrea's face floods with red; her capable hands lock into fists. "That bastard! He's *lying*! Can't you see that?"

"Why would he do that?"

"Because he's a skirt-chasing son of a bitch and a pathological liar!" She starts to turn away, then looks at Neely speculatively. "You said you called him at home?"

"Yes. This morning, about eight-thirty."

"Was his wife there?"

"She answered the phone."

Andrea nods, a bitter smile tugging at her lips. "Wait here."

Before Neely can respond, she disappears through the door on the west wall. Neely follows her, turning left down a hall to a bedroom. Andrea doesn't object. She's too intent on searching a dresser drawer. Finally, she finds a ring case covered in midnight blue velvet.

She hands it to Neely. "So Donald says I was *just* a customer, that he never gave me *anything*?"

Neely opens the box. Inside is a diamond solitaire, and it's impressive—at least two carats.

Andrea says, "The jeweler's name is inside the lid. See it? Nathan Jansen—Westport, Oregon."

"Well, that tells me where the box came from, but not whether the ring originally belonged in the box, or how you acquired either one."

"Well, then, I would suggest that, first, you look inside

the band and read what's engraved there. Second, talk to Nathan Jansen, for God's sake. He'll remember who bought a rock like that. Besides, Don made such a production of it, Jansen could never forget."

The band is gold and wide enough for an easily legible inscription: "Don and Andrea, always and forever."

"Take it!" Andrea insists. "Take it to Jansen and *ask* him."

"I will." Neely puts the ring in the box and slips it into a pocket, then uses her notebook to write a receipt and hands it to Andrea. "You still haven't explained why Don would lie to a sheriff."

"Because he's a bastard!" She closes her eyes a moment, then adds, "Probably because his wife was there. He wouldn't want her to know we'd lived together or been engaged. He damn sure wouldn't want Wifey and me comparing notes. I might tell her that when he bought me that diamond, he had two other bedmates on the side—including one of the girls from the Jade. I was lucky I didn't end up with AIDS. When I found out, I threw him and all his junk out, including that stupid gun. But I kept the ring. I figured I'd earned it."

There is in Andrea's expressive face something Neely recognizes: grief. But in Andrea's case, it isn't grief for a loved one's death, but grief for the death of love.

Andrea lifts her chin in splendid defiance. "So, you're welcome to search for that gun. You won't find it *here.*"

Neely knows Andrea may be right, but as an officer of the law, she can't take a suspect's word for it. And at the moment, there are the other items on the search warrant to consider. She asks, "Where's your computer?"

Andrea hedges: "I do most of my computer work in my office at the center."

Neely doesn't argue, but leaves the bedroom and walks down the hall, opening every door she passes. Closets, two baths, two more bedrooms. The bedroom with the view of Chinook Bay has been converted into a home office, equipped with a computer, printer, and fax. Andrea shadows Neely every step of the way, glaring now from a few feet away as Neely surveys the office.

"Andrea, you deleted every document on *Medusae kotii* from Jan's computer and took his backup discs and notes. Where are they?"

"I don't know what you're talking about."

"Then I'll have to find them myself." She goes to a bookshelf stacked with boxes of discs, takes a box off the shelf, pulls the discs out one by one, reads the labels, then tosses them aside like Frisbees.

"What are you *doing*!" Andrea shrills. "Those are in *order*!"

Neely takes another box from the shelf, flips through the discs, tosses them, reaches for the next box. "I don't have time for a neat search, Andrea."

"You bitch! Stop it! *Stop* it!"

"You have two alternatives. You can refuse to cooperate, in which case I'll have to keep looking—and disrupting your filing system. Or you can tell me where you put the stolen discs and notebooks."

"Stolen! I had a *right* to that information! We worked on that project *together*! This is personal, isn't it? You're still *jealous* of me! You always were." She looms, taut and immensely fit, physically powerful. "And you figure the damn jelly is going to be worth a lot of money, and you want your cut! This so-called search doesn't have *anything* to do with a police investigation!"

Neely feels her body responding to Andrea's tension, readying itself, her feet planted for balance and leverage. "The damn jelly is all yours, Andrea. If it does turn out to be worth anything, it should be shared with Jan's sister's sons, but that's up to you. And this search has *everything* to do with the investigation. Jan was working at his computer before he was attacked. I want to know what he was working on. If it was just field notes, fine. But if the last thing he typed has something to do with his murder, I want to see it. And if that means I have to arrest you for impeding justice, I'll do it."

Andrea doesn't move, but gradually the tension seeps out of her, until she's limp and visibly shaking. "Okay."

The word is spoken so softly, Neely can barely hear it. And, unexpectedly, Andrea is crying, her mouth an aching grimace. "We worked so *hard* on that project. Oh God, I just wanted something that was *ours*—Jan's and mine— even if he *didn't* love me. Colleagues and friends, that's all we could ever be. That's what he told me. So sweet and so devastating . . . And the next day—he was dead."

Neely's skin feels chilled, as if she were immersed in cold ocean water. She can't speak. She can only wait in silence until Andrea gets herself under control.

Finally, Andrea looks at her, a hard look full of pain. "How do you *do* it? You talk about him like it's just another case to you. He didn't love me, but I can't stop crying. And he *did* love you."

Neely shivers in the cold currents, and she's surprised she can speak. "I don't have the luxury of crying for him. Not yet."

For a while, Andrea seems to consider that; then she nods. "He did love you. If you ever were jealous of me, you had no reason to be."

"I know. Thank you, Andrea."

"Yeah." She pulls in a deep breath, goes to her desk, and opens a drawer. "These are his backup discs and field notebooks. I haven't looked at them since I put them in here Thursday morning after . . ."

Neely forces herself to go to the desk and look in the drawer. "Any idea which disc was in his computer that morning?"

"Yes." She pulls out a loose disc from between two of the boxes. "This one." Then she sits down and boots up the computer, slides the disc into a slot, and clicks up its window. Neely leans over her shoulder to read the titles under the icons.

There.

CORRES W/ DR. NIRI RE S. CLAUSII.

Niri. Niri-san. She can hear him speaking the word, dragging out the vowels. And *S. Clausii*? Santa Claus.

Dr. S. Benjamin Nicholass.

She points to the icon."Can you—date and time."

Andrea highlights the document, then runs the arrow down the FILE menu to GET INFO. She whispers, "Oh, Neely, this is it. Last modified Wednesday, November sixth, ten-twenty-one P.M." She clicks the document open.

It's short. Half a page, single-spaced. Neely's name is at the top. She turns away, her breath stopped in the icy currents of remembrance.

Hold on. Damn it, you've *got* to read this. Jan's last words.

Ain't electronics grand?

Neely—
Something strange going on. I finished in the darkroom twenty minutes ago and was on my way to my office when I saw the loading dock doors were open and a car parked outside. Headlights on. Couldn't see anything for the lights. Heard a voice say something like Twelve hundred this time. Somebody answered, couldn't tell who or what they said. Then first voice said, That's not enough anymore. I hid in my office, looked out window in door. Heard car drive off, doors close. Saw Ben and Curtis come down hall. C. carrying Intel carton full of Pentium processors. I know because he stumbled, spilled some. Missed one when he picked them up. I found it. Followed, listened outside Ben's office. He said something about microscope case, and don't drop any more of them. I think Ben hiding processors in Just saw Ben leave C still here doesnt know Im

here cant call you he might see light ona phone Ben mustbe
smugling procssors to baja in case takesit every trip never
usesmicroscoe never does any resear

Neely tries not to think about why the message ended
at that point. She asks levelly, "Would you make me a printout, Andrea?"

Chapter 46

THE DISK AND PRINTOUT ARE in Neely's shirt pocket—over her heart.

She drives away from Andrea's apartment in a rage. But not at Andrea. Never again will she feel rage for Andrea Olenick—not even the atavistic, jealousy-threaded rage black women sometimes feel for attractive white women for whom everything seems to come so easy. Especially men. But nothing comes easily for Andrea.

Before Neely left the apartment, she returned the ring to her.

No, this rage isn't for Andrea, and there's an element of calculation in it. Without it, Neely would dissolve into helpless agony. She can't let that happen. Not now, when she knows the truth.

But the question is, How can she *prove* the truth?

Precisely.

The Whisperer used that word more than once, and it's one of Ben Nicholass's favorites. She should've caught that.

She brakes as she reaches Highway 101, makes a right turn, and drives north over the arc of the Chinook Bay Bridge.

Proof is a catch-22. Heathman has access to the expertise for voiceprint comparison between the tapes of the Whisperer's calls and Nicholass's voice, as well as DNA comparison with the saliva on the payoff envelope, both of which would provide some of the proof. But she can't ask for voiceprint comparisons or DNA profiles on a pillar of the community like Dr. S. Benjamin Nicholass.

Not without proof.

Culpepper would wet his pants at the idea. And Judge Lay would wet his pants at the idea of issuing a search warrant for Nicholass's house. Yet that's probably where the Pentium processors—proof of Nicholass's involvement in smuggling—are hidden now. He wouldn't leave them at the center after murdering Jan, knowing it would be crawling with cops the next morning. And he can't board *Poseidon* until the captain unlocks the gate to the boarding ramp.

What a sweet scam it was.

Nicholass must have an accomplice at Intel, who stole the processors and delivered them to the center on the eve of *Poseidon*'s voyages to Baja—and left an unidentified fingerprint on the processor in Jan's pocket. Nicholass hid the processors in his microscope case, where it was unlikely Mexican customs officials would look, and if they did, he could afford to cross their palms liberally. In Cabo San Lucas, he exchanged the processors for a caseful of virtually priceless artifacts. When he returned to Westport, he called George Tarbet from a pay phone, and the next day, Tarbet and Spinski left for the Caymans, returning a few days later with the cash to pay Nicholass for the artifacts. Then Tarbet set up shop in his secret showroom.

Not that the scam always went smoothly. Last year on December 28, Giff Wills somehow stumbled onto it and began blackmailing Nicholass.

And last Wednesday night, Jan Koto also stumbled onto the scam. Was he murdered because Nicholass didn't think Jan would be as "cooperative" as Giff? Or simply because Curtis McMinn always hits or shoots first and thinks later— if he ever thinks at all.

Neely bangs her fist against the steering wheel.

Where is the *proof* ? The last words of a murdered man?

Neely stops at the red light at the junction of Highway 13, waits impatiently for the right-turn signal to change.

The problem is, Jan said he saw Nicholass *leave* the center.

Of course he left the center. It was Curtis McMinn who discovered Jan in his office; whose face and the knuckles of his right hand were bruised in a struggle with Jan; who shot Jan with a 9-mm gun—the caliber of his duty weapon; who had handcuffs handy to secure the wounded and perhaps unconscious Jan to the leg of his desk—that was the ligature that bruised but didn't burn or cut Jan's wrist. And later it was McMinn who disposed of a bloodstained painters' tarp at the recycling center, where Danny Murchison mistook him for a ghost. Or an angel.

And it's McMinn whose loyal, ever-pregnant wife will swear that he was home all of Wednesday night. Sick as a dog.

But it wasn't McMinn who conceived the plan to drown Jan in the medusa pool. He doesn't have that much imagination. Nor the imagination to conceive the graffiti that made Riker a suspect, although McMinn probably provided information about Riker's history of vandalism.

Ben Nicholass may have left the center after the delivery of the Pentium processors, but he returned. Neely is sure of that.

After McMinn shot and hit and handcuffed Jan, what would he do?

He would phone his boss.

Uh, Ben, there's been a little glitch here at the center.

McMinn is the weak link. If she could interrogate him . . .

Sure, Neely. Just send a couple of deputies to arrest him. Or arrest him yourself. And find out the true meaning of the word *mutiny.*

We take care of our own.

Someone is honking in the line of cars behind her; the light has turned green. She swings onto Highway 13 and begins signaling for a left turn into the courthouse parking lot.

Then there's Giff's murder. And the white sports car seen driving west from Giff's house at 5:30 A.M. She has no doubt one of the tires on Nicholass's Mercedes SLK will be a perfect match for the track in the mud next to Giff's driveway, and the footprints in the sawdust in the garage will be a perfect match for Nicholass's Nikes. Neely turns into the parking lot, drives slowly toward the TCSO slots.

But Nicholass didn't kill Giff. The MO was too coolly efficient. That was Spinski's work. Still, she's sure Nicholass made the frenzied search for the evidence Giff was blackmailing him with.

But how does she *prove* that Giff was blackmailing Nicholass?

Well, there's Giff's evidence: the jade figurine and the photographs—*if* there are any recoverable fingerprints on them.

She turns into the parking space next to the blue Toyota pickup.

It's too much to hope that Buck caught the man who shot Heather Blessing: the Whisperer. *S. clausii.* Dr. S. Benjamin Nicholass.

Buck is leaning against the tailgate, apparently watching her from behind his mirrored shades as she gets out of the patrol and asks, "Any news about Heather?"

"Yeah. Sally called. Heather'll need surgery to get the slug out, but the doc says there'll be no permanent damage. You served the search warrant."

It's a question, even if he gives it no questioning inflection. Neely only nods, frowning at the pickup. "Where'd you find it?"

"In the parking lot at the East Village Mall. Nobody in it."

"Sure. Probably left his own car there earlier. All he

had to do was roll up the bottom of the ski mask, and he had a cap to cover his hair. People might notice that otherwise. Of course, the beard—"

Jesus, what is she doing running off at the mouth to Buck? Tired. She's getting too damned tired to think.

She asks, "Was it hot-wired?"

"No." Buck's mirrored gaze stays with her for a few seconds; then he reaches into his pants pocket. "This was in the ignition." He hands her a key ring ornamented with a polished water agate.

For a moment, she feels light-headed. "These are the extra keys Jan and I kept in the top drawer in the chest in our bedroom—the chest under the samurai sword."

"Well, Riker has what you'd call an airtight alibi for the drive-by, since he's in our jail. So, how did the drive-by perp get those keys?"

"From Riker. I'd better have a talk with Yew-gene. No. Lisker first. He's more likely to cave."

"I'll sit in," Buck says, and follows her into the lobby.

·

Chapter 47

WHEN BURTON "LASH" LISKER IS brought into Interrogation A, he attempts a cocky stance, but his bald head and the orange T-shirt and sweatpants hanging on his scarecrow body give him a clownish aspect.

Buck is standing by the door. He says, "Sit down, Burton."

Lisker glares at him, but he sits, choosing the chair across the table from Neely. Buck takes the chair at the end of the table, leans back with his arms folded, muscles straining at the seams of his sleeves. Neely gives the tape recorder the requisite information, then places a small tan envelope, sealed in a plastic evidence bag, in the center of the table.

"You and Yew-gene look to be coming up in the world, Burton," she says amiably. "You're in the torch-for-hire business now. Trouble is, that's the kind of felony judges get really uptight about."

"Don't know what're you talkin' about, bitch."

Neely pushes the envelope an inch closer to him. "Where'd you and Yew-gene get this, Burton?"

"Don't know nothin' about that money."

"What money?"

"In the fuckin' enve—" He stops, his Adam's apple bouncing.

"How did you know there was money in the envelope?" When he only stares at her in sweating silence, Neely says, "Burton, arson carries five to ten hard time. Now, I know arson isn't your style. Graffiti, cross burning, vandalism, yes. But arson is in another league. You're just lucky no one was in the house, or you'd be up for felony murder."

There's the look of a cornered animal in Lisker's eyes, and an involuntary grunt escapes him, but otherwise he remains silent.

Neely shrugs. "Well, maybe you'll like the state pen, Burton. Regular food, regular hours, regular work. Of course, some of the inmates have strange ideas about entertaining themselves, but you'll have *plenty* of time to work out and build up some muscle."

With that, he emits a mewing moan between clenched teeth, then wails, "I didn't want nothin' to *do* with it! Bomber'd already bailed. I shoulda bailed, too, but, shit, Dirk'd go postal! He'd *kill* me!"

Neely catches Buck's brief smile, but she remains focused on Lisker. "Okay, Lash, if you help us, maybe you won't have to do as much time, and you won't do it in the same place Yew-gene is going. So, where did this money come from?"

"I don't *know*. Don't figure Dirk does, neither. See, we was just hangin' out in the Dog—"

"When was that?"

"Uh, musta been Thursday afternoon. Anyway, Dirk gets a phone call. Somebody asks for him by name. Afterward, he tells me we got a job of work to do, and we're supposed to go to the men's john in the state park, and there'd be an envelope underneath the trash can."

"Did Dirk say who this caller was?"

"He didn't know. Said whoever it was whispered everything."

Neely nods. Now she can add conspiracy to commit arson to Nicholass's roster of unprovable crimes. "So you picked up the envelope. Did you see anyone? Someone in a car—a white sports car?"

"Didn't see nobody and no cars. And right then, I *told* Dirk, I told him we oughta just keep the money and forget the fire. What could the guy do? I mean, whoever it was on the phone. But Dirk kinda liked the idea of torchin' your place. Said it'd be a totally excellent high, watchin' the coon's house burn. 'Course, we didn't get to see much of it."

"Too bad. Did the Whisperer give Dirk any other instructions? Like to retrieve something from the house before he torched it?"

"Yeah. Said to look for spare keys and leave 'em where we found the money."

"And when you found the spare car keys, you just couldn't resist that samurai sword, could you?" Lisker's face and scalp go pink, but he makes no response. Neely asks, "Did you see anyone pick up the keys?"

"Shit, no. We was long gone. Headed up River Road."

Neely looks at Buck, but apparently he has no questions. She rises and goes to the door, knocks for Swenson. "Okay, Lash. I'll put in a word for you with the DA."

When Neely and Buck reach the lobby, she notes the circles on the wall penned around craters where bullets have been dug out. "Chief, what was the caliber of those bullets?"

"Nine millimeter."

Again, the caliber of McMinn's duty weapon. But McMinn was in the TCSO at the time of the drive-by, searching her office. She asks, "Has Curtis showed up with a nonissue weapon lately?"

"Yeah. Said a neighbor kid stole it. Hell, I meant to check today to make sure he got it back. How'd you know about his duty weapon?"

She doesn't feel ready to tell Buck that she thinks McMinn shot Jan, or that she has now come to an even more far-fetched conclusion: that Nicholass, knowing McMinn's passion for guns and how difficult he would find it to dispose of any gun, took the Glock away from him.

She shrugs and says, "Lucky guess."

They part company, and Neely goes to her office, checks the moth orchid, then sits down at her desk to call Giff's house. She learns that Heathman returned to Portland, but he'll be back tomorrow. He left two messages: First, the tarp found at the recycling center has paint smears matching the fresh paint in the center's museum, and bloodstains matching the victim's blood type.

And the second message: The bullet fired at her on the beach came from the same gun Jan was shot with.

She keeps gathering more evidence, but none of it will convince the DA that Nicholass should even be regarded as a suspect, much less that he's guilty of murder, conspiracy to commit arson, smuggling Mexican antiquities, and trafficking in stolen . . .

Pentium III Xeon processors . . .

Person doesn't keep his eyes open, he's going to fall into the first pothole he comes to.

Well, Gramma, I've fallen into a lot of them lately.

If Jan was right, if Nicholass did hide the processors in his microscope case Wednesday night, ready to carry on board *Poseidon* the next morning, when the ship was scheduled to sail, they're *not* at his house now; they're still in his office at the center.

Thursday morning, the day Jan's body was discovered, the day her world shattered around her like a cage of mirrors, when Neely first went into Nicholass's office, the microscope was on a bookshelf, the case on the floor in front of the shelf, and next to the case . . .

A cardboard carton marked with an Intel logo.

Yes. But she doesn't remember seeing the carton again. The microscope case, however, was still there when she interviewed Nicholass. And later Thursday morning, Nicholass tried to leave the center with the microscope case and a briefcase. But Heathman refused to let anything leave the building and followed him to make sure he returned them to his office.

Nicholass hasn't been allowed into the building since.

But why didn't he take the microscope case and its incriminating cargo home Wednesday night after aiding and abetting Jan's murder?

Perps always fuck up, sooner or later.

And Nicholass isn't a pro, although he has access to one. But Spinski had nothing to do with Jan's murder. He'd have made a cleaner job of it. So, maybe Nicholass was a little strung out after killing a man he'd known and worked with for two years. Maybe he forgot the case.

And the next morning? He had at least twenty minutes after he got to the center and "discovered" the body before Neely arrived. But Andrea was in the building. Maybe he was afraid she'd see him and wonder why he was carting equipment out to his car. In fact, he could easily have gotten it past her: She was busy in Jan's office deleting his computer files. But Nicholass wouldn't know that.

Or maybe it was simply arrogance that made him decide to leave the case in plain sight in his office, assuming the representatives of the law would be too stupid to even notice it.

Neely takes a long breath. The microscope case, at least, is still in Nicholass's office, and that plus Jan's message should be enough to convince—

She's staring at the closed door into Heather's office, but not seeing it, and when it opens, suddenly and forcefully, it startles her.

Speak of the devil . . .

Owen Culpepper charges in, topcoat on, his briefcase in his left hand, and demands, "Have you questioned Riker yet?"

"No, sir, but I—"

"Good, good. I'll handle the interrogation. The public defender's office says Carl Harding has agreed to defend

Riker. He'll be here tomorrow morning." Then the DA's tone and attitude shift into uncompromising sternness: "Neely, I've made a decision."

Good for you. "Yes, sir. What about?"

"The oceanographic center. It's intolerable to keep it sealed off so long. If Heathman and his team haven't found everything they need by now, they'll *never* find it. I just called Dr. Nicholass to inform him that the center is now officially unsealed."

"You *what?*" Neely bolts to her feet. "Mr. Culpepper, you're making a *serious* mistake."

He stiffens at that. "May I remind you that as head of law enforcement in this county, the decision is mine to make."

"But I have new *evidence!*" She fumbles in her shirt pocket for the printout, then thrusts it at him. "Read this!"

"What is it? Where'd you get it?"

"From Andrea Olenick. She had the disc that was in Jan's computer the night he was murdered. There was a message on that disk, addressed to me. It was the last thing he typed. *Read* it!"

Culpepper tips his head back to get his bifocals in focus on the paper. His frown intensifies as he reads, and Neely expects some expression of consternation or at least amazement when he finishes it.

The last thing she expects is laughter.

But that's what she gets as Culpepper tosses the printout on her desk. "Nice try, Neely."

She stares at him, bewildered, while his amusement reverts to anger. "Neely, you must think I'm a total fool! This is a pitiful subterfuge. Really, I never expected you to sink so low, but after your accusation against Giff, I'm not surprised that you'd try to tar Dr. Nicholass and Sergeant McMinn. Well, you *won't* get away with it!"

Neely holds on to the word *subterfuge.* "You think I *invented* this message?"

"Don't look so insulted. Of course you did! Now, I realize you've been under considerable strain lately, and I can understand—"

"You don't understand *anything*!"

"I understand that you're going off the deep end, and I advise you to take some time off. If you persist with this libelous behavior, I'll charge you with malfeasance. I *mean* that, Neely!"

Is that a glint of triumph in his myopic eyes? Does he think he'll be rid of the nigger who would be sheriff so easily?

She says tightly, "I did *not* invent that message. You can ask—"

"Spare me." He heads for the door, but there stops to add, "The Westport Oceanographic Center is no longer a crime scene, and you have no authority there. If you want in, you'll have to pay admission like everybody else." Then he storms out, slamming the door behind him.

Chapter 48

AGAIN AND AGAIN, THE SLAMMING door echoes in Neely's mind, until her head aches with it.

Yes, I think you're a fool, Mr. Owen Culpepper, sir, the honorable district attorney of Taft County. *Fool.*

But I have nothing to lose, Mr. District Attorney.

Can you even imagine what that means?

Freedom.

Oh, yassuh, us nigger bitches truly *do* like the sound of that word.

I *will* have justice. You, Mr. District Attorney, the honorable honky hick good ol' boy bastard fool—*you* can't stop me.

Neely takes a deep breath and lets it out slowly. She's still standing behind the desk. She checks her watch: 6:10. Looks to her right, out the window. Already dark outside, and the pink-orange streetlights are on. A sheet of newspaper blows along the asphalt, shifting shapes with the wind. Storm coming in.

The question she must consider is, What will Nicholass do now?

Go to the center. Retrieve the microscope case.

She can't go *into* the center, because she can't risk tainting any evidence she might uncover. But she *can* wait outside the building until Nicholass leaves with the evidence.

If she intends to wait in ambush for him, she must move now. He's got a head start. How much of a head start, she doesn't know, but she has no time to waste. Neely reaches for her Stetson on the file cabinet, and it's only then that she realizes the door to the briefing room is open, and Buck Dolin is standing just outside the Dispatch Center.

Watching her. Big hands curled ready at his sides. Waiting.

Waiting for her to ask him for backup?

She knows now that he wasn't involved in Jan's murder or Giff's or anything else in this tangled web. She can trust him. At least she can trust his honesty. But can she trust him to follow *her* orders if that means arresting Sgt. Curtis McMinn?

We take care of our own.

No. She might trust *him* but why should he trust *her* that far?

And that means that once again she must confront a suspect without backup.

Neely heads for the lobby, grabs her jacket from the coatrack by the door, shrugs it on as she strides through Heather's darkened office, and, as she crosses the lobby, hones her resolve with the memory of Heather lying bleeding on this floor.

Outside, the wind hits hard and cold. No rain yet, but its electric scent is in the wind. She looks down the row of patrols and personal vehicles. McMinn's T-bird is missing.

She gets into the Toyota, pushes her key into the ignition, and turns on the headlights. The dash lights glint on her key ring and remind her that one of the keys on the ring is the master key for the center. Heathman has the other master key, and he's in Portland.

She finds herself laughing. No humor in it. Only irony.

It doesn't matter. Ben Nicholass will get into the center to retrieve the incriminating evidence one way or another.

BY 6:30, AFTER CRUISING THE three streets bordering the Westport Oceanographic Center twice and seeing neither a car in the staff parking lot nor a light in the building, Neely finds an observation point near the south end of Frigate Street, which runs along the east side of the center's property. The house she chooses is across the street, with a clear view of the staff parking lot and the loading dock at the end of the far wing. It's an old gentrified cottage, one of three in a row displaying short-term rental signs, which means it's unlikely at this time of year that any of them are occupied. She backs between tall unkempt hedges into the narrow driveway of the middle house.

Then she turns the motor off, watching with a sinking feeling as the first drops of rain explode against the windshield.

Chapter 49

THE WINDSHIELD WIPERS WHIP BACK and forth furiously as Buck Dolin squints over the steering wheel of his black Bronco into the murk of rain. It doesn't help that his headlights are off.

Neely's headlights were off, too, but he saw the blue Toyota pickup in the corner streetlight when she turned south on Frigate Street. She's settled in somewhere on those two blocks. That's a guess, but he saw her drive around the three sides of the center twice.

Irritably, Buck turns on the defroster. Now the sky is dumping frozen rain, and the windshield's fogging up. Lousy night for surveillance, or whatever it is she's got in mind.

He puts the Bronco in gear and drives east along North First past Frigate to Gull Street. There he turns right, and after two blocks makes another right on South Second. But he doesn't continue to Frigate. Instead, he turns right into the alley behind Frigate.

Shit, he's going to have to scout for her on foot.

Buck is willing to let Neely do her thing, whatever it is, but he knows about grief, knows the tricks it plays with your head. He remembers Neely on her knees with that sword in her hands.

Like she was ready to commit hara-kiri.

Jan Koto was a good man, and what was between him and Neely was something special. Only a person lucky enough to have that kind of special thing in his life could recognize it in somebody else's.

Buck recognized it.

If Val hadn't been killed by cancer, if she'd been murdered, he would've had the killer's blood on his hands. Or died trying.

Well, if Neely figures she knows who did Jan Koto, Buck can understand her heading out on her own. That asshole Culpepper cut her off at the knees, and besides, who would she call for backup? The guys hadn't been exactly enthusiastic about her taking over Giff's office.

And Buck Dolin? Does she have any reason to think she could look to him for backup?

Trouble is, it's all messed up with the black thing. You can't deal with people in black and white. Not *real* people. Real people go to shades of gray.

But maybe he just doesn't get it.

Buck sighs, reluctantly facing the prospect of sloshing around the neighborhood in the rain trying to find Neely's pickup. She must have her radio on her. He has a notion to call her.

Where the hell *are* you, Neely Jones?

No. She'll have to play this out her way.

Chapter 50

THE HOT TUB SMELLS OF cedar and is set in a bay of floor-to-ceiling windows. This is George Tarbet's favorite place in his luxurious lower-level apartment, the only place where the pain that eternally burns within his bones is quenched to any degree.

Sandy Spinski calls this room the gym, and behind Tarbet, he's grunting and sweating in his red bikini trunks. Lifting weights, straining in pursuit of bodily perfection.

Tarbet floats in the warm, bubbling currents and regards the twisted imperfection of his own body with sardonic irony. All things are relative, and with any luck, Sandy will grow old and one day find his perfect body a white gnarl of aching bones under fragile flesh.

Of course, this disease isn't a matter of age, and Sandy will probably escape its ravages. In fact, he'll probably never reach old age at all. Life expectancy is short in his line of work.

Replacing him will be difficult.

Tarbet looks at the windows. His lovely view is lost to pounding rain. The interior lights reflect on the glass in cascades of blue and green—the color of the walls and floor tiles. The music on the sound system is *La Mer*. Sandy hates it. Can't work out with that wimpy shit.

A discreet ring: the phone. Tarbet doesn't move. He listens to Sandy grunt and drop his weights, pad across the room to the juice bar.

"Yeah? Just a minute."

Sandy brings the cell phone to Tarbet. "Nicholass," he says, and pads back to his weights. Tarbet winces as he grasps the phone and brings it to his ear.

"Ben. You're calling from a pay phone?"

"Of course, Mr. Tarbet. I thought you'd want to know: The center and *Poseidon* have been officially unsealed."

"Then your influence with the DA finally prevailed?"

"Finally. I'll phone the scientific staff this evening. I've already called Captain Olsen. He'll alert the crew and be here early tomorrow morning. We should weigh anchor by noon. You'd better let Rivas know I'm coming. ETA, twenty-one days. Anyway, I'm going to the center now to check on the processors."

Tarbet's colorless eyes narrow as he tries to decide why that sounds an alarm in his mind, other than to remind him that Nicholass was incredibly negligent to leave the processors at the center after the unfortunate incident with Dr. Koto.

"Do they need checking, Ben? Wouldn't Curtis know if they'd been discovered?"

"Well, uh, probably. I just prefer to be safe, rather than sorry. In fact, I think I'll take them home."

"Why not leave them at the center, if it's no longer a crime scene?"

It takes Nicholass too long to answer that. "Well, I just . . . I don't trust Neely Jones."

Could it be, Tarbet wonders, that the esteemed Dr. Nicholass is planning to do a bunk? Those processors are worth at least a million on the black market. Señor Rivas is Tarbet's man and won't deal solely with Nicholass, but no doubt someone else will.

And Nicholass is the one who has the contact at Intel.

Tarbet says, "You assured me Sheriff Jones would resign."

"I may have, uh, underestimated her. But there's nothing she can do now. According to Curtis, she can't count on any backup from any of the deputies *or* from Culpepper. You don't need to be concerned, Mr. Tarbet. Everything's under control."

Tarbet finds that assurance less than convincing. But he sounds almost jovial when he says, "I'm glad to hear that. Good night, Ben."

He cuts Nicholass off and puts the phone on the rim of the hot tub.

Amateurs! This was an elegant scheme, but he shouldn't have let it become dependent on amateurs. Perhaps the time has come to move on. Or retire? Now, that *would* confound Sayson and associates.

Tomorrow, he could be on Grand Cayman. Tarbet closes his eyes and imagines a white-hot tropical sun warming his aching body. He's tired of Oregon's cold sodden winters. Sick to death of them.

Yes, the time has come.

But it would be a shame to leave a million dollars in purloined processors behind. Waste not, want not.

"Sandy, I have an errand for you."

"You ready to get out?"

"No. I want you to go to the oceanographic center—bearing in mind that you must lose the tail the DEA so thoughtfully provides—and when Ben arrives, which should be in the near future, I want you to take the processors off his hands. Bring them to me."

Sandy only nods, as if Tarbet had asked him to go out for a loaf of bread. "I'll get dressed."

Tarbet adds, "Quickly, I hope, Sandy, and you'd best arm yourself."

"Always do."

Chapter 51

THIS IS NOT GOING TO work.

Neely stares through a windshield opaque with rain and a salting of ice pellets. She turned the wipers on once, even at the risk of someone seeing them working on a supposedly empty vehicle, but that offered only distorted glimpses of streaked lights.

Damn it, damn this storm!

Never since she moved to the Oregon coast has she said that. She loves the ocean storms in all their exhilarating variation. But not now. Not when she needs so desperately to see what's going on in that parking lot and at the loading dock.

Well, there's only one alternative.

Neely opens the door against the wind, pulling her Stetson down tight. She eases the door shut, then makes her way to the end of the hedge-lined driveway. She can see the globe lights in both the public and staff parking lots as dim blurs. But no headlights.

She sprints across Frigate Street, slipping on windrows of sleet, splashing through water-filled potholes and a curb-deep stream in the gutter, then sloshes across a soggy lawn, and, with her shoes sodden, her pants soaked to the knees, reaches the building. The wide eaves cut off some of the rain, but not all of it, not with the wind behind it. She leans against the cedar siding and peers around the corner.

The staff parking lot is still empty. On the bay, *Poseidon* shines white, rocking in storm-driven waves.

She checks her watch: 6:50. Where the *hell* is Nicholass?

Or did she begin her vigil too late?

Chapter 52

DEA SPECIAL AGENT SCOTT SAYSON sits down at the kitchen table, contemplating a bucket of the Colonel's extra-crispy chicken, while Agent Joe Mirka works his way through a thigh, crumbs sifting down on the paper towel he's using for a plate. Joe loves the Colonel's chicken. Sayson is reaching the point where he knows that if he sees another take-out meal, he'll throw up.

But none of them are cooks or like washing dishes.

Sayson peels the flaky, oily skin off a drumstick and bites into the gray flesh. It's at that moment, with his mouth full and his hands greasy, that he hears Roger Levitt call out from the living room: "Got some action here."

Joe, who's going off duty, keeps chewing. Sayson wipes his hands on a paper towel as he heads for the darkened living room. Roger is at the west windows, a pair of infrared binoculars up to his face.

"What's happening?" Sayson asks.

"Looks like Sandy's taking the Porsche for a spin."

Sayson looks down the slope to Tarbet's house. His goddamned fortress. The rain on the windows distorts everything, but he can see the light in the open garage and Spinski's white Porsche backing out. Sayson's pulse accelerates. Damn, after all this time, it's amazing he can get excited about anything Spinski or Tarbet do.

Levitt says, "Sandy's probably just headed for the Jade. It's Saturday night, after all."

"Yeah, but the girls don't start their show till eight. I better see what he's up to." Sayson returns to the kitchen, grabs a couple of pieces of chicken, and wraps them in paper towels as he continues to the garage. "See you later, Joe."

"Say hi to the girls for me. Specially that little Latino babe."

Mirka's kidding. Or he expects Sayson to think he's kidding.

Sayson backs the maroon Ford out of the garage, drives south a block to intercept Spinski at the corner of Abalone and North Fourth.

There it is, fountaining into Sayson's headlights: the Porsche. And there's Spinski giving him the finger and a big grin.

Sayson is getting tired of the game. As tired as he is of take-out meals. Spinski expects Sayson to tail him, and he'll do his best to lose him. And Sayson will let Spinski lose him. What Spinski doesn't know is that on one of his visits to the Jade, his car, parked outside, acquired a non-factory-authorized piece of equipment: a radio locator.

Sayson plays along for a while, up and down the rain-swept streets of Westport; then he drops back and lets Spinski think he's lost his tail. Sayson returns to Highway 101 and drives south to the Jade. He waits near the sleazy neon-lit building for five minutes; then, when Spinski doesn't appear, drives north, listening for the ping.

Yeah. There it is. The courthouse?

No. Losing him.

Sayson U-turns in the middle of 101, goes back to the traffic light, and turns east on Highway 13.

The signal's coming in strong now.

He turns right on Ebbtide Street, switches off his headlights, and slows to a crawl, while the pinging gets louder and faster. He turns left on North First, in front of the Westport Oceanographic Center. The lights in the public parking lot are on, but it's empty. No lights in the building.

Jesus, there's the Porsche, parked on the left side of the street, just ahead. Sayson drives past, turns left at the next street, and parks the Ford, then, taking a deep breath, steps out into the wind and rain.

It's a damn monsoon. How do people *live* in a climate like this?

Soaked and chilled to the bone within seconds, Sayson works his way across lawns and finally reaches a bush a few yards from the Porsche.

It's empty.

Shit!

The oceanographic center? Why would Spinski be hanging around here?

Chapter 53

Neely takes her cold-numbed hands out of her pockets and turns her flashlight on just long enough to check her watch: 7:10.

Where *is* Nicholass?

The parking lot is dusted with melting sleet, but it's only raining now. Only? It's hard to think of this deluge as *only* anything. On the roof, the rain sputters like frying bacon, gurgles down the drainpipe at the corner. She leans against the damp cedar, closing her eyes to take in its clean, spicy scent.

And something else.

Her body reacts with a fight-or-flight quickening before she consciously identifies it.

The sour smell of human sweat. Male sweat.

She spins around, flicking on the flashlight in her left hand, her right hand going for her gun, but she doesn't reach it. Like light strobing on photographic film, fixing an image in a thousandth of a second, Sandro Spinski's face is burned into her mind.

Blond hair trailing wet on his smooth, unlined forehead.

The cutting edges of perfect teeth bared in a predatory smile.

Blue eyes so devoid of life they might as well be glass.

And she knows those eyes were the last thing some people saw before they died.

A huff of effort; he snaps the barrel of his gun across her face.

Her left cheek explodes in pain, crackling, jagged as lightning. Mouth full of liquid copper, blood spattering the sidewalk, raining blood and pain.

But she doesn't fall.

Spinski catches her, jerks her around, her back against him, pulls her gun out of the holster, and twists her left arm behind her.

"Stand *up,* bitch!"

Knees won't hold; face is coming apart. Right hand pressed to her throbbing cheek warm with blood pouring through her fingers.

But terror is a great clarifier. It puts pain in perspective.

What braces her rubbery knees and brings her mind and eyes into focus is the sensation of something cold and hard jammed against the back of her neck at the atlas joint. She can't see it, but she knows what it is: Spinski's Desert Eagle .44 Magnum automatic.

And she knows exactly what a bullet from that gun will do to her skull and brain.

Spinski pushes her forward. She stumbles, reaches out with her right hand for the wall. He's looking around the corner. His breath on her right ear is shallow, too fast. He's pumped.

Is this how you get your kicks, you bastard? Does this make you feel like a man?

Arrogant people make mistakes. They underestimate their victims.

Hold that thought.

Right. While you hold your face together.

Special Agent Scott Sayson, do you know where your subject is tonight? Or did he slip past you while you brooded on George Tarbet's sins?

Spinski whispers, "Yeah . . . here they come."

Headlights. Twin beams shaped out of needles of silver rain.

McMinn's T-Bird swings in from the entrance on the other side of the parking lot and stops in front of the loading dock, where the light over the door glitters on the gold. A few seconds later, Ben Nicholass's white Mercedes SLK appears. Nicholass parks next to McMinn. They get out of their cars and run up the three steps to the loading dock, where they stand in the rain, talking. Arguing, maybe.

"Come on, bitch. Let's go." Spinski wrenches her arm just short of the breaking point and prods her toward the loading dock.

He laughs—a sound as devoid of life as his glass eyes—and shouts, "Hey, Ben! Look what I found!"

Chapter 54

BEN NICHOLASS BLINKS, BUT IT doesn't go away: the apparition emerging out of the whipping curtains of rain into the pink glow from the light over the loading dock. At first, it seems to be one person moving with a strange gait; then it becomes two in a sort of lockstep.

Spinski?

What the hell is *he* doing here?

And that's Neely Jones he's pushing ahead of him, her left arm behind her back. She's got her right hand to her face, and her uniform is not just soaked, it's stained with something dark.

And what's *she* doing here? Anyone else would've taken the money and waved good-bye to Taft County long ago.

Nicholass shouts, "Sandy, where'd you find *her*?"

"Round the side of the building. I figure she was waiting for *you*. Come on, bitch—up the stairs." Spinski's grip tightens on the arm behind her back, and she stumbles on the steps and reaches out with her right hand to brace herself against the wall.

That's *blood* on the front of her uniform. Nicholass

stares at the three-inch-long gash across her left cheek, the streak of white bone.

Oh, God . . .

Spinski gets Neely up on the loading dock, and to Nicholass's relief, she again covers the wound with her hand. And looks at him. She stands there, soaked and bloody, with her clipped Negroid hair glistening with rain, and stares at him like a voodoo conjuror, her black eyes huge, hooded, emanating such potent hatred, Nicholass feels his pulse pounding, and he understands one thing very well: She knows.

She knows everything.

Spinski asks, "So, how come we're standing around in the rain? Open the goddamn door."

Nicholass glares at Curtis McMinn, who's standing slack-jawed under that silly mustache, staring at Spinski. Curtis always was afraid of him. Nicholass says curtly, "Because neither of us has a key. The police took—" Then he remembers that it was Neely he surrendered *his* master key to.

But before Nicholass can do anything, Spinski says, "Shit, that's no problem," and fires two shots through the lock. The metal implodes, and within the building, an alarm screams.

"You *stupid* ass!" Nicholass jerks open the door and races for the alarm panel, hands shaking as he punches the code to turn it off. That *moron*! This system sends a signal directly to the TCSO. But maybe he got to it in time. There's a thirty-second allowance for accidental alarms.

He flips the first light switch, and the fluorescents at this end of the hall go on. Spinski has Neely inside, and McMinn is behind him, closing the door. Neely looks as if she's close to passing out, and yet those voodoo eyes are still fixed on Nicholass.

"Sandy, you'll have to . . . dispose of her."

"Yeah?" He nudges the back of her head with his enormous gun, and she stiffens. "Want me to do her now, Ben?"

Neely's hand drops away from her face. The hand is dripping blood on the floor. Can't wash it out. They can still find the blood, just like they found Jan's blood, and after McMinn scrubbed that damned floor—

"No! For God's sake, not *here*."

Spinski laughs. "Yeah, I'll do her, but I want the stock first. Mr. Tarbet sent me to get the stock."

"The what? The processors?"

"Yeah."

"But *why*?"

"Don't know. Where are they?"

Damn Tarbet! Nicholass pushes his dripping hair back from his forehead. Yes, he *had* thought about taking the processors and leaving town tonight. Canada, maybe. Only about four hundred miles to the border. But why throw in the towel on a highly lucrative business? With that skinhead taking the blame for Koto's murder, and nobody making any connection with Giff's murder, they're home free.

Except for Neely Jones.

And now Tarbet is getting paranoid. He wants the "stocks."

But since it's Sandro Spinski doing the asking, Nicholass says, "They're in my office. I'll go get them."

"Wait just a fuckin' minute! I'm going with you." Spinski turns on McMinn. "You! Yeah, fuzz mouth. I want you up ahead where I can see you. Move!"

McMinn moves. Quickly. He's a pace ahead of Nicholass when they start down the hall.

Never should've hired that cretin, Nicholass thinks bitterly. Seemed such a good idea. A greedy man willing to follow orders without asking questions. A mole in the local sheriff's office.

And a certified idiot.

I'm going to get out of this clean, Nicholass promises himself, but maybe not with Curtis McMinn.

And definitely not with Neely Jones.

Damn it, she had her chance to get out alive.

Chapter 55

BUCK DOLIN COULDN'T BE SURE what he heard a couple of minutes ago was gunshots—not with rain rattling on the metal roof of the porch where he'd taken shelter. His only shelter now is his Stetson, and he's having a hard time holding his temper. He's wet and cold and muddy, and he damn well hadn't planned on spending the evening like *this*.

But he's found Neely's Toyota—in the driveway, just ahead. He feels his way between the hedge and the pickup to the cab and peers inside.

Empty.

Teeth grinding painfully, Buck squints across the street at the center. A couple of cars in the parking lot. One looks like Curtis McMinn's T-bird.

Bastard. Shoveling shit about how he got his Glock back, but the neighbor kid jammed the clip, so Curtis's uncle is fixing it. He'll have it back Monday for sure.

Right. And Monday, Curtis just might lose his sergeant's stripes.

Buck splashes across the street and the saturated lawn, and as he gets close to the museum wing, he turns on his flashlight. Nobody inside can see the light here. He reaches the cover of the eaves, and that's when his flashlight catches something half-hidden under a rhododendron.

A tan Stetson.

He goes out into the rain to pick it up. It's Neely's. Her name is on the tag sewn inside.

Cornelia Faith Jones. He always wondered where she got that *Neely.*

But nobody leaves a hat this expensive out in the rain on purpose.

And now he can see a dim light under the bushes. He reaches through wet leaves, and his fingers close on a flashlight just like his. He flicks it off as he puts it in his jacket pocket and steps back under the eaves, where he moves the beam of his flashlight in methodical circles. There. On the concrete, dark stains. And on the wall . . .

A handprint. In blood. Buck holds his right hand up, hovering over the print. It's too small for a man's.

Jesus X. Christ, Neely! What did you get yourself into?

He pulls his transceiver off his belt. When he gets through to dispatcher Wayne Gerlach, he can barely hear him for the static.

"Wayne! Dolin here. You reading me?"

"Yeah, Chief."

"I need some backup at the oceanographic center."

"Nobody here but Brad and Kev."

"Send 'em down. Tell 'em to stay out of sight and wait for my orders. And see who else—"

"What's goin' on, Chief?"

Buck doesn't respond to that question. He turns the radio off.

He can see a shadow: somebody moving toward him along the side of the building.

Chapter 56

STUMBLING INTO DARKNESS. LIGHTS BEHIND, shadows ahead. Cold. She's shivering with the cold.

Focus, damn it!

Two moving shadows ahead of her: the bastards who killed Jan, who left him floating forever in her memory in pink water surrounded by pink moon jellies.

Where's your rage?

It's still here, waiting in the gray embers of pain and fear. Breathe grief on the embers, and the rekindled fire flashes into flame.

But don't let Spinski feel the heat.

Hold the flame in a grip of ice. Stumble a little. Moan. Fall back against him.

"Keep moving, you stupid cunt!"

The glass-eyed man will break her arm if he twists any harder. But when she leaned back against him, she felt the gun stuffed into his belt.

Her gun.

The timing will have to be exact.

Nicholass will use the private entrance to his office. He has the key. She didn't take that one away from him.

Yes, when he unlocks the door, but before he turns on a light.

Is there a light switch by the private entrance? No, not there. Next to the door into the secretary's office. Nicholass will have to cross to that light switch. Or to the lamp on his desk. He'll probably head for his desk. Doesn't matter. She needs darkness.

And a distraction.

They've reached the corner. Turned it. Dim light in the distance seeping in from the public parking lot through the glass doors at the entrance. She hears the murmur of pumps from the museum wing.

Nicholass stops at his private door.

Spinski growls, "Hey, Ben! You got a key to your office, or do I have to shoot off that lock, too?"

"Shut up, Sandy! I *have* the damned key!"

"Then *use* the fuckin' thing! Bitch, don't you pass out on me, or I'll do you right here—even if ol' Ben *does* puke at the sight of blood."

Neely calls up a whimpering moan. Oh, I'm so afraid, big, strong glass-eyed man. Just a weak little woman, and so afraid . . .

Believe it, you bastard.

And now the flame of rage burns blue-hot, courses through her arteries and veins, floods every muscle, and at this moment, she wouldn't be surprised if the blood pouring from her torn cheek turned incandescent.

Chapter 57

BUCK REACHES FOR HIS GUN, his flashlight still in his left hand, but he's suddenly blinded by another flashlight, and he makes a flying leap behind the nearest rhododendron, landing on his belly in an explosion of bark dust and mud.

"DEA! Don't move, Spinski!"

Buck spits out wet bark dust. DEA? That's the federal agent—what's his name?

"Sayson?" Yeah, that's it. Shit, somebody could've got killed. "This is Chief Criminal Deputy Buck Dolin, TCSO. Just hold your damned fire!"

"Dolin? Oh, my God."

Sayson hurries toward Buck while he gets himself on his feet and resettles his Stetson. He leans down to pick up his flashlight, then shines it on the DEA agent.

Sayson is putting a semiautomatic back into a shoulder holster. He glances up at Buck as they move back under the eaves. "Sorry about the scare, Chief."

"So, what're *you* doing out on a night like this?"

"Wishing I was inside. I'm tailing Spinski—Tarbet's bodyguard and sometime hit man. His car's across the street. You seen him?"

"No. But maybe I've seen his work. Right about . . . here." Buck shines his flashlight on the bloody handprint.

Sayson whistles. "What's going *on* here?"

"Well, I figure we better find out—fast."

Chapter 58

A DISTRACTION. SHE NEEDS A distraction, and she doesn't know what it will be.

When Nicholass's key clicks in the lock and he opens the door, Neely feels a slight relaxation in Spinski's grip on her wrist, an easing of the pressure on the gun at her head.

Is this it? The distraction?

No. Not yet. She takes deep, silent breaths while Nicholass moves into the darkness of the office, with McMinn right behind him, and Spinski pushes her forward on McMinn's heels. Nicholass says, "Curtis, watch out for the microscope case. It's right—"

"*Shit!*"

A thud: McMinn stumbling over the case, his fall punctuated with thumps and curses. *This* is it . . .

And Neely spins left into a crouch, while Spinski's gun discharges like a dynamite blast inches from her ear. His hand clamps hard on her wrist, but her turn robbed him of leverage. She jerks him toward her, her left leg raised and unleashed, ramming her foot into the side of his knee. He yelps, fires again, and her right arm arcs down, the energy in every muscle in her body flowing like electricity into the knife edge of her hand, and she *feels* where he is, where he'll be in the next millisecond, and the focused power explodes at the back of his neck with her exultant *kiai*.

He falls like a boulder.

Neely drops to her knees, ears numbed from the blast of the gunshot. Shouts, something falling, shattering. Every sound is distorted and muffled. She fumbles for her duty weapon in Spinski's belt. Someone moaning? Not Spinski. He doesn't move. With the gun in hand, she rises and strikes out for the other door and the light switch. She has to get to that switch before Nicholass turns on his desk lamp. Her outstretched hand encounters the locked door, then the doorjamb. And finally the light switch.

In the sudden glare, Neely puts her back to the door, arms extended, her gun in a two-handed grip, and shouts, "I can take *one* of you out before you can kill me!"

Wide-eyed and slack-jawed, McMinn half-crouches to the left of the desk, the gun in his right hand trembling. It's not his duty weapon. Close, but no Glock.

Nicholass is behind the desk, leaning with his left elbow on the glass top. The lamp lies broken on the white carpet in front of the desk. And apparently, one of Spinski's wild shots found a living target: Nicholass is grimacing in pain, right hand pressed to his backside.

But the gun in his left hand is aimed at Neely.

Glock 9-mm. McMinn's duty weapon.

She centers her sights on Nicholass. "Maybe I should take *you* out, Ben. You gave the orders for Jan's murder. And for Giff's."

The Glock wavers, and to her numbed ears, his voice seems to come from an echoing distance. "Neely, the *carrot* . . . it's still available. Name your price! I'll make you rich, Neely—rich!"

She could kill him now. Gut-shoot him. Make it slow and painful. McMinn might kill her, but would it matter? Not if killing Nicholass would turn grief into satisfaction, even for the few seconds left to her.

But it won't. Nothing will change the fact of Jan's death.

And she wants more than death for Dr. S. Benjamin Nicholass.

She wants this Santa Claus hung out for public display, stripped of everything but his sins.

"Or should it be you?" Neely shifts to put McMinn in her sights. The weak link, so tensely rigid, it seems he might at any moment splinter into hysteria. "Curtis, you shot Jan, but you didn't kill him. Not then. That came later, when Ben arrived and told you what to do, when you dumped Jan in the medusa pool. And he was still *alive* then!"

"Alive?" McMinn's head twitches in a negative motion. "No! He wasn't—I mean, I didn't . . . Ben told me he was *dead*!"

"You *idiot*," Nicholass yells. "Shut up!"

McMinn's face swells red, and he does the one thing Neely didn't anticipate: He turns his gun on his boss. "*You* shut up, bastard!"

"Drop it, Curtis!" Neely shouts, at the same moment McMinn fires one shot, a hollow thump in her numbed ears.

Then he drops the gun.

It thuds on the carpet while the Glock slips out of Nicholass's hand, hits the glass with a sharp crack, and he slides backward and collapses on the floor like a sack of seed.

But McMinn's shot missed him.

It hit the window and left a small black hole in the miniblinds. Neely isn't sure how McMinn managed to miss at a distance of a few feet, but the great gun lover always was a lousy shot. She moves around the desk, keeping it between her and McMinn, and looks down at Nicholass, sprawled on his back, mouth open.

But he's breathing. He passed out, fainted.

She wants to give herself up to gales of laughter, to laugh until she cries, but she can't risk laughter *or* tears right now.

"Curtis, pick up your gun and put it on the desk." He

obeys, and she adds, "Back up against the bookshelf. Good. Hands on your head."

With her left hand, she hooks the trigger guards of the two guns and slides them toward her. Got to cuff McMinn, read him his rights. Get an ambulance for Nicholass. Backup. Now's the time to call for—

Her eyes come into focus on the open door, and her heart pounds erratically. Someone's standing there.

"*Damn* it, Buck, you've got to stop sneaking up on me like that!"

Buck Dolin strolls into the office, his gun pointed at the ceiling. Scott Sayson is right behind him. Buck surveys the room, eyes slitted, his gaze lingering on McMinn, who hasn't moved, except to fix his gaze on the floor. Buck holsters his weapon and says, "Hell, Scott, we could've stayed home out of the rain."

Sayson nods. "Doesn't look like anybody needs rescuing." He kneels beside Spinski, feeling for a pulse. "He's alive. Barely. There's the Desert Eagle. Look at the *size* of that thing."

"That thing" is Spinski's gun, lying on the carpet only a few feet from his motionless right hand. Neely considers the vanity that made Spinski treasure this monstrous weapon, and it seems fitting that the gun will condemn him to prison or even a lethal injection when the crime lab runs a ballistics comparison with the bullet that killed Giff.

Buck turns his squint on Neely. "What the hell came down here?"

"It's . . . a long story." Damn, she's getting dizzy. She adds irritably, "You might as well make yourself useful. Call for backup."

"Brad and Kev are on the way."

"Then cuff Curtis and read him his rights."

"Curtis?"

"Yes." She meets Buck's doubtful gaze steadily.

And McMinn chooses this moment to demand, "I want a *lawyer*!"

Buck's sudden disgust is so intense, Neely expects him to spit on McMinn. But he only asks her, "What's the charge?"

"Start with aggravated murder," she says. "Same for Nicholass and Spinski—when they wake up enough to hear anything."

Buck begins the ritual of arrest, his attitude indifferent, as if McMinn were just another punk off the streets.

But Neely wonders what it's costing Buck, that indifference.

Her ears are beginning to clear, but the dizziness is getting worse. If she could just sit down a minute . . . She goes to the couch, sits at the edge of the cushions. Buck's talking into the phone. "Wayne, we need an ambulance. Got a couple of perps down. And the sheriff's hurt."

The sheriff? Is Buck Dolin referring to her as *the sheriff?*

That calls for a celebration, except she hurts too much. She presses her left hand to her cheek. Someone at the door, but she doesn't have to deal with it: Brad Skinner and Kevin Locksey. Buck talks to them, hands McMinn over to them. They take him away.

Neely squeezes her eyes shut, opens them. The lights seem to be flickering. She begins "Scott . . ." and has to clear her throat. "Scott, the connection between Nicholass and Tarbet—part of it—is in that microscope case. Ben probably has the key on him."

Nicholass doesn't stir when Sayson bends over him to search his pockets and after a few seconds announces, "Here's his keys. Anybody got some gloves?" He pulls on the latex gloves Buck hands him, lifts the case onto the desk, and begins trying keys. The fourth one works.

When he opens the door on the front of the case, layers of small, flat, black rectangles spill out with a slippery rush. Sayson breathes a soft "Wow!" and reads the label on one of the processors: "Pentium III Xeon. Must be a thousand of these suckers here."

"Twelve hundred, according to Jan's letter." Neely looks around the room. She's beginning to shake, and it's getting past her control. "Buck, that briefcase on the floor by the bookshelf—see if it's unlocked."

He finds the briefcase and snaps it open. "What the hell? Nothing but pieces of cardboard in here."

"The Intel carton, torn up for disposal," Neely says. "Might have some interesting fingerprints. Nicholass. Curtis. Whoever delivered the processors."

"Damn, Culpepper's going to love sorting *this* thing out." Buck smiles wryly, but it fades when he focuses on Neely. He crosses to the couch and sits down beside her, gently pulls her hand away from her face. "Who did this to you?"

She covers the wound again. "Spinski."

"Figures." Buck glances at Sayson, who's happily counting processors, then asks, "Neely, why the *hell* did you walk into something like this without any backup?"

"If I'd told you this afternoon I wanted to arrest Sgt. Curtis McMinn, would you have volunteered as backup?"

"Maybe if you told me *why* you wanted him arrested."

"Would you have believed me?"

He considers that a moment, then shrugs. "Next time, try me."

Neely nods, and somewhere in the distance, she hears a siren wavering against the throb of the wind. Probably be a beautiful ocean tomorrow. But she'll see it alone. The sea was Jan's gift to her, but forever after, she'll see it alone.

And she wonders, Is this when I finally get to cry?

She feels Buck's arm around her shoulders, and he says, "It's okay, Neely. It's time."

Chapter 59

A PERFECT DAY, IT LOOKS to be, for those who love empty skies. The rising sun casts the geometric shadows of houses across the sand, and the breakers turn in ermined glory with a roar that never ends. At six o'clock on this exquisite Monday morning, Neely Jones isn't running. She's walking. Strolling.

The new ER physician who stitched and bandaged her cheek was adamant: no violent movement, no running. With any luck, the gash will heal with only a thread of a scar.

Dr. Daya Wheatley was a refreshing surprise in the sterile confusion of the ER. Like Neely, the doctor is also a black female in a profession dominated by white males. Daya joked that she decided to take the job at Westport General Hospital when she heard that Taft County had elected an African-American woman sheriff.

Then the doctor explained that the real reason she decided on Westport was to get her thirteen-year-old son out of Portland and away from the temptations and dangers of gang culture.

Neely didn't tell Daya that her son would find temptations and dangers here, too. Nor did she mention that she wasn't sure she intended to continue wearing the mantle of Taft County's first African-American woman sheriff.

She still isn't sure this morning.

She needs time to think, and she had none yesterday. Sunday wasn't a day of rest—not with depositions and interrogations and conferences with Culpepper, Heathman, and Scott Sayson, assessing the evidence available to prosecute four suspects on charges ranging from assaulting an officer of the law to aggravated homicide.

Sandy Spinski and Ben Nicholass are still in the hospital. Nicholass is recovering from the removal of a .44 Magnum slug from his right gluteus maximus. Spinski suffered spinal damage and might end up a paraplegic—a prospect that doesn't concern Neely.

Curtis McMinn is now in a cell in the TCSO jail. He spent most of Sunday spilling his guts while his lawyer rolled his eyes heavenward.

George Tarbet occupies another TCSO cell, but his silence has been resounding.

Tarbet's house was searched Saturday night, and Buck reported that the showroom—the unaccounted-for space between the living room and kitchen—still contained pre-Columbian antiquities left over from *Poseidon*'s September voyage.

Finally, after a press conference in which the annoyed DA was virtually ignored by the journalists, Neely informed him that she had three weeks vacation due her, and she was taking it now. Buck Dolin would serve as interim sheriff. With that, she left the courthouse, took her aching face to the motel, and slept for twelve straight hours.

Now Neely revels in the luxury of walking the beach, knowing she won't have to return to the TCSO today or the next day or maybe not ever. Saturday night's storm left the sand cluttered with driftwood and piles of bull kelp like brown tangles of hibernating snakes; the high-tide line is littered with broken jellyfish and other marine life that didn't survive. The gulls are feasting.

And, up ahead, they're providing a game of chase for a sheltie.

The dog hasn't a chance of catching the gulls, who hover lazily out of reach above her, but no doubt the object of the game isn't actually to catch a bird, but simply to run and dance in the sun, to rejoice in an invisible cornucopia of scents for her keen nose.

Vixen.

And if Vixen is here, Willow Thornbeck can't be far away.

There. Sitting on a weathered log near the bank, her short white hair glowing in the sunlight. She waves, and Neely walks up the gentle slope of the beach toward her. Willow has two more dogs on leashes: a shorthaired brown dog a little larger than Vixen—must be the basenji—and a foot-high longhaired black dog of vague ancestry. When Neely reaches the log, the basenji responds with coughing whines, and the mutt with brazen yaps, looking up at the sky to Neely's left.

Willow hushes them. "This is a friend, so don't put on such a show. Sheriff, I guess you haven't met Kili and Abby."

"Not in person." She extends the back of her hand for them to smell. Abby, the black mutt, is blind, she realizes, or nearly so.

"And the whirling dervish out there," Willow adds, "is Vixen."

"Yes, I recognized her." Neely sits down on the log. "How are you, Willow?"

"Well, I'm fine, and much happier now, thanks to you and Deputy Locksey. I saw you on the news last night. Made me proud just to know you." She frowns slightly. "But I hope that cut doesn't leave too much of a scar."

"Dr. Wheatley says it'll be a very small scar—if I behave myself."

"Then you really must." She reaches out and tentatively touches Neely's hand. "There'll be other scars, I know, and I'm so sorry."

Neely takes Willow's hand, and it's only then that she realizes how seldom she has actually touched other people— except for Jan—since she's lived here. Gramma Faith would say that's the white in her; Gramma maintains that whites are afraid of touching.

Willow smiles, and Neely gives her hand a squeeze before releasing it. "I'm flying to San Francisco tomorrow," Neely says. "I need some time with my mom and with my dad's family. He had two sisters and a brother, so there's lots of family."

"Oh, that's wonderful, Neely. Yes, at times like this, you need to be with your family. Are you coming back?"

The question takes Neely by surprise. She's been asking it of herself, but no one else has asked it of her.

"I don't know."

Willow nods. "I just wanted you to know that the other half of my duplex is available, since Mr. Wyland has vacated it, so to speak."

Neely looks down the row of houses on the bank to the shingled duplex. She's never been inside, but she has no doubt it's warm and comfortable. And the view . . .

"What are you asking for it, Willow?"

"Well, I've had to raise the rent. Property taxes on the beachfront are getting ridiculous, you know. I'm asking three fifty."

"A week?"

"Oh my, no! A month."

Neely shakes her head. "Willow, *that's* ridiculous."

"Too much, do you think?"

"Too little."

"Well, it'll cover the taxes. Besides, if you moved in, I should get a break on the insurance. I mean, it ought to mean something to have the *sheriff* next door."

Neely doesn't respond to that, but Willow doesn't seem

to notice. She's watching Vixen, who's running headlong toward them.

"Here she comes! Oh, isn't she beautiful when she runs?"

She is indeed beautiful, like a golden magical mix of wolf, fox, and gazelle. Kili goes out to the end of his leash to meet her, but she ignores him and runs to Neely, where she stands panting a moment, then shakes herself, spraying seawater and sand, and Neely laughs.

It feels good, the laughter, as if it's something she's forgotten.

She reaches out to the sheltie, who puts her head between Neely's hands and looks up at her with luminous brown eyes. Neely knows she can't understand what goes on in this animal's mind, any more than Vixen can understand what goes on in hers. Yet there's something—

"I'm just fostering her, you know," Willow says.

"What?" Neely frowns uneasily.

"Well, Vixen is a young dog and full of beans. She needs someone who can run with her, which I certainly can't."

"But what will happen to her? I mean, if you don't find anyone to . . . run with her?"

"Oh, don't worry, I won't let her be put down. It's just that I don't feel she's really mine."

Then Willow looks at her watch, takes a leash out of her jacket pocket, and secures it to Vixen's red harness. "Well, I must get home and back to work. Come on, kids, time to go. Neely, you have a good trip, and take care of yourself."

"Thanks, Willow. You, too."

Neely watches her walk south, deftly keeping the three leashes untangled. Then Neely turns her gaze to the sea, savoring the icy clean scent of the west wind, watching the waves rise to glassy blue-green peaks and spill in white waterfalls while the sun makes rainbows in the veils of spray. When she looks south again, Willow and the dogs have vanished. There isn't another human being on the beach.

Jan used to say, "Nothing here needs us. This scene won't change if *Homo sapiens* should disappear overnight. It would all be here—water and waves and gulls and sea lions and the tiny creatures that live between the sand grains— whether we're around or not."

Jan found that concept reassuring. He considered understanding that vast indifference necessary to understanding the sea.

At this moment, Neely finds the concept profoundly lonely.

She feels tears cold on her cheeks. She hasn't had time yet to grasp the enormity of her loneliness.

One thing she's sure of: She'll go to San Francisco for the funeral. She'll be her mom's hurt child as long as she needs to. She'll visit the observatory with Dr. Helene Cleary-Jones, learning and stretching her mind. She'll go to church with Gramma Faith and Aunt Esther and the cousins, and sing the old hymns she knows all the words to but can't really believe. She'll visit her uncle Gabe at the Road to Light Shelter and listen to him play his trumpet like the angel himself. She'll sightsee and eat and shop like a tourist.

But she won't find an answer to loneliness there.

Will she find it here?

She needs some time.